THE FAITHFUL

THE FAITHFUL

The Chronicles of Trinian

Terrence L. Rotering

XULON PRESS

Xulon Press
555 Winderley Pl, Suite 225
Maitland, FL 32751
407.339.4217
www.xulonpress.com

NOVELS BY TERRENCE L. ROTERING
Available from Xulon Press
STAND
FOREVER
www.xulonpress.com

Paperback ISBN-13: 978-1-66289-717-7
Hard Cover ISBN-13: 978-1-66289-764-1
Ebook ISBN-13: 978-1-66289-718-4

✝✝✝

This book is dedicated to:

God, The Father, The Almighty, Maker of Heaven and Earth,
of all that is, seen and unseen.

Our Lord and Savior, Jesus Christ, The Redeemer, The Lion of Judah,
The Lamb of God, The Good Shepherd, The Prince of Peace,
The King of Kings and the Lord of Lords!

The Holy Spirit, The Counselor, The Comforter, The Spirit of Truth,
The Spirit of Wisdom, The Spirit of Knowledge and Understanding,
The Spirit of Counsel and of Power, The Spirit of Holiness,
The Spirit of Grace, The Spirit of Life.

†††

"The Lord has established his throne in heaven and his kingdom rules over all. Praise the Lord you his angels, you mighty ones who do his bidding, who obey his word. Praise the Lord all his heavenly hosts, you his servants who do his will.
Praise the Lord, all his works everywhere in his dominion.
Praise the Lord, O my soul."
(Psalm 103: 19-22)

"The Lord reigns, let the nations tremble;
He sits enthroned between the cherubim, let the earth shake.
Great is the Lord in Zion; he is exalted over all the nations.
Let them praise your great and awesome name — He is holy."
(Psalm 99:1-3)

†††

"Now faith is being sure of what we hope for
and certain of what we do not see.
This is what the ancients were commended for."
(Hebrews 11:1-2)

†††

"For the Lord loves the just and will not forsake his faithful ones.
They will be protected forever,
but the offspring of the wicked will be cut off."
(Psalm 37:28)

AKNOWLEDGEMENTS

†††

T hank you Mom and Dad for loving me and raising me to know my God — this is the greatest gift a parent can give their child.

To my pastors and teachers; thank you for teaching me of God's justice, God's love, and the truth of God's plan for our salvation through Jesus Christ, our Lord and Savior.

To Theresa, my wonderful wife, my best friend, and my partner on this so temporary walk upon the earth; thank you for loving me despite my many imperfections, for keeping me on the straight and narrow, and for constantly reminding me of the eternal retirement we have waiting for us in heaven. I will love you always.

To my two noble sons, Tanner and Thomas, godly men and sure to be my lifelong best friends; I am so honored to be called your father. Run a good race and may the Lord always bless you and keep you in his loving care.

To my magnificent daughter-in-law, Shannon, a godly woman and a wonderful addition to our family; we are so blessed to have you in our lives. May the Lord always be with you and bless you in everything you do.

To all my extended family, friends and fellow Christians; God has richly blessed me to have you in my life. You inspire me, comfort me, bring me great happiness, and sweeten my hope of eternity in heaven with the Lord.

Finally, and most importantly, thank you, God, for creating me, saving me, and bringing me to faith in you. Thank you for all the blessings you have given to me in this life and in the next.

Thank you for bringing this book — this story — to completion. May it always bring honor to your name and accomplish that which you have prepared for it to accomplish.

PROLOGUE

†††

God has a plan.

We cannot see it. Except where he has made his plan known to us in his Word, his plan is beyond our ability to observe and beyond our ability to fully comprehend.

This should not be contentious, for it should be obvious to each of us we are not God or equal to God. This universe clearly reveals his majesty and power. If we did not speak of God's power, his faithfulness, and his love; the very rocks around us would cry out! Indeed, the symbiotic diversity of his creation, the critically precise orbits of the celestial bodies and the very laws of nature testify to God's awesome wisdom, power, and love for his creation — his love for us.

God has told us everything we need to know about his plan for man — His-story — through his Word, and he has given us a great bounty of promises on which to anchor our faith. He has promised that he loves us, that he will always protect us, that he will always take care of us, and that all things will work together for the eternal good of those who love him and are called according to his purpose. God is faithful to always keep his promises; all of his promises. The great cloud of witnesses — those who have gone before us as well as those who surround us even now — assures us of this truth.

God's people are faithful to their God. God has chosen and called his people, saving them by his grace through faith alone. Our faith — our faithfulness — is a blessing from a faithful God. Though the faithful will make mistakes in their walk, God is faithful to keep and preserve those whom he has chosen. The faithful will praise God for their faith, their salvation, and their eternal inheritance in heaven. All the glory belongs to God and to God alone.

The faithful put their trust in God. Unlike the unbeliever, whose god is their stomach and whose focus is temporal; the focus of the faithful is on serving their heavenly king and on eternity. They recognize their protection and help does not come from any earthly king but from their heavenly king. The faithful wait on the Lord of the heavens for all their needs, and the Lord of the heavens never disappoints. God is, has always, and will always be faithful.

The Faithful Stand Forever

†††

"Be alert and of sober mind. Your enemy the devil prowls around like a roaring lion looking for someone to devour. Resist him, standing firm in the faith, because you know that the family of believers throughout the world is undergoing the same kind of sufferings." (1 Peter 5:8-9)

"From one man, he made every nation of men that they should inhabit the whole earth; and he determined the times set for them and the exact places where they should live. For in him we live and move and have our being." (Acts 17:26, 28)

†††

"Your word, O Lord, is eternal; it stands firm in the heavens. Your faithfulness continues through all generations." (Psalm 119:89-90)

"I believe that almost two thousand years ago, there lived a man such as the world has never seen before and has never seen since. He was God the Son in a human body, at times laying aside his divine power, and at times shaking off his human limitations, but always obeying God's law perfectly.

†

"I believe that he was put through the mockery of a trial, unjustly sentenced, and quickly put to death in order to get him out of the way. I believe that he died on a cross, and his body was laid in a borrowed tomb, which was sealed and guarded.

†

"I believe that on the morning of the third day after his death, his friends came, intending to take care of his lifeless body, but instead found an empty tomb, because he had risen from the grave. I believe that he showed himself alive to his followers on a number of occasions, convincing them all, beyond a shadow of a doubt, that he was alive.

†

"I believe that his death paid the price for my sins, and that his resurrection has opened the door of eternal life to me and all who believe in him. I believe that Jesus Christ is my Savior, that he is living and ruling forever, and because of his life, death, and resurrection, I too shall rise from the grave and live forever with him! Amen." (Easter Creed)

"We believe in one God, the Father almighty, maker of heaven and earth, of all things visible and invisible.

"We believe in one Lord, Jesus Christ, the only Son of God, eternally begotten of the Father, God from God, Light from Light, true God from true God, begotten, not made, of one being with the Father. Through him all things were made. For us and for our salvation, he came down from heaven, was incarnate of the Holy Spirit and the Virgin Mary, and became fully human. For our sake he was crucified under Pontius Pilate. He suffered death and was buried. On the third day he rose again in accordance with the Scriptures. He ascended into heaven and is seated at the right hand of the Father. He will come again in glory to judge the living and the dead, and his kingdom will have no end.

"We believe in the Holy Spirit, the Lord, the giver of life, who proceeds from the Father and the Son, who in unity with the Father and the Son is worshiped and glorified, who has spoken through the prophets. We believe in one holy Christian and Apostolic Church. We acknowledge one baptism for the forgiveness of sins. We look for the resurrection of the dead and the life of the world to come. Amen." (Nicene Creed)

†

"If you love me, you will obey what I command. And I will ask the Father, and he will give you another counselor to be with you forever — the Spirit of truth. The world cannot accept him, because it neither sees him nor knows him. But you know him, for he lives with you and will be in you." (John 14:15-17)

"I believe in the Holy Ghost; the holy Christian Church; the communion of saints; the forgiveness of sins; the resurrection of the body; and the life everlasting. Amen.

✝

"I believe that I cannot by my own reason or strength believe in Jesus Christ, my Lord, nor come to Him; But the Holy Ghost has called me by the Gospels, enlightened me with His gifts, sanctified and kept me in the one true faith; In like manner as He calls, gathers, enlightens, and sanctifies the whole Christian Church on earth, and keeps it with Jesus Christ in the one true faith; In which Christian Church He daily and richly forgives all sins to me and all believers; And will at the last day raise up me and all the dead; And give unto me and all believers in Christ eternal life.

"This is most certainly true."

(The Third Article, Doctor Martin Luther's Small Catechism)

"If you love me, keep my commands. And I will ask the Father, and he will give you another advocate to help you and be with you forever — the Spirit of truth. The world cannot accept him, because it neither sees him nor knows him. But you know him, for he lives with you and will be in you. I will not leave you as orphans; I will come to you. Before long, the world will not see me anymore, but you will see me. Because I live, you also will live. On that day you will realize that I am in my Father, and you are in me, and I am in you. Whoever has my commands and keeps them is the one who loves me. The one who loves me will be loved by my Father, and I too will love them and show myself to them —

"Anyone who loves me will obey my teaching. My Father will love them, and we will come to them and make our home with them. Anyone who does not love me will not obey my teaching. These words you hear are not my own; they belong to the Father who sent me.

"All this I have spoken while still with you. But the Advocate, the Holy Spirit, whom the Father will send in my name, will teach you all things and will remind you of everything I have said to you. Peace I leave with you; my peace I give you. I do not give to you as the world gives. Do not let your hearts be troubled and do not be afraid." (John 14:15-27)

"And you also were included in Christ when you heard the message of truth, the gospel of your salvation. Having believed, you were marked in him with a seal, the promised Holy Spirit, who is a deposit guaranteeing our inheritance until the redemption of those who are God's possession — to the praise of his glory." (Ephesians 1:13-14)

"I am sending you out like sheep among wolves. Therefore be as shrewd as snakes and as innocent as doves. Be on your guard; you will be handed over to the local councils and be flogged in the synagogues. On my account you will be brought before governors and kings as witnesses to them and to the Gentiles. But when they arrest you, do not worry about what to say or how to say it. At that time you will be given what to say, for it will not be you speaking, but the Spirit of your Father speaking through you.

"Brother will betray brother to death, and a father his child; children will rebel against their parents and have them put to death. You will be hated by everyone because of me, but the one who stands firm to the end will be saved —

"The student is not above the teacher, nor a servant above his master. It is enough for students to be like their teachers, and servants like their masters. If the head of the house has been called Beelzebub, how much more the members of his household!

"So do not be afraid of them, for there is nothing concealed that will not be disclosed, or hidden that will not be made known. What I tell you in the dark, speak in the daylight; what is whispered in your ear, proclaim from the roofs. Do not be afraid of those who kill the body but cannot kill the soul. Rather, be afraid of the One who can destroy both soul and body in hell. Are not two sparrows sold for a penny? Yet not one of them will fall to the ground outside your Father's care. And even the very hairs of your head are all numbered. So don't be afraid; you are worth more than many sparrows.

"Whoever acknowledges me before others, I will also acknowledge before my Father in heaven. But whoever disowns me before others, I will disown before my Father in heaven —

"Anyone who loves their father or mother more than me is not worthy of me; anyone who loves their son or daughter more than me is not worthy of me. Whoever does not take up their cross and follow me is not worthy of me. Whoever finds their life will lose it, and whoever loses their life for my sake will find it.

"Anyone who welcomes you welcomes me, and anyone who welcomes me welcomes the one who sent me. Whoever welcomes a prophet as a prophet will receive a prophet's reward, and whoever welcomes a righteous person as a righteous person will receive a righteous person's reward. And if anyone gives even a cup of cold water to one of these little ones who is my disciple, truly I tell you, that person will certainly not lose their reward." (Matthew 10:16-42)

"Do you not know that in a race all the runners run, but only one gets the prize? Run in such a way as to get the prize. Everyone who competes in the games goes into strict training. They do it to get a crown that will not last, but we do it to get a crown that will last forever. Therefore I do not run like someone running aimlessly; I do not fight like a boxer beating the air. No, I strike a blow to my body and make it my slave so that after I have preached to others, I myself will not be disqualified for the prize." (1 Corinthians 9:24-27)

†

"However, I consider my life worth nothing to me; my only aim is to finish the race and complete the task the Lord Jesus has given me—the task of testifying to the good news of God's grace." (Acts 20:24)

†

"But the fruit of the Spirit is love, joy, peace, patience, kindness, goodness, faithfulness, gentleness, and self-control." (Galatians 5:22-23)

†

"A thousand years in your sight are like a day that has just gone by, or like a watch in the night." (Psalm 90:4)

†

"What once was, as well as what will someday be, are not limited by what currently is; and none are limited by man's limited ability to understand."

†

For the Spirit ALWAYS points to the Son!

TIMELINE

†††

Creation and Fall

|

8000 years

|

Tophet

The Great Awakening   **The Faithful**

The Great Struggle I

|

1000 years (Scribes)

|

Veteris (Truth Keeper — 1st Age)

|

Jonas and Tessia

|

Louis (Truth Keeper — 2nd Age)

|

The Great Struggle II   **Stand**

(Truth Keepers — 3rd Age)

|

The Great Unraveling   **Forever**

contents

†††

Chapters:

Part 1: Beginnings

Part 2: A New Home

PREFACE

†††

A young boy named Abner kneeled in the tall grass on the mountainside hill that overlooked his modest countryside home. It was a moonless night, and he was alone in the dark beneath the glimmer of a million stars.

As he had done so many nights before, he dreamed of his future wife, his future children, and the difference he might make in the world.

What will my wife be like? Will she be beautiful? What gifts will she have? How will I know her when I see her? What will my children be like and what will be their gifts? What is my calling? Will I make a difference?

In awe of the night sky and the one who had made it, Abner, looking through the eyes of faith, raised his hands and his prayers to the God of the heavens and the earth.

"Father, it is I, Abner. I come before your throne tonight to pray for the one you have prepared for me, the one who will one day be my wife. Though I do not know her yet, I know you know her well. You have knitted her together in her mother's womb and have known her for all of eternity. Bless her with the gifts she will need to do your will and to serve you faithfully in her life. Shield her from the evil one and all his minions. Guide her Father, protect her, and never leave her side.

"I also pray for our children, the children we will one day know, the children you will bless us with. Help us, Father, to raise them in a way that is pleasing to you. Help us teach them to love the truth and to honor you with their lives. Now, this night, long before you have given them to us, I dedicate their lives to you. You know them, Oh God, and you love them more than I will ever know how to love them. Hold them in your almighty hands and allow their lives to be a living sacrifice in service to you. Show us all how to love, even as you have loved us?

"I ask these things, Father, in your almighty name, trusting that if these requests be in your will, then they are already done, for you are the Faithful and Almighty One!"

A soft breeze moved across the field of moonlit grass like an invisible wave. It blew quietly through his blond hair and softly caressed his youthful face.

Abner remembered the words of the 73rd Psalm.

Yet I am always with you; you hold me by my right hand. You guide me with your counsel, and afterward you will take me into glory. Whom have I in heaven but you? And earth has nothing I desire besides you. My flesh and my heart may fail, but God is the strength of my heart and my portion forever.

"I love you God. You are my first love and my last love. Above all, I will ever love, here in this place, I will always love you. One day I will leave this place, and when I do, I will go to live with you forever. Help me always to remember this. Help me never to forget."

Abner stood, gazing into the night sky in awe and wonder, excited to see how the Lord would bless him and change the world through his life.

You, Oh Lord, are faithful.

Below the night sky, the boy smiled, and heaven smiled with him.

MAP

HEATH   GWAIR

LAKEN

NORTHERN SEA

N

MECH

ATLANTIS

DARK
SEA

KRIEG

(OMENTIA)
DEXILIA

LUKE

Ramot

CHATTAIN

KAN

DEVIA

TANSHIRE

PAX

CRYSTAL VALLEY

SHEP

GOLDEN
FIELDS

PLATTOS

KANDISH

TOBAR

BIORN

PFERD

SONTE

ROTHING

STRANGE
LANDS

PARLANTIS

LANDS
END

SOUTHERN SEA

PARLANTIAN
SEA

PART I: BEGINNINGS

CHAPTER 1

REMEMBER

†††

This time did not differ from a hundred times before. Wee little ones had asked the old man the question countless times through the years, usually as they bounced on his knee and pulled with both hands on his long, gray beard.

No one knew how old the gray-bearded man was except that he surely must have been ancient in his years. He looked ancient, walked ancient, and talked of things that were ancient. He had always been around, as long as any could remember, and he seemed to know the answer to every question asked regarding their long, nearly forgotten history.

"Tell us, tell us again, won't you? What was it like way back then?" asked Ka'elee, a sweet little girl with freckles and a turned-up nose.

"There is so much to tell, little one, and I fear it will be your nap time long before I can finish."

"Oh please, please?" All the children now surrounded him and joined in by pleading with the old man to tell them the story.

As the children tugged on his old, brown coat and at the ends of his worn sleeves, several young men and one young woman joined the growing group of enthusiastic listeners.

One of the young men assisted the children in their request. "Veritas, God has told us through the words of the Apostle Paul that 'The man who thinks he knows something does not yet know as he ought to know.

But the man who loves God is known by God.' We do not yet know as we ought to know. Won't you teach us?"

Another of the young men added to the plea. "Please tell us one more time. We will listen to your words, and we promise to remember every one, always. We will pass them on to our children, so our people will never forget our history."

The old man's bushy eyebrows rose and a look of seriousness covered his face as he proclaimed, once again, his signature quote for moments like these. "I will tell you again, once more, and then I will tell you no more. For what has been will soon pass with me to a hidden place, found only on foggy, winter nights and in early morning dreams, unless you remember, and remember it well."

Of course, he knew this was probably not entirely true. The truth of times gone by would live on in the memories and the witness of the many that he had taught their history to over the many years of his life. Indeed, the Republic's scribes had meticulously recorded his words countless times, corroborated them with ancient texts, and would protect and carefully reproduce them for Trinian posterity.

And so the old man deliberately leaned back and carefully resting his back against the sole remaining oak tree that had long towered high above the apple orchards on Outlook Hill. He searched his memory and carefully repeated the ancient words that a truth keeper had given him many years earlier.

The children gathered around him on the soft carpet of velvety grass that spread plentifully amidst a wide assortment of gold, purple, pink and yellow spring flowers — vibrantly displaying their splendor in the late morning sunshine. Butterflies fluttered about as the old man, led by the Spirit, told the children of a time and a place that again came to life through his words.

"It was an age of eminent men, heroic battles, and an epic struggle between the forces of good and evil. As you know, our struggle is not with flesh and blood, but with the evil forces of the spiritual realm.

Never the less, both good and evil have their earthly servants, servants composed of flesh and blood, like you and me.

"The men of this age were powerful, powerful in ways beyond your understanding. Their faith and trust in good and in evil gave them strengths and abilities rarely witnessed today, if witnessed at all. They possessed powers beyond those of your fathers, mothers, sisters and brothers of this current age.

"Men with simple minds dismiss these facts as exaggerations. Do not let their ignorance mislead you. What once was, as well as what will someday be, are not limited by what currently is; and none are limited by man's limited ability to understand."

"You have heard it said that men of our time use but a small percentage of their minds?"

The children nodded in response.

"Well, in the age I will now tell you about, man used much, if not all, the mental abilities God had given him. Though man no longer lived for multiple centuries as he did shortly after the fall into sin, his intelligence was still available to him, not having yet been so dulled and corrupted by centuries of sin, disease, and interbreeding. Indeed, man could not only access areas of his mind that today he cannot, but by using those areas of intellect, he could accomplish great wonders in architecture, mathematics, problem solving, etcetera. Even rudimentary communication with birds and beasts of the field was possible; ability all but lost in this age."

"I speak to you of a time we will never see again, except in my memory and in your imaginations; a time much like all times, in that it will never repeat."

The old man had their undivided attention. It was not his command of language or style of speaking that held their interest as much as his knowledge of things that had once been. He was not the greatest orator of his time, but one who spoke with authority on the events of another time. His words had weight and meaning and were not just the drivel of fools spouting their opinions or thoughts. It had been this man's lifelong mission to preserve, for future generations, the history of their people and God's story; His-story itself.

In addition, when the old man spoke to the children, he spoke their language, not attempting to impress them with his grownup words, but to talk to them on their level, so they would best understand. They loved him for this.

"It is a time that we must remember! For if we forget, we will leave undefended the gates of truth to the whimsical assaults of future ages and the targeted arrows of the great deceiver himself. For you see, children, you can't rewrite the truth, but you can hide it. If the light leaves, darkness can move in unhindered. Darkness is, after all, the absence of light and it flourishes in the absence of truth."

Ka'elee crawled up in the old man's lap and got comfortable. The other children listened intently as the words poured from the wise old man's lips like golden honey from a sweet jar.

"It had been approximately eight thousand years …"

CHAPTER 2

LIGHT AND DARK

†††

It had been approximately eight-thousand years since the time God gave the promise of a Savior to mankind. It had been approximately twenty-five hundred years since God had punished man for his wickedness and put the rainbow in the sky for all to remember both man's history of wandering from the truth and the mercy God had shown to man by not completely erasing mankind from existence. Once again, man spread across the face of the planet.

I take you back to a land known by our fathers as Omentia. Our history officially begins there. It was a place we once called our home.

The light was strong there, but men took the light for granted. They dabbled in things that were evil, thinking them a curiosity; and their amusements, harmless. As generations passed, they grew more and more complacent, opening the door to evil and its acceptance of the abhorrent. Omentia's conscience atrophied until the light faded to only a dim flicker.

Darkness is powerless against light, but darkness is also cunning and patient. In the absence of light, darkness thrives. In the absence of good, evil reigns.

Soon, Omentia, very short on memory, had almost completely forgotten their God, the promise of a Savior, and their troubled history. Thus, Omentia became vulnerable to the lure of evil, and evil, always on the watch for opportunity, moved.

Evil set its gaze on Omentia and soon sunk its talons into her purposefully. As the light continued to fade, darkness continued to increase its presence, filling the void left by the departure of the light.

Then it was time.

CHAPTER 3

WEAPONS

†††

The father of lies looked down on the inhabitants of the earth; hating all that was upright and true, he despised them all.

He gathered the darkest of his angels, those who, like him, had rebelled against the Holy One. They were all condemned to eternal punishment and would soon burn in the fires of hell forever, but for a short time, they remained free to rule the skies over the planet of men. They were invisible to those who walked upon the earth.

Meeting in the pitch black of darkness, much like the absolute void which filled their being, their fiery-red eyes turned to the great deceiver of men for their instructions.

The prince of darkness spoke to the commanders of his legions. "The land to the west is the prize; Omentia will be the means. Omentia is nearly ready to fall. Soon it will be ours, and it will do our bidding to take the rest."

"Many are the weapons we have at our disposal to use against these mortals! They are weak and have forgotten that we are here. We will take advantage of every opportunity to divide them, destroy their spirits, and negate their role in the great battle."

Scum, one of Satan's commanders, spoke. "Master, do they not learn from the mistakes of others? Do they not learn from their past?"

They possess Adam's seed, and their eyes easily entice them, their stomachs lead them, their emotions derail them, their thirst for knowledge seduces them, their anxiety over temporary things distracts them, and their quest for power and wealth controls them. They want to know the future. Give them a taste of the forbidden fruits, and they will follow us to hell like dogs. These are your lures. These are your weapons against them. Use them all!"

"Do they not know of their weaknesses?"

"They know of their weaknesses, but alone they are powerless to control them. Denial is how they cope. Though they number their days, they live as if they will never die. Ignoring what has come before, as well as what follows closely behind, they choose to see only that which is right in front of them. They know their path will destroy them, and yet they do nothing to change their course. They are flesh, and flesh is weak."

"This will be easy, master!" Scum snarled amidst the howling of the others, who energetically showed their agreement and eagerness to begin the attack.

"Go. Find those who have the void in their hearts and fill it! Give them what they want and bring as many of them to me as you can! They will all burn with us eternally in hell!"

Their eternal destiny, already decided by the Holy One, the fallen demons made it their sole mission to bring as many souls with them as possible to the pit. At Lucifer's command, the demented demons departed their dank dungeon, their crimson-red eyes darting off in all directions in search of the unsuspecting souls that awaited them.

CHAPTER 4

POWER

✝✝✝

P otentus, drifting through the clouds high overhead, sensed a void he could fill.

The dark angel of power entered the cave from the deep shaft that exuded poisonous fumes from the intense flames burning within the mountain. Those within the caves of southern Omentia would prove easy prey for Potentus. He would pull them to the darkness by satiating the hunger for power that stirred deep within each of their souls.

One soul below was especially vulnerable. His parents had decided, whether out of laziness or an honest desire to not interfere in their children's beliefs, to let him and his siblings learn for themselves what they should believe. In effect, his parents were telling him that there wasn't any absolute truth and whatever he believed in was fine — that they as parents hadn't found truth and thus thought it irrelevant to pass anything on to him or that they simply didn't care enough for him to teach him what they had learned. Maybe it was all the above. Either way, this nonchalance in parental leadership and instruction left a spiritual void within him that someone or something else would eventually fill.

For Pete, that someone — that something — had just arrived.

✝✝✝

Pete paused from his labors, sat down on the hard, rocky floor of the cave, and took a drink of water. As he did, he let his mind wander to better days; days before he started working in the dark, damp caves.

Those were the days! Long days spent playing the pretend games as he and his friends liked to call them. In these games, they would fantasize about being whoever or whatever they wanted to be, and they could acquire awesome powers and do amazing things. He and his friends would often lose themselves in the pretend games for days on end. Those days of freedom and happiness had ended all too abruptly.

Pete Petite, as everyone called him, now had a dirty job, and he knew it. Pete Petite, the son of a poor miner, had followed in his father's footsteps, even though he would have chosen another profession if given the choice. He had helped his father support the family at the young age of thirteen by working in the "hole."

Pete, now fifteen, hated the hole. It was dark, cold, and hard to breathe in the mines. In addition, Pete was small, and the work was hard. Though his father had assured him he would grow bigger in time, it didn't seem like it was going to happen. His mother thought the lack of sunshine and poor breathing conditions of the mine were stunting Pete's growth, but every time his mother brought it up, his father would reply, "That's rubbish! The hardy work will make a real man out of him!" So, Pete went to the mines.

This morning, like every morning, Pete and the other workers entered the mines just before sunrise to spend the next twelve hours extracting kerogen. Crowding into the creaky elevator that brought them deep into the hole, Pete all but disappeared amidst the large frames of the other miners. As they made their descent, Pete realized that the only light he had seen for a week was that of a miner's lantern.

One hour into the shift, Pete found himself alone in a small tunnel. The light of his lantern provided the only source of illumination in the absolute darkness. He began thinking about the kerogen and how important it was to all of Omentia. Omentia needed the kerogen to burn for power. He looked at his lantern. The beam of light emanating from its flame darted about the cave walls with every little wisp of air that made its way through the tunnel. As Pete worked, his mind focused more and more on his growing discontentment.

Power. All this work for power. Power for Omentia.

Pete's thoughts turned selfish as he swung his pickaxe and slammed it into the kerogen wall of the cave.

No power for me! No power to get out of these caves!

He swung the axe again.

I wish I had some power!

He swung the axe harder and chipped a piece of kerogen rock from its place in the rock wall.

Power to be somebody!

As his pickaxe impacted the cave wall again, the kerogen splintered and flew in all directions. Pete did not notice the fiery-red eyes peering at him from the darkness of the tunnel. All Pete could think about was how he hated the mines, hated his life, hated being small, and hated being insignificant. His thoughts blinded him to everything else.

His anger soon turned into a rage. Pete cried out. "I want power! I want POWER!"

The words brought fiendish pleasure to the ominous creature lurking in the shadows behind Pete. The demon smiled in the darkness; its eyes focusing intently on Pete.

From nowhere, Pete thought of the words. Words he had never thought of before. Words he had certainly never spoken. Strange words.

Like the make-believe words he and his friends would sometimes speak during the pretend games, these words were gibberish; or so Pete thought. And yet, this time, he longed to say them out loud — he had to say them out loud.

He gave little thought to the words, thinking them harmless. But unknown to Pete, the words that would soon echo quietly through the cave were anything but gibberish and anything but harmless. The words paid homage to the demons, praising them and calling on them to act in the world of men. The words did more than make the simple sounds heard by human ears. They summoned demons that wielded much power in the physical world and grew even more powerful when called upon by the lips of flesh.

From out of nowhere, more unfamiliar words found their way into Pete's head and out through his mouth. Things happened as he said the peculiar words; strange things; amazing things. Things he could not let the others see; at least not yet. They would not understand — not like he did. He must keep them as his secret for now.

Secret.

Potentus whispered from the darkness, "Our secret."

CHAPTER 5

LONELINESS

†††

Soluson, the dark demon of loneliness, descended into the outskirts of the small town and searched for his prey. As the light drained from the land, the fruit of men grew ripe for the picking. The land was overflowing with souls that had everything they needed, but selfishly found themselves unsatisfied and wanting more, and more, and more. Soluson had found that flesh never felt satisfied. No matter what level of affluence, prosperity, or success it attained; it always wanted more.

Soluson valued his specialty weapon of loneliness. All men, at some point, were susceptible to it. Men set unrealistically high expectations of their acquaintances, friends, and lovers, only to ultimately realize their disappointment. This disappointment leads to loneliness. Just like all sin centers on "I," loneliness also focuses human thought on itself and its own selfish needs.

Once a human directs their attention towards themselves, leading the sinful mind down the path of self-pity, burdening it with sinful thoughts, and sowing faith-destroying doubt becomes much easier. The momentum can build into a downward spiral until guilt and shame completely cloud the soul. Then despair appears. Once despair is present, the mortal is of little use to the Holy One. He is so concerned with himself that he can bear little fruit, let alone care for the needs of those around him. Getting those upon the earth to focus on themselves and abandon service to the Holy One was Soluson's specialty.

Soluson spread his cloud of loneliness across the darkening skies, letting it fall like a gloomy cloak over the countryside below. Soluson loved his job, and he was good at it!

Destroying flesh is so satisfying!

✝✝✝

As the sun leisurely set on the horizon in a somber blend of gold and red, a man walked laboriously up the stone path that led to his modest wood and rock home on the hill. Yellow, brown, and red leaves reached the appointed time for their downward spiral and fell quietly from the surrounding trees. They now covered the ground below the man's feet, gradually draining of life; curling up and dying. Their silent cries were inaudible to the man as he made his way up the path.

The man stopped at the top of the knoll and watched the sun go down behind the hills to the east as a mockingbird sang the last song of the day. His unsettled tune proclaimed to all who would hear that a change was coming. Abner rubbed his left knee and let out a soft sigh. His legs were still strong, but the cool fall breeze was giving him fair notice his bones would not appreciate the coming winter chill.

The man's eyes then turned to his home a little farther along the stony path. The colors of the aged rock and wood of the home faded amidst the long shadows of the approaching darkness, and the warm stream of smoke rising from the chimney appeared to turn to ice in the moon's cool light.

Abner had walked the land for forty-seven years and had worked very hard for most of that time. A believer in the truth, he had taught the Word faithfully to his family. He had accomplished much and had succeeded at most everything that he had set his mind to; thanks be to God. He had a fine wife, two gifted sons, a lovely daughter, and a nice plot of land with a warm home. Abner was indebted to no man.

Abner was the only son of an immigrant named Anters who had miraculously arrived on the shores of Atlantis one cold winter day from

Mecca, across the Northern Sea. A winter storm had caught the mishap crew of the small fishing vessel unaware, proving disastrous to them. Despite being found very near death and frozen to the mast of the ship, Anters survived the ordeal. The other crewmembers either got washed overboard by the icy waves or froze to death en route.

Abner had tried very hard to live a life worthy of his father's legacy, and anyone appraising Abner's life would surely have thought he had done so. He had every reason to be happy and satisfied with his accomplishments.

Suddenly, though, Abner thought about his life differently. Thinking that maybe his life hadn't worked out for him the way he thought it was going to work out, he felt like something was missing. As Abner stood in the shadows of the setting sun, a tear rolled down his cheek.

The only thing I ever really wanted was to feel loved. But after all these years, I just feel alone.

Despite being blessed with a wonderful family, Abner longed for more. He longed for the warmth and affection that he thought would follow. Deep within Abner's mind, he believed that his efforts over the years should have earned for him a greater amount of affection from his family. But it had not. Instead, his efforts had simply become the status quo; the normal and expected. To his family, he became invisible; nothing more than the provider — taken completely for granted.

The more Abner had provided for his family, the more his family's interests and hobbies occupied their time and attention. Abner had faded into the background of their lives. Though he had given his all for them, he now realized he could and should expect nothing from them in return.

These thoughts had troubled Abner on and off for weeks, and they had profoundly affected his spirit. His constant battle with loneliness had, over time, coated his heart with layer after layer of sadness, anger, bitterness, and depression. He did his best to fight these feelings by remembering his many blessings and constantly thanking God for giving him the ability to provide for his family. Still, the loneliness was unrelenting. With time, hopelessness took hold, separating Abner from those he loved and deliberately entombing his heart.

Abner withdrew from his family. As he perceived his withdrawal of little notice or consequence, the hopelessness grew in strength, leaving Abner feeling more and more detached. Soon, Abner felt little more than a stranger as he returned to his home from the fields after a hard day of work.

As he slowly opened the front door of his home, his two sons, Ka'el and Truin, were sitting at the main table, eating a healthy portion of pork-potato stew. His wife, Evelin, was in the upper loft of the home with their daughter, Elin, and from the sound of it, the girls were making Elin a new winter dress.

A chilly breeze entered the door behind Abner before he quietly closed and latched the door behind him. Unbeknownst to Abner, a stranger with a heart of ice had entered the home with him.

Truin greeted his father with a smile. "Hello Father."

"Hi Pa," Ka'el added.

"Hello boys." Though the two young men before him would always be his boys, there would be no doubt in the mind of an outside observer that the term "boy" no longer described the two brawny lads.

Ka'el was seventeen and the older of Abner's two sons. His wavy blonde hair covered his ears, and he tied it together in the back, which was customary for their village. He had dark blue eyes and broad shoulders from years of helping his father harvest potatoes and tend to the livestock.

Truin was Ka'el's younger brother by one year and also had blonde hair, but he kept it cut short; except at the top, where it grew straight toward the heavens for about two inches. He, too, was strong, though not yet as strong as his big brother. What Truin lacked in strength, he more than made up for in wisdom.

From the boys' point of view, it had taken much too long to grow into young men. Abner and Evelin couldn't help but feel the inevitable pull the outside world was exerting on them. It wouldn't be much longer before outside interests would entice Ka'el and Truin to attend to the activities that young men attend to as they approach manhood.

"Feels like winter is sending us a greeting," Truin offered cheerfully.

"Before we know it, the snow will be falling," Abner responded with less enthusiasm.

Ka'el said, "Hungry Pa? We saved you some of Mom's pork-potato stew. If you don't want any, I'm sure I could finish it up for you."

"Thanks son, but I'm afraid I'm going to have to at least try some of Eve's stew or I'll be sleeping out with Thor tonight."

Thor was their 110 pound sheepdog, the four-legged member of the family. No one in the family really knew for sure where Thor ranked them in the pack. Thor seemed to obey them all very well, most of the time, but every once in a while he would show his independence; usually when he sensed something the two-legged members of the family did not.

"Besides, I've been thinking about pork-pot and biscuits for hours now."

Ka'el and Truin looked at each other and responded simultaneously. "Bummer!" Evelin had earned village-wide recognition for her pork-po-tato stew, or as they liked to call it, "pork-pot."

Upon overhearing the conversation, Evelin promptly appeared at the top of the loft balcony, excited that her husband was home for dinner. "Great, because I have a second pot of pork-pot on the stove, and I don't want any leftovers!"

Her words brought the intended reaction. Two young warriors and one seasoned veteran of the dinner wars scrambled for the stove in the back of the room for the sustenance their bodies craved after a long day of physical labor. It warmed Eve's heart to see that the fruits of her labors were so appreciated. Men didn't always remember to show their appreciation with words, but their actions spoke volumes.

"Mom, how long do I have to stand here?" Elin waited impatiently in the loft.

"I'm coming honey," Evelin said, unfazed. "I'll be there in just a minute."

Sons and daughters were different, but not that different. Evelin understood her role of mother was one of service to her family and to the Lord. Selflessness was a genetic trait of women when it came to caring for their children. If it wasn't clear to a new mother during her pregnancy that the number one priority for the rest of her life would be her children, then it would abruptly become obvious as soon as she went into childbirth.

Being a mother was not for the weak. Raising boys had only reinforced this lesson for Evelin. That her children were healthy and strong spoke volumes of Evelin's childbearing ability and her child-rearing prowess. She had done very well.

What is wrong with Abner?

Evelin pondered this question as she finished the hem on Elin's dress.

He has seemed so distant lately.

Abner was just finishing his pork-pot stew, and though he had been engaged in conversation with the boys about the day's events, he remained plagued by the intense thoughts and feelings of loneliness.

This had been happening more and more often lately. It was like he was navigating through the rooms of his mind and somehow frequently got stuck in a room called "lonely." He could still hear the sounds of his other thoughts as they traveled the hallways of the house—the house he knew was his brain. His thoughts entered different rooms named "funny," or "interesting," or "happy," etcetera, but his focus usually found its way back to this room; back to this prison.

Sure, he could get out of the — lonely room — eventually. But as he visited it more and more often, he found it more difficult to leave; locked in the room for longer and longer periods of time.

Soon it became more than the lonely room, it became the "scary room." The more that he visited, the more the way out became more difficult to find. The walls got harder, the light in the room faded, and it started feeling like someone or something else was in the room with him. Eventually, he realized there was a shadow in the room — a hideous and sinister shadow.

The thought sent a shiver down his spine.

"Father."

Abner remained lost in his thoughts, staring out the window.

"Father."

A distant, gentle voice pulled Abner out of the scary room.

"Father, it is time for devotions."

The thought of time with the family and the Word led Abner out of the scary room; out of the clutches of the shadow that kept the prison and into a bright and warm room — a peaceful room

"Yes, devotions — time for devotions," Abner said.

Abner, Evelin, Ka'el, Truin, and Elin gathered together on a round rug that Evelin and Elin had made the previous year for the floor of the family room. Thor took advantage of the opportunity to cuddle with his pack. He plopped down across Truin's lap as he did most every night during devotion. It was a warm and cozy room, but even cozier now; now that Thor had joined them.

The fire crackled in the fireplace as Abner read aloud from the Word. "Yet I am always with you; you hold me by my right hand. You guide me with your counsel, and afterward you will take me into glory. Whom have I in heaven but you? And earth has nothing I desire besides you. My flesh and my heart may fail, but God is the strength of my heart and my portion forever." (Psalm 73:23-26)

Abner pondered the words deeply, and he realized, once again, that the Lord was all his soul needed to be happy and content. The Lord was his full-time friend and confidant; his helper and redeemer.

Who have I in heaven but you? How could I have forgotten?

Almost immediately, the loneliness departed Abner, like smoke caught in a stiff wind. Accompanying the loneliness expelled from Abner's heart were the hostile feelings towards Evelin that Abner had allowed to fester and grow; the feelings that Evelin had not been a loving mate. Abner could now see that these feelings were selfish and sinful. They were poison arrows to his heart, and he quickly sent them out the door into the cold, dark night where they belonged. He saw Evelin once again as the loving mother and wonderful life-partner that she had always been.

Love God above all things and love your neighbor as yourself. These are God's commands. Evelin is doing her best to fulfill them. She, the boys, and all of us are here for God; to love God, to serve God, and to give glory to God.

Abner realized he had been making his loved ones, those given to him as blessings from God, into his idols. This was especially true of Evelin. He had longed to make his wife the number one object of his affections. However, though his spouse was to fill a special place in his life, she was not to be the prime object of his affection; lest she become an idol before God. Rather, Abner's only hope of finding and remaining happy in a sinful world was to love God with all his heart, with all his soul, and with his entire mind. Loving God was the true purpose of man's existence, and only in fulfilling this purpose could a man find happiness and contentment.

Abner realized that if he was faithful to God and again focused on his love for God rather than on his unfulfilled, sinful and selfish desires, he could resist the devil. The temptations of lust, self-pity, despair, and loneliness would then flee from him!

Evelin notice Abner's countenance change as he read the Word, and she smiled at him lovingly. Abner, noticing her gaze, lifted his eyes to hers and did the same. It was suddenly very clear to him how much she loved him.

How could I have doubted? How could my thinking have gone so far off track? Thank you, God, for your Word! Thank you for calling me back when I stray. Help me love and serve those you have entrusted to my care.

Abner remembered King David's prayer and repeated it aloud. "Create in me a pure heart, Oh God, and renew a steadfast spirit within me."

Then, basking in the love of his God and the warmth of his family's company, Abner joined Evelin in teaching Ka'el, Truin, and Elin from the Word.

Abner quoted Joshua, "As for me and my household, we will serve the Lord." Abner added. "This is how it has always been, and this is how it will be until the Lord takes us home."

They all joined in song, singing praises to the Lord. So it was with Abner, Evelin, Ka'el, Truin, and Elin. Good stewards of this time of light and peace, they studied the Word, grew in their faith, and learned to trust more and more in the Lord their God.

Unbeknownst to them, a time of darkness and war was coming. They would need their faith to get through it.

✝✝✝

"…The first foundation was jasper, the second sapphire, the third chalcedony, the fourth emerald, the fifth sardonyx, the sixth carnelian, the seventh chrysolite, the eighth beryl, the ninth topaz, the tenth chrysoprase, the eleventh jacinth, and the twelfth amethyst." (Revelation 21:19)

Unperceivable by rudimentary human senses, majestic beings with mighty wings and glowing countenance watched from another dimension. They paid attention to and pondered the words of those they served and protected.

They had seen other weak and sinful mortals serve the Master in great ways, and they knew they would soon again witness mighty acts in the unfolding of His-story. What would the legacy of these flawed and frail creatures become during their brief journey within time — the blink of an eye in eternity before their time would be no more? Surely, these creatures must be significant, for the Father of Light had sent his servants to keep special watch over this family.

The largest and most beautiful living being, shining in countless colors like those of a rainbow, and yet in many more hues than any earthly rainbow had ever displayed, communicated to the others. "The Lord allows this soul, known as Abner, to be tested."

A second living being, nearly as large and beautiful as the first and possessing six mighty golden wings, spoke. "This Abner remains faithful to the study of the Word, to prayer, and in trusting the one true God." Its wingtips burned even more brilliantly as it responded.

The Chief Being's thoughts echoed. "I will now minister to Abner. The Lord directs you to keep watch over the others for they are all special within His-story. I am told that Ka'el and Truin, the two sons of Abner, will meet much opposition along their path, but their paths will bring much glory to the Master. Elin, the daughter of Abner, is no less special; though her greatest significance will be in another time."

The living being with the golden wings set his jasper gaze on the family kneeling in prayer and then looked to the others. "I will do as the Lord has willed."

As they spoke, a small child met with an accident in a distant land.

The Chief Being directed another with sapphire wings. "Go now, as a child had lost an eye and needs to be taught to see."

A spectacular blur of sapphire instantly followed.

Others, whose eyes burned brilliant emerald, topaz, and amethyst, spread their mighty wings and disappeared in a multicolored blaze of light. They too had faithful to protect.

Chapter 6

Youth

†††

They were like two peas in a pod. Their childhood could not have been better for the sons of Abner. Together with their sister, Elin, the boys enjoyed a wonderful childhood.

Elin spent most of her time with her mother, Evelin; learning how to sew, cook, clean, and take care of the household. Some young women found homemaking mundane and others considered it degrading, but Elin trusted her mother's belief that women are essential for men's well-being. Evelin believed nothing happened in the household without a woman around. The reason the family is healthy and strong is because of the woman's clean home and great cooking. With her wisdom and caring, the woman takes care of the children's education and ensures their father's contentment. If there is happiness and hope in the family, it is because of the woman's warmth and love. A household without a woman is simply not a home.

"Remember, charm is deceptive, and beauty is fleeting, but a woman who fears the Lord is to be praised."

Elin took her mother's words to heart, diligently worked to learn all she could, and fervently prayed to someday have a family of her own. Until she had a family of her own, Elin decided she would do her best to care for her father and brothers, as if doing so was her responsibility.

Ka'el and Truin showed less responsibility in their teenage years. Though they too spent a large amount of their time in home

instruction—learning God's Word, reading, writing, and mathematics—
they spent most of their time just being boys. They gained much of
their early wisdom by adding valuable experience to the knowledge
they gained in their home schooling. While Abner and Evelin were
often up into the early morning, wondering if their boys were still alive;
their daily adventures kept the family entertained around the fireplace
in the evenings.

As soon as the boys were old enough to help around the ranch,
Abner showed them the ropes. Soon, their assistance became essential
in harvesting the crops, feeding the livestock, and the day-to-day heartbeat of the homestead.

One of the weekly activities for the boys was to go hunting and
fishing with Abner. The nearby streams were teeming with a wide
variety of fish, and the forest was rich with grouse, rabbit, pheasant,
and deer. Abner taught the boys how to set traps for rabbit, and how to
use the bow for taking grouse, pheasant and deer.

Throughout these weekly hunting and fishing trips, Abner and the
boys made many lasting memories, and Abner passed on more than
just his knowledge of hunting and camping. Indeed, to the best of his
ability, Abner passed as much of his wisdom as possible to the boys on
these excursions. There was so little time to train them in the way they
should go. Before long, they would be men and others would count on
them to be knowledgeable of the things of the world as well as have the
ability to make wise decisions. Any major gaps in their training as boys
could lead to poor judgment and unintentional missteps as young men;
even the smallest missteps as young men could be fatal.

On one occasion, Abner, Ka'el, Truin, and Thor joined three other
men and their sons in tracking down a pack of wolves that were terrorizing local farms and killing their sheep herds. Abner took advantage
of the opportunity to teach the boys a valuable lesson he had learned
many years earlier from Grandpa Anters.

"There are three types of people in this world. People will behave like
sheep, wolves, or sheepdogs." The boys listened carefully as they walked.

"Some people think they can go through their life minding their own business and avoiding trouble. They think if they don't bother others, others will likewise leave them alone. Holding firmly to this belief, they disregard the need to prepare for the day that trouble will come looking for them. They are people of peace, and I do not fault them for being so. They are the sheep.

"Then there are those who take advantage of these peaceful sheep. They lie in wait for them. If given the opportunity, they gang up on the sheep, kill them and take all that they possess. These are the wolves. The sheep live in fear of the wolves, feigning tranquility, but knowing that they cannot defend themselves if the wolves come to their door.

"Someone must protect the sheep. Someone must be there when the wolves come looking for sheep to devour. This is the sheepdog. The sheepdog shares the peaceful desires of the sheep and lives at peace with all those around him. Yet, he prepares for the day when the wolves will come, and he is ready to defend not only himself but also the surrounding sheep."

They held their bows all the firmer as Abner spoke to them. The boys listened intently to his instruction.

"We are sheepdogs!"

With Thor's help, the men found the wolf pack they had been tracking, and they cut the pack down to the last wolf with their bows. They skinned the wolves and took the hides back home with them to make winter coats for the family.

The sheep were once again safe.

✝✝✝

The children of Abner and Evelin grew strong and wise.

Assisted by one of Abner's closest friends, a very talented and spiritual man named Noa, Ka'el and Truin fashioned walking sticks, then fighting sticks, and finally advanced weapons with which to both hunt and defend their family. Having taught them how to perfect their wood making skills, Noa taught the boys their village history through the playing of musical instruments and the singing of songs. He was also very musically talented. The boys respected and admired Noa, treasuring the times they shared with him.

Ka'el showed unparalleled strength for a young man of his age. He became especially proficient with the knife and the staff. Not only could no one take him in a wrestling match, but it soon became clear that there were few beasts that could match him, either.

Once, while Abner and the boys were out hunting, Ka'el inadvertently wandered away from the hunting party. Instinctively taking advantage of Ka'el's misfortune, a young tiger on the prowl attacked him. Most young men in Ka'el's situation would have perished beneath the tiger's claw, but the Spirit of the Lord was with Ka'el. Though Ka'el had his knife and staff with him, he found no need for them. Instead, he tore the tiger apart with his bare hands.

Though Ka'el recognized his power was from the Lord, he enjoyed the popularity that he had gained from it. He secretly grew proud of his physical stature, spending a considerable amount of his time exercising to increase his physical strength. In fact, Ka'el's priority became furthering his physical abilities. His reputation grew, and soon his name became synonymous with power in all the surrounding villages. As his reputation grew, so did his pride.

In some respects, Truin followed in his big brother's footsteps. Though not as strong as Ka'el, he became quite skillful at wielding two swords at once. His physical speed and agility also made him a challenge that few could hope to match. He became as formidable as a team of two armed men.

However, physical training was not Truin's priority. Besides furthering his physical skills, Truin continued to prioritize growing closer to the Lord and gaining wisdom; recognizing that these were his genuine sources of strength. He studied the Word faithfully, prayed often, and considered his relationship with the Lord his number one priority. He relied on the Lord for all things and downplayed his own untrustworthy abilities. Rather than boasting about his strengths, he remained humble, reserved, and thoughtful.

Elin, the youngest of the three children, grew fair and unblemished into womanhood. She was as beautiful within as she was without. She learned much of how to be a good woman from her mother, but most importantly, she learned to fear and love the Lord. Elin's warmth and caring were unsurpassed. She loved unselfishly, and her presence was a blessing to all around her.

Elin, Truin, and Ka'el remained the best of friends, sharing countless happy memories together during their childhood.

†††

Abner continued to spend many days and nights teaching the boys how to camp, how to survive off the land, and how to hunt. Around the campfire, he would teach his sons what life was all about.

He would say that every man and woman is here for a reason. Every single one of us is part of a story that is unfolding; part of His-story.

Abner was a large man, a powerful man, and a smart man. The boys listened closely to their father's words; words of wisdom from a man who had experienced much throughout his years. Abner had studied the world in great detail and learned God's Word well, letting it successfully direct the course of his life. In their hearts, the boys felt the best they could ever hope for was to be like their father, and his approval meant the world to them.

"No man can see the complete picture. Each of our lives is but a drop of water in a fast-moving stream. The stream has a beginning, and it has an end. We are all part of it. Only our Father in heaven knows where the stream is going and what part we are to play. He has given us the gifts and opportunities to do what he has prepared for us to do. We must be faithful to the calling of our maker and preserver. He controls the stream, and it will flow where he has planned for it to flow."

These were heartfelt words of a father to his sons, and they sunk in deep; helping to form the very essence of the men the boys would soon become.

"We are all family; all God's sons and daughters. We are here to love one another and give glory to our Father in heaven. A man can show no greater love than to lay down his life for a friend."

The boys would remember.

CHAPTER 7

OMENS

†††

One day, while the boys were hunting with bow and spear in the forest, they explored an area they hadn't ventured into before. They thought a little exploration was good for building confidence and pushing the envelope of their life experiences.

The brothers started towards home after a successful hunt. The sun had set, and a full moon had already risen into the dark blue sky.

"What is that?" Ka'el noticed a strange light glowing ahead of them in the forest.

"Looks like a fire."

"Let's check it out."

"Wait Ka'el. Are you sure we should? It's late, and we should get back to our campsite; it will be pitch dark before you know it."

"C'mon. It won't take long. We'll be fine."

As they drew closer to the fire, the forest smelled of a foul odor, like one they had never smelled before. In addition, they noticed the temperature dropping rapidly. Frost was on the ground and on the trees all around them.

"What in the world?" Truin crept through the thick underbrush.

"Truin, there; through the trees, see them?" Ka'el pointed.

Truin kneeled down next to Ka'el and peered through the brushwood. Up ahead, about two hundred feet in front of them, he saw a fire blazing at the center of a clearing. Thirteen motionless figures, wearing crimson hooded cloaks, stood in a circle around the fire. Only the ends of their noses and chins emerged from their dark hoods, eerily reflecting the pale moonlight and darting flames of the fire. The scene made the silent, still sentries look like fiery goblins keeping vigil as they awaited a sinister master.

"Who are they and what are they doing just standing there around the fire? And what is up with the frost on the trees and that putrid stench?" Truin asked.

"No idea, little brother, no idea."

As they watched from what seemed to them to be a safe distance, they heard a low, garbled resonance emanating from the mysterious group. A moment later, the resonance became an incoherent chant in a language they could not understand.

Unknown to Ka'el and Truin, the hooded group of teenagers met in this place every full moon, and the dark ceremony they would soon perform would call upon an evil that Ka'el and Truin had never even imagined.

The group of teenagers had played together for several years. Their amusements had started out harmlessly enough, playing *innocent* games that actively used their imaginations. They ignored the truths of their fathers and chose instead to look for a new truth in the stars, in nature, and in their own imaginings. They played games with dark, fantastic characters of various powers and desires. By doing so, they unwittingly empowered the dark forces around them and within them.

In the beginning, it had all been in good fun, but they soon found out that their imaginary creatures actually existed in the spiritual realm. Ignoring God's warnings to stay away from such activity, they ignorantly opened their souls to the influence and control of these dark spiritual forces.

They played with evil and gradually allowed it to sear their consciences. First, they allowed depraved thoughts to inhabit their minds. Then, by accepting the thoughts as their own, they embraced the darkness that was so deviously planted within the fertile soil of their spirits.

They opened their hearts and minds to darkness, and the unseen demons in their midst readily accepted their invitations to begin the harvest of their souls.

As Ka'el and Truin watched, it readily became apparent that one youth was leading the others in the ritual. The leader's name had been Pete, and he had, until recently, worked in the mines with his father, providing for his family. However, something had happened to Pete, and he no longer resembled the young man he had been, inwardly or outwardly. In a very short time, Pete's thoughts, words, and actions had taken a menacing turn. Pete had run away from his home, left all concern for his family behind, and begun living among the animals in the forest.

Physically, Pete had grown unnaturally large, his countenance became very threatening, and his voice had sunk much deeper; matching his sinister appearance. He had rapidly risen to a position of leadership among his longtime group of game-playing friends and successfully guided them into experimenting with ever-increasingly darker fascinations.

As the group of teenagers enthusiastically chanted around the fire, a rudimentary Ouija board, carefully placed at the center of the large pentagram they surrounded, spelled out a name.

K-A-R-Y-A-N.

Once the Ouija board had spelled out the name, the group began chanting the name repeatedly; their voices growing in intensity with each repetition.

"Karyan."

"Karyan."

"Karyan!"

The sound of the chanting seemed to feed the flames of the fire, whipping them up in untamed excitement; while, paradoxically, the chill in the air grew more and more frigid. The horrific smell became unbearably bitter and noxious.

Simultaneously, Ka'el and Truin reached up and pinched their noses, cringing at the repugnant smell.

"We have to get out of here, Ka'el! I don't know what is going on here, but this is definitely not a good place to be."

"We are fine, little brother. Don't worry, I'll protect you."

"Really, with those long locks of golden blonde hair, and—"

A sudden swell in the chanting cut his words off. The boys' attention snapped back to the strange happenings before them.

"Karyan!"

"Karyan!"

"Karyan!"

The leader of the group stepped out from the rest of the circle and approached the raging fire. Then, standing in front of the fire, the shadowy figure deliberately removed his heavy hood. As he did so, the chanting ceased, the fire flared in angry intensity, and the winds circled ominously around the fire. Dirt, leaves, small rocks, and other forest debris from the surrounding area joined the frenzied torrent of matter and energy swirling around the dark assembly.

The fire transformed itself into different animal shapes, each shape morphing into another with no rhyme or reason. Suddenly, a much more ominous creature appeared in the fire, feeding upon the flames in which it stood. In some ways, it resembled that of a man, but not a man like anyone had ever seen. The fiery creature was enormous, a full three times that of the now un-hooded man standing before it. Though its shape changed continuously as the flames of the fire twisted, the boys could see that the fiery creature had large wings, a tail, scaly limbs, and enormous claws. Its face was that of a man, but of a man terribly disfigured. It had long, thin, spiky ears; a cavernous mouth with pointed teeth; and gigantic eyes that burned even a brighter red than that of the fire in which it lived.

The fire creature appeared to be communicating with the hooded gathering in words indecipherable to Ka'el and Truin.

"Ka'el! Let's beat feet!"

The vision before them mesmerized Ka'el. "What could this be?"

"Evil. That is what it is. Pure evil! We have to go, now!"

As Truin spoke, the fire creature's gaze snapped in their direction. Its blazing eyes locked on to them, and its mouth snarled in a devilish grimace. The faces of the hooded followers all turned together to look directly at Ka'el and Truin; their previously cloaked features glowing beneath their hoods in reflected moonlight like ghoulish corpses. Their sunken eye sockets remained black chasms; completely void of any light.

This shocked Ka'el out of his trance.

"Run." Ka'el's protective concern for his little brother seized its rightful place over his youthful overconfidence.

"What?" Truin's eyes remained fixed on the foreboding image before him.

"Run, Truin, run!" Ka'el was no longer concerned with their futile attempts to be stealthy.

Truin did not have to be told twice; well, at least not three times. He stood, pivoted, and departed the area as swiftly as humanly possible. Ka'el stood promptly to follow him, but turned back for just one more look. He made eye contact with the beast. A shiver ran down Ka'el's spine as the beast snarled his name from the flames. "Ka'el."

As Ka'el took off after his brother into the shadows of the forest, a solitary hooded figure with green eyes repeated his name. "Ka'el."

†††

Not long after the strange events of that night in the forest, Ka'el and Truin set out on the hunt. This time they headed south, to the Omentian plains. After their last encounter, they wanted to ensure they had plenty of warning of anything unusual that might head their way.

Ka'el and Truin had spoken often about that night in the forest, yet they had kept it a secret from the rest of the family. Why, they weren't exactly sure. On the one hand, they didn't know what to make of it. It was just so unbelievable. They doubted whether anyone would believe them if they shared what they had witnessed. On the other hand, they didn't want to scare Evelin and Elin. The women overreacted to such things. So, even though they felt bad not telling their family, especially their father, they conveniently rationalized that they should keep it a secret; at least for the time being.

The strange sightings in the forest profoundly affected Truin. The Spirit stirred within Truin, and he saw the evil behind all they had witnessed that night and the threat it posed to the family. He always knew that the peoples of Omentia worshipped false gods, but he had never witnessed such a manifestation of their dark rituals in person. After the experience, he realized more than ever the false sense of security his family had been enjoying as they lived in the pagan land. They had been ignoring the heathen beliefs of the peoples around them and trusting that their family would remain unaffected by their practices. Truin could now see that eventually they would be in direct conflict with their neighbors; his bet was sooner rather than later.

Ka'el's take on the whole forest experience was much different. What they saw had initially brought him much anxiety. But in retrospect, he was more curious about what they had witnessed than fearful.

What is that mysterious group doing in the forest? What is with that creature in the fire? How did it know my name?

Ka'el thought often of going back on some other moonlit night to learn more about the strange practices of the cloaked ones.

After they traveled across the Omentian plain for most of the morning, the young men spotted a lake in the distance. The area surrounding the lake appeared to be quite fertile, densely covered in foliage of many types. The boys thought there must surely be an abundance of wildlife there for the taking. Unfortunately, they had to first pass across a relatively barren stretch of land, basically desert, in order to get to the lake.

Discussing their alternatives, they decided they had all the water they needed to make their way across the stretch of wasteland. They would then simply refill their water bags once they reached the lake, and they would then have plenty of water for the return trip.

After reaching a consensus, they set out across the barren wasteland. About an hour later, as the sun rose high in the sky and their skin felt the full assault of the harsh rays of an early afternoon sun, something went terribly wrong.

"Oh, oh!" Truin said, as he looked down at the ground with a bewildered look on his face.

"What is it, Truin? What's wrong?"

Truin's demeanor abruptly changed. He held his hands high above his head. "Stop Ka'el, stop! Don't come any closer!"

Ka'el froze. When he did, he noticed Truin was shrinking. A second later, Ka'el could comprehend what his eyes were telling him. Truin wasn't shrinking; he was sinking into the earth!

"What is this?" Truin cried in desperation as he struggled to pull himself back out of the shifting sand beneath his feet.

His protective instinct kicking in, Ka'el lunged forward to grab his brother's arm and hand, hoping to pull him from the sinking sands that had already consumed both of Truin's feet and calves. However, as he did, the sinking sand snatched one of Ka'el's feet and ankles. Instinctively, Ka'el fell backwards upon firm ground and with his backwards momentum could pull himself free from the deadly menace.

"Stay back Ka'el! Stay back, or you will get trapped as well!"

"I can't reach you, Truin, I can't reach you!" Ka'el watched his brother sink another foot into the ground below them.

Their minds raced for a solution as Truin continued to struggle to get free.

Ka'el noticed the struggle had only made Truin's predicament worse and that with every bit of energy and effort Truin employed to get free, the sinking sand advanced its hold on him. "Stop fighting it Truin! Stop fighting the sand and just relax."

"Relax? That is easy for you to say!"

"Trust me, it is difficult for me to say it, but you have to stop fighting the sand!"

"I know it sounds crazy, but struggling is working against you and advancing the sinking sand's hold. We need to buy time to find help. Stop fighting it! The more you fight it, the more it quickens!"

It was very difficult for Truin to control his fear as he continued to sink deeper. Truin took several deep breaths and forced himself to stop struggling against the sand that had pulled him under the ground to his waist.

Ka'el saw nothing in the area that could readily help them. Then he remembered some broken tree limbs they had passed a couple of miles back.

"I'm going back for those tree limbs we passed. Maybe I can reach you with them, and I can pull you out of there."

Truin tore his focus from the sands consuming him and looked into Ka'el's eyes.

"You're leaving? Really?"

"I hate to leave you Truin, but we have to do something. We are running out of time!"

Truin assessed the situation and took a few breaths. He calmed down and clearly understood his brother's intentions. "I understand brother, go."

Ka'el turned and began running to retrieve the tree limbs he hoped could save his brother.

"And Ka'el!"

Ka'el stopped and turned back toward Truin, almost falling over from his sudden change in direction.

"I'll wait for you right here, ok?"

Ka'el, amazed at Truin's witty quip, responded with his own attempt at levity. "You better wait for me! Right there!"

Truin frowned nervously. He knew for all of Ka'el's strengths, speed had never been one of them. It wasn't looking very good for the home team.

As Ka'el took off in a sprint, Truin's reality shifted. In an instant, his priorities turned upside down and inside out. The trivial daily wants and needs that had preoccupied his mind just moments before were now completely gone. None of them seemed remotely important anymore. His thoughts turned instead to his short life, and how he had spent his days.

What was it all about? What difference did I make? How have I served the Lord? Is this how it will end?

Alone, under a blazing sun and rapidly sinking into the hot depths of the earth, precious tears flowed from Truin's eyes. Falling, they promptly turned to mist as they impacted the hot sand engulfing him.

Truin prayed out loud.

"Lord, God almighty, the great I AM, Lord of my father, and my father's father before him; all praise, all glory, all honor, and all power be to you! Maker of the universe, the sun, the earth, and all upon the earth; giver of life and all good things; to you I lift my voice. Save me from the grip of the earth. Surely, I have not done all that you have planned for me to accomplish in my life. Surely, there is more that you wish for me to do to serve you. But if it is your will that these sands take me, your will be done, Oh Lord. You give and you take away. Blessed be your name! Into your hands, my God, I commit my spirit."

When Truin opened his eyes, he could see that he had sunk even deeper into the sinking sand. It appeared it was the Lord's wish that he leave this land and go to his eternal home.

So be it. Whether I live or I die, I belong to the Lord.

Truin remembered the many nights around the fire with his family, studying the Word. He remembered all the promises God had made and a sudden peace came over him.

"Need some help?"

The voice caught Truin by surprise, and he wasn't sure where it came from. He looked up, squinting into the bright sunlight. He could barely make out the figure of a man standing over him on the sand. The man was young and strong in appearance. His hair looked blonde, even blonder at the tips, with a band of silver streaking through it.

"Yes sir. I would appreciate that." Truin was much more relaxed than anyone in his situation should be.

Without delay, the stranger pulled Truin out of the grips of certain death. Mysteriously, the blonde stranger was having no problem keeping a firm footing on the shifting sand. This struck Truin as odd, but he really didn't care how the stranger was doing it. The exuberant realization that he would live overwhelmed Truin's senses, and he couldn't process much more than that.

As the stranger lifted Truin to firm ground, he could now see the blonde man's complexion was as white as a cloud, with no sign of any sun coloring or damage. His features were pleasant, like those of a child. Yet this man was certainly not a child. He lifted Truin out of the quicksand as if he was lifting a small sheep out of the river. No child could do that.

Truin was exhausted. The intense heat of the sun and the panicked struggle against the unrelenting sands had combined to deplete all of Truin's energy. The best he could do was to sit up as he tried humbly to thank the stranger for liberating him from the sands.

"I thought it was the end of the road until you came along. My brother went to find some help, but I don't think he would have made it back in time. I thought I was going to die right there, all alone."

"Alone? Oh no, you are far from alone."

The strange response surprised Truin, but he let it slide.

"May I ask your name, my friend?"

"My name? My name is Engel."

"Well Engel," Truin said as he pointed toward the area up ahead, "my brother and I were heading towards that lake over yonder."

It was at that point that Truin realized a few things. First, as he looked and pointed toward the lake up ahead, he saw that there wasn't a lake up ahead.

Where did it go?

It then struck him, again, that the stranger had been standing on the same sands that he had been sinking in.

How can he do that?

As he turned to look back toward Engel, his new friend was no longer there. Engel had vanished.

Did I imagine the whole thing? I'm free from the sinking sand that a moment before had all but consumed me. If no one pulled me out, how did I get out?

As he tried to figure out what had just happened, Ka'el approached, running faster than Truin had ever seen him run. He arrived with a six-foot tree limb in tow to use in pulling Truin out of the sand.

As Ka'el reached Truin, he collapsed beside him, exhausted from his desperate run. Ka'el could barely catch his breath. "What happened? How did you get out? I mean, I'm happy to find you alive. I thought I might not make it back in time, but how?"

"A stranger pulled me out. His name was Engel."

"Who? What stranger?" Ka'el scanned the horizon for the man he apparently missed.

"The stranger. Didn't you see him as you returned?"

"I didn't see anyone besides you, Truin." Ka'el was growing somewhat concerned that his little brother might have been in the scorching sun too long.

After a few minutes, Truin could stand on his feet with Ka'el's help. They both stared off into the distance where the lake had once been, or so they had thought. Confused and exhausted, but alive; they called it a day.

What do all these things mean? What strange purpose lies behind these happenings? Who is behind them?

So many questions needed answering, but the brothers decided the answers could wait until they had made it back to the secure surroundings of their home and their family.

As the young men made their way back across the flat wasteland toward the security of the green forest ahead, Ka'el looked at Truin and made light of the entire ordeal. Ka'el sported his renowned smile. "We sure have fun on these little adventures, don't we?"

Truin tried to keep from grinning for as long as he could; after all, he had almost died. But seeing the giant smile on Ka'el's face, he couldn't keep a straight face for more than a few seconds. "If you say so, big brother. If you say so."

†††

The family did not know what to make of Ka'el and Truin's stories from the forest and the plains. Elin, who had been the recipient of many of their pranks over the years, found the stories just a little too unbelievable to be true. She thought her two older brothers were manufacturing yet more wild tales for their own amusement.

Evelin, knowing her boys better than Elin, could see they were telling the truth; or at least they were telling what they believed to be the truth about what they had experienced. She pondered their words, but soon found the events her boys described too disturbing to dwell on. Trusting that Abner would do what was required to settle the situation, she also overlooked their stories.

Upon hearing the stories of both the forest ritual and the desert event that nearly took Truin's life, Abner became disturbed by what he recognized as telltale signs. He could clearly see the signs of the impending dangers that were rising in their own backyard; signs of a hidden war that was raging in the shadows all around them. This war would soon force everyone in the land to choose a side; either stand against evil or give in to it.

Gone was the time a man could postpone the decision by simply looking the other way. Should his family remain in this land; a land in which he and Eve had planted their roots so long ago, made a beautiful home, raised three fine children, and made so many wonderful memories? Or should they pack up and move west to a land free of this growing evil and start their lives anew?

Abner knew most, if not all, of his neighbors would say he should stay. They would call him foolish to even consider leaving after all that he had built in Omentia. "Why would you leave, because of some children playing games in the forest and one minor accident in the desert?"

However, Abner saw things they didn't see. He saw a changing culture in the land all around him and the obvious warnings that no good would come from that change.

Still, Abner decided he should give more thought and prayer to such a significant decision.

CHAPTER 8

TRAGEDY

†††

All the trees were falling.

"What in the world?" Truin stood frozen in place, staring up into the highlands. "What is going on up there?"

Ka'el followed Truin's gaze to the distant hills ahead. All the trees on one hill were crashing to the ground, one after the other, like dominoes. "I've never seen anything like that happen before. What would cause that to happen?"

Ka'el, Truin, and Thor had been hunting rabbit, quail, pheasant, and deer all morning. Both of Abner's sons became quite accomplished with their bows, knives, and slings. Ka'el had taught Truin well, and Truin had more than matched Ka'el's hunting skills; though Ka'el would never have admitted it.

This day's take had been plentiful, and each of the young men carried some of the morning's bounty. The hills and forest were teaming with game of all sorts, and the family would eat well that evening.

As the brothers tried to figure out exactly what it was they were seeing, they heard a low rumble coming from the hills ahead of them. Thor stood at alert, watching the brush up ahead.

"What is it, boy?" Truin stood next to Thor, trying to see what he saw.

The hair on the back of Thor's neck and upper back stood; his tail froze. A low pitch growl emanated from deep within his throat, and his jowls rose.

Ka'el deliberately drew his bow. Truin, following Ka'el's lead, readied his knife. The low rumble grew louder and louder, like a monster approaching at high speed through the trees.

"I don't like this, Truin."

Suddenly, without warning, a thunderous wind swept through the area, knocking the boys from their feet. Branches and leaves blew from the trees. Rocks and ground debris flew in every direction.

The boys turned on their stomachs and covered their heads for protection. Thor tumbled into a gully, where his instincts told him to remain. The ground shook like they had never felt it shake before!

After a minute, the boys picked themselves up off the ground. Thor was quick to join them.

"Tru, are you alright?"

Truin brushed himself off and checked on Thor. "Yeah, I guess so. Are you OK?"

"Yeah."

As they looked around, they couldn't believe their eyes. The whirlwind had toppled a line of trees a hundred paces wide, beginning in the hills far above them, continuing through their current position, and running down the hill to the stream far below. It was a miracle they had survived the blast, let alone remained unscathed.

But where one threat had come and gone, another still approached. An enormous boulder in a towering rock face above them, shaken from its foundation by the mysterious blast, broke free and began its unobstructed freefall towards the brothers. As it plummeted, the tumbling rocks that had broken free just ahead of the boulder caught Thor's attention; his ears and tail stiffening as his head snapped to the left and his eyes locked on the falling rocks. Thor's instincts sent the otherwise fearless canine darting for the trees.

Truin noticed stones and pebbles falling past his eyes and landing at his feet. It took a moment to comprehend what was happening; a moment they didn't have.

Truin looked up and saw. His eyes widened, adrenaline pumped, and without hesitation, his reflexes did what came naturally; he saved his brother.

"Ka'el, look out!" Truin lunged forward and pushed his surprised brother towards the gully where Thor had once again taken refuge.

As Ka'el flew through the air, he locked eyes with Truin. The look was surprise, fear, concern, love, and dread all rolled into one.

This event was totally unforeseen and totally unpredictable. In a moment, everything changed — forever.

✝✝✝

As Ka'el hit the ground and rolled into the gully, the preponderance of the falling rock ledge reached Truin. Standing defenselessly beneath its onslaught, Truin was out of time and ideas. Ka'el watched in horror as Truin took the brunt of the falling rock. It smashed into Truin like ten charging bulls and tossed him into a nearby tree like a discarded rag doll.

"Tru! No!"

A few seconds later, the avalanche abating, Ka'el and Thor rushed to Truin's side. He was in terrible shape. His body was badly beaten and cut up. The force of the avalanche crushed Truin's left arm.

"My brother, what have you done? What have you done? No! It should have been me!"

Carefully taking his brother into his arms, the tears flowed like streams from Ka'el's eyes. Love, a rush of childhood memories, and excruciating guilt overwhelmed Ka'el. Yet, this was not the time for emotion. This was the time for action. Truin needed help, and he needed it now!

"Thor! Run ahead, get help!"

Thor snapped to attention on Ka'el's words, then after but a moment's hesitation, dashed toward home.

As Ka'el lifted his unconscious brother onto his shoulders and raced for home, he felt helpless and alone.

He was not alone. Beyond his limited physical senses to perceive, they stood beside and all around Ka'el. A whisper echoed like thunder in another dimension. "Master, help them?"

†††

Two months had passed since Truin's life had undergone the life-altering change. Still, he was alive.

The most terrifying moment for Abner and Evelin was the moment they saw Ka'el emerge from the forest with Truin in his arms. The sun was just peaking over the western horizon as Ka'el and Truin strenuously made their long approach through the wheat fields to the ranch.

Thor had arrived alone hours earlier, barking and howling as if to announce that something terrible had happened, but Abner did not think it wise to head off into the darkness in the middle of the night in search of the boys. He prepared as best he could to set out at first light to find them and was just about to follow Thor back into the forest when the boys appeared at the far edge of the fields.

Abner and Evelin ran into the fields to meet Ka'el. When they finally took Truin into their arms, Ka'el collapsed, disappearing below the heads of wheat. Ka'el was exhausted. He had used every bit of his strength to carry Truin home without stopping even once to rest.

Truin had been close to death. He had lost a lot of blood, and was unconscious. Abner carried him back to the cottage, where Evelin and Elin immediately tended to his injuries.

The first two weeks had been touch and go. No one thought Truin was going to make it, though no one dare say the words. With the help of Doctor Phil, Truin regained consciousness. That is when the reality of his injuries truly hit home; Truin would never be the same.

Initially, Truin felt thrilled to be alive. He remembered little of the accident, but Ka'el filled him in on the specifics.

"Tru, you saved my life! You are a hero! You pushed me out of the way of the falling rocks, even though that meant you would take the full brunt of their assault and pay the full price."

And pay the price he had. Doctor Phil could stabilize Truin's injuries and patch up his wounds, but he wasn't a miracle worker. The many internal injuries, not to mention Truin's crushed left arm, were far beyond Doctor Phil's or any healer's abilities to mend. So Doctor Phil, Abner, Evelin, and Elin turned to the best and only hope they had; they turned to God in prayer. Morning, noon, and night, they prayed over Truin; they prayed to the God they knew would hear and answer their prayers.

It broke Abner's and Evelin's hearts that Truin would have to go through the rest of his life handicapped, without the use of his left arm — if it was God's will, he even lived. Truin loved jousting with his brother in the fields each day; it brought him so much joy. How would this accident ultimately affect Truin's future? How much of a burden would it be for him? They did not know. What they knew was that God could use even the least of his servants for his purpose, and that God's strength was greater than any handicap Truin might have.

The Lord has a plan, and the Lord will be faithful in its unfolding. We must trust God's omnipotent wisdom. We must see past this tragedy.

Ka'el had a unique set of troubles. He felt overwhelmed with guilt on the one hand and consumed by jealousy on the other — both rooted in sinful pride. His younger brother had saved his life, and that was a bitter pill for Ka'el to swallow. He should have been the one protecting Truin — the one saving Truin's life.

It should have been me. I should have taken care of my little brother.

Ka'el felt as if everyone he met was thinking the same thing. Forever, he would have to live with this shame. In addition, he would forever live in the shadow of his hero brother and the constant deference given to Truin for his sacrifice that day. Truin had stolen the honor that should have been his. Again, Ka'el's pride raged within.

Ka'el knew these thoughts and feelings were wrong, but he couldn't get them to leave him alone. The more he tried, the worse they plagued him. So, emotionally, he left. He spent more and more time out hunting on his own, avoiding all contact with Truin. The bond that he had once shared with his brother faded until it was effectively gone.

Elin became Truin's best friend. The moment her parents brought Truin into the farmhouse, Elin's maternal instinct kicked in; she never left Truin's side. She did everything Doctor Phil and her mother requested she do to care for her brother and much, much more. Truin recognized and appreciated her efforts. The long days, weeks, and months on the tortuous road to recovery gave him ample time to internalize all that his sister was doing for him; all she had given up in her life to make his life bearable.

"Someday you will become a prominent leader, Truin," she would tell him when he felt like giving up. "God will use you in great ways. You just wait and see."

Truin would never forget Elin's example of unselfish love, and he thanked God for his sister dozens of time every day. He couldn't imagine how he would ever make it up to her.

It took several months under Evelin and Elin's constant care and attention for Truin to heal both internally and externally. Though the left side of his body was and would remain covered with ugly scars that would forever remind him of the incident, Truin would regain at least partial use of his arm. Doctor Phil had done a terrific job of setting and stitching it up, but it would never be quite the same. Truin could straighten his arm, but anything else was just not possible; at least not for the foreseeable future.

At first, Truin was very depressed. So much had changed so rapidly. The sudden changes forced Truin to rethink all of his hopes and dreams, leaving his future uncertain.

What will become of me now, now that I am but half a man?

With the constant attention of his sister and the incessant prayers of his parents, Truin pushed back the dark clouds of worry, fear, and sadness that relentlessly attacked him both day and night. Through the eyes of faith, he found hope.

One day I will see the purpose of what has happened to me. One day I will again dream.

So Abner and Evelin prayed, Elin nursed, Truin persevered, and Ka'el hunted. Time passed, but it would take more than time to heal these wounds.

Chapter 9

Bad Signs

††††

D arkness extended its grip over Omentia. Men turned away from the truth that their fathers had passed down to them and, seduced by the fascination of the unknown, abandoned the truth they knew for the allure of strange new ideas and wonders they did not understand. Their minds turned toward their wealth, their luxuries, and the feeding of their carnal desires. They abandoned the one true God who had created all things and instead worshipped the things he created.

They elevated their selfish concerns for convenience, pleasure, and earthly opportunity far above the preservation of the truth and morality handed down to them. Turning their spirits over to demons; they dishonored their bodies with one another; and sacrificed their defenseless children, both born and unborn, to their new gods. Unrepentant, they sealed their destinies; both in this world and in the one to come.

††††

"We have been very successful in the land," Satan proclaimed to his winged followers. "Good work Viscere, Pecunius, Glutonus, and Scire. The men of Omentia are growing weaker by the moment. They are only concerned with what they can see; the wealth in their hands, the food for their gut, and the accumulation of their knowledge; as trivial as it might be. They have traded the worship of God for the worship of his gifts. Perfect!"

"We are now ready for you, Doldrus, you Terrus, and you Metus! Go into the land and bring the Omentians the desires of their selfish hearts and the fruits of their menial labors. Then we will give them the suffering their foolishness deserves!"

As he spoke, wave after wave of demon, led by Satan's closest lieutenants, descended on the land of Omentia like the rains that fall in dark sheets over the plains and bring life to all the creation. However, this cloud did not bring life. Instead, it brought slavery, destruction, and death.

Cottage by cottage, settlement by settlement, and village by village fell into the darkness; first the parents and then their children. Depravity in thought, word, and deed became the rule instead of the exception. The darkness transformed neighbors into strangers, friends into foes, and the Omentians' love into anxiety, fear, and hatred. Chaos would soon take hold of Omentia, as men, no longer trusting each other, quit working together for the common good.

Satan was pleased. The land was ripe for the harvest of those who would do his bidding. They would learn his dark arts, speak his dark words, and gladly obey all of his dark commands.

CHAPTER 10

A MARRIAGE

†††

One summer afternoon, while Ka'el was out hunting alone in the forest, he heard a terrifying scream. Tearing toward the screams as fast as he could, he found a young woman pinned against a rock wall by a very large, brown-hump bear.

Without hesitation, Ka'el ran toward the bear, waving his hands and yelling at the top of his lungs. He had been told that running toward the bear, waving his hands and yelling at the top of his lungs, would often scare it away unless it was angry, had previously tasted human flesh, or was exceptionally hungry. To Ka'el's dismay, this bear wanted lunch, and he was now on the menu.

"Run, to the high rocks!" Ka'el directed the young woman. Ka'el charged the bear at top speed. He had two seconds to figure out what to do next. He knew the bear — a ten-foot tall, two thousand pound killing machine — was a formidable opponent. To say that Ka'el was confident about the outcome of this encounter would be inaccurate. Still, hesitating at this point in his attack would show fear, and both the animal kingdom and the kingdom of man universally understood that showing fear was the first step in a brief journey to failure. Failure in this case meant certain death, so there was really only one thing to do; charge the bear. This caught both the woman and the brown-hump bear completely by surprise.

The bear rose on its hind feet, tearing at the air with its powerful front claws and letting out a bellowing roar.

Ka'el had drawn his eight-inch hunting blade and was formulating his attack plan. The bear's instinct and experiences most likely taught it that rising on its hind legs and roaring always terrorized its prey. It was no doubt confused by Ka'el's speedy and audacious attack. By the time the monster lashed out at Ka'el with its mighty claws, Ka'el had already maneuvered abeam the beast's position and slashed across its right hind shank with his razor-sharp blade. This had severed the key muscles and tendons in the bear's right hind leg that allowed the monster to stand erect.

As Ka'el rolled out of his tactical attack, the bear's right leg gave out. The bear crashed to the earth, still sweeping its claws through the air, trying to contact Ka'el. The bear's claw tore into the earth as it crashed to the ground. Ka'el now stood between the writhing bear and the young woman. Facing the bear, Ka'el instantly assumed a fighting stance and planned his next move. He didn't want to kill the bear, but since it was a man-hunter, it was a menace to all life in the area and needed to be dealt with appropriately.

There was also, of course, the matter of the girl. Though Ka'el had not yet had the time to fully ascertain the young woman's — specific features, he had noticed her basic shape and appearance. Since he had stormed a savage beast without hesitation, something about the girl had obviously appealed to him; not that he wouldn't have done the same for any damsel in distress. He couldn't leave the girl with an angry and wounded killer bear. Besides, a bear with a wound like the one Ka'el had inflicted would not last long in the wild. Before long, a pack of wolves or another bear would certainly have taken its life.

I'm considering it a mercy killing!

Ka'el's preemptive attack and superior speed had given him the advantage over the much larger predator. The furry hunter was now the furry prey.

Ka'el moved swiftly in a circle around the bear. Though the bear tried to turn with him, its injury did not allow it to keep up. It didn't take long before Ka'el was behind the bear and in position to make his next and hopefully last attack. The maneuver was bold. The timing would be critical.

Ka'el ran and jumped on the back of the brown-hump bear, grabbing hold of the scruff of its back above its hump and wrapping his legs about the bear's upper torso as tightly as he could. The beast was not happy. It threw its head and upper body about in anger, intensely frustrated that it could not reach its attacker.

As Ka'el hung on with all his might, he again drew the bloodstained, eight-inch blade and thrust it repetitively into the neck and throat of the beast. Blood sprayed in all directions from the lethal wounds.

To the bear's credit, the wounds inflicted by Ka'el did little to deter it from continuing the fight. However, the rapid drainage of precious fuel from its major arteries was too much for it to endure for long. Previously the uncontested master of its territory, the great bear succumbed to the blade and its wielder. As the life-light faded from its brown eyes, the bear and Ka'el collapsed together to the earth. A cloud of dirt rose around them as they hit the ground, momentarily obscuring them from the young woman's sight. When the dust settled, a tired but elated Ka'el stood over the dead carcass of the magnificent beast.

Well, this should get me some attention.

The young woman, amazed at her champion's courage and a bit surprised by his success, ran to Ka'el and threw her arms around him, giving him a big hug.

The demonstration of the woman's gratitude surprised Ka'el, but he accepted the hug gratefully. After all, he had earned it.

A moment later, the young woman, abruptly realizing that she was hugging a total stranger, stepped back, embarrassed.

"Oh, I am so sorry. Please excuse my boldness."

"No problem, really," Ka'el then noticed the beauty of the woman that he had just saved. She was about six inches shorter than he was and had an exceedingly attractive figure. Her hair was as black as the forest on a moonless night, her skin had a deep brown tan, and her eyes glowed a dark emerald green color.

She is stunning! Ka'el like!

"My name is Tala. What is your name?"

"My name is Ka'el, and my family lives over the ridge, beyond the river. Where do you live and how did you ever find yourself out here all alone?"

"I am alone. My whole family died in a fire two years ago. I was traveling through this land trying to find a place to start a new life."

Ka'el could not stop looking into her eyes. She was so incredibly beautiful. Every word that was exiled from her lips — none would ever leave voluntarily — did so in the most intoxicating way! Her beauty captivated Ka'el!

"You shouldn't be out here all alone. Come with me to my home tonight. My family has plenty of room, and you're welcomed to stay with us for as long as it takes to find a suitable place to live."

Tala smiled. "Thank you Ka'el. Thank you sincerely. I don't know why fate has brought us together, but I am eternally indebted to you."

So Ka'el brought Tala home to dinner that evening, to the great surprise of his family. It would have been inhospitable of Abner to not offer Tala a room, as his son had already extended the invitation. And so Tala stayed.

†††

It wasn't easy to find a suitable place for Tala to live, and it didn't take long for Tala and Ka'el to become inseparable. Tala always said the right words, wore the right clothes, and did the right things in all the right ways, but something just wasn't quite right. Truin could see it clearly; Ka'el could not.

Before long, Ka'el and Tala were courting. Truin attempted to intervene, pointing out to Ka'el that Tala did not share his core beliefs in the one, true God; that this difference would lead to major problems down the road.

"What do you really know about her? At least give it some time, Ka'el."

But it was too late for Ka'el to change course. Ka'el couldn't think of living a day without Tala in his life. His desire and longing for Tala grew with every passing day and soon it outweighed what he knew in his mind was right; what he knew the Lord had directed concerning such things. Because of his disagreement with Truin, the brothers grew even farther apart.

One day, unbeknownst to the rest of the family, Ka'el and Tala ran off and were married. They returned home and shocked Abner and Evelin by announcing they had become husband and wife. Realizing there was nothing they could do to change what had already been done, Abner and Evelin accepted Tala into the family and did all they could to make her feel welcome.

Truin felt let down by Ka'el's hasty and imprudent choice of a wife. Truin believed that choosing an unbeliever for a life-mate could only lead to a life of trouble.

What have you done, brother? What will you teach your children?

Truin felt partially responsible for the direction Ka'el's life had turned. He should have been there for Ka'el, and tried harder to dissuade him from this marriage; shown him the error of choosing this course of action. He longed for the days when he and Ka'el were side by side in the forest hunting. Those days seemed so far away. So much had changed so rapidly.

Abner gave Ka'el forty acres of prime farmland as a gift on the occasion of his marriage to Tala. On this land, Ka'el built a small cottage for Tala. Though Ka'el wanted to complete the cottage by himself, winter was swiftly approaching. So the entire family, including Truin, helped Ka'el finish the home before the winter snows.

Ka'el and Tala's new home was a picturesque dwelling on a small knoll, nestled up to the foothills. Behind the cottage, ancient and majestic trees shaded the house from the sun in the summer and shielded it from the north winds in the winter. It was beautiful, and the newlyweds couldn't wait to begin their new life together.

With each passing week, Tala became more and more accepted as a member of the family. Ka'el conscientiously instructed her in the way of truth, determined to have spiritual unity within his family and to have his future children raised — knowing the true God of their fathers. Despite not being taught the Word in her childhood, Tala showed openness to hearing it and soon started taking part in regular worship with the family.

However, Tala had already learned another way. Several years earlier, she had dabbled in the mysterious dark arts. Following a young miner boy named Pete, who overnight had gained extraordinary powers and abilities, Tala had joined a secret group for monthly meetings in the forest. There she had witnessed amazing things; things her parents would simply not have understood. Soon, she too had done things she should have never had the power to do.

Tala wanted to tell Ka'el about this incredible source of power that she had discovered, but the right time had never quite presented itself. So Tala continued to make reasonable excuses about where she was going every month on those nights when she and the others would meet in the forest under the full moon. She felt bad for not telling Ka'el; essentially lying to him. But Pete, or Karyan as he was now called, agreed that the right time for full disclosure had not yet come.

There was an even deeper secret that Tala withheld from her new husband. It had been Karyan that had encouraged Tala to meet Ka'el in the first place, immediately following the night Ka'el and Truin had discovered the group's secret meeting place in the forest. Tala had shown an immediate interest in Ka'el, and Karyan had selfishly seen it as an opportunity he could not pass up; an opportunity that would reap a glorious return in the future. Arranging the chance meeting of the two in the forest, and even controlling the basic movements of the enormous bear that had threatened Tala, Karyan had manufactured a scenario that had successfully spiked Ka'el's interest in Tala. Tala's extraordinary beauty, combined with the orchestrated play in which she and Ka'el had met, had produced an elixir that had completely overwhelmed Ka'el's senses, undermined his reason, and filled his heart with an uncontrollable desire for Tala. This desire had prematurely resulted in their hasty union as husband and wife.

†††

When Tala and Ka'el had been married for approximately six months, Ka'el discovered Tala had been lying to him about her monthly jaunts into the forest. When he confronted Tala, she told him everything. Against Karyan's specific instructions, she told Ka'el about her meetings with the others in the forest and the specifics regarding their very first meeting.

Ka'el was furious. He felt deeply hurt and betrayed. He couldn't believe that Tala had been there that night; the same night he and Truin had witnessed the monster in the fire. In addition, his new wife had lied to him repeatedly over the previous six months about where she was going and what she was doing.

Ka'el doubted Tala's sincerity, her integrity, and her beliefs. He wondered if he had ever really known Tala at all. Could he ever trust her? What kind of evil is she mixed up in? He deeply regretted having taken Tala so hastily for his wife and wondered how he could ever break this news to his family.

Tala tried to ease Ka'el's suspicion, ensuring him that her feelings for him were true and that she had never meant to deceive him. She insisted she had wanted to tell him the truth all along, but that she was simply afraid that he wouldn't have understood. She assured him she had planned on telling him the truth as soon as she knew how and when to do it.

Tala took advantage of the opportunity to persuade Ka'el to come with her to the meetings in the forest and to learn of the power that he too could hold in his hands. She showed him some of what she had learned, speaking the dark words Karyan had taught her, but instead of having their intended effect, these demonstrations further alienated Ka'el and filled him with fear.

Though Tala continued to entice Ka'el to study the dark arts with her and learn of their power, Ka'el resisted. Ka'el couldn't help but be curious as to the power the dark arts held; he had been curious ever since that first night in the forest. But he prayed to God for strength to defend against the temptation to feed his curiosity, and God answered his prayers.

Ka'el kept all these events from his family because of embarrassment and shame. He wanted to talk with Truin about the terrible situation he now found himself in, but the crevasse between him and Truin had grown too wide; his pride, once again, got in his way.

Ka'el now saw Tala and her beliefs as a threat to his family; a cancer that he must protect them from. Instead of asking his parents or Truin for help, he bore the daily struggle alone. And so, to insulate them from Tala, Ka'el drifted even further away from his family.

†††

Fractos watched from another dimension, a dimension invisible to those with mere physical eyes. His job was to divide those who would pose a threat to Satan's plan to eradicate all believers in the one true God.

The first step in conquering mortals was always to divide them. Together, mortals could support each other, hold up the weakest among them, and stand. However, once divided, they would have no one to turn to when attacked and would fall much more easily to the persuasive power of darkness.

Fractos had successfully teamed up with Viscere and Arrogante to divide the strong young warriors of this family, and the time of their destruction was close at hand.

CHAPTER 11

EAGLE FLIGHT

†††

As the sun peaked across the western horizon, a powerful eagle took flight from its nest high in the cliffs of western Omentia. It flew over Abner's land, Ka'el's cottage, and the sheer cliffs on the water's edge. It rapidly gained altitude and climbed high above the puffy white clouds before heading west over the Dark Sea.

The eagle's name was Talon, and he was the leader of the orn or eagles. Talon peered down at the countryside below. The golden farming hills of Abner's ranch abruptly changed to dark blue as the land gave way to the tumultuous waves of the sea that constantly battered the jagged rocks of the Omentian coastline. He moved swiftly about the large billowing clouds, enjoying the frequently traveled trip west by periodically alternating between high energy, acrobatic maneuvers and gentle gliding bliss.

It seemed like everything was changing in Omentia and not for the better; of this, the orn became keenly aware. They had sensed an evil presence growing in the land, and because of this impending darkness, the orn had migrated west to the great island across the Dark Sea.

Talon set his wings for a rapid descent as the morning fog broke on the eastern shoreline of the great island below him, and he saw clearly through the morning haze. Talon soared between snow-covered peaks as he plummeted down through the crisp and chilly morning air of the northern mountains. He then glided through the large redwoods of the thick green forests, and hunted for fish along the dark blue rivers that ran endlessly through the yet unblemished paradise. Well fed, Talon found his normal resting spot high in the rocky mountain cliffs.

The orn had surveyed most of this land. High mountains dominated the northernmost terrain, dense forest covered the central portion, and a diverse range of terrain characterized the southern territories. The land was bursting with life and unrivaled in abundance. A wide variety of small to large game flourished throughout the island.

The presence of those made in the maker's image was still very low here, and from what Talon and the others had seen, the men that lived here still loved the maker and respected his creation. They took from the land only that which was needed for their survival. Man and the rest of the creation lived here in harmony, as the Creator originally intended.

This place was good, very good for the eagle. Soon, all the orn would make this their new home. In fact, large-scale migration and nesting had already begun.

CHAPTER 12

DREAMS

†††

A bner had been having many restless nights as of late. His mind was always going, trying to decide what he should do in the various areas of his life.

It had been a year since Truin's accident and six months since Ka'el had brought Tala into the family. Abner did not expect these events at all when the year started, and if he had the chance to choose, they would definitely not have been his preference. But Abner, in his aged wisdom, knew that the twists and turns on the road of life — even the twists that brought short-term pain or suffering — always had a purpose. Though he often struggled to find the silver lining in the less than optimal or even harmful events that befell his family, he had lived long enough to see the wisdom of being patient; letting the events of life and their consequences unfold. He trusted God's hand would guide all things for their ultimate good.

Abner found that the hardest part of planning was often just letting God be God. He was a man who loved to be in control. He thought he knew the best way for life's events to unfold. As such, he was most naturally disappointed when things happened in a way or at a time that was not in line with his plans. Truin's accident and Ka'el's hasty choice in a wife were hard for Abner to accept. Abner and Evelin had no choice but to trust in God and give these events and their ultimate consequences over to him, knowing that he could both see and control the events of the future. To this God, the only true God, they entrusted the lives of those they loved so dearly.

But Abner's trust in God was to be tested further. One night, while Abner was fast asleep, the Lord came to him and spoke his name. "Abner."

Slowly opening his eyes, Abner heard the voice, but wasn't sure where the voice was coming from.

"Abner."

He knew he wasn't awake, and he also knew he wasn't dreaming; at least this wasn't like any dream he had ever had before.

The still, soft voice called out to him a third time. "Abner."

"Here I am."

"Abner, take you wife Evelin, your sons Truin and Ka'el, and your daughter Elin. Leave the land of Omentia with haste. Take your family and all your possessions. Move west, across the sea, to the great island beyond."

"But Lord, everything we know is in this land. Will we not lose everything we have built here?"

"Be still Abner. A storm is coming to Omentia. Evil has made Omentia its home. It is no longer safe here for you or your family. I will protect you, and you will prosper in the land that I will show you."

Abner realized he was sitting in his chair next to the bed. His eyes were open, and he was gazing out the window at the moonlit clouds to the west.

He looked over and saw that Eve was still curled up under the covers, sleeping soundly. He did not know when or why he had moved from the bed to his chair by the window.

Abner looked out the window at the clouds swiftly moving across the moon high above. At that moment, he realized everything had just changed. He had gone to bed thinking it was just another night. Without warning, the God of the heavens—the God of all creation—had spoken directly to him.

Joy filled Abner's heart as he realized the Lord knew him and his family by name. Actually, filled with joy was a vast understatement. Every bone, muscle, and fiber of his being was completely ecstatic. He could barely sit still as the words the Lord had spoken echoed through his memory, filling up his mind and his heart.

God spoke to me! God promised he would be with me, prosper me, and protect me!

Abner's mind raced as he reflected on what he had been told. Over and over, the words echoed in his mind.

A storm is coming — it is no longer safe. I will protect you.

Abner sat for hours, completely unaware of the passing night. Ever so slowly, the excitement of the event wore off as physical fatigue overpowered the rush of adrenaline that had surged through his veins. Abner's thoughts then turned to his home, the land that he had known for so many years, his friends, and his neighbors.

What will happen to them?

Abner awoke to a gentle voice. The warm rays of a morning sun baked his body as Eve's soft voice welcomed him to a new day.

"Abner, honey, wake up. Sweetie, wake up."

Abner's eyes opened. He was still in the chair.

"How long have you been there?" Eve kissed Abner on the forehead. "Weren't you cold?"

Abner struggled to wake up. He squinted into the bright golden rays shining through the window.

"I'll make us some breakfast." Eve gave Abner a warm hug and then scurried out of the bedroom like a woman on a mission.

Abner sat in the chair, once again fully aware of what had happened, while Omentia had slept. He struggled with how to tell Eve; how to tell his family. It should have been easy, but Abner had doubts.

Will anyone believe the Lord spoke directly to me? Won't they think I am crazy?

Abner knew he had to trust the Lord. Not trusting the Lord would mean certain failure and probably much, much worse. Yet, it was so hard to leave behind everything he knew, everything he had labored to build for so many years. And what of Ka'el and Truin?

Will Ka'el and Truin follow us?

††††

Abner sat with Evelin on their porch, enjoying the early evening breeze that flowed like an invisible stream off of the foothills to the north of their home. His heart ached as he told Evelin his dream and the decision that he had made to leave Omentia.

Abner was trying his hardest to feel what Evelin's heart was thinking. It had taken Abner years to learn that although men think with their minds, women think with their hearts. This was just one of the many differences between men and women that he had observed over the years.

Evelin sat quietly, listening to Abner's words. Her heart told her she would miss their home. It told her she would miss their friends. But mostly, her heart told her she loved the Lord, that she loved her husband, and if it was time to move to a better place that the Lord had chosen for them; then so be it.

Evelin answered her husband with the words of Ruth from the Word. *"Where you go I will go, and where you stay, I will stay. Your people will be my people and your God my God. Where you die, I will die, and there I will be buried. May the Lord deal with me ever so severely, if anything, but death separates you and me."*

Tears ran down Evelin's cheeks. Tears filled Abner's eyes. They sat on their porch watching the sun set in the east over the land the Lord had given them; over the land, the Lord had directed them to leave behind. Smiles crossed their faces as they remembered all the blessings the Lord had showered on them over the years.

Abner gazed into his wife's eyes. "We must trust him."

Evelin placed her hand on Abner's hand. "There is no other choice."

††††

Tala was not happy, and she let Ka'el know it. "I refuse to leave! Everything I have ever known is here. My life is here, and my friends are here!"

Ka'el had just returned from his parent's home where Abner had sat him and Truin down and informed them of his decision to leave Omentia. Truin had readily accepted Abner's concerns about Omentia and his rationale for leaving. Ka'el resisted. He fought the idea, citing several reasons why the move was not wise. However, after realizing that his parents had made their decision, Ka'el did what respectful and faithful sons do; he signed on to the plan.

Ka'el understood Tala's emotions. After all, he had much the same feelings about leaving Omentia; he had just voiced them to his father. But Ka'el questioned Tala's honesty.

Does Tala really not want to leave because this is her home, or is it for other reasons?

Ka'el confronted Tala point blank. "You just don't want to leave your secret friends, the ones you meet at night in the forest!"

"That is ridiculous!" Tala's eyes called into question her sincerity; she could no longer hold Ka'el's gaze. Her dark eyes fell to the ground as her face flashed with anger, clearly revealing her divided loyalties.

Ka'el softened his tone. True, Tala had deceived him about her trips to the forest, but Ka'el didn't think there was really any malice involved on Tala's part. Instead, Ka'el decided Tala was simply misguided and needing his help to break free from her shady acquaintances and their very disturbing practices.

Ka'el took Tala's hands in his. "Tala, honey, I know it is hard to change, but you don't need that group and their dark arts anymore. I am here for you, and I will take care of you. You are my wife now. We are family."

Tala's furrowed brows relaxed as she reluctantly raised her eyes to meet Ka'el's. She loved him, as she understood love, and she knew she couldn't leave him. She told her husband she would go with him, all the while knowing Karyan would never allow her to leave the fire-worshippers.

CHAPTER 13

A CRY FOR HELP

†††

Alone, cold, hungry, and very frightened; she cried silently in the darkness. Her memories and her tears were all that kept her company in this dark and lonely place. Ever since they had taken her from her family two months earlier, her life had been a living hell.

Christina was a blond-haired, blue-eyed girl who had lived in the small town of Laken in the land of Heath. Heath lay far to the west of Omentia across the Northern Sea.

One evening, as Christina was walking home along the river, she was savagely abducted by slave traders. These evil men were sweeping the countryside of Heath, taking the defenseless by force, and selling them to the highest bidder. Her abductors told her that if she didn't go along with them quietly, they would go to her home, kill her parents, and take her brothers and sisters, too.

Christina was terrified. She had two older sisters and one younger brother; just three years old. She knew that the first few minutes would be the best time to escape her abductors. Yet she couldn't stand the thought of anything happening to little Benjamin.

Christina didn't know what to do, so she froze and did nothing. She was bound, gagged, blindfolded, and tossed like a bag of garbage into the back of a wagon with several other bags of garbage.

At seventeen years of age, Christina had recently noticed that many men around her village had taken a keen interest in her. She was sure these men were no different. Not knowing exactly what they wanted from her, she had her suspicions and was thankful for every minute they left her alone. Yet, she feared that at some point she would face the inevitable; young women rarely became slaves to perform cooking duties.

For several days, Christina's captors shuffled her and the others from wagon to wagon, mostly traveling at night. They remained blindfolded the entire time and given very little to eat or to drink. Before long, because of either lack of food and water or lack of sleep, Christina's mind drifted. She was so tired and so hungry that she no longer cared what they did to her.

Her captures carried Christina aboard a ship and threw her into another dark and damp place to shiver alone in the cold. Though she hadn't actually seen other captives aboard the ship, she knew that there were others. She heard their whimpers through the wooden walls of the cramped box that was now her home. She tried to contact with them by knocking on the walls, but every time she did so, a large and quite filthy seaman would burst into her wooden cell and assault her. Christina stopped trying. She withdrew inwards, conserved her strength, and took advantage of the opportunity to pray.

She had many questions that didn't seem to have any answers.

Why? Why is this happening to me? Will I ever see my family again? What is going to happen to me now? Do you have a plan for me, Lord? What do you want me to do?

Christina's parents had taught their children to know God loved them and would always take care of them. They had taught Christina and her siblings to grow strong in the faith through the Word, because they didn't know when their faith would be called upon to see them through one of life's many storms. Her father would say that it was just a matter of time — be ready. Her parents were right, the storm had come unexpectedly, and it was good that she had prepared well for it.

Though confused and disheartened by the events that had befallen her, Christina continued to trust in the one true God. She knew the Lord had a plan for all those who loved him; that all of God's children had value; and that no matter where a person might find themselves in the world and in no matter what the condition, all remained within God's caring hands.

Christina loved God and knew that he was with her, even though she now felt so alone. Though it was very hard, she resisted the temptation to trust her feelings. She knew her temporal feelings were shifting sand and would betray her. Instead, she must trust God's promises, for they were the only solid ground there was to stand on.

She remembered the passages from the Word. *Because of the Lord's great love we are not consumed, for his compassions never fail. They are new every morning; great is thy faithfulness. I say to myself, 'The LORD is my portion; therefore, I will wait for him.'*

Christina prayed out loud. "God have mercy on me. Please defend and deliver me from my enemies. I trust you and the purpose you have for my life. Please let me serve you well. Give me the strength to be who you want me to be and to do what you have called me to do. Save me my God, for I am yours."

Meanwhile, the slave ship headed east at top speed for Omentia, where in recent months slavery had become much more profitable and in high demand.

Christina was to be sold as soon as they arrived at port.

†††

"Prepare," the Chief Being commanded Golden Wing. "Soon you will minister to this little one and let her know her God has not forgotten her. Her prayers will be heard, her prayers will be answered, and she will be instrumental in the Lord's plan for this land. She has been chosen."

Golden Wing spoke. "They are so small, so weak. Yet they can be so big, so strong and so faithful."

"Their bodies — their vessels — break easily, but that which they hold within is from the Lord. That which they hold within is their true power. It will never pass away or fail. As they become more about what they hold within and less about what they see without, the stronger and more faithful they become."

"It is amazing to watch the Lord's plan unfold; amazing to minister to these fragile creatures, the children of the King."

"Yes, it is truly amazing. Prepare."

CHAPTER 14

DEPARTURE

†††

Once they decided they were leaving, they wasted no time making preparations. Fall was in the air, and soon the winter seas would prevent a safe passage. They sold their land and prepared for the journey.

Truin secured the services of a boat captain known throughout Omentia to be a god-fearing man, though being a Christian was unfortunately becoming a commercial liability instead of an asset. His name was Papa Johnson or PJ for short.

PJ had long made his living by providing transportation for families looking for a better life or fleeing from trouble. The trouble often took the form of religious persecution. In those instances, PJ didn't mind not being paid for his efforts. The chance to make such a difference in the lives of fellow children of the Master was payment enough; though the liberated families usually paid PJ and his family back once settled in Adonia. Though this move for Abner's family didn't yet qualify as persecution, PJ agreed it was a wise, precautionary move.

PJ had seen the warning signs that permeated Omentia before. Many a land changed almost overnight from worshipping the one true God one day and worshipping a false god the next. Sometimes this happened when evil rulers extended their clenched fists over a territory and mandated a change by force, creating a wave of fear and unbelief that overwhelmed a people like a tidal wave. Sometimes it happened more gradually, when apathy and indifference stole a population's soul long before outward, visible danger arrived. Defeat in these cases was quiet and subtle. Either way, darkness was on a constant advance; never sleeping, never resting, and always wanting more. Only the light could stand against darkness, and though PJ was a humble man, he still saw his part as important to God's purpose. People had overheard him say, "I am but a small light, but even a small light has a significant effect on a sea of darkness."

PJ had himself taken his family and moved to the western island two years earlier, setting up a small homestead on the coast of Delvia. He provided for his family by fishing off the eastern shores of Delvia in his schooner, La Gina, and by making several journeys a year to rescue families in desperate need of transport from lands of persecution. There, at their home on the shore of Delvia, PJ's wife and sons waited for him to return from this his fifth such journey of the year.

And so it was on that brisk fall morning. An icy breeze blew in from the frosty Northern Sea, assaulting the small port of Atlantia on the northwestern shore of Omentia. Below the dark blue-gray clouds, shouting out their warning of the approaching darkness; and the rising sun opposite them, promising refuge in the west; a small family of travelers and their miscellaneous belongings boarded La Gina. The travelers took a leap of faith, placing their trust in their God rather than in the material blessings of land and fortune they had painstakingly accumulated over many years.

Also accompanying Abner's family was Truin's best friend, Khory. Khory became like a brother to Truin, filling Ka'el's absence after the accident in the forest. Abner had sought Khory, an expert in self-defense and various fighting techniques, and requested he meet with Truin soon after Truin was well enough to get back on his feet. Abner, concerned that Truin's new disability would cause him to spiral into a deep depression from which he would never recover, thought Khory could help Truin learn to compensate for his disability.

To everyone's delight, Truin remained very positive about his future, not lamenting over his new disability at all. Rather, he considered himself blessed to have been in the position to save his brother's life. Thanks largely to Elin's support, Truin faithfully held that God had even more planned for him and eagerly charted a course to prepare for that eventuality, insisting he would be ready for whatever God had planned for him next.

Truin saw Khory as a godsend. Khory was ten years Truin's senior and had learned much about the art of war by traveling extensively throughout foreign lands and learning from the many warriors that he encountered. He assured Truin that he could regain much of his fighting ability and learn to outmaneuver most potential opponents. Khory was instrumental in helping Truin rethink how he could use his other strengths to compensate for losing much of his fighting ability with his left arm.

When Khory first began training Truin, Khory would often say, "Here is but half a man. What is it that but half of a man can do that I should be concerned with him?" Khory assured Truin most men would have this initial opinion of Truin, and their miscalculation of his abilities would give Truin an instant advantage in any fight. By using this initial advantage, Truin could swiftly dispense with an enemy before they ever realized their erroneous assessment. Truin had always possessed great speed and agility, and now that his opponents would underestimate his abilities, he could be even more successful against them.

Between the time of Truin's accident and the family's departure for Delvia, Khory and Truin became as close as brothers. Truin had taught Khory about the one true God, and God had opened Khory's eyes to the purpose of his life. Evelin and Elin had made Khory feel very welcomed, and before long, Abner had invited Khory to stay with them.

When it came time for Abner and the family to leave Omentia, it took no time at all for Khory to announce. "I have always wanted to see the western island. Besides, I have no intention of letting my one-armed brother explore a new land all by himself!"

Khory believed Truin had given him the greatest gift he could ever have received from anyone. He knew the one true God. Although he knew he could never fully repay this debt to Truin, he was determined to try. He promised he would remain at Truin's side as long as Truin wished. He promised to defend Truin with his life, if required, for it was the least he could do to repay Truin for the eternal life that he had received through Truin's witness.

"Truin, I will never desert you. This I promise."

And so Khory became part of the family, much to Elin's delight, as she had carried a fancy for Khory ever since the first day he arrived.

Truin was excited about a new start in Adonia, hoping the change in surroundings would help put the forest incident well behind them all, maybe even Ka'el.

A new start in a new land will surely be good for everyone.

†††

The small family of the faithful huddled together on the deck of La Gina. Abner led them in prayer.

"Almighty God in heaven, please be with us on this voyage to the land you will show us, the land you will give to us for our new home. Please be with us on this journey, as we are defenseless without you. Take away our anxiety and calm our fears. Reassure us with your presence and lead us in the way you would have us go. We are yours, dear Father. Please show us how we should best serve you. So shall it be."

The group all responded as one. "So shall it be."

PJ stood at the bow of La Gina as she forged her way west through the enormous waves that pressed back with all the Dark Sea offered; as if the sea was attempting to prevent their escape. PJ could feel there was something about this group of travelers that was different, and he was happy God was allowing him to play a small part in the contribution they would no doubt make in the future.

As the sun peaked above the whitecaps in front of them and the storm clouds formed behind them, the small band of travelers with faith in God and high hopes for the future said goodbye to the land of Omentia and set sail for a new life across the sea.

Part 2: A New Home

CHAPTER 15

RESCUE

†††

"We must not allow this flesh to reach land. Destroy them! Send Bestia to rouse the Wezen."

†††

It awakened.

They had no forewarning of the destruction that would soon befall them as the creature, summoned to do the bidding of its evil master, silently moved deep beneath the surface of the Dark Sea; far below the La Gina.

†††

Ka'el and Truin helped as much as they could. Though they had never really sailed before, PJ hurriedly taught them the ropes. Soon they made valuable contributions, reducing the workload for the crew of the La Gina. PJ appreciated the extra help, and the brothers appreciated learning how to sail.

Abner and Evelin did the best they could to relax. They had never sailed before, and it seemed harder for them to grow accustomed to the rhythmic motion of the sea's waves than it was for the rest of the younger voyagers. Sitting on the deck, keeping their eyes on the horizon, and breathing in the salty, fresh air seemed to help. Evelin also insisted that applying pressure to the inside of her wrists helped with the symptoms of the seasickness. Abner couldn't see how the action could help, and therefore, it didn't help him at all. He was happy it worked for Eve, though.

Khory, though he wanted to help Truin and Ka'el with the sailing, became somewhat sidetracked. After being confined aboard the schooner for a couple of days, Khory, with a little gentle nudging from Elin herself, became aware that Truin and Ka'el had a little sister. Khory's priorities changed. Before long, Khory and Elin were inseparable; of course, this wasn't earth-shattering news considering their situation aboard a small sailing vessel.

Tala, kept largely to herself, choosing to stay below deck and dwell on her self-proclaimed misfortunes. Though Evelin and Elin attempted to include her in various activities, Tala simply didn't seem to fit in with the rest of her new family. She didn't share their history, their beliefs, or their optimism regarding their future home across the sea. As far as Tala was concerned, she would remain miserable and make everyone else around her miserable.

If I'm not happy, why should anyone else be happy?

It was midmorning as Truin and Ka'el joined their parents near the bow of the schooner. It had been a tough morning on the very rough seas, and as the waves settled and the sun broke through the passing storm clouds the brothers took a break from their labors, joining Abner and Evelin for some fresh air and a well-deserved rest.

Though they had been at sail for eight days, there was still no land in sight for as far as the eye could see. The sky and water blended together to form a single shade of light blue; making the horizon completely indiscernible. The complete lack of a horizon was like being on a foggy plain, with no proper sense of direction. Fortunately, the crew could ascertain the position of the sun, so they knew west was still off the bow, or roughly so. As the sun heated the air and it contacted the sea water, a thin fog formed on the surface of the water, and the dreamy effect became even more pronounced.

"It feels like we are the only people in the world," Evelin whispered. The dreamy conditions made her feel like speaking any louder than a whisper would somehow shatter the surrounding fog.

"It does," Truin said, in a whisper. To Truin, the conditions were beautiful, peaceful, and a perfect moment to rest from their labors.

"I am glad Captain PJ knows how to tell which way to go, because out here, I am as lost as a hound with a head cold," Abner said. Wouldn't it be great if our new home had mountains we could use for reference? I hate this feeling; I've been feeling lost ever since we set sail.

"I'm going to check on Tala." Ka'el rose to his feet. He grimaced as his sore muscles reminded him he wasn't used to many of the motions that his duties had demanded of him in the last few days.

"Ship!" cried the lookout, unexpectedly. The cry shattered the peacefulness of the scene and shook all aboard out of their foggy daydream.

"Ship directly ahead," announced the spotter, poised high above them on the forward mast.

Several of his shipmates swiftly joined Abner, Evelin, Ka'el, Truin, and Captain PJ as they scanned the murky void in front of the ship. They cut through the sea fog with their eyes, searching intently.

Captain PJ was well-seasoned in spotting land, icebergs, and ships on the horizon. He instantly spotted the newcomer at about five miles, dead ahead. Though difficult to see through the fog, the others soon saw the faint outline of the ship; though they would not have seen it at all had they not already known it was there.

Everyone was glad they had spotted the other ship, reducing the possibility of a collision in the dense fog. Once they knew the ship's track and corrected La Gina's course, they considered the knowledge of the other ship's presence became merely a curiosity. In the next few minutes, that would rapidly and dreadfully change.

†††

The crew of the slave ship worked feverishly to get to their destination in Omentia as hastily as possible. After all, to them, time was money, and money was everything.

They had been at sea for two weeks, and it would be three more days before they would be in the port of Atlantia, offloading their human cargo.

The clamor of the recent abductees, now slaves below deck, had tapered off more than a week earlier as their substandard diet of bread and water, as well as the realization of their future prospects, took its toll on the captives. Instead of having to calm the prisoners down, effort was now required by the ship's crew to ensure that those caged below remained alive and in good enough condition to fetch a decent price at auction; at least enough to compensate their captors for the cost of their effort.

Most of the crew never considered the moral aspect of what they were doing; not really. The ones who occasionally felt sympathy for the slaves had little trouble rationalizing away any personal responsibility for what was happening to the poor souls below.

Surely I play a small part in this human tragedy, but it is going to happen with or without me, so why not put food on the table for my family? If I had my way, I would set them all free, but what can I do?

And so the crew, committed to keeping their schedule and fulfilling their mission, pushed forward at full speed; their ship cutting through the waves like the sharp edge of a blade through butter. Suddenly, however, the ship stopped. One second she was at full speed and the next her forward motion ground to an abrupt halt. The ship listed dramatically to port, violently propelling most of her crew from their posts and tossing some overboard into the tumultuous waves below. The ship's hull violently tore open, ripping two-foot thick timber planks from their appointed place like toothpicks in a child's model ship.

"We must have hit land!" screamed the Captain as he rushed to see how they could have run aground in the open waters.

Bewilderment gave way to incapacitating fear as the cause of the calamity became all too apparent to the slave ship's captain and his crew. Before anyone had time to get their bearings, the ferocious beast was upon them. The creature's massive twenty-foot tentacles were sweeping across the deck, tearing the masts from the ship, toppling her sails, knocking her crew overboard, and pulling her down into the depths from which it came.

The slaves beneath the ship were terrified by the initial jolt, and found themselves pressed against the forward wall of their wooden cells, while the screams of the crew and the deafening sounds of the shattering hull echoed around them. Thousands of gallons of frigid seawater then filled their cages, fully awakening them from their stupor, despite being dehydrated and malnourished, and they too joined in the chorus of screams, crying out for help!

The guards below deck had no intention of helping the prisoners survive. Those guards, still conscious, scrambled to escape what was soon to be their watery tomb. They clawed and climbed over each to reach refuge, only to find that the ship had already capsized and there was no escape to be found. Chaos, fear, and death reigned both above and below the deck of the ship.

Christina did not know what was happening. Her portable prison had broken loose from the floor and had tumbled around the cargo hold. Seconds later, a large rupture in the hull had ushered in a deluge of freezing seawater, ensuring the ship would never escape the Dark Sea's deadly grip. Christina was helpless as her floating coffin tumbled about with countless others inside the hold of the sinking ship. There seemed to be no hope of surviving whatever was happening, and Christina wasn't even sure she wanted to live.

"My God, please do not forsake me. Have mercy on me, your servant."

Others around her screamed in horror as the ship continued to crumble around them. Shattering timber that, but moments before, was the ship's skeletal system, swirled around in the tumultuous waters, impaling and crushing everything in its path. The torrent of water trapped everyone, causing them to struggle for the smallest, life-sustaining breath of air. But none besides Christina raised their petitions to the God of heaven and earth.

As the ship came apart, the powerful tentacles of the giant beast tore at its remaining structure, savagely dismantling it like a toy. Its enormous eyes now glaring at its prize from above the surface of the water, it searched out its prey. The monster's sinewy limbs seized screaming sailors, who futilely pleaded to their pagan gods for mercy and deliverance, and ruthlessly pulled them into its deadly jaws of death. They found no mercy or deliverance.

†††

As the La Gina came within a mile of the slave ship, all aboard saw what was happening in the turbulent waters ahead of them. They could not believe their eyes.

They watched in shock, wondering what, if anything, they could do to help. They cried out to each other, "Look at that monster! Are we next?"

†††

As the sea monster's attack forced the mighty slave ship to crumble into pieces, Christina's wooden cage plunged beneath the water that had flooded the hull. One of the ship's mighty masts forcefully drove through the center of the hull like a stake going through paper, shattering Christina's wooden cage into pieces. Christina freed herself from the wreckage just in time to avoid being dragged to the depths with her fellow captives. Twenty feet below the surface of the sea, she struggled with all her might to escape the cold, silent darkness of the void below her and reach the warmth and light of the surface above. As the ship and its prisoners departed into the shadowy depths, Christina pushed for the surface.

Christina gasped frantically for air as she reached the tumultuous surface of the sea. Death and debris were everywhere. Exhausted and only seconds from blacking out and sinking forever below the merciless waves, she latched on to a piece of floating timber. She could not hold on for very long; her body shook uncontrollably in the frigid waters.

Barely clinging to the edge of consciousness, Christina noticed a man floating toward her and also clinging to a piece of debris. The man, about her age in appearance, had blonde hair; even blonder at the tips. He reached Christina and secured their two tattered timbers together. Christina did not recognize him from the ship and didn't know if he was a prisoner or a prison keeper. Either way, they were both in the same boat now or, to be accurate, not.

The man efficiently rigged a larger gathering of debris together and assisted Christina in crawling partially on top of it.

Christina's arms and legs were burning with exhaustion. Had the man not shown up when he did, Christina's fatigue would surely have overtaken her, and she would have slipped away to join the rest of the prisoners in the depths below.

The young man hung to the side of the floating sanctuary while Christina regained her senses.

"What is your name?

"I am Christina." Christina thought of asking the stranger's name, but before she could muster the will, he continued.

"We must have courage; everything will be all right. Fear not! God is nigh!"

These words took Christina totally by surprise. Christina recalled distant, hidden memories from her childhood as she drifted again to some vague place between consciousness and unconsciousness. She remembered accompanying her mother as a young child to listen to visitors that had arrived from a faraway land to share the truth of God with them.

These visitors, a husband and wife, had made a profound impact on their village. The man, Juddin, had worked primarily with the adults of the village and his wife, Barbille, had ministered primarily to the children. Juddin and Barbille told them about the Creator of the heavens and the earth, of his plan, of his promises, and of his love. They showed the people of her village how God wanted them to live and why his plan was the best plan to follow.

Juddin and Barbille lived in Christina's village for seven years, teaching them and serving them. Both young and old alike underwent a transformative change during those years. Turning from the old ways, their hearts now beat to a different drum; desiring only to love and serve the true God and each other.

Christina was only twelve when they left, but she remembered the visitors' departing words to the village as their small boat floated down the river. Barbille shouted, "Fear not! Be Faithful! God is nigh!"

These were the words she now remembered as she found herself in this — the direst of circumstances.

The stranger watched Christina as she silently recalled her childhood memories. Then he spoke the words aloud.

"Fear not."

"Be faithful."

"God is nigh."

As the turmoil that surrounded them raged, the stranger smiled at Christina. His face beamed a gentle calmness through and above the surrounding chaos. His words were peaceful; and as Christina returned the stranger's gaze, she focused intently on the young man's words.

"Are you afraid?"

The question seemed silly.

Of course I am afraid. How could anyone not be afraid? How can you not be afraid?

"Yes, I am terribly afraid." The fear and stress of current events had taken their toll on her senses.

As they spoke, gigantic waves, created by the thrashing of the great sea beast, erupted in all directions, colliding with the floating debris and carnage all around them.

"Are you a believer?"

The question rattled her as she recounted the seeds of faith that had matured and blossomed in her life.

"Yes, I am." Christina's voice was uneasy and anxious.

The stranger's smile widened. "Everyone believes in something, whether or not they admit it."

He spoke to Christina in a warm and calm voice, quite unlike the scene of chaos, death, and destruction that surrounded them. "What is it? What is it you believe?"

The words struck her head on, reaching deep inside to the most private recesses of her heart. She remembered her family, their shared faith, and the promises God had made to all who believe and put their trust in him. She remembered that the Master always remains faithful to his children, despite his servant's unfaithfulness. Finally, she remembered God loved her.

As she looked into the young man's eyes and remembered the God she trusted, peacefulness embraced Christina. The anxiety drained from her body as she steadied her voice and put her thoughts into words.

"I know God loves me, and that all of this has a purpose. I know I am not alone."

"Are you afraid?"

"No, I am not." Her answer surprised her.

"Trust him now."

Christina closed her eyes and slipped off the makeshift raft into the raging, blue waters of the Dark Sea; beginning her long, cold descent into the black depths below.

†††

The multi-legged beast from the deep was not yet content as its deadly tentacles searched the surface for any remaining survivors. Most of the screams of the ship's crew had subsided, though some still called out from the fog in terror as the creature found them and permanently ended their suffering.

Captain PJ and the rest looked on in horror. They wanted to assist the other ship and its passengers, but what could they do? While they had watched, frozen in fear and indecision, the La Gina had closed to within one-thousand feet of the creature.

Captain PJ trumpeted orders to his crew to change course and "high tail it out of here!"

But it was too late. The enormous eyes of the monster had found them, and it lunged forward through the water on a collision course with the La Gina; determined to make her its next prize. All aboard knew there would be no escape. The monster would be upon them before they could even turn the boat and begin their retreat. Abner and his family watched in alarming amazement as the creature advanced like an arrow through the water.

Truin, Ka'el, and Khory readied their weapons to do what they could to protect their loved ones, while Evelin and Elin secured themselves; preparing for the inevitable impact of the creature with the ship.

The next few moments were surreal. As they watched the deadly monster approach, Abner's mind wandered.

Why did God have us leave Omentia just to have us die in the sea?

Abner trusted in God's promises and knew that dying here in this dreadful place could not be the fate of his family.

Surely this is not your plan, Oh Lord. Yet, if it is, I accept it.

Abner prayed.

Who am I to know your ways, Oh God? Who am I to direct your footsteps? You give and you take away. Blessed be your name!

The sea boiled. Waves bubbled as hot air rose all around the ship, bursting forth from somewhere deep beneath the sea. The La Gina began to shake and toss back and forth upon the waves.

As Abner's attention turned away from the approaching monster to search for the source of the boiling cauldron beneath them, a new menace rose from the depths below.

Whereas the monstrosity they had just watched devour the doomed ship had been like nothing they had ever seen, the creature they now saw rise from the waters beneath them was like nothing they had ever imagined. It filled them with both awe and fear.

The waters before them parted, and the creature's massive head rose from the sea. Its gaze swept back and forth, scanning the horizon with eyes that burned like fire.

When the dreadful eyes locked onto the rapidly approaching threat, its enormous jaws opened, releasing an earsplitting roar that caused all aboard the La Gina to fall backwards and cower on the deck.

The enormous creature continued its rise from the sea, the waves breaking away from its scaly back to reveal massive shield-like ridges covering its entire flank. The titan's chest appeared as if made from solid rock; its limbs as forged from iron.

Propelled by the massive displacement of seawater off the creature's back, the La Gina soared across the surface of the sea away from the titan, causing her passengers and the crew to hold on to anything within reach to keep from being thrown overboard.

Never had they seen or even heard of such a creature. It rose effortlessly out of the sea, its ferocious appearance without equal. With one wave of its powerful tail, it propelled itself across the sea toward its approaching nemesis. Its massive jaws opened to reveal row after row of razor-sharp teeth. Fire shot from its mouth; smoke and ash poured from its nostrils. The sound of its roar pierced the ears of all within sight, forcing them to cover their ears, once again, with their hands.

As they watched in awe as this great emissary arose from the depths, Evelin ran to Abner's arms, Elin clung to Truin, and Tala rushed to Ka'el for protection. Captain PJ and the crew of the La Gina froze, staring in disbelief at what they were witnessing.

Seeing the fear and trembling around him, Truin shouted for all to hear, "Don't be afraid! The Lord will fight for us this day! All we need to do is to be still and know that he is God." Truin didn't know where the words came from; he just knew he had to say them.

Though they all heard Truin's words, everyone but Evelin continued to stare at what they knew would soon be a clash of titans. They could not tear their eyes from this once in a lifetime event. Who had ever witnessed anything like this?

Evelin, however, even amid this extraordinary event, turned her gaze to her son.

Look at his faith!

And in that moment, she knew, for the first time since his accident, that the Lord still planned great things for Truin.

Truin's words echoed in Abner's mind as he continued to watch the battle unfolding before them.

The Lord will fight for us today. Surely, this is why we are here. Show us your power, Oh God.

Seconds before the multi-legged monster reached the La Gina, the leviathan intercepted the murderous menace and buried multiple rows of its teeth into it. The leviathan now held the monster by what appeared to be its head, its teeth grasping it right between its massive eyes. Huge fountains of black spray spewed from openings behind its bulging eyes as it thrashed in panic. The monster wrapped all of its tentacles around its armor-plated attacker to squeeze the life out of the leviathan. The leviathan rose even higher out of the water, tearing at the creature with its deadly claws. It tore away enormous pieces of clammy flesh with every sweep of its claws.

Without warning, the leviathan dove back beneath the sea with the colossal sea creature still within its jaws, and with a whip of its powerful tail, it was gone back to its home deep beneath the sea.

The churning of the waves and the boiling of the water gradually subsided, but no one aboard the La Gina could move. They just stared out at the sea; still in shock from what they had just witnessed and unsure if they should let down their guard in case another completely unforeseen and unbelievable event take them by surprise.

Truin scanned the horizon and thanked God for what he had done to deliver them from the fate that had befallen the other ship. Truin wondered what sort of people had been aboard the destroyed ship; a ship that had not been an equal recipient of the Lord's mercy and deliverance that day.

Before Truin could finish the thought, he spotted something in the water. Though debris still floated all around them, rising and falling in chaotic patterns upon the rough waves, Truin's eyes focused on a small patch of wreckage floating about three-hundred feet off the port side of the La Gina. It appeared to Truin to have a person clinging to it.

Truin rushed to lower a dinghy. "Over there, on the water; I think there is a survivor!"

Truin shot a quick glance at Captain PJ to ask for permission, and without hesitation, Captain PJ returned a nod of approval. Wasting no time, Captain PJ's first mate, Mikole, joined Truin and another, and together the three men set out fearlessly across the treacherous waters to pick up what appeared to be the only survivor of the doomed ship.

"Hurry, it looks like a girl, and she is slipping away!"

†††

As Christina slipped deeper into the depths of the sea, a bright figure followed her down, took her by the hand, and ever so gently pulled her back to the surface.

"Have faith, little one, have faith."

Christina's eyes opened to a burly, bearded man named Spencer, who had grabbed hold of her arm and was now pulling her out of the water into a dinghy.

"Hang on, little one, hang on!" another man said as he gently took hold of her other arm and helped to lower her to safety within the small boat.

Truin looked down with tender eyes. "It is going to be alright. You're safe with us."

CHAPTER 16

LANDFALL

†††

The ship dropped anchor in the bay. They couldn't believe their eyes. Never had they imagined a place of such beauty. Overwhelmed with excitement, everyone hastily prepared to go ashore. Abner and Evelin could do nothing but stare from the deck of the ship at their new home. It was so beautiful!

"The Lord has been good to us," Abner said.

"He has been very good to us, and he will continue to be faithful," Evelin said as she looked up into her husband's hazel eyes.

"Thank you for being faithful."

Evelin pulled Abner in close. As they embraced, time stood still. It was as if it was their very first kiss. The chaotic activities of the ship's crew, the preparations of the passengers, the waves splashing against the sides of the ship, and the gulls flying about all attempted to disturb the moment; but this moment would allow no company. Abner and Evelin remained alone in a moment outside of time, and it was special; one of those special moments that are remembered for a lifetime.

Everyone went about their business; everyone but Truin. He had noticed his parents' embrace and stopped to savor the moment. From across the ship, another had also noticed. Christina looked longingly at Abner and Evelin from afar, wondering if she would ever again see her parents. Her eyes wandered past them and met Truin's gaze. Christina held Truin's gaze a bit too long. She looked down, embarrassed. A second later, she glanced back up. Truin smiled, and Christina bash-fully smiled back.

It was at this moment that Elin noticed Truin and Christina smiling at each other. Her heart leaped for joy at the sight.

Could it be?

Elin was ever ready to take another lost soul under her wing. She had gladly taken on nursing Christina back to health; much like she had done with Truin after his accident. In the days since, Elin and Christina had grown quite close, and Elin had hoped Truin might take an interest in Christina. To date, this interest hadn't presented itself. But now —

Could it be?

Time soon reclaimed its hold on Abner and Evelin, and Truin and Christina's moment passed. All the dreamers joined the hustle and bustle of eager passengers and crew. It would be some time before anyone would speak of the glances exchanged, and many would argue they meant nothing but meaningless happenstance. Yet, many a future had been determined by fleeting moments such as these; for it is often the unplanned moment, the unintended look, and the unspoken truths that seal the covenants long before the conscious thoughts ever even form. Was this one of those times? Only time would tell.

CHAPTER 17

EXPLORATION

†††

The new land was largely unsettled, though no one could understand why. Abner and his family carefully constructed a settlement on the eastern shore of Delvia, ensuring shelter and a defendable source of food and water. The next order of business was to explore their new surroundings, discover what the land offered, and decide on where to settle permanently.

Truin had long considered exploration his specialty. He volunteered to lead an expedition into the great unknown, since he had not yet become responsible for providing for a wife. Evelin would have nothing to do with this suggestion, arguing that Truin was not yet ready for the rigors of navigating the unknown terrain. She was quite adamant that her injured son should remain safe for a little longer. This would be the opinion of any mother.

Christina was also concerned for Truin. She was still careful to not let her true feelings for Truin show, but Elin's discerning eye could see Christina's affection for Truin in more subtle ways. Christina's careful observation of Truin when she thought no one else was watching, and the understated ways Christina's voice changed when she spoke of Truin were dead giveaways.

Abner felt differently about Truin's desires. He shared Evelin's concerns, but as a father, he had other things to consider besides Truin's safety. The family had journeyed to a new land, and getting settled would not be easy. They could not afford to coddle Truin for long; needing the contributions of everyone if they were to survive. Abner saw the progress Truin had made in the months following the accident to include regaining the use of his bow. Knowing that Truin needed to reestablish critical confidence in his own abilities, he agreed it was time for Truin to spread his wings. However, he also realized he had to live with Evelin while Truin was out, risking his life as Evelin so deliberately put it. So, he insisted Khory and two of Khory's best fighting men accompany Truin on his journey of exploration. This, of course, went without saying, as Khory would not have let Truin venture off without him, anyway. After much convincing, Evelin signed on to the plan.

Abner expected it would be difficult for Truin alone to map out all the land. Therefore, he sent out several groups of men in various directions. He chose these men from several faithful friends and neighbors that had also read the writing on the wall and left Omentia with them; hoping to build a better life in a new land. Abner trusted every one of them with his life.

Truin headed south along the eastern coast. Five other four-man groups set out on different routes to explore their assigned areas. Each group received instructions to travel forward for two weeks and then return to the settlement. The plan was for all to reassemble back in the village in four weeks and share the information that they had gathered.

Truin, Khory, and Khory's handpicked fighters set out with the others at sunrise. They planned to journey south along the coast for the entire fourteen days allotted to see how far the island stretched.

Along the way, the men discovered a wide variety of terrain. South of Delvia, they crossed fertile plains and rolling hills; plentiful with both fruit and vegetation. At the three-day point, they passed through a large, shiny valley with steep, rocky cliffs on either side. At the seven-day point, they carefully negotiated their way along sheer cliffs that plunged to the rocky ocean coastline below.

On the thirteenth day, they could faintly see the ocean to the south of them in the distance. The following day, reaching the southernmost tip of land, Truin suggested naming the region "Land's End." All agreed, and thus it became so.

The group turned back again to the north, and ventured more inland for the return leg, believing it useful to learn more by investigating uncharted territory. They set their course on a northwesterly heading. They planned to deviate from the coast for a day or two to offset inland appropriately.

Two days later, they entered a distinctly different region. Crossing a small river, they encountered a foggy marshland where strange gases bubbled up from below the murky waters. The gases heated the air significantly. The swampland forced them to travel farther west than they had intended, and in doing so, they soon noticed creatures much different than those they had ever encountered before.

First, they heard roars in the distance and eerie screams from deep within the steamy swamplands. These sounds made their skin crawl, but they pushed on. They were on a mission to discover a strange new land, and that meant they must learn both the good and the bad of it. If there was something within the swamps that posed a threat to the family, they believed it was better to know about it now and prepare for it than to remain ignorant and surprised at some later date.

As they pressed into the foggy swamplands, the sounds of the beasts there grew louder and louder, until they seemed to encircle the explorers completely. It was then that they caught the first glimpse of the enormous creatures that lived there. Beasts as long as ships with necks that reached up into the tallest of the trees inhabited the swamps. Mighty birds with wings the size of ship sails glided through the air; their high-pitched shrieks terrifying the burliest of the explorers. Many other monsters, previously seen only in the nightmares of children, roamed freely in the distance. The monsters reminded the men of the colossal creatures they had encountered crossing the Dark Sea.

Though the creatures remained undisturbed by the minuscule presence of the tiny human intruders, discretion finally overrode the explorers' sense of wonder; they left the place as quietly as possible.

Because of the mighty creatures that lived there, they named the land Serendopolus, and each man made a vow to never set foot there again. They didn't want to give these creatures any reason to leave their land, track them north, and potentially put the settlement's existence in jeopardy.

As the group continued north out of the swampy marshes, the temperature again cooled. A range of bluffs and high hills appeared on the horizon as the air cleared. They made camp at the foot of these hills at dusk on the seventeenth day.

As the sun set over the Dark Sea to their east, the men heard what sounded like the beating of wings; thousands and thousands of wings. They each grabbed a torch and followed the sound for a short distance toward the hills. In the twilight, they discovered what appeared to be a whirlwind of creatures. The creatures flew in a circular pattern and ascended into the moonlit sky from a large cave entrance. Astounded, they watched the creatures for hours. The endless stream of flapping creatures remained unabated. Eventually, the novelty of the event wore off, as the men recognized their fatigue and returned to their campsite. They decided unanimously to investigate the mysterious cave in the morning.

All were restless that night as they replayed the events of the unforgettable day over and over in their dreams. Truin, however, awoke from his rest and was sure he had seen some gruesome beast flying overhead in the darkness, peering down upon him with burning red eyes.

He convinced himself he was simply letting his imagination run wild and talked himself into closing his eyes to catch a bit more sleep. The only way he found peace was to remember the words of God. The Lord had said for men to "be fruitful and increase in number; fill the earth and subdue it. Rule over the fish of the sea and the birds of the air and over every living creature that moves on the ground." Though God had given this directive before the fall, he still loved his children and promised he would be with them always. There was no reason for

Truin to fear anything that walked on the land, swam in the sea, or flew in the air.

If God is with me, nothing can defeat me. The Lord's will, whatever it is, is alright with me.

With these thoughts in mind, Truin let his mind wander to a safer place where monsters existed only in his imagination.

As they slept, the wind carried the devilish chatter of countless hideous creatures through the night sky; creatures that spied on the travelers and planned their demise. The demonic babble swirled between the twisted, moonlit branches of the trees that towered over the travelers, carrying upon it the barely audible sound of many sinister voices. They chanted the same phrase repeatedly. "The son of Abner must die."

When the explorers arrived at the cave, they discovered a stream flowing rapidly out of the center of the cave entrance. Many large fish traveled out with the current from the dark interior of the cave. The fish were so numerous in the stream that it appeared a man could walk across the stream, solely on the backs of the fish; if one was foolishness enough to attempt such a thing.

"Wow, look, those fish are enormous! I wonder where they come from," Truin said, as the group stood staring at the large opening in the rocks and the schools of super-sized fish exiting from it. "Let's go inside."

"Do you think that is a good idea?" Khory was not all that excited about going underground after the previous sightings of quite hefty herbivores.

"Oh, come on. We won't know if it's a good idea unless we give it a shot, now will we?"

"Ah, ok — yeah, sounds good," Khory said, displaying an over-exuberant swagger; his facial expression telegraphing a completely different sentiment entirely.

"Do you want to go first, old friend, or —?"

"I'm good. After you." Khory motioned politely with his hand for Truin to proceed.

They lit their torches and began the ascent; Truin in the lead. They followed the stream that ran through the center of the cave. Further and further they went, higher and higher, deeper and deeper into the darkness of the cave and into the unknown within. Before long, their torches provided their only light.

The cave started out as a rather small opening at its entrance, and it stayed that way for a hundred feet. After that, its dimensions expanded exponentially, rapidly growing to be enormous. It was difficult to tell its size exactly, but by Khory's rough estimation, the ceiling of the cavern must have reached a hundred feet or more in height.

Though the light of a small candle can make an enormous difference in a black room, the light emanating from their torches seemed to be swallowed up in the darkness of the voluminous cavern around them. The explorers' torches barely lit the sides of the cave; the light rarely, if ever, reaching the ceiling. In addition, the flickering of the torches gave the illusion that every stalagmite and stalactite were alive; jumping back and forth as they progressed deeper into the cavern.

Also adding to the unsettling scene around them, the fins of the fish swimming downstream reflected the crimson-orange glow of the torches, dimly casting multiple shades of moving color against the cave walls.

"This is really quite beautiful, though disconcerting," Truin commented. "An unbelievable find! We must remember this place. My mother would love this."

"Yeah, sure, if you say so," Khory said. "So, how much farther do you think we should go? We are on a timetable, you know."

"Really Khory? This is awesome! We can't just stop now. We have to see where this leads. Maybe it's a shortcut?"

"Ah. Ok. Sure. A shortcut."

The other two men, Achilles and Xenon, just looked at each other, wondering what they were doing in a cave. Their training focused on fighting, not exploring holes in the ground. Still, they accompanied good men, and good men were scarce; so they kept their grumbling to themselves.

The men journeyed into the cavern for another hour, amazed at all the beautiful things they encountered. The temperature steadily decreased as they progressed deeper into the cave, and farther into the mountain. Soon, it was just downright cold!

"Maybe we should come back when it is warmer," Khory offered.

Aside from a quick glance as if to say, don't be a wimp, Truin ignored the comment. His attention focused on a faint glow ahead of them.

"Hey, look at that," Truin said to the men, pointing into the glowing tunnel.

Not far ahead, the cavern forked in two different directions. The river flowed out from the tunnel to their left, while the tunnel to the right appeared to have its own glowing light source.

They reached the split in the tunnel, and Truin led the expedition to the right, intent on investigating the light which emanated from that tunnel.

The glowing tunnel amazed them. Embedded in the walls of the cave were many veins of glowing rock. The veins of rock ran vertically up the cave walls. They glowed a brilliant, bluish hue, such that the torches were unnecessary.

Truin checked out the tremendous find. "Despite being cold to the touch, this rock glows in the dark! This could provide us with another source of light for our villages! This is truly unbelievable!"

The men marveled at the strange ore, chipping off pieces to take with them out of the cave. Even Achilles and Xenon were excited and filled their pockets with the new glowing rocks.

"Maybe caves aren't so bad after all," Xenon said.

"Maybe not," Achilles agreed.

Between the mysterious fish, the glowing rock, and the seemingly endless cavern; this was truly a spectacle, the likes of which none of them had ever witnessed.

After having scrutinized the shaft and taken time to rest and eat, the men again advanced up the other tunnel to find the origin of the mysterious stream. As they progressed, they noticed many pockets or holes in the walls and the ceiling of the cavern. This seemed odd enough to tweak their curiosity, but they focused their attention elsewhere; distracted again by the many strange and wondrous sights within the cave.

As the reddish glow of their torches lit up the cavern ahead of them, they realized they were not alone. They could see the shapes of many fighting men perched among the stalagmites up ahead.

Truin, Khory and the men immediately drew their weapons and assumed a fighting formation. However, it did not take long for them to realize that the would-be ambushers ahead remained motionless. Other than the optical gyrations caused by the light from their torches, the strangers remained as still as stone.

Weapon still drawn, Truin approached the first of these men to find that it was nothing more than a large stalagmite. He wondered how a stalagmite could so closely resemble the shape of a man. Truin told the rest of the men to spread out and investigate the area.

Khory and the others dutifully complied, carrying their torches to the different quadrants of the cavern to assist Truin in checking out the man-shaped stalagmites and other interesting oddities. Achilles found a large recess in the far wall of the cave and studied the strange hieroglyphic he had found there. It appeared as a crimson hourglass carved into the rock. Xenon stood in the center of the cavern, close to the stream, staring up at the ceiling of the cave and wondering about the many tunnel openings there. Truin continued to check out his stalagmite, chipping away at the layers of the composite minerals that seemed to include organic material.

Khory had just noticed that the roof of the cavern also had man-shaped stalactites covering it, when, without warning, everything changed. The men's senses told them something bad was happening, but sudden disbelief and sheer terror momentarily incapacitated that part of their brains that initiated the fight-or-flight response. As they each tried to figure out the visual puzzles that lay before them, they all became distracted by the faint sound of something, or more accurately, many somethings encircling them. It was like the pitter-patter of thousands of raindrops dancing on the rock floor of the cave; the syncopated serenade echoing through the cavern. Their eyes darted about as they searched for where the tapping and scratching sounds were coming from.

Unexpectedly, the cave wall Achilles had been studying moved. Though he instantly realized that the red hourglass was not a cave marking but the ruby-red marking on the underbelly of a colossal arachnid, he realized it too late. Without warning, he was tumbling inverted. A split second later, he was being hoisted up into the air by his right ankle.

The arachnid had struck! It used two of its hind legs to entrap Achilles' ankle in its webbing, and was now winching him higher and higher towards the ceiling of the cave; there Achilles would defenselessly hang, awaiting his captor's lethal injection.

"Help me! Help me!"

The sound of Achilles' tortured plea reached Truin's ears just as he too solved his puzzle. He had just realized the stalagmite that he was so frantically chiseling on was actually the cocooned remains of a hollowed out human carcass; a carcass encased in mineral deposits for decades, preserving its last moments and echoing its agony for all of eternity.

Instantly, Truin sprang into action, racing to the place that he knew Achilles had just been a moment earlier. He did not expect what he would see.

Achilles hung perhaps a hundred feet above him, clawing at the gooey webbing that held him suspended in midair; preferring to fall to a certain death upon the rocks below over enduring the unimaginable misery that would be his in the intimate presence of the bloodsucking monster that studied him from above.

A massive black widow spider hung just above Achilles from the cavern's ceiling; her eight, red eyes glowing in the dim light of the cave. She was holding on to the major portion of her web with her front legs and using her hind legs to heave Achilles higher and higher into the air, away from any hope of refuge he might have on the ground.

Now, seeing Truin below him, Achilles again screamed for help. "Truin, help me! Help me, please!" All Achilles' pride as a warrior had instantly vanished. The terror that had totally overtaken him shattered Achilles' arrogance like an icicle cast upon a rock.

Truin struggled to find a solution, but there was no time to think. Action was required! Without delay, Truin did the only thing he could do. He drew his bow and fired a volley of arrows into the black demon that was orchestrating Achilles' looming demise.

Gracefully, the widow moved her legs, preparing each strand of web. With fine precision she prepared to cocoon Achilles; to entomb him within his own body. Soon she would inject him with the potent toxin that would both paralyze him and simultaneously reduce his organs to jelly; turning Achilles into the sweet mush that she would later suck from his lifeless shell. She elegantly continued her work until she felt the first of Truin's arrows pierce her clammy flesh. Screaming in rage, the bulbus widow scrambled down her web toward Truin, who faithfully held his ground and barraged the widow with his death darts.

While this was happening, several other spiders emerged from the tunnel holes in the cavern ceiling above Xenon and had dropped their webbed netting down upon him and several large fish that had been passing by him in the river. As Xenon struggled against the sticky strands, the web enclosed him and he, too, was soon on his way to the ceiling of the cave. There, he would serve as the evening entrée.

Khory could not believe his eyes. He stood frozen in fear against the side of the cave, taking in the entire scene and unable to move a muscle. Normally fearless and dependable, Khory would fight in any situation; any situation but this one.

For as long as Khory could remember, he had been afraid of spiders; terrified of spiders. When he was five, he had snuck away from his mother's careful watch and found his way into the family barn. Somehow, he had made his way into a neglected corner of a horse stall and fallen backwards into an underground storage bin. Normally, this would not have been a big deal. However, he was too small to get out of the stiflingly humid tub, which, over time, had become infested with arachnids of various types. Khory soon found himself covered in a thick web and countless spiders, unable to escape.

For several hours, Khory screamed for help, but no one came. His mother thought he was with his brothers. His brothers thought he was with their mother. It took hours for them to realize that he was wandering around on his own. Finally, after a frantic search, they found him and pulled him out of the hot hole of hybrid horror.

Khory learned two things that day that he would never forget. The first was to listen to his mother. The second was that he did not like spiders.

As Khory watched Xenon and Achilles being entangled in the web, his mind succumbed to the terror it had successfully suppressed for so many years. The horrific memories came rushing back to him in an instant, overwhelming his senses. It had been so long since he had felt fear of this magnitude that it took him by surprise, shutting down his ability to move even a muscle.

Amidst Xenon and Achilles' terrified cries for help, Truin called for Khory. "Khory, Khory, help me! We must save our brothers!"

Khory wanted to answer, but he could not. He remained flat against the side of the cave, eyes as wide open as humanly possible, and hyperventilating.

The situation was rapidly deteriorating. Two spiders that had netted Xenon fought over him high above the cavern floor, tearing at each other over the prize. Xenon had entirely capitulated after being bitten repeatedly by both of the monsters, and now he no longer felt anything except the mental anguish and horror of witnessing the end of his own life through paralyzed eyes.

As the spiders twisted and tore apart the two separate halves of what had once been Xenon, the glowing ore from his pockets joined the lifeblood that now poured out of him, splattering together against the rocks that bordered the stream below.

The large widow spider, finding Truin's arrows annoying, had once again ascended back to Achilles and had begun rapidly wrapping him in a tomb of web as he screamed in agony. Completing her deadly task, she had sunk her large fangs into his chest, cracking his breastbone in half and slashing open several major organs. Achilles' eyes remained open, darting back and forth, but his body surrendered; giving up its struggle for freedom and giving up its struggle for life.

Now the sinister eyes of the crimson-marked spider shifted to Truin. Truin could see that there was nothing more he could do for Xenon or Achilles.

"Lord, help us!" Truin cried as he ran towards Khory. But before he made it halfway to Khory's position, he too became caught in the strands of web previously laid out by the widow. Truin struggled to get free, but the sticky strands of spider spew had stopped Truin in his tracks. He had lost his bow and could not reach his sword. His torch, like those of Xenon and Achilles, now burned uselessly before him on the cavern floor; a gloomy harbinger of the fate that soon awaited him.

There was only one whose torch remained at the ready.

"Khory, help!"

Khory remained frozen, cocooned within a shell of fear. All he could do was look on helplessly as the giant widow moved in methodically towards Truin for the kill.

Khory made eye-contact with Truin.

"Khory," Truin said quietly. His voice echoed as it skipped across the cave floor, blending harmonically with the gentle sounds of the stream flowing through the cavern.

At that moment, Truin understood. He remembered the story; the story from Khory's childhood. "Father, have mercy on Khory, your son. Father, show mercy to Khory, your son, and help him escape the dungeon of fear that traps him. And if it is my time, do not let my fate imprison him even further in guilt."

"Khory, get out of here, now!"

Khory felt torn. Every bone in his body told him to run away as fast as he could. Truin was even telling him to run. He backed away, toward the exit of the cave.

But then he remembered the love that he had for his friend and the promise that he had made to him.

I will never desert you.

"Father in heaven, please help me. I know I have nothing to fear. No matter where I am, I am in your hands. Help me do what is right. Help me trust you and obey. I have given my word to never abandon this man — my friend. If it is your will, please save us? My life is yours. Your will be done."

A quiet resolve settled over Khory, and peace filled the room in his heart where fear once reigned supreme.

"Hang on Truin, I am coming!"

Truin's attention had shifted back to the shiny, black beast that was almost upon him; its huge fangs and eight eyes now clearly in view. Fear tugged on Truin's mind with a ferocity like he had never experienced. He had faced death before—in the forest—but this was different. He had risked his life to save his brother. But this, this seemed like such a waste; like a useless way to die!

Father, what purpose would it serve for me to die here in this place? Then again, it may not be for me to know why; to know your plan. I may not see your faithfulness right now, but I know you are faithful! I will trust that you love me and that there is a purpose in whatever happens here. Whether I live or whether I die, I belong to you!

When he had finished his prayer to his maker, Truin resolved to fight until every bit of life was gone from his body. He faced the approaching monster, and tore his arm free of the web, drew his sword, and prepared to strike at the beast as soon as it moved within range. Unfortunately, he could see the creature's long front legs preparing strands of web; web with which to defend against Truin's first and almost certainly only assault.

Truin knew he would probably reach none of the dark monster's vital organs with one strike. Still, there was no other alternative. He was stuck with the cards dealt. That is when the great dealer dealt him another card; an ace.

"Need a little help buddy?" a transformed Khory rushed to Truin's side and began slicing him free from the widow's sticky trap.

The widow noticed and halted its advance, furious that Khory had interrupted its deadly dance with Truin.

"Khory? What are you doing? I told you to get out of here!"

"Kind of dark down here; I guess I got turned around a bit. Thought you might know the way out, so I came back to get you. Any problem with that?" Khory took the time to stop and smile at Truin for effect.

"Works for me, but maybe we should hurry; time is running out!"

Khory made a few more critical slices with his sword, while holding his torch high in the air directly in the path of the approaching widow. The spider felt the heat of the torch as it rose to meet her, and withdrew momentarily, giving Truin just enough time to break free of the web and begin running toward the exit of the tunnel. Khory was right behind him, covering the retreat.

Truin and Khory knew their comrades were beyond helping, and ran their best speed, but it would not be good enough. The giant spider, unwilling to be denied of its catch, was gaining on them rapidly.

To make matters worse, the walls of the cave had come alive with activity. First, the spear-like tips of legs appeared, soon followed by burning, red eyes and finally by grotesquely bulbous torsos. Through countless holes in the walls and ceiling of the cavern, enormous spiders emerged as if they had heard the dinner bell being rung. These famished spiders, tired of eating fish from the river below, squealed in excitement as they realized there was a rare item on the menu this evening. Unfortunately for Truin and Khory, they were the entrée. Countless spiders repelled from their ceiling lairs. They hit the ground and joined those already in pursuit; racing after their new prey as if to win the prize.

It wasn't looking good for the visiting team.

That is when Truin and Khory heard thunder coming from the entrance of the cave. Strangely enough, the thunder was drawing rapidly closer as if to converge on their location. A moment later, the men realized it wasn't thunder, but the thunderous sound of a stampede.

A stampede of what?

They couldn't believe what they saw as they made out the shapes of the stampeding beasts converging on their location — giant ants! They found themselves directly between two armies; an army of giant spiders to their rear; an even larger army of giant ants in front of them.

They had little time to react. Truin and Khory joined the fish, hoping the stream would shield them from the inevitable collision of the two militias and the carnage that would undoubtedly follow. Truin dove into the river. Khory followed him a moment later.

Their timing was perfect. They no sooner hit the water than the two armies met in battle, and the fight ensued.

The ants and the spiders are natural enemies, as the spider is a constant threat to all the insect-kind. Normally, an insect would find itself alone in its struggle against the spider, but not this day; not this fight. This day, the insect invited his friends to the party, and they outnumbered the spiders three to one. Still, it appeared to be a fair fight, as the two armies appeared equally matched.

Large, flying ants hit the arachnids from above, joining their soldier-ant brothers as they tangled with the eight-legged enemy on the ground in a savage fight to the death. The arachnids fought back hard, attempting to defend their lair against the coordinated onslaught of the ant colony; a colony determined to reclaim the ancient hole which the spiders had stolen from them decades earlier. Why the clash of these titans had occurred at that exact moment in time was both obvious and amazing to Truin and Khory.

Truin and Khory hit the icy waters of the stream, and their bodies instantly convulsed in avid protest to its bitter and icy touch. The stream was freezing, and their muscles screamed in misery; but they were very thankful they still had bodies and for the much needed refuge.

The current swiftly escorted them towards the exit of the cave as the battle raged all around. In little to no time, they lost all feeling in their extremities. Once the frigid current had adequately separated them from the main mêlée, they painstakingly pulled themselves out of the stream and onto the rocky floor of the cavern. Thankfully, they were now close enough to the cave entrance to make their way out of the cave without their torches.

Carefully staying to the edge of the tunnel to avoid interrupting a long line of supply ants carrying food and eggs into the cave, they stealthily approached the cave exit. As they did, Truin supposed that perhaps this cave had once been a giant anthill, taken over by the spiders. Miraculously for Truin and Khory, the ants had chosen this day, and precisely this time, to reclaim it. Thank God they had or the men would have surely perished within the cave, sharing the horrible fate of Achilles and Xenon.

They emerged from the cave, exhausted but still wired. Truin and Khory praised God for their deliverance and thanked him for saving their lives. Then they prayed for the souls of their two lost comrades, asking God to have mercy on them and to welcome them with open arms into their new home with him in heaven.

CHAPTER 18

ADONIA

†††

The next morning, after carefully marking the entrance to the cave and annotating its location in their journal, Truin and Khory resumed the return leg of their journey. The rest of their trip was relatively uneventful. They joined the other explorers in Delvia and reported all they had discovered.

All the explorers had astounding stories to tell of the areas that they had explored. In the north, majestic mountains towered over frozen sapphire lakes. To the west, vast deserts led to a tremendous gorge, where sharp cliffs dropped many hundreds of feet to the raging sea below. The southwest's rolling hills and marshlands gave way to countless coves with endless supplies of fish. Great forests dominated the center area of their new home. In addition, rolling hills and vast plains supported an abundant variety of both large and small game.

This land was everything Abner had hoped. It was abundant with food and natural resources to include wood, stone, iron, silver, gold, glowing rock and many brilliant gems. The soil was rich in nutrients, and the new arrivals had every reason to expect a plentiful and prosperous annual harvest of crops.

Abner named the land Adonia and dedicated it to the Lord. His family and close friends settled the land, intending to make it their permanent home. The family built the first permanent settlement in Adonia in the foothills of the northern mountains. It provided the best overall location for climate, defense, food, and the abundance of pre-cious natural resources. The city of Aanot, as they named it, became the Capital of Adonia. Here, nestled in the mountains of a new land, Abner, Evelin, and their children made a new home and found a new future.

Abner's family feared the Lord, and God blessed them greatly. God rewarded their labors with abundant harvests and complete protection from both disease and calamity. God's powerful hand protected Adonia, and Adonia prospered.

†††

Golden Wing and the heavenly host smiled down on the inhabi-tants of Adonia, and kept a watchful eye to the east, where darkness was tightening its grip on Omentia.

CHAPTER 19

DARK COVENANT

†††

Pete never knew God. The little voice within Pete that gave him a natural knowledge of his Creator, as well as a sense of right and of wrong, should have caused Pete to search for the truth. He should have seen God's invisible qualities and divine nature in all that God had made on the land, in the sea, and in the skies above. Instead, Pete resisted what his conscience and his senses told him. He remained blind, and in his blindness, he chose a different path.

More than anything in the world, Pete longed for power. As a youth, working in the caves, this thirst for power became an obsession.

The absence of light in Pete's heart soon attracted evil. The dark angel, Potentus, seeing Pete was vulnerable, exploited Pete's desire and equipped him with the power that he so longed to wield. Potentus placed his mark upon Pete, giving him a new name; for Pete was no more. His new name was Karyan.

As Karyan's power grew, his control spread. Like an ever-expanding cloud, his unnatural demonstrations of power drew in more and more of the curious. Fascination kept them coming back. Eventually, their lust for power and pleasure drew the lost sheep to the darkness, as their foolish hearts and their sinful desires led them to exchange even the truth of God for a lie.

Omentia's morality effectively crumbled under Karyan's hand. Karyan's disciples put their trust in magic and then in all things vile.

Their men and women abandoned natural relations, choosing instead to commit indecent acts with one another. Those who once knew of the true God turned their back on him, turning instead to godlessness and wickedness. Since they suppressed the truth with their wickedness, God's wrath turned against them; he gave them over to their depraved minds.

The evil angels descended upon Omentia by the thousands, seizing Omentia's inhabitants and filling them with every kind of wickedness and depravity. Though they knew God had said these evil things were wrong and deserved a punishment of death, their darkened hearts condoned and approved of all those who committed such deeds.

The dark cloud spread across Omentia, and soon all of Omentia fell to Karyan's dark control.

CHAPTER 20

Truin and Christina

†††

Anot, the city of light in the new land, glimmered on the edge of the great, blue mountain cliffs of northern Adonia. It was here, towering high in the clouds, that love bloomed.

Christina had captured Truin's heart the moment that she had first looked into his eyes. He didn't know it, of course, but Christina, with the help of her new best friend, Elin, soon made it very obvious to him.

Ever since Truin's accident in the forest, Elin became increasingly protective of him. After nursing him back to health, Elin took it upon herself to see that nothing bad would ever again happen to her brother, at least as far as she could control.

In the months that followed Christina's miraculous rescue from the jaws of death in the frigid waters of the Dark Sea, Elin saw Christina as the sister she never had. Naturally, it didn't take long before Elin had the idea that Christina and Truin, being of similar age, beliefs, and circumstance — were perfect for one other. Actually, Elin couldn't take all the credit for the idea. She had seen the way Christina had watched Truin when he wasn't looking, and she had seen the way Truin had watched Christina when she wasn't looking. They both asked her about the other incessantly, and everyone realized around them that the two were in love, even though they didn't seem to know it themselves.

It was about this time that Truin met a young man named Jonn. Jonn had lived in Adonia for many years and had an extensive knowledge of the various peoples that inhabited the land. Since Abner's clan was not the first to settle in Adonia, information about the peoples already inhabiting the land was of vital importance.

Various small clans existed in several pockets around Adonia, and each had its own unique commodity for trade with the others. Trade was paramount in Adonia for survival, especially when a family was new to the land and not yet well situated.

Jonn, being a trader, possessed valuable knowledge of the goods that could negotiated, where to find them, and their prices. This made him invaluable to the family as their mediator, negotiator, and ambassador to the diverse peoples of the land.

Initially, Truin met with Jonn, weekly, for business and administrative discussions only. However, their friendship flourished, and soon they began meeting on a much more regular basis for an assortment of activities. Before long, Jonn began accompanying Truin and Khory on the hunt.

One brisk, fall day while the trio hunted bear in the mountains to the north of Aanot, Jonn and Truin's young friendship faced a test. Khory had stopped to set up camp while Truin and Jonn took one more stab at the surrounding countryside for a prize to bring back to Aanot the following day. The sun was getting low in the sky, and though it would still be awhile before it set, a lofty peak to their east was casting a long shadow over them and the light in the forest was fading to black.

Hot on the tracks of a large, brown bear, Truin and Jonn split up. The plan was to converge on the bear from two different directions, ensuring one of them was downwind from the bear; remaining undetected to take the shot.

The plan worked, though arguably it would have worked better had the bear not got the jump on Truin before Jonn was in position to take a shot with his bow. Truin had closed on the brown from upwind and the beast had sensed his approach. As such, when the two of them met, Truin found himself unprepared for close contact with the two-thousand pound killer. Before Truin could react, the eight-foot tall predator was in a full charge and not twenty-five feet away. Not having time to draw his bow for a shot, Truin attempted to dodge the assault by diving behind a nearby boulder. He knew in his heart that this would provide only a temporary refuge, but temporary would have to do until a better option presented itself.

As Truin dove for cover, the brown beast lunged for him. Both Truin and the bear were airborne simultaneously, and at that moment, time seemed to move in slow motion. As Truin prepared to hit the ground and roll behind the boulder, his arm outstretched to cushion the impact with the ground, and he looked back into the eyes of the monstrous beast intent on consuming him for dinner. Every muscle and tendon in the massive beast's body flexed in the attack, its powerful jaws were wide-open, and its teeth were at the ready to saw Truin's flesh apart with ease. With its front legs outstretched and its six-inch claws fully extended, the beast aimed to tear at Truin's soft, unprotected skin. The brown was but feet from its objective. Given time, Truin could have counted the individual hairs that bristled on the creature's hide; given time.

At that moment, still in slow motion, an arrow appeared in Truin's peripheral vision. It moved ever so deliberately with perfect intent across his field of vision until it contacted the throat of the charging bear. Penetrating a few milliseconds later with meat and then vein, blood spurted fiery red from the point of impact. As the arrow continued to penetrate, it emerged from the backside of the beast's throat, bringing a shower of flesh and blood with it as it exited.

At that fleeting moment, Truin thought he saw something change in the bear's eyes. A light that was there just an instant before flickered, before ebbing out. It was as if the beast's moment, its designated time, had come.

As rapidly as time had slowed, it returned to normal speed. Truin hit the ground and rolled, coming to rest painfully hard against the side of the boulder. The brown bear's body continued in flight behind Truin, barely missing him as it passed. Its momentum alone drove its trajectory as the massive muscles that a moment before propelled its attack had gone limp. It hit the ground, crumbling into a monstrous pile of meat and fur on the ground to the side of Truin; its neck nearly torn from its lifeless body.

A split second later, Jonn was at Truin's side, looking more pleased with himself than concerned with Truin's close encounter.

"Not a bad shot, wouldn't you say?"

Truin couldn't have agreed more. He considered teasing Jonn about the timeliness of his shot, but before he could, the situation changed yet again. As Jonn helped Truin up, they found themselves surrounded by five men, clothed in heavy furs and wearing unwelcoming countenances. Several hunters from another tribe had been tracking the same brown bear. The hunters discovered Truin and Jonn standing over what they fairly considered their prize; they were not very pleased.

"Dunkned overstad lam baden trenchkuft!" One of them exclaimed as he pointed irately at the still warm carcass of the hairy beast on the ground in front of them.

Jonn could see that Truin, emotionally a bit off balance from almost being eaten a moment earlier, was about to resist handing over the furry trophy, so Jonn skillfully stepped in as a necessary, diplomatic go-between. Understanding their tongue well, as he did most of the various dialects in the land, he stretched out his open hands and offered them the beast with a smile. "Mesckala tem diest — la monta kullo."

Jonn, noticing Truin still looked angry and resistant — no doubt based in confusion over the rapidly changing situation and his recent fight-or-flight experience — overstated his smile and repeated his gracious gesture. He subtly suggested Truin respond in similar fashion or risk both of their hides accompanying the bear's back to the strangers' village as trophies from their hunt. Truin finally caught on, and his expression instantly changed to one of welcome and friendship. He echoed Jonn's invitation that their new friends take the brown.

The anger quickly faded from the strangers' faces, and friendly smiles abounded. Four of their group prepared the fallen creature for transport. The largest of the men, presumably their leader, standing at least a foot taller than either Truin or Jonn, approached Truin. Towering over Truin, the hunter presented Truin with an ornate dagger made of a material that glowed a bright blue.

"Forst ameno couractea — mucktos."

Dumbfounded, Truin accepted the gift, which felt very cold to the touch. All he could think to do was smile. "Thank you."

The hunting party departed as stealthfully as they had arrived. Truin was still unsure of exactly what had transpired. He looked at Jonn. "Now what exactly was that all about?"

Jonn grinned. "Well, it appears you are a hero."

"Huh?"

"Well, any man who would purposely use himself as bait to stop a man-eating bear from terrorizing the people of this mountain, and then choose not to take the glory or even the spoils of the hunt, but give it to the people of the mountain for food and clothing; that is the definition of a hero to these people."

"But, I didn't —"

Jonn interrupted. "Ah, now stop being so modest! We all saw it. You are a hero. These men pledged their tribe would know of your bravery and your friendship to their people. The dagger was a token of their friendship with you and all that may accompany you in this land. They also look forward to future trade with you and your people."

At that moment, Truin realized Jonn had done quite an unbelievable job of turning a potentially violent situation into a quite profitable one with his quick thinking, diplomatic expertise, and masterful use of his fluent language skills. Indeed, his new friend would prove to be a tremendous help in this new land. "Thank you, Jonn."

"All in a day's work. Should we get to camp? I am sure Khory will be quite upset he missed out on the action."

"I'll bet he won't believe any of it happened."

Truin looked down at his new blade. "But he'll have a hard time denying this."

"Good point. No pun intended."

†††

It wasn't long before Elin and Khory conscripted Jonn into their scheme to bring Truin and Christina's budding love affair out of the shadows of denial, where it had remained through the winter and into the light of spring. Jonn, worth his weight in gold in all diplomatic affairs, proved once again to be just the catalyst needed for spring fever to take root in Aanot.

Improvements in Aanot had progressed steadily since building had begun a year prior, and Abner decided it was time for a celebration; a thanksgiving for all the blessings God had given the new inhabitants of Adonia. Evelin suggested throwing a banquet and a dance to kick off the weeklong event, and soon preparations were in full swing.

Khory made sure that Truin invited Jonn to the event, clarifying that all of Aanot's new friends must attend; doing otherwise would be quite rude.

"Quite rude indeed!" Truin had agreed.

Unknown to Truin, however, Elin and Khory, already planning on attending the dance as a couple, had casually suggested that Christina must also attend. Elin had asked, "What would a celebration at Aanot be without the most beautiful girl in the land?" Blushing at the comment, Christina had humbly agreed to attend; finally accepting the notion that she could start a new life in Adonia.

Both assuming someone would invite Christina to the ball as his official date, Elin and Evelin began work on an extraordinary dress, designed to ensure Christina would be the talk of the event; that she would be the young woman all the ladies envied as well as the young woman all the gentlemen would want to have by their side.

Two weeks before the dance, Truin was still dragging his feet. Though he wanted more than anything to ask Christina to the dance,

Truin had never really talked to a girl in a boy-girl kind of way, and his shyness was getting the best of him. He was downright miserable!

Khory tried all the usual techniques to encourage Truin to ask Christina to accompany him, but Truin always had some convenient excuse for putting it off.

Truin needed a nudge, and this is where Jonn came in. Truin was unaware that Jonn was courting his own sweetheart in his home village, and what Truin did not know was critical to the plan.

Khory, Elin, Evelin and Jonn were all key characters in the play that was now unfolding. Christina was too, though she was completely oblivious of her part. The goal was to arrange for Truin to see Jonn calling on Christina and subtly plant the idea that Jonn was asking Christina to accompany him to the dance. The conspirators thought that the sight of Jonn and Christina together, as well as the idea that those next few moments might forever determine an unalterable course of romantic events, would force Truin into action.

It was a well-orchestrated play, yet very simplistic. Though some might see their little plan as a manipulation of sorts, the intent was simply to get Truin to see how he truly felt about Christina and force him to act upon it. In reality, they were doing Truin a favor that he would undoubtedly appreciate for the rest of his life; so the conspirators hoped.

The various acts of the play fell together like pieces of an elaborate puzzle. First, Evelin ensured Christina was present on the back patio of Abner's hacienda, overlooking the gardens and vineyards of Aanot, at the precise moment that Jonn came to meet with Abner to discuss various trade agreements that they had been negotiating with the local tribes. Evelin also ensured that Abner was busy when Jonn arrived and requested Jonn wait for Abner on the patio. This put Jonn and Christina together on the patio, alone if you will, to discuss heaven knows what. The patio was well visible from Truin's home, and Khory ensured that he and Truin were behind Truin's place, working on a project at the same time Jonn and Christina met on Abner's patio. Finally, at just the right time, Elin dropped by Truin's place to mention casually to the boys that she had seen Jonn and Christina together on Abner's patio. She then said the words to light the fuse. "I wonder if Jonn is asking Christina to the dance."

Truin froze when he heard Elin's words. He looked towards Abner's patio and saw Jonn and Christina together. Instantly he knew he had to do something immediately! Tere was no time for thought, only action. His mind offered no excuses for delay. Adrenaline surged through Truin's veins. His heart raced, and before Elin could finish her prepared lines, Truin was gone like a flash. Elin looked at Khory with a smile. "Fuze lit." They watched as Truin sprinted away.

Truin raced across the gardens between his home and his father's hacienda, jumping over vines, and dodging workers.

I have to get there before he asks her! I just have to!

Truin was resolute in his mission as he leaped over the wall onto the patio next to Jonn and Christina. Had he had time to think about what he was doing, about the surprised look on Christina's face, or about what an idiot he was no doubt making of himself; reason would have triumphed and proper decorum would have demanded that he apologize for his abrupt arrival, cut his losses, and retreat in the utmost embarrassment.

However, in that moment, love — not reason — was in control. Nothing mattered to Truin except releasing the feelings of love for Christina that he had kept pent-up for so long; revealing the truth — his secret love for the girl that they had found alone in the ocean on that terrible and yet most wonderful of days!

"Christina, Christina, I have to tell you. I'm sorry, I just have to tell you!" Truin announced, still trying to catch his breath.

"I'm sorry to interrupt," Truin said. He looked at Jonn. "Excuse us for a moment?" Truin purposely escorted a wide-eyed and surprised Christina to the far side of the patio. After feigning surprise himself, Jonn watched the act unfold with inner delight. A small smile broke across Jonn's face, sending a small but obvious signal — to any would-be observers of the play — that he approved with how the plot appeared to be unfolding.

Not thinking, just feeling, Truin's emotions gushed from his mouth. "Christina, ever since that day on the boat, I haven't been able to stop thinking about you. You are — you are so wonderful!"

Christina loved what she was hearing. She had shared the same feelings of infatuation for Truin, but thought that she would never hear these words come from Truin's lips. She beamed; her eyes lit up, her smile widened, and her face flushed. She took it all in, hanging on every word Truin spoke.

"Would you go with me to the celebration dance? Please, please go with me to the dance?"

Christina paused, letting the words ring in her ears, and in a way making Truin pay for waiting so very long to ask her.

Then she could stand it no longer. "Yes, I will go with you Truin! Of course I will go with you!"

They laughed as they looked into each other's eyes; tears of joy ran down their cheeks. Truin took Christina in his arms and swung her in circles. They laughed and shouted for joy, like two children playing in the rain. Then, abruptly, Truin stopped. He wondered what his friend Jonn was thinking of this sudden turn of events. They both turned to find Jonn was no were to be seen. The unbridled joy returned. Overcome with emotion, they continued to carry on like foolish school children.

Elin and Khory watched from Truin's backyard with joy and prideful satisfaction in a job well done!

"I love spring," Khory said as he turned to Elin and gently took her into his arms.

"Me too," Elin said. Her teasing smile fading as they embraced.

Evelin returned with lemonade to find two very filthy youngsters dancing about on her patio. Her heart leaped for her son and for this wonderful, young girl she had come to know and love. Both Truin and Christina had already seen too much heartache in their young lives. It was good for them to have each other.

Thank you, Lord, for bringing these two together. Who could ever have foreseen these two meeting, being from such distant lands? Only you, Oh God, could work out such a thing. You, Oh Lord, are so faithful!

†††

The celebration in Aanot was spectacular! Everyone that had come ashore with Abner and his family a year earlier, along with all of their new friends from the surrounding countryside and adjacent regions, were on hand to celebrate a year of God's rich blessings. The weeklong event also provided an excellent opportunity for Abner and his family to give witness to the love and faithfulness of the one, true God to their new friends in the land; those who did not yet know him.

Abner could not believe how much God had changed his life in the past year. He had never seen it coming. A little over a year ago, he didn't even know that change was on the horizon. Still, God's plan had unfolded in quite a spectacular fashion. They had a wonderful new home in a wonderful new land. Their home life had also changed and for the better. Abner and Evelin had again grown very close. They frequently shared each other's company, leaving many of their old pastimes behind in Omentia. They worked together on various projects, and remembered why they had married so many years earlier. They no longer took each other for granted, and their love grew stronger with every passing day.

Abner had learned an important lesson, and he shared it at every opportunity with as many people as possible.

All any child of God ever needs to do is trust and obey their Heavenly Father. He always knows what is best and will take care of the rest.

Christina, as expected, was the most beautiful flower in the bouquet of women at the celebration dance. Evelin and Elin had truly acted selflessly in ensuring Christina stood out, sparing no expense or effort to adorn her richly. They spent a tremendous amount of time on Christina's dress in the days leading up to the dance and on Christina the day of the event, making sure she looked glorious. And breathtaking she was! Truin about fell over when he first saw her. She was radiant, and there was not an unattached male present that didn't wish to dance with her.

Christina, however, only wished to dance with Truin. Truin had rescued her from stormy seas, and Christina believed God had brought Truin into her life for a truly significant purpose. She only had eyes for Truin.

The celebration was just the beginning of a love affair that became the talk of Aanot. The courting between Truin and Christina continued for a year with the blessing of all.

Meanwhile, Jonn was happily courting the love of his life, a young maiden named Robinelle. Many were the days when Truin, Christina, Jonn, and Robinelle would leave their work and the troubles of the world behind to head off into the beautiful Adonian countryside for days of hiking, fishing, camping, and just enjoying God's beautiful gifts of nature. They discovered many amazing vistas and made many unforgettable memories on the outings.

Truin asked Christina to spend the rest of her life with him in their favorite place, a hillside not far from Aanot. It overlooked a dark blue lake that they had found while camping with Jonn and Robinelle. Without hesitation, she looked into Truin's eyes and told him God created her to be his partner and would love him until her last breath left her body.

They married six weeks later in another celebration that dwarfed any previous. Khory was Truin's best man; Elin was Christina's maid of honor. Jonn and Robinelle were also in the wedding party.

Elin and Khory made the day ever more special by announcing a surprise of their own. That evening, at Truin and Christina's wedding reception, Khory announced that Elin and he were engaged to be married. The ballroom erupted in even greater jubilee. It was truly a night to be remembered!

Though Ka'el and Tara attended the wedding reception, they missed the actual wedding ceremony. Everyone wondered why they hadn't attended. It was definitely rare for the brother of the groom to miss the wedding ceremony, especially when the groom had asked him to be a groomsman. Ka'el claimed they had tried to make it to the wedding ceremony, but because of unforeseen circumstances that he could not elaborate on, they could not make it in time. This excuse didn't float very well, and Ka'el's apparent lack of consideration for important family events further alienated him and Tara from the family.

Abner thought maybe Ka'el was reluctant to attend the ceremony, because he and Tara were having difficulties in their own marriage; though no one knew the specifics.

Evelin's sixth sense told her more was going on than met the eye, and this troubled her greatly. She gave her anxiety to the Lord, entrusting it to his almighty will. She continued to pray earnestly that God would take care of her strongest, firstborn son; the one she now feared needed the most help of all.

†††

Truin built Christina a house on a hillside, shaded by a large oak tree that overlooked the dark blue lake that was their favorite place in the world. Now it was even better.

Truin and Christina complimented each other fully, cared for each other selflessly, and loved each other unconditionally. Every night they watched the sunset over the east end of Blue Lake and thanked God for bringing them into this new land of beauty and peace; most of all for bringing them together. Before long, God blessed them with another gift, the gift of their first son. They called their son Geoff, which means the peace of God.

CHAPTER 21

SEVEN SONS

†††

Now these are the sons of Truin, son of Abner. The first bundled blessing given to Christina and Truin was a son they named Geoff, born soon after establishing their home on Blue Lake. A year later, the Lord blessed him with a brother named Skottie, who was born with a good-sized birthmark, resembling a lion, over his heart. Daniel was their third son, born two years after Skottie. Bigaulf and Gareth followed Daniel; they were both exceptionally large at birth. Finally, in the tenth year of their marriage, Christina gave birth to twins, Cusintomas and Moesheh. Seven sons were born in all to Christina and Truin. They were all happy and strong, and their parents loved them dearly.

Truin entrusted the safety of the boys to two lifelong friends that had accompanied him from Omentia; McBob and Black Bart. These men had gained the reputation of being two of the bravest and most trustworthy warriors in all of Omentia. Originally from the Glen of Braden, they had trained under the master of martial arts himself, Sifu Rodriguez. People throughout the land knew them as the brothers of a lion. They considered it an honor and a privilege to accept such a responsibility. McBob had told Truin, "No doubt these boys will one day be future leaders in this land. We cannot overstate the importance of protecting them. One cannot lead if he no longer draws breath. On my life, I will keep them safe."

Many men and women assisted Truin, and Christina in teaching the boys as they grew. Truin spent as much time as he could with his sons, but the duties and responsibilities that came with settling a new land stole away much of the time that he would rather have spent with them. He prioritized teaching them the Word and passing on to them the things that he had learned in life; but he needed help in raising his sons the way they needed to be raised and fully teaching them what they needed to be taught. For this, he called upon friends he could trust.

Noa, one of Abner's dearest friends, taught the sons of Truin integrity, duty, and discipline; much like he had done when assisting Abner in teaching Truin and Ka'el many years earlier in Omentia. Not getting any younger, Noa enlisted the help of his nephew Melkione, who taught the boys self-defense. Along with McBob and Black Bart, these god-fearing men followed Truin's lead in being an excellent role model for the boys to emulate. They helped teach the seven sons to be men of honor, men of courage, and men of service; service to God, to their family, and to their new homeland.

Their mother Christina; along with Melkione's wife, Margerie; and their Aunt Elin taught the boys the "softer," yet equally important characteristics of being godly and honorable men. First, they too prioritized God's Word, focusing on what the Word meant to the boys in their daily lives. Next, they helped each of the boys discover and develop their own God-given talents and skills. They taught the boys to read, to write, and to use mathematics. Finally, they taught them to never forget where their gifts came from.

For every good gift is from the Father of Lights.

They prayed and sang praises continually to the Lord of the heavens.

God blessed Truin, Christina, and their sons with an abundance of love, joy, and prosperity. The seven sons of Truin grew up strong and wise, each with their own individual skills; but all with a heart of love, a will of iron, and a spirit of power.

As the boys became men and each made their own adventures, they head out into the unpopulated areas of Adonia to discover the land "beyond." At Truin's request, Jonn prepped each of them before they left on the various clans that inhabited the land, what their different customs were, how to best make a good first impression, and, most importantly, how to avoid conflict.

Christina was always teary-eyed, seeing another of her sons go into the great unknown, but years of hunting expeditions and "great adventures" as the boys liked to call their frequent outings had eased the sudden impact of their inevitable departures from her nest. Christina rested in the assurance that God would bless and protect her sons. She often repeated to herself out loud — because it helped to hear the words — "God loves them even more than I do. He will be with them, as he has promised."

Truin echoed her sentiment as he blessed each of his sons, sending them on their way with words traditionally repeated from the Word on such occasions. "Be strong and courageous. Do not be terrified; do not be discouraged, for the Lord your God will be with you wherever you go."

As would become the tradition for each on their eighteenth birthday, Abner would have an enormous feast prepared within the walls of Castle Armon for the young man's coming of age. Castle Armon had, over the twenty years since their arrival, grown into a mighty fortress; the greatest in all of Adonia.

The first of such feasts was for Geoff. Geoff was the first to reach eighteen, and setting the example for the rest of his brothers, he set out shortly after the feast in his honor, traveling south to the large, forested areas of central Adonia. Since he had been old enough to walk, he had loved to climb trees and truly loved being in the forest. He loved the smells, the colors, and the rich variety of life to be found in the timberland. Now, with endless forests before him, he explored the land. People often overheard him singing tunes as he walked. The large forestland he settled became known as Tobar, named after the province's dense forests. They were so thick with vegetation and fantastic creatures that a quick passage through them was nearly impossible.

When it was his time, Skottie headed southeast to the rolling hills and valleys that awaited him there. This land reminded him of his youth in the foothills around Blue Lake, minus the white-capped mountains, of course. Skottie couldn't stand the thought of ever living in the flatlands or "flats" as he called them. He loved this hilly land's variety of terrain, to include the caves his father had discovered with Khory years before. Skottie named this territory of rolling hills, valleys, and caves, Kandish, after the beautiful crystals or kan found underground. Skottie surmised that one day someone would discover the true value of the kan crystals, causing Kandish's importance to skyrocket.

Daniel followed his brothers' lead and headed south, but he headed southwest to the flats. He had always loved the open skies and flatlands, where a man could see forever. Despite his youth, he possessed a wisdom beyond his years and took great pleasure in the simple blessings given by God. This included witnessing rainstorms replenish the plains, a rainbow in the sky confirming the promise, and the breathtaking sight of a radiant sun ascending in the west and a vibrant sun descending in the east. He became well known for his great wisdom, often being asked to settle the most controversial of disputes. His land became known as Plattos.

Bigaulf grew to be the largest of the sons born to Christina. He loved to work the land, and his strength became that of legend. Bigaulf returned to the land where his family had first come ashore twenty-five years earlier. This land was exceptionally fertile, and Bigaulf enjoyed an ever abundant harvest of crops that he readily shared with his entire family. His land became known as Delvia.

Gareth also grew very large and strong, second only to Bigaulf. He loved the land to the north; the mountains, the snow, and the ice. While his other brothers favored hunting to the south where it was warmer, Gareth, or "Koldas" as they often called him, would head north to the ice-lands to hunt. When it was his time to leave the fold, Gareth settled in the high country, where the grade was steep and the air was pure. This land became known as Chastain.

The twins, the youngest of the brothers, favored western Adonia. Cusintomas settled in the northwest and Moesheh in the southwest.

Cusintomas favored the blowing sands of the great desert and the sheer cliffs of the western shore. He liked to hike along the cliffs that towered over the Northern Sea and spend his time scaling the steep rock faces while perfecting his climbing techniques. Bands of wild, dark-tan horses roamed freely in this land, and the region became known as Tanshire. When not climbing the cliffs of Tanshire or taming a wild bronco, Cusintomas often visited Gareth. Together they would scale the snow-covered mountains of Chastain.

Moesheh loved the water. He spent most of his early years fishing and swimming in Blue Lake. Moesheh chose the southwest coast of Adonia because it offered red rivers, red pastures, and countless schools of redfish. He loved the tropical climate, the sandy beaches, and the endless variety of fish. This land became known as Rothing.

The sons of Truin lived god-pleasing lives, married god-fearing women, and had many god-fearing children of their own. They settled the land, gave all glory to God for their successes, and were careful to treat everyone they met with honesty and respect. In return, all the inhabitants of the land trusted and respected them. Their many adventures were indeed legendary and, as time passed, they became the leaders of their respective provinces.

CHAPTER 22

PROSPERITY

†††

For decades, Adonia prospered and grew. Aanot thrived as the sparkling gem of Adonia and became the center of trade and commerce for the region. Though Abner was the patriarch of the newly thriving land, Truin effectively took the reins of leadership in uniting Adonia and directing its efforts toward common goals.

As each of Truin's sons settled the lands they had chosen, their wisdom, honesty, courage and charisma placed them on paths of leadership in their respective territories. Villages thrived and provinces took shape; the inhabitants soon looked to the sons of Truin for management and guidance.

Truin gathered around him many wise advisors for counsel. In time, these advisors would form the core membership of the first Council of Adonia, but in the early days of its formation, these meetings remained much more informal; more like a family gathering than any kind of official meeting.

Among these advisors were Khory and his brother, Daev. Because of their training and knowledge of metallurgy, they became Aanot's first blacksmiths, or "smiths." They assisted in the manipulation of metals for many important uses, not the least of which was the manufacturing of the weapons to be used in the defense of Adonia.

Jonn continued to be a key advisor to Truin regarding trade and relations with the various peoples of Adonia. In time, Jonn assumed an official ambassadorial role, working out differences between the seven newly formed provinces as well as representing the provinces in talks with the native tribes of Adonia.

Jonn's brother, Gladsel, also became a special advisor to Truin; though primarily as an ambassador to the lands and peoples outside of the land of Adonia. This was a tough job, but Gladsel handled the task with honor and class.

Abner, Truin, and his sons, though geographically separated, continued to prioritize their family ties. They visited as often as possible and coordinated their efforts. Under Jonn's keen business eye, all their endeavors flourished. They founded new villages across the land and prospered, while simultaneously being a blessing to all those around them.

CHAPTER 23

STRANGE LANDS

†††

Though their relationship remained rocky at best, Ka'el and Tara raised two sons. Tala named her first son Toro. He was a surprise to both Ka'el and Tara, arriving during a troublesome time in their marriage. Toro's arrival, however, drew Ka'el and Tara closer once again, reminding them each of the love that had united them in the beginning and giving them another on which to focus their mutual love. Weiphal arrived two years later, officially making them a family of four.

While growing up, Toro and Weiphal enjoyed the company of their cousins immensely. Though they could always feel the tension that existed between their father and their uncle Truin, it never impacted their relationship with their cousins. The sons of Truin and the sons of Ka'el were like brothers. They played together, laughed together, and hunted together.

Toro and Weiphal had a special affinity for animals. Toro was most impressed with the beasts that roamed the land, while Weiphal was most taken with the birds of the air. Since the time they were young lads, Toro and Weiphal appreciated the beauty and abilities of all the creatures that surrounded them. They respected and dealt kindly with the animals, and it often seemed that the animals behaved differently around them; almost as if they trusted Toro and Weiphal more than they did other men.

When it came time to leave home, Ka'el's sons felt a powerful pull towards the south, where strange creatures roamed. The lands of excitement and danger is where they wanted to be.

Few explorers had explored the Strange Lands; more accurately, few explorers returned to speak of their exploration. Those who did return, returned with unbelievable stories of fantastic creatures that few believed still existed; if they ever existed.

The intellectuals of the time firmly believed that men who claimed to see such creatures were nothing more than avid storytellers fabricating fantastic fables.

To Toro and Weiphal, these amazing stories were exactly the exciting quest they had been dreaming of all of their young lives, and they couldn't wait to begin their adventure into the great unknown.

The time of waiting had been agonizing for the boys. Then, almost without warning, the waiting ended. It was time.

†††

"Unbelievable!" Toro could not help but say it out loud.

"Incredible!" Weiphal responded, as he too looked on in amazement at the beautiful landscape in front of them.

They had just entered the uncharted Strange Lands, directly south of the forests of Tobar. As they exited a deep gorge, marking the southernmost region of the forests; the temperature and humidity rose, a peculiar smell filled the air, and they witnessed the most breathtaking view.

The early morning sun was casting orange rays of light between the various layers of gray fog that covered the swamplands ahead. Enormous trees jutted skyward above the highest fog bank and into the tranquil, dark-blue heavens. Despite the morning sun invading their domain, the stars still twinkled across the great expanse above it all.

The sight alone was enough to demand undivided attention, but what happened next put the exclamation point on awesome!

As the golden rays of light bounced across the fog bank and lit up the giant trees in its path, the unexpected addition of many snake-like necks with massive heads disturbed the serene scene. The necks punched out of the fog and stretched nearly as high as the top branches of the trees. As one creature would burst into view, another would disappear, sinking back down beneath the surface of the fog. All across the horizon before them, this dance ensued, and it was unlike anything Toro and Weiphal had ever seen before. Adding to the incredible panorama, giant winged creatures glided across the horizon just above the treetops, screeching out their high-pitched cries in response to the long, low sighing of the longnecks below them.

"I can barely believe what I am seeing," Toro said. "To be honest, I had my doubts about the stories being true; I hoped they were, but I didn't truly believe — until now."

Weiphal was speechless. He just stood motionless in the early morning mist.

They stood there in absolute wonder. The sun rose higher into the sky, and the fog melted away. With each passing moment, more and more of the countryside before them came into view. Every moment brought more bewilderment. They could now see the massive creatures in their entirety. These were the largest creatures they had ever seen; the largest they had ever even heard mentioned. They walked on four large legs; legs as thick as the trunk of a great redwood. They had necks twice the length of their giant torsos; necks they used to reach the very tops of the highest trees for food. Every step they took shook the ground beneath them.

The magnificent beasts paid no attention to the men, as if to say that the men meant nothing to them. Toro and Weiphal could not have been happier with the creatures' indifference. The last thing they wanted was for these giants to perceive them as a threat; or, even worse, an enemy.

With the thought came another that Toro shared ever so quietly with his brother. "I can see that finding food will not be a problem in this new land, though I am not so sure I look forward to the hunting."

Weiphal turned to face Toro, and together they contemplated the scenario. "Ah, but who would be the hunter and who would be the prey?"

†††

For twenty days, Ka'el's sons and their scouting party carefully traversed the swamps and low-lying forests of Serendopolus, charting the land and discovering many new species of creatures there. It was at this time that Weiphal announced his desire to break off and explore a land even farther to the south and west. As the brothers crossed the high hills separating these two distinctly different lands, they parted ways, determined to meet up again in the spring.

It was now well into fall, and discovering that most of the larger creatures lived in the low-lying swamplands in the center of Serendopolus, Toro stayed in the highlands. He contended that sometimes observing from a distance was the best formula for success.

While hunting for game one night, Toro separated from his men. As he awaited the arrival of his dinner under the pale blue light of a full moon, a chill overcame him. He broke off the hunt in favor of much needed rest and headed back towards camp. Disoriented, he wandered off into the darkness and soon found himself quite lost. As he stumbled along, alone in the eerie shadows of the moonlight, he became all too aware of the peril of his situation. He was lost, ill, alone, and the temperature had dangerously dropped to a level much lower than he had expected. Before he knew it, storm clouds had hidden the moon from sight. The wind howled, and a heavy sheet of snow fell from the sky. He needed to find cover, and he needed to do it now!

Toro discovered a shallow cave in the side of a rocky hill that provided him with some shelter from the snow and wind, but he didn't have the proper equipment for spending the night in a storm. Shivering uncontrollably, then not at all, hypothermia set in; he became delirious. He curled up into a ball in the back of the cave and prayed to God for help. As he lost consciousness, he had all but given up on surviving through the night.

As Toro fell into a deep sleep, he dreamed. He dreamed of being encased in a coffin of ice; the ice growing thicker and thicker around him with each passing moment. He tried to move, but he could not. He tried to scream, but his mouth wouldn't make any noise. The world grew darker and darker as the light fought to penetrate the nearly opaque shell of frozen death that entombed him.

The light faded, and strange shadows darted around him. He tried to see the shadows' masters in the dim illumination, but his eyes always seemed a moment behind and unable to focus on the illusive creatures — unable to discern their shapes.

Then he heard the howling.

Is that the wind or some strange beast?

In his weakened condition, Toro grew keenly aware of his own fear; fear of the unknown forces that now encircled him. Hopelessness took on a life of its own, further entombing Toro in an icy grave of dread; devoid of warmth and light.

Cold —
Dark —
Alone —
Help me.

Then something changed. A sliver — just a sliver of light. Then another sliver, joining the first. Then a third. Suddenly, a bright beam of light penetrated the ice. It refracted, reflected, and spread in all directions through the ice that encased him, shattering it into pieces.

So bright. So warm. Not alone.

His eyes opened, slowly and painfully. He could see bright light reflecting off the mounds of snow outside the shallow cave. He peered between his eyelids in disbelief that he was still alive. Afraid to move, he struggled to make sense out of what was happening.

How can I be alive? Why didn't I freeze to death?

As his senses returned to him, he wondered why he was so warm. It was then that the rest of his body reported in. He was warm; his whole body was warm. He felt like he had a fur coat on. But he remembered he had nothing warm to wear when he drifted off, when he faded away from consciousness.

Still afraid to move his head, his eyes darted about to gather the much needed information. What he learned both amazed and terrified him.

A pack of wolves filled the cave, surrounding Toro and wrapping his body snugly in their fur coats. They had him wrapped up more snuggly than a newborn wrapped in warm blankets by its mother. Though he couldn't be sure exactly how many wolves there were, he thought he could count six — six enormous wolves.

His mind raced.

Did they also seek shelter here from the storm? Do they know I am here? Of course they know I am here. They are wolves, and wolves know stuff like that! Don't they know our kind hunts their kind? Why haven't they attacked me? Do they intend to eat me?

Toro's heart raced. The sound of it beating thundered in his head.

No, no, settle down, settle down! They will hear!

Toro held his breath, hoping it would quiet his heart, but it was too late. Toro's eyes widened as he realized the largest of the wolves had opened its eyes, raised its head, and was looking directly at him. His eyes met the wolf's large, green eyes, and Toro's racing thoughts stopped dead in their tracks; petrified like the rest of his body.

At twenty-five, Toro was a big man. He was strong, and he could fight well, but he knew he could do nothing in this situation. Surrounded by a pack of wolves, unarmed, and weakened; there was really nothing he could do. He couldn't even think of what to attempt. He had no plan.

I'm dead.

Toro, again, prayed to God for help. As he prayed, the large black wolf rose to its feet. The other wolves, which until now had appeared to be asleep, awoke, and followed the black wolf's movement with their dark brown eyes.

The green-eyed wolf lowered its head until its nose was only a few inches from Toro's face. Toro could feel the creature's warm breath as it exhaled. Still staring into the wolf's eyes, it was a moment unlike any Toro had ever imagined.

Without warning, the beast moved, but it was not the movement Toro expected. Toro expected the monster to release a ferocious attack, tearing off his face with one snap. Instead, the wolf purposefully pushed its furry head along the side of Toro's face, letting out a faint and peaceful growl as it did.

Toro had closed his eyes, expecting the worst. As he felt the soft caress of the wolf's fur across his face, he carefully opened his eyes to see the wolf turn toward the opening of the cave. The rest of the wolves, seven of them total, carefully unwrapped themselves from around Toro and rose; making their way out of the cave and out of sight. Only the large black wolf remained at the entry to the cave. It turned its head again, looking directly at Toro one more time before raising its head to the sky and letting out a loud and dominant howl. Then, it too disappeared from the cave entrance; leaving Toro alone and confused as to what was going on.

What just happened?

Toro sneezed and, feeling like everything might just be alright, allowed himself to smile. *Allergies.*

Toro remembered something his dear friend and spiritual mentor, Nomen, had once told him long ago. "We fear that which we do not understand, but God fears nothing. God understands all, for he is the architect of all. All things are in his hands. All creatures do his bidding. Trust him and remain faithful unto death, and he has promised you a crown of life."

Unexpectantly hearing the black wolf's howl, Buke and several other searchers from Toro's hunting party felt compelled to investigate the sound. They had looked all night for Toro, fearing the worst. They arrived to find Toro safe, uninjured, and professing yet another unbelievable story of the Strange Lands.

As Buke and the others brought Toro safely back to camp, they listened intently to Toro's account. Many of Toro's men refused to believe Toro's story, initially unable to understand how such a thing could have taken place. Nomen, however, recognizing the Lord's fingerprints when he saw them, spoke the Word of God to the men — and they believed.

After being rescued so extraordinarily from the certain jaws of death, Toro could do nothing other than praise God for his life and the second chance he had received.

†††

Weiphal and his men knew right away that this new land was unique and, to be frank, quite unnerving. The very first morning they had ventured into the grassy plains that bordered the southernmost province of Adonia, they had heard eerie screeches emanating from the horizon; from distant patches of enormous trees that towered over the rolling hills ahead.

The trees themselves seemed unusual because something had removed branches from the ground level up to about one-hundred feet in height. Above one-hundred feet, the trees became very dense with branches and leaves, altogether forming a treetop canopy that few rays of sunlight penetrated.

Not knowing what was causing the terrifying sounds above the canopy was disheartening to the explorers and increased their anxiety as they traveled. They almost questioned whether exploring this new land was worth facing the mysterious creatures that lived in the trees before them. At these times, they looked for strength from Weiphal. He stood a good foot taller than most of them and displayed no sign of fear whatsoever. Instead, he appeared to be quite curious about the origin of the ominous noises.

Weiphal was the kind of man who simply did not believe in dancing around an issue. Rather, he believed in meeting things head on. Seeing that his men grew more and more shaken by the ever-increasing volume of the treetop disturbances, he rather nonchalantly broached the subject.

"Men, what do you think is causing that incessant squealing up ahead?"

At first, there were no responses. The men just looked at each other apprehensively.

"C'mon now, surely you have some ideas. I'll start. Let's see, it could be the wind blowing through some kind of strange tree cone up there, making those high-pitched sounds."

"Right, that is a possibility," said Mitch, Weiphal's right-hand man. Mitch was the rugged, outdoorsy type with a flair for humor. "Then again, it could be a horde of giant, horned tree snakes; waiting to descend upon us in wrath, snatch us up, and devour us as we pass by!"

This reply, of course, did not help, since by this time the group of ten explorers was making their way through a waist high, grassy plain. None of them could see what was at their feet as they pressed forward.

"Horned, tree snakes? Is that the best you can do? Shoot, as boys, we used to hunt rattling snakes with y-sticks and sell their skins to old Mr. Higgins. We used their rattlers to make toys for the little children of the village. Surely we will not let a few tree snakes rattle us."

Mitch wasn't done. "Sure, but those snakes weren't twenty feet long. They didn't have horns, and they didn't hang out in trees waiting for unsuspecting travelers to wander by!"

"I think they're bloodsucking bats!" said Austinian, a courageous and oversized member of the group. "They sound like bats — big ones with big fangs!"

"They aren't bats," Mitch said with a smirk as he stopped and faced Austinian. "Bloodsucking bats don't hang out in the daylight at the top of trees. They hang out in caves under the ground and only come out to eat at night."

"Oh, ok, so bats don't hang out in trees, but when was the last time you saw a twenty-foot long, horned, man-eating, tree snake?"

Austinian and Mitch argued their ever-increasingly entrenched positions, and the rest of the group could not help but laugh. It appeared as if neither of the feuding men cared if a deadly creature descended upon them from the trees; all that really mattered was being correct in forecasting the true nature of the creature that was there.

"That's enough ladies," Weiphal injected with a grin. "Save it for the bloodsucking, horned, snake bats! Be alert! We are nearly at the first patch of trees."

As they approached the trees, the squealing hit yet a higher level of intensity.

They could see that almost without exception, something truly powerful had snapped the lower branches of the trees, from the trunks of the trees — some six inches across. Standing at the edge of the trees, they could see that something truly powerful had torn the branches from the lower levels of the trees and used them to strengthen and fortify the canopy high above.

Beneath the dense umbrella that now covered them, little light penetrated the canopy, creating a shadowing and gloomy climate all around them.

Chase, another member of the group, broke the silence and said, "Maybe some tree folk live up there, and they have removed all the lower branches to keep the horned tree snakes from climbing up there and sucking their blood."

Everyone looked at Chase in disbelief at the apparent sincerity in his speculation.

"What?" He responded defensively. "It could happen!"

Then all the strange sounds stopped, and there was silence. Not just a brief silence, but complete silence, like when you say something stupid in a crowd of people and everyone has to stop and look at you. Instantly, the men felt like they had captured someone's or something's attention — like they were being watched.

††††

Talon glided south over Adonia. It had been twenty years since he had led the orn from Omentia to Adonia. His instincts had been good. This land was a wonderful home for the eagle.

Since their arrival, they had observed much. Every thing that took place, took place under the watchful eye of the orn flying high above. Their vantage point was unequaled from their lofty nests high in the mountain peaks and the treetops.

Talon and the orn had prospered in this new land. They had raised their young in safety, grown in number, and lived in peace with the men of peace that walked below them upon the ground. These were good men; Talon's instincts told him so.

The orn had never pressed south of the forests of Adonia. There was never a reason. They had been more than content with the high places in the north. This day, however, Talon was told to fly further south. He obeyed.

††††

They had been the rulers of their land for two millennia. They had ruled the skies long before these trees—these trees that were now their home—had even sprouted from the earth. Over that period, many immense creatures had crawled and walked on the ground. These many diverse creatures would have threatened their offspring if they could reach their nests. Because of this threat, they took to the highest trees of the land, removing as many of the lower limbs as possible to reduce unwelcome guests from reaching their homes. Now, having no natural predators that could seriously threaten them, they feared nothing.

They had watched the new, two-legged beasts approach their tree patch; their keen eyesight tracking every movement of the beasts. Fearing nothing, they felt no need to keep quiet. They continued their morning songs. Not until the strangers stopped below their tree patch was the attention of the leader warranted. Then, all the singing stopped.

†††

Bestia circled high above, eager to do his master's bidding. His mission was to turn the ancient creatures against the Adonians, and he couldn't wait to get started. He spied the winged giants perched high in their nests, and his body tingled with excitement. Soon, their powerful claws and sharp beaks would tear open the flesh of the Adonians. He wished it were his claws and his teeth dealing out the deadly blows, but orchestrating the event would be the next best thing to doing it himself.

Across Omentia, Bestia and his fellow demons had deceived the followers of Karyan into thinking they were gaining special powers, and that through the use of special words, they could do magic, work illusion, and control the elements—even control the beasts. Karyan's disciples thought themselves powerful, when in fact they were already slaves to the demons.

These fools are too dumb to realize that they are but our slaves! We have the power, and they are nothing; nothing more than our puppets!

Bestia enjoyed deceiving Hussein, the Omentian, into thinking that he was in control of the beasts. Taking Hussein had been easy. He had a weak mind that thirsted for power; power he could not gain through his own intellect and talents. Once given a taste of power, Hussein became an instant disciple of evil, willing to do anything to keep his newfound skills. He had readily sold out his family to destruction in Omentia and spent the last six lunar cycles traveling secretly throughout Adonia, gaining valuable information for his master.

Now, perched on the rocks below, Hussein waited for Bestia to speak, to pull the strings and work the magic. Bestia would give Hussein the words; Bestia's minions, his fellow demons, would then enter the winged giants and direct them to do his bidding.

143

†††

Hussein hid in a cluster of large boulders at the base of a large bluff overlooking the grassy plain and the towering tree patches. The boulders had accumulated there over the ages, having dislodged from a rocky wall above and fallen to their present position over the period of a millennium. No one could see Hussein as he watched from above, but he could clearly see the explorers approaching.

This will be an excellent test of my power.

Hussein had practiced his influence over various lesser creatures in the past, steadily growing stronger and stronger.

If I can control these magnificent creatures, I will be the most powerful man in the world; maybe even more powerful than Karyan himself!

Hussein spoke the mystic words.

†††

The giant ancient took to flight. Its huge wings made a deep and powerful thumping sound with every beat they made in the cold air. The air shook violently as the shockwaves from the monstrous beast's movement emanated out from around it.

The ancient circled high above, again focusing its keen vision on the invaders. It set its wings for a rapid descent and attack. With lightning speed, it would strike and seize one or more of the unwelcomed guests from the earth before they even realized what had happened. It would then crush their bones in its powerful talons and feed the leftovers to its newborn chicks.

†††

As Talon approached from the north, he noticed a small band of men had gathered under one of the tree clusters below. Talon could see that one of its ancient relatives, a giant raptor or graptor, had spotted the men. If Talon's instincts were correct, the graptor had begun a rapid descent on them. The graptor no doubt considered the men a threat to its nest and would do what came naturally to eliminate the threat. Talon found no fault in the graptor's defensive actions.

Talon was unsure of the reason behind his summoning to this place, but his instincts provided him with a simple course of action. Without delay, Talon darted down toward the men. He must reach them before the graptor.

†††

When the sounds in the trees above abruptly stopped, the anxiety level of the band of Adonians rose rapidly. No one knew what threat might appear from the treetops, and after the earlier discussion of possibilities, no one was too willing to find out. The men looked frantically around for any sign of what might happen next.

Suddenly, a vast shadow caught their eye as it passed over the ground behind them. Weiphal and his men ran back to the edge of the tree patch and looked up into the clear, blue sky to see what had caused the enormous shadow. Their eyes, now accustomed to the dim light beneath the tree patch, could not adjust rapidly enough to make out what had flown over, but whatever it was, it had been large enough to block out a huge portion of the sun as it passed.

Weiphal directed the men to take cover, but then realized there was nowhere to take cover. Instinctively, Mitch, Austinian, Chase, and the rest of the men formed a defensive circle around Weiphal. Drawing their swords and shields, they prepared for the worst.

The sheer size of the creature struck the men with awe and wonder as the graptor emerged from the sun, heading directly for them. Never had they imagined that a flying beast of this size could exist. They stood frozen in position, unable to move. They knew that if this beast intended to harm them, then they had already forfeited their lives. Thoughts of loved ones flashed through each of their minds as they prayed to God for help. They prayed they could stand with their comrades and not flee at the last second; either way would bring death, but far better it would be to die a courageous and honorable death, standing tall and unafraid, then to die in fear and retreat.

The graptor closed on them, and Weiphal could see the look of angry resolve in its eyes. It appeared his team would soon pay dearly for whatever they had done to antagonize this majestic creature.

Without warning, and from out of nowhere, a large eagle burst onto the scene. It spread its six-foot-wide wings in a flare and unexpectedly came to rest on Weiphal's shoulder. Weiphal nearly fell over because of the sudden addition of the great eagle's weight. The eagle faced the approaching graptor and screeched a loud warning to the majestic bird approaching at high speed from above.

†††

Suddenly, the ancient orn saw only a beautiful angel where a moment before, a small band of men had stood. The angel had six wings, sapphire eyes, and emitted a blinding light. It held a flaming sword high in the air, and the graptor knew instinctively to break off its attack. It immediately did so, swerving past the band of men before soaring up into the heavens. Weiphal and his men covered their ears as the graptor let out a deafening shriek while passing them.

†††

Bestia screamed in anger, frustration, and fear at the arrival of the protector! His plan had been foiled, and the giant orn was returning to its nest high in the treetops. Bestia could not control himself. He had come so close that he could almost taste the Adonian flesh, and his bloodlust had to be satisfied!

Someone must die! If not the Adonians, then —

Enraged, Bestia broke free a large boulder from the cliffs high above Hussein and sent it hurtling down towards him.

†††

Weiphal and his men, blown to the ground from the forceful wake of the giant raptor as it flew by them, struggled to their feet, trying to come to terms with what had just happened. One minute, they thought they were all dead. The next, the giant raptor had broken off its attack, and it appeared this eagle had played some part.

The men looked in astonishment at the eagle that now stood on the ground next to Weiphal. After a momentary pause, the eagle flapped its wings and climbed into the sky, disappearing into the bright light of the sun above.

"What does this mean?" Weiphal looked at his men. Silence —

Then Mitch answered. "It means we don't have to fear the horned, bloodsucking, tree snakes anymore!"

No one noticed the large boulder that had broken free from the rock ledge some ways away, crushing an Omentian named Hussein beneath it. Hussein's whimpering plea for help remained unheard and unanswered as the life oozed out of him. His screaming spirit left his broken body; dragged away to the scorching fires of hell.

†††

Bestia smiled in momentary satisfaction as he basked in Hussein's torment. Then his insatiable appetite to inflict pain and misery on flesh returned like a flood.

The species of great orn or gorn now belonged to the light, but there were other beasts in this land, beasts more powerful than the gorn, that could be called to serve his master.

He smiled and left in haste, leaving a thick trail of smoke and fire behind him.

CHAPTER 24

THE RISE OF ADONIA

†††

It was a time of great wisdom, peace, and prosperity. From Aanot and the small villages founded by Abner's offspring, the Adonians rapidly expanded. The children married, were fruitful, and multiplied. The descendants of Abner grew very great — very great indeed!

They remembered the truth of the God who lives in the heavens, the promise he had given them of a Savior, and the need to be faithful to him; and him alone. They kept the commands that God had given them, sacrificing the cleanest of their animals to him in remembrance of the penalty for their sin and the hope they all shared in the coming Savior; a Savior who would cleanse them of that sin forever.

The people lived together with each other in peace. Competition for goods was all but nonexistent. The provinces engaged in fair trade to meet everyone's needs, as the land offered every natural resource imaginable. Everyone had an abundance of food, clean water, and shelter.

The men of the villages met together weekly to pray to their faithful God, proclaiming to all that their dependence rested solely on his power, provision, and protection. These prayers rose to the heavens from throughout the land. Like the smoke from a thousand fires against a multicolored sunset on a cold winter evening, they gave unquestionable testament to the loving relationship the Adonians had with their maker. These prayer warriors became the backbone of each community as it grew, and eventually, these gatherings transformed into village councils. God saw the faithfulness of the Adonians, heard their prayers, and blessed them with his love and protection.

God often used his power over his creation to amaze and bless those he loved. He had created all of nature, as well as its natural laws, through his word alone. He alone held it together through his unlimited power. Therefore, at times, he altered the laws of nature, the laws he had created, as a sign to the inhabitants below of his sovereign majesty. Some of the native peoples of the land found these unnatural events unbelievable. However, aided by the insight and instruction of the Adonian believers, they came to understand that all is possible for the one who holds all creation in his hands. Through these events and the witness of the faithful, most of the native peoples of Adonia came to believe in the one true God.

The creatures of Adonia also prospered. Because the land of Adonia was so rich in natural resources, many creatures lived and thrived there. These creatures had, since the time of the flood, remained mostly undisturbed in their natural habitat; growing quite sizeable and numerous. The time was soon coming when man would clash violently with the creatures that inhabited Adonia. Without God's protection, man could not survive.

God used his angels to protect the Adonians. It was not unusual for angels to walk among the Adonians without their knowledge. The Adonians knew of the angels' presence in the heavens, but because of their overreliance on their senses of sight and sound, they could not appreciate the extent to which angels interacted with them in their daily lives.

And so it was in the land of Adonia. All prospered, but none so much as the sons of Truin. Geoff, Skottie, Daniel, Bigaulf, Gareth, Cusintomas, and Moesheh each settled his own province, fell in love, married, and had children. Their respective provinces entrusted each of them with leadership positions. They formed provincial councils and justly governed their provinces, facilitating peace throughout the land.

In time, Truin asked Jonn to work with the seven provincial councils to optimize trade among the provinces. Each province had its own valuable resources and contributed to the prosperity of the others. As such, each depended upon the others. Soon, the provinces established active trading routes among themselves, and the seven council chairmen began meeting twice a year in Aanot to discuss the issues that required attention.

This arrangement especially pleased Christina. Though each of her sons would regularly return to Aanot with his family to visit, it was rare that these visits aligned with each other. It was good to spend quality time with each of her sons separately, but Christina truly missed having them all home at the same time. The biennial Council of the Seven, as it became known, gave Christina a great opportunity to have all her sons together under her roof once again as a family.

Evelin and Elin shared Christina's excitement at the prospect of the family reunions. Elin's two daughters, Kaye and Salli, had married and settled with their husbands in Aanot. Kaye had married one of Jonn's friends, Gladsel. Salli, the youngest of Elin and Khory's daughters, had married Willieim, a young apprentice of the Brothers of a Lion. Kaye and Salli had borne many children, and gave Evelin many great-grandchildren. Kaye and Salli brought the great-grandchildren to the reunions to see all their aunts, uncles, and cousins. Evelin loved to see her grandchildren and great-grandchildren; the reunions gave her the perfect opportunity.

The family reunions became quite the semiannual event. Kaye and Salli arranged all the food and festivities for the parties. Each time they held the family reunions, they put out such a diverse spread of delicacies that the celebrations lasted longer and longer. The aroma of the grilled poultry, beef, fish, crab, lobster, fruits and vegetables rose throughout Aanot, bringing young and old alike to join in the celebrations. Kaye's specialties were the baked goods, pies, cakes, and breads; they brought her renown throughout the land. Salli's specialty was her knack for making others feel welcomed, and she ensured no one left wanting for anything.

At one such family reunion, Geoff conspired with the brothers to give their father a very special gift. For this gift, precious stones from each of the seven provinces, one for each of the seven sons, were required. It was essential to take very precise measurements for each of the stones regarding size and weight to ensure that their suitability for this very special purpose.

The perfect stones of just the right size and weight would be a very daunting task to acquire. However, at just the right time, a solution materialized. Out of the blue, a precious stone collector presented herself to Jonn. Her name was Thalmir. She had moved to Adonia from Omentia about a year prior and had been traveling through the provinces, collecting precious stones from throughout the land. She was sure that she had the perfect stones in her collection. Jonn put her in touch with Geoff, and he found all the stones needed in Thalmir's collection.

The brothers wanted to give Truin a gift that he could cherish forever, one that would transcend time, and one that would remind him of his sons whenever he saw it. They arranged for a special timepiece to be assembled, one smaller than any constructed before. They plated this timepiece with the finest gold and fitted it with precious stones, one for each of them. At the top of the face of the timepiece was a brilliant diamond, the most indestructible of gems, symbolizing a family bond that would last forever. Each of the other seven precious stones on the timepiece was symbolic of one of the diverse provinces found in their new home of Adonia. Emerald was for the beautiful forests that flourished so plentifully in the province of Tobar. Sapphire represented the deep blue lakes that covered Kandish's rolling hills. Topaz was for the white peaks that crested the mountains of Chastain. Amethyst was for the beautiful purple sunsets of Plattos. Beryl was for the endless expanse of grain that waved in the fields of Delvia. Sardonyx was for the countless brown and tan ponies that inhabited the land of Tanshire. Finally, Jasper was for the reddish-brown waters that flowed freely in the land of Rothing. The watch-maker finely engraved the name of each of Truin's seven sons on the back of the timepiece, behind the stone for their province.

Late on the final night of the reunion celebration, after most attendees had retired to their cottages with their wives and children, Geoff, Skottie, Daniel, Bigaulf, Gareth, Cusintomas, and Moesheh joined Truin around the fire. The seven sons of Truin, along with their father, formed a circle around the fire as innumerable stars burned brilliantly in the night sky above them.

It was good for Truin to be alone with his sons. These opportunities happened far too rarely. He dearly loved his wife and his daughters-in-law, but just as there was value for women to get together and visit occasionally without men, so there was also a time for the men of the family to gather and speak to each other; man-to-man.

Truin felt overwhelmed as he looked across the fire at his sons, who were now men and leaders of men. How richly God had blessed him and his family! The time had flown by so swiftly since they had arrived in Adonia. In that time, God had blessed Christina and Truin with seven healthy and god-fearing sons. Again, God had blessed these sons with god-fearing wives and children of their own. He had blessed them all with peace, an abundance of natural resources, and a booming population of young men and women faithful to the one, true God.

Truin bowed his head to pray, and his sons followed his lead. "Dear Father in heaven, almighty God, maker of the heavens, the earth, and everything in the heavens and upon the earth. We praise you for all that you are and all that you have done. You depend on nothing; you have created everything, and everything is subject to your will. We praise you for your power and your wisdom. We have no fear; you love us and you control all things.

"Thank you for your Word. Through it we know you, the truth, the promise, and our glorious future with you in the kingdom you have prepared. We have no fear; you secure our future.

"Thank you for preserving the brilliant lights in the sky, the life that they bring us, and the natural laws that exist in our world. Even though we do not yet fully understand them, we know you have put them in their place to preserve our lives. We have no fear; you preserve us.

"Thank you for our bodies, our health, and our families. We are grateful to you for the rich and daily preservation of our lives and the lives of all the creatures you have created around us. Thank you for giving us the earth for our use and giving us dominion over it. Please help us use the resources you have entrusted to us wisely, in accordance with your will. We have no fear; you number our days.

"Thank you for giving us our clothing, homes, land, cattle, goods, and all that we need. Thank you for defending us from all danger and guarding and protecting us from all evil. All this you give us out of your divine goodness and mercy with no merit or worthiness resident in us. We have no fear; you are our Good Shepherd.

"Please Father, be with us. We humbly acknowledge our dependence on you for all things. Please help us serve and obey your precepts and never abandon the truth. Protect us from thinking too highly of ourselves, lest we wander from the truth and your protection. Please protect us from those in the world who have turned their backs on you; those who are in league with the evil one and would lead us away to our destruction. Please send your protectors to defeat them wherever they may lie in wait. Please use us to do your will. We have no fear; you are here.

"We love you Father. Thank you for being our God. Whether we live or die, we pledge ourselves to serve and obey you. Please help us to this end. Amen."

Without exception, the sons echoed, "Amen, this is true, so may it be."

Smiles surrounded the fire as a renewed sense of wellbeing settled on the men. They had already fully discussed the business they had needed to discuss regarding their respective provinces. Now a father and his sons relaxed and reminisced about a time when they were children, long before they had left Aanot to build lives for themselves—a simpler time.

After two hours of recollection and laughter, stillness fell over the assembly as the stars flickered overhead by the millions in different colors.

Daniel said, "Father, we have something for you."

The atmosphere instantly turned to one of deep reverence and devotion as the seven sons of Truin turned their attentive gaze to their father.

Cusintomas rose and approached Truin; he held something in his right hand behind his back.

"Father, we wanted to give you something."

As Cusintomas brought the gift into view, the firelight reflected off the gems upon the timepiece's face.

"We wanted you to always remember us, to remember the faith we share, to remember the love we have for you and each other. No matter how much time may pass; no matter our differences or what may separate us; these things will never change."

Truin was caught off guard. He was not expecting anything like this, and it showed. Truin's eyes reflected the twinkle of the gift's gems as tears filled his eyes. Even in the dim light of the fire, the boys could see Truin's eyes sparkle as he gazed upon the most beautiful gift he had ever seen.

Truin was speechless, which brought immense happiness to his sons. He stood; they stood with him. As he looked around the circle of his sons, now men to the last of them, his pride and love for them all was exceedingly apparent.

"I will treasure this all the days of my life. It is a symbol of our family, our unity, and our love. We will keep this in our family and our family will protect it for as long as we exist upon this earth.

In the firelight, below the stars, Truin and his sons reaffirmed their commitment to God, their family, and their home. They pledged their lives to defend the truth of the one, true God; the safety of those they loved; and their freedom in this land — at all costs. They pledged, with God's help, to always stand.

Even as they spoke, the darkness closed its grip like a dense, midnight fog on the land of their forefathers far to the east.

CHAPTER 25

FALL OF OMENTIA

†††

I am Reynold. It wasn't always like this.

There was a time when my homeland was good. In those times, families prospered, children laughed, men helped their neighbors, and all honored God. That day has passed.

It did not happen overnight. It did not happen because all turned towards evil at once. There were many who were still generous, many who were still kind, and many who were still decent. However, they grew careless. They grew lazy. Like unwatchful sheep, they wandered away from home; away from safety. They wandered from the light until they became lost in the darkness. Unaware and uninterested in truth, they lost it.

They accepted a philosophy that truth was whatever they wanted it to be, and that one man's truth was as valid as another man's truth. The concept of absolute truth itself—disappeared. Though God's invisible qualities of eternal power and divine nature were clear to us all, so that none of us had any excuse, some suppressed the truth. Though they knew God, they turned from him, neither glorifying him nor thanking him. First, they denied his decrees, and then they denied his existence all together.

Nature hates a void, and so it is also with the spiritual. Where there is a void of light, the door is wide open for darkness, and the powers of darkness are never idle. In this way, Omentia's thinking became futile, and Omentia's heart became dark.

Men cared only for themselves. In their arrogant rebellion against their maker and in the name of their individual freedom, they turned their desires to sexual impurity and shameful lusts, degrading themselves with one another — first in the darkness and then in the light of day.

Like a small hole in a dam erodes away at the protective foundation of the barrier, gradually at first and then at an ever-increasing rate; thus the philosophy of spiritual tolerance gave birth to and nurtured a cancerous tumor within my land. First allowed, then accepted, then embraced; the cancer soon ate away at the very fabric of Omentia like a ravenous monster. There was no stopping the destructive offensive once it could thrive.

Omentia began the practice of worshipping created things instead of the Creator. The way was then open for the dark ones to move in, and they did. The practice of divination spread like a wildfire across the land. Sorcery, the dark arts, witchcraft, and child sacrifice became common practice as the Omentians spiraled downward in an ever-increasing thirst for the vile. They commended each new level of depravity as a new stage of human freedom and enlightenment; progress.

In Omentia's denial of God, she rejected the value of all life. The Omentians eradicated their old without a second thought; not wise enough to even realize they too would someday be old.

They are no longer of any value to us. Why waste our resources on them?

They slaughtered the weak for sport. They soon became so wicked that they even killed their defenseless, unborn babies for the sake of convenience, with no shame at all.

It would just be a burden for me to have a child right now. I'm having too much fun. It's not fair to me or the baby — better to kill it now.

Many left and warned their fellow Omentians to leave. Following the example of the god-fearing among them, they departed for the lands to the west before the black scourge tightened its malevolent grip. They remembered and heeded the Lord's warning.

"Let no one be found among you who sacrifices his son or daughter in the fire, who practices divination or sorcery, interprets omens, engages in witchcraft, or casts spells, or who is a medium or spiritist or who consults the dead. Anyone who does these things is detestable to the Lord, and because of these detestable practices, the Lord your God will drive out those nations before you. You must be blameless before the Lord your God."

The tide of sinfulness swept over Omentia like a tsunami. The magnitude of the decadence exceeded anything witnessed since the days of the Great Flood, when the earth was last cleansed of its depraved unbelief. Like the other sleepers of their time, the ignorant thought naively that it could not happen to their land. They were unprepared to stand and resist when the plague of unbelief came. While they slept, the torrent of darkness covered their land and swept them away. The evil ones took those who could not flee and sacrificed them if they would not give their souls over to the darkness.

I am Reynold. My neighbors are gone. My people are gone.

I stayed behind as long as I could — I and many others. We stayed behind to save the children. When the practice of child sacrifice became widespread, we did everything possible to stop this obscenity.

But it was of no use. Karyan and the dark ones blinded the people to the perversion of their sinful acts. Those left behind cared only for themselves, and in keeping with Karyan's decrees, they sacrificed the innocents to the dark ones in return for their favor.

We had to go underground. We saved the children we could by hiding them during the day and sneaking them out of Omentia at night. Secret transport ships took them to freedom and safety in the west.

There were many who risked their lives to save the children and the babies of Omentia. Many of these servants of God gave the ultimate sacrifice of their lives in the furnaces of Karyan so that the defenseless among us might have the chance to live. But there were so very many we could not save. God have mercy on their souls and on the souls of the murderous butchers who snuffed out their tiny lives!

I fled to Adonia below a moonless sky with the last of the children we could save. Still, the cries of the children we had to leave behind resonate in my ears. I can still smell the stench of death carried on the east wind that filled our ship's sails and brought us to safety. Their memories haunt me; their cries echo in my mind every waking hour and every sleepless night.

Our land is gone. Lust, greed, hatred, lawlessness, and pure evil occupy Omentia now. Evil will not long satisfy itself with the souls it has consumed there. Soon the darkness will advance on Adonia. God have mercy on us.

CHAPTER 26

PARLANTIS

†††

It was late May in Adonia. The trees and flowers were in full bloom. The homestead and surrounding hills on Blue Lake were breathtakingly beautiful.

At midday, Christina and Truin were resting on their patio in the shade of the oak trees, enjoying a pleasant conversation with Evelin and Abner; they had come to visit for the weekend. Visitors approaching their home by the road from Aanot surprised them. As the visitors drew near, Truin could see that their son, Bigaulf, was among them. Truth be told, it was pretty hard to overlook him in any group of people, for even with the large and rugged size of most Adonian men, Bigaulf towered well above the majority of them. In addition, Jonn and Gladsel were among the group.

"It's Bigaulf — Jonn, and Gladsel too!" Truin wondered why they would all travel up from Aanot during the heat of the day.

"Excellent!" Christina jumped to her feet. "Are the girls with them?" She peered out into the distance, wanting to find the answer to her own question.

"I don't see them, but there is another with them I don't recognize. They seem to be in a hurry. Wait here. I'll go meet them and bring them over."

Truin ran down to meet the visitors. Bigaulf alone carried the group's weapons and supplies, but he dropped them as soon as he saw his father approach. Truin greeted his son, and Bigaulf gave his father a bear hug that just about squeezed all the breath right out of him.

"Good to see you, son!"

"You too, father!"

"To what do we owe the pleasure of this visit?"

Bigaulf turned and looked behind him where Jonn, Gladsel, and another man were just joining them.

Truin greeted them. "Jonn, Gladsel, welcome."

Bigaulf interrupted the reunion. "Father, we have brought with us a man from across the sea. His name is Phillip."

Before Bigaulf could continue, Gladsel said, "He washed up in Delvia six days ago, and as soon as he could travel, Bigaulf brought him to Aanot. Bigaulf says that he has a story that you and Abner must hear immediately. I am afraid that he brings us grave news from Parlantis."

Truin could now see that the man accompanying them looked like he had once been very strong, but was now very weak. He looked like he had just been through a terrible ordeal. Cuts, burns, and blisters covered his face, arms, and legs. His condition appeared in stark contrast to his clothes, which were fresh; Gladsel had given the man new clothes. Jonn and Gladsel were helping the man along; each taking an arm as they walked.

Truin helped his friends with Phillip. They brought him up to the cottage and back to the patio, where Christina and Evelin were waiting with water, clean bandages, and ointment. They set the man down on a chair and began tending to his wounds.

Christina gave her son a hug, but realizing the weight of the moment, kept her visiting for a later time. Abner greeted the men and sat back down, ready to hear the urgent news. Evelin simply smiled at her grandson, conveying all her love to him with the one simple gesture and filling Bigaulf instantly with the peace and warmth of being home.

Truin, Abner, Jonn, and Gladsel sat patiently next to the man as the women cared for him. Bigaulf sat in the background, reflecting on the man's story, as he prepared to hear it once again.

When Phillip was ready to speak, he began.

"My name is Phillip. I am Parlantian."

"Parlantian?" Abner looked inquisitively at Truin and then back at Phillip. "Why are you so far from home? What happened to you?"

The man was forty years old, but looked like his recent ordeal had added fifteen years to his life. Tears filled his eyes as he relived the horror of his memories.

"Parlantis is gone."

"Parlantis is gone?" Evelin spoke aloud, as both she and Christina looked at each other in disbelief. Jonn and Gladsel instantly realized the impact this news would have, if it were true, on Adonia. Parlantis was a major trading partner with Adonia, and Parlantian grain supplemented Delvian grain as a major source of food for many of the provinces.

Parlantis had begun long ago as an agricultural community. Parlantians considered themselves the sons of the plow. Trading their food with the lands surrounding them had brought Parlantis great riches and prosperity. With these riches, they had built amazing cities, unrivaled in the entire known world. Parlantis became renowned for its amazing feats of architecture and science: towering pyramids, endless underground dwellings, elaborate bridges, and many other wondrous achievements—achievements that surpassed the understanding or abilities of the lands that surrounded it.

The thought of Parlantis being gone was simply unfathomable.

Phillip continued. "Not more than one month ago, we received an ultimatum from Omentian messengers. They said we must surrender control of our crops, our homes, and our cities, or face the wrath of Karyan."

"Our leaders did not understand this ultimatum. They wondered, 'Who is this Karyan?' We had always lived in peace with Omentia. Omentia had no authority with which to make these demands of us, and we had no intention of submitting to them."

The men listened intently to Phillip's words.

"We refused their ultimatum, of course. Our leaders assured the people that we had no reason to fear Omentia or any other land. Though we were a peaceful people and wished none ill, we had always prepared for the day when trouble would come to our shores. No land or people had ever successfully attacked our land — never."

Phillip stopped to take a drink. Christina helped him. Then he continued.

"As I am sure you have all heard, our cavalry was most feared in battle. No one had ever defeated our cavalry."

Abner had heard stories of the Parlantian cavalry in battle ever since he was a child. The Parlantian cavalry was like a force of nature. None had been victorious over them throughout Parlantian history. It was Abner's belief that none would ever choose to meet them again in battle; none would dare.

"When the day of battle came, we were ready. I was there. I saw it all. As a doctor and trainer of horses for the guard, I helped prepare the guard for the battle. I accompanied the guard to the Golden Fields one week ago as they prepared to face the invaders.

"That fateful morning, the women of Parlantis — the mothers, sisters, and daughters — had ceremoniously assisted the dressing of their sons, brothers, fathers, and husbands in Parlantian battledress. Even the horses wore equine armor, passed down through the ages within each family for just such an occasion. Few of these men, even fewer of their sons, had ever ridden in battle; they too believed that they never would have the need. They had trained for this day for most of their lives; there is no greater honor than to fight for the freedom and safety of your family, your home, and your land."

Phillip seemed to drift back in time, his eyes staring into space and his thoughts fixing on a painful place deep within his mind. An agonizing mix of emotions was clear on his face as he spoke every word.

"Our cavalry lined up for battle, four hundred across and twenty deep. It was a beautiful sight to behold; the elite of Parlantis, the very best of the best. Men and their steeds, dressed in black and gold battle

163

dress, lined up in historic formation on the Golden Fields as Parlantian grain gently waved in the breeze beneath an early morning sun. Above them, the battle flags of Parlantis fluttered high as the gentle morning breeze blew in from the northern shore. The beauty and majesty of this sight alone should have turned away any invader.

"The enemy had already landed on the northern shores under the cover of darkness. However, the golden rays of the rising sun had exposed their positions. As the tops of their ship masts became visible, poking through the ceiling of the morning sea mist, the columns of the Parlantian Guard deployed to repulse the invading army.

"The Parlantian Guard formed their battle line on a mile-wide peninsula that jutted north out into the sea. All Parlantians knew this peninsula as the Golden Fields, which had witnessed many historic victories for the Parlantian Guard. To the east and west of the Parlantian Guard's formation, the sheer cliffs of the peninsula denied the enemy any port of entry onto the Parlantian isle. The invaders had to come ashore from the north, across the Golden Fields, and Sir Briean the Brave, the Commander of the Parlantian Guard, knew it.

"Families of the Parlantian Guard cavalrymen gathered atop the rolling hills behind their fatherland's military forces to watch their Parlantian heroes be victorious in battle. This is the way it had always been of old, and surely, it would be this way again. The women and youth of this time were resolute in their determination not to be denied the honor of watching their Parlantian Guard emerge victorious in battle once more, as it had always been in the past. There was little perceived danger to the citizens of Parlantis in being so close to the actual fighting; everyone believed the Parlantian Guard would continue their undefeated streak. What a glorious occasion it would be!

"The morning rays of sun rose over the Dark Sea, slicing through the morning fog that rolled in heavily over the ships and onto the shore. The light partially blinded Sir Briean's view of the Omentian forces, causing him some concern. Still, he drew comfort from the obvious fact that the Parlantian Guard could not lose and everyone knew it."

Phillip continued as all those present listened intently. "The Parlantian Guard waited in silence, beautiful in stature on the fields of gold. Loved ones watched and prayed, assured of yet again another historic victory to be passed down through the ages to their descendants by both word and song.

"The sea fog continued to darken, thicken, and extend its encroachment deeper inland; nearly reaching the forward Parlantian positions. Though extremely disciplined, the men of the Parlantian Guard wondered just what forces they would meet on the field of battle. The expanding sea fog did not help assuage their growing anxiety. Even though the Parlantians knew there were a dozen Omentian ships offshore, no one had any idea about the number of troops that had come ashore during the night or how well equipped they were. The darkness and sea fog had eliminated any accurate intelligence on the enemy's strength, and even the column commanders were growing uncomfortable with the uncertainty.

"Still, everyone knew the Parlantian Guard could not and would not lose in battle. This the men repeated to themselves over and over, successfully masking their growing concerns by allowing nothing but courageous resolve to show on their faces. The sheer strength of their number, the precision of their formation, and the elegance of their uniforms — as well as each man's false bravado — reinforced the confidence of the entire force.

"The sea fog continued its approach. Sir Briean could no longer see more than one hundred yards in front of him. He knew full well that he could not at this late time reorganize the formation or change his battle plan. So, he did what all the renowned commanders before him had done; he commanded a full charge. Whatever awaited them within or beyond the fog would certainly succumb to the overwhelming power of the Parlantian Guard; for once they were in full assault, they were always victorious.

"The cavalry began their charge towards victory, causing the very earth below them to shake, and their families cheered in the background."

Tears that had formed in Phillip's eyes now ran down his cheeks as he continued. "The Parlantian Guard moved forward as one giant wave of men, stallions, and steel to meet the unknown enemy. As they did, the fog darkened, taking on a life of its own. At the ominous sight, a concerned silence fell over those faithful assembled to witness the glorious event, replacing what had moments before been the exuberant cheers of women and children.

"A moment later, sounds never heard in Parlantis or any other place this side of Hades abruptly replaced the uneasy silence. Unnatural and indescribable sounds began emanating from the fog.

"Regardless, the men of the Parlantian Guard had their orders, and they always followed their orders to the letter. It was unthinkable that a guardsman would ever break his charge or retreat before the enemy.

"A favorite tool of the cavalry was to use its speed of maneuver to sweep around the enemy at both ends and outflank the enemy's forces. Once again, the rear flanks of the Parlantian Guard broke formation and initiated this tactic by sweeping to the east and west; first to pincer and then to envelop the invaders.

"However, as the darkness moved in and blanketed the peninsula, it hid the edge of the cliffs, making it quite perilous for the Parlantian Cavalry to complete their maneuvers; the riders simply could not tell how close they were to the edge of the cliffs as they executed the maneuver. They bravely rode at full speed into the fog, blindly following their village banners. The fog enveloped them like a fish swallowing a fly.

"Fear finally bubbled to the surface and turned to terror as the cavalryman entered the blackness before them. Swords drawn, the men of the Parlantian Guard lashed out at whatever they could find, thinking it must certainly be the enemy. In their fear and confusion, they saw only their deepest and darkest specters before them. On the outer edges of the battle, countless Parlantian riders rode at full speed right off the sheer cliffs. Men and horses plunged to their deaths on the jagged rocks far below.

"Apprehension and fear now stretched out their clammy tentacles and latched on to the old men, women, and children that had gathered on the hills to observe the battle. We could hear the Mêlée, but we could not tell what was happening or who was winning. In silence, we held our collective breath.

"Then we heard the terrible high-pitched whistle of a thousand arrows being unleashed from somewhere beyond the fog; by archers awaiting the command to cut down our forces. A fraction of a second later, a cloud of arrows rose out of the fog deck at various angles, some on a high trajectory for distant targets and some nearly level for close in marks. They disappeared again as they reentered the fog deck in search of hose targets.

"The terrifying sound and horrible sight of volley after volley of Omentian arrows rising from and falling back into the fog deck to strike down our men assaulted our senses. Omentian archers rained down death on our fathers and sons, uncles, and brothers. The screams of agony from within the dark cloud were heart wrenching as the flying daggers of death found their victims. Our last and only hope for freedom was perishing before our eyes.

"Silence and disbelief turned into misery and wailing as the women of Parlantis fell to their knees in uncontrollable grief and pain. The rest of us simply looked on in shock, frozen in time and unable to move; as if we were observing some Heathian tragedy.

"Time seemed to stand still, and the slaughter continued for what seemed like an eternity. But for the occasional horse without its rider, nothing emerged from the darkness of the fog.

"Soon the battle cries and fleeting sounds of distant skirmishes died off. Deafening silence replaced them. All hope of a positive outcome from the battle had departed. Still, we stood motionless, hoping beyond hope of a return to the blissful expectations of the morning: the Golden Fields, the glorious battle, certain victory — a hope no more.

The terrifying and humiliating sound of laughter shattered the somber silence. It began as one voice and then grew to be the sound of many voices laughing all at once. The sound was that of a man, then that of many men, and finally not the sound of men at all. It was the unmistakable sound of devils and demons. The laughter grew in volume, and objects appeared above the cloud. Dirt, swords, belts, helmets, rocks, and pieces of men — men dismembered in the battle — emerged from the cloud and then disappeared again. The cycle repeated over and over; objects circling within the cloud, occasionally emerging, and then disappearing.

"As the mass of circling objects reached the forward edge of the fog, the fog retreated. It pulled back toward the sea to reveal our worst fears. The beautiful Golden Fields became bright red with the blood of Parlantis' sons. Thousands lie upon the field, writhing in the last spasms of death, their agony being drowned out by the thunderous laughter of the many phantoms that surrounded them.

"Countless numbers of hooded Omentians with axes and scythes glided over the fallen guardsmen like shadows, severing limbs and disemboweling those who had survived. The agonizing screams of their victims added to the sadistic symphony of satanic celebration.

"In the center of this sea of slaughter stood a towering form, hooded in black with his arms outstretched to the sky; an immobile figure of seemingly superhuman strength. The many objects from the battle orbited around him, spinning eerily as they flew.

"The winds blew toward us, and they carried with them the most hideous of stenches conceivable to man. I cannot accurately describe it to you. It was more than the smell of death; it was the smell of hell itself.

"As the screams of the women and children rang out at the sight of their loved one's dead and dying on the battlefield, the blazing, red eyes of the evil one in the center of the Crimson Fields locked its focus on the innocents beyond. The hideous laughter stopped as he dropped one of his arms and pointing at us. His voice thundered the command. 'Kill, maim, and destroy!'

"Instantly, the ghoulish shadows crossed the plain towards us at a frightening pace. The terrifying sound of many arrows pierced the sky as the archers once again, unleashed death from above. This time, we would not just be spectators in the carnage that ensued.

"The mourning of the women for their loved ones lost in the battle instantly changed to terror as they lifted their small children into their arms and began running for their lives. We men who accompanied them were unsure of what to do next. We tried to decide whether we should mount a defense or retreat with the women. Without armor or weapons, we knew we could not offer a fight; not for long. The enemy had just destroyed our finest!"

Phillip's eyes closed and tears ran down his face as he bowed his head and spoke the words. "So we ran."

"As I turned to run, the last thing I saw was two Parlantian Guard soldiers, barely alive. Possessed by demons and driven by madness, they continued to slash away at each other amidst the carnage. Between them and us, the hooded demons were swiftly advancing.

"The waves of razor-sharp arrows indiscriminately fell amongst us. The waves of razor-sharp arrows struck down women and small children from behind. They fell helplessly wounded as their frenzied neighbors, fleeing the deadly onslaught, trampled them underfoot. Even ignoring the cries of their children calling out to them for help, panic-stricken women continued their retreat, only to be cut down by the blade. They were the fortunate ones. They carried away the less fortunate, alive and screaming.

"The demons dragged away many survivors, like myself, to the villages where the hellish onslaught of raping, pillaging, and destroying continued unabated. I cannot speak to you any further of the things I saw there. I will not."

Phillip's face twisted in horror. His breathing became erratic and his demeanor was one of incredible anger — and incredible shame — as he recounted the horror of what he had witnessed. It was plain to see that he was being eaten away from the inside by what had happened to his people, as well as by his own helplessness to do anything about it.

Abner, Truin, Jonn, and Gladsel grimaced in righteous anger at what they were hearing. Evelin and Christina could not help but sit in shock and tears. Evelin had to leave, unable to listen any longer.

"I should have died with my people!"

The men looked at Phillip, searching his eyes.

Is this man a coward?

They wondered what they would have done.

Would I have died fighting the Omentian onslaught, or would I have run with the women and children to survive? What is the right thing to do in an impossible scenario such as this?

Truin asked, "Why do you live?"

The words hung in the air as if to echo the unspoken accusation the men held in their hearts. *How could Phillip have fled and left the women and children behind to die?*

"I wanted to die, but that was not the plan for me."

They all looked skeptically at him, wondering if indeed the experience had driven him mad.

"Tell us."

"I was alone, imprisoned in a cell. For two days, I heard the screams of those being taken away for sacrifice. The women cried out for mercy. The children screamed in terror. They were drug away to God only knows what. It was driving me mad!

"I prayed to the unknown god, 'Please, god of the heavens, if you are there, take my life from me. I cannot bear this any longer!'

"As I prayed, a man appeared before me. As I prayed, a man dressed in white appeared before me. He spoke to me and said, 'The one who made you has numbered your days.' Your time to leave this place is not now. I am a messenger. You, too, are now a messenger. Go to Adonia and tell the one known as Truin all you have seen.'"

Jonn and Gladsel looked at each other in disbelief.

"You have got to be kidding!" Jonn exclaimed in anger.

Gladsel echoed Jonn's disbelief. "That is the best this coward can use for an excuse for why he lives!"

"No, wait, there is more. Let my father decide if he speaks the truth."

"Bigaulf, what is it you expect of me?"

"Father, this is why I have brought him to you. I remembered a story you told us once. Listen to him, please?"

For Bigaulf's sake, Truin looked back at Phillip, trying to decide whether to believe his story. "Is there more?"

Phillip closed his eyes. "Just one other thing, and I hope this means something to you. If not, I too will believe that I am insane."

Phillip clung to his words as his life depended on them. He lifted his head and looked directly into Truin's eyes. "The man said you and he were friends. He said his name was Engel."

Engel. The sound of the name hung in the air. It was familiar. Truin turned his gaze to Christina, and it hit both of them simultaneously like a lightning bolt!

Christina looked like she had seen a ghost. "Could it be?"

Truin looked at Bigaulf, who stared back at his father. Bigaulf wondered if he had correctly remembered the story that Truin had told him and his brothers so long ago.

"Yes, Engel and I are friends."

Tears again rolled down Phillip's face as hope again burst through the darkness of pain and remorse.

Maybe there is a purpose behind why I live. Perhaps there is a purpose for my life.

Even more than this, the realization struck him that there was a God in heaven who heard his prayers! Phillip's demeanor transformed.

Jonn and Gladsel looked at Truin in shock, trying to sort out what was going on.

Truin looked at Christina and grinned. "Honey, your son has an excellent memory. Thank God that he does."

Truin no longer saw Phillip as a stranger but as a brother and one of God's messengers. He grinned and said, "Please, friend, finish your story."

Revitalized, Phillip continued. "After Engel opened my cell, he led me out into the night. I could hear the Omentians all around me. I could see them. But as we passed between them, they seemed to look right through us as if we weren't even there. It all seemed like a dream to tell you the truth; I didn't really know what was happening.

"We made it to the shore, and from there I don't remember too much. I can't tell you how long I drifted on the sea before washing up in Adonia. I don't remember any of it. Bigaulf says he found me unconscious, drifting on a tree limb. He nursed me back to life, I told him my story, and he brought me to you."

Everyone fixed their gaze on Truin as he contemplated what Phillip had told them. Then Truin spoke. "Today, God has given us a new brother."

Truin looked at Christina, who had regained her composure and was again tending to Phillip's wounds. Truin smiled. "Our home is his home."

Christina smiled at Phillip. "I would have it no other way."

As Truin rose to his feet to talk with the men, Phillip said, "We were Parlantians! We trusted in our military might, in our accomplishments, our scientific advances, and our history. We thought we were strong, and that we did not need the protection of a god."

All eyes turned to Phillip.

"We were wrong. Man cannot stand alone against evil. Engel said there is a god in Adonia. Is it true? Is there a god here that can protect us from this evil?"

Though any of them could have answered the question, Abner said, "There is a God in Adonia, the only true God. He has always protected us, and he will always protect us. We welcome you to stay here with us, brother. You will be safe here."

Overwhelmed by their immediate acceptance of him and the love they extended to him so freely, Phillip buried his head in his hands and cried. As Christina consoled him, Truin and the men gathered on the other side of the patio and discussed the revelations.

It didn't take long before Truin stated what they all knew to be true. "The Lord has blessed us today with a warning. Trouble is coming. We must be ready when it arrives."

CHAPTER 27

BE STILL

†††

"Attack them now!" Karyan commanded his general.

"But Master Karyan, we have just taken Parlantis. The men are still enjoying the fruits of their labors and the spoils of war."

"Do not disobey me!" Karyan thundered. The building shook as objects in the room launched from their resting positions and flew against the walls as if to emphasize the wisdom of heeding Karyan's words.

"Yes, master. Yes, master. Right away." The Omentian general's demeanor changed instantly from flippancy to the seriousness required when being in their new leader's presence.

Many of Omentia's generals had recently lost their positions of leadership, along with their lives, by considering themselves irreplaceable; nothing was further from the truth. There was only one leader in Omentia, and his commands were not to be disobeyed.

"Take the ships across the sea and crush the Adonians! Do not return until you have accomplished this task. Do you understand?"

The general sheepishly avoided any eye contact with Karyan. "Yes, Master Karyan. I understand."

The next morning, fifty ships packed with Omentian light infantry, archers, and supplies departed Parlantis for Adonia. The men, exhausted from their merrymaking with the spoils of war, were now confident that they could defeat anyone that stood in their way. After all, who had successfully stood against them so far? They had defeated the Parlantian Cavalry! No army had ever done that before.

Karyan, too, grew arrogant; so much so that he sent one of his lieutenants with the fleet to do his bidding in Adonia. Kala Azar had been with him since the early days in the forest when he had discovered the dark arts and joined with the spirits who gave him his power. He trusted Kala Azar's abilities. Though incomparable to his own, the power of darkness was strong with his lieutenant.

Karyan thought little of the Adonians. Almost forty years earlier, several families had left Omentia for this island across the sea. There was no logical way this handful of deserters could mount any kind of defensive capability against his army, especially considering the supernatural power that now assisted him and his lieutenants.

Karyan had instructed his underlings well in using the dark words. "Use them wisely and only when necessary." He knew they did not understand how the dark words worked — not like he did. The dark spirits only gave that knowledge and power to a select few; only to those chosen — like him. Still, he had instructed the inner circle well, and with the dark words, they had power; though limited. Kala Azar's power would give him what was necessary to bring the Adonians to their knees — if he even needed help from the dark ones.

†††

The La Gina was the first of the twelve trading ships sailing north from Delvia for the ports of Heath. PJ was still her captain, and the years of Adonian growth and prosperity had brought him much opportunity and a very profitable business. He now had some forty vessels under his command, though only twelve were with him on this trip. They were bringing Tobarian lumber to Heath to exchange for Heathian cacao pods. The cacao trees only grew in Heath, below the tropical rain forest canopy. The Adonians used the cacao pods to make chocolate; considered a delicacy in Adonia and in most places throughout the world.

Mikole was PJ's second-in-command and captained the seventh ship in the convoy. He had joined up with Captain PJ soon after the La Gina had brought Abner and his family out of Omentia decades earlier. Captain PJ had recognized Mikole's natural sailing skills, and it hadn't taken Mikole long to earn PJ's trust. They became full partners soon after and were like brothers.

Word of Omentia's fall had spread rapidly throughout Chastain and Delvia, reaching the crews of the vessels sailing this day right before they had left port. Everyone was on edge with all eyes on the lookout for trouble.

Both PJ and Mikole had sailed to Parlantis for Parlantian grain within the last few months, but those days, apparently, were over. An unsettling darkness hung over the eastern horizon, as if the lands of Omentia and Parlantis perpetually burned, sending a continuous plume of smoke and ash into the air. It reminded Mikole of the volcanic eruption he had seen as a child. Everything under that cloud of death had died. So it seemed with the current darkness to the east; nothing within its shadow would escape its suffocating grip.

Every evening, as the sun set in the east, the ship crews had a reminder of what was happening on the other side of the Dark Sea. As the sun's fading rays tried to break through the dark cloud that hung on the horizon, only a few rays were successful in penetrating the blanket of oblivion. The result was a blood-red sky. Aided by its cohorts of cool, twilight breezes, it never failed to give the crews of the trading ships the chills.

The darkness of the night often brought a glorious display of stars overhead. The stars joined the northern lights that danced in columns of blue and green as Mikole dreamed of his wife Pamela. Mikole had two loves, Pamela and his schooner, the Sirenian. When he was with one, he dreamed of the other. Mikole understood he was very fortunate to have both the love of a good woman and a job that he truly loved.

Still, as time had passed and Mikole had aged, more and more things became clearer to him. The initial, idealistically romantic feelings that vex all men in their youth had matured into a truer and more lasting love for Pamela. The adventurous excitement that had once enthralled him as he set out to sea had lost much of its luster as the time spent at sea took its toll on his bones.

Mikole saw that something was missing. There was a hole in Mikole's heart that the things of this world couldn't fill—not even by Pamela or the Sirenian. As he grew older, this "missing something" bothered him more and more, like an ache that never goes away.

Mikole thought more about the inevitability of death, and how death would one day take his two great loves away from him. He thought more and more about what followed this life.

What will happen to me? Where will I go after I die?

He soon realized that his life was just a vapor in the wind, and that it would soon pass like the lives of those before him and those after him. There simply had to be more.

Is this all there is? If so, what was it all for? If these fleeting days upon the earth are all there is, then life is ultimately meaningless. There has to be more to it.

This is when the God of the heavens touched him and filled the hole in his heart. PJ taught Mikole about the Creator, how man had rebelled against him, and how the Creator had promised a Savior to mankind. He taught Mikole the history of God's people and showed Mikole how death was not the end of all things but simply the door to much, much more. It was on that day — the day when Mikole learned the truth — that Mikole's fear of death disappeared, and his life truly began.

Mikole learned that what a man would do during this short time on earth to serve his Creator and his fellowman was all that was truly important. Mikole committed his life to service. With this new commitment, his love for both Pamela and for the sea found a new richness that he had never known before.

Now it is all complete. Now it all makes sense.

Aided by the light of the stars in the heavens, the commercial flotilla sailed through the night, moving smoothly and safely northward. Soon, the sun peaked over the water on the western horizon. Its red, orange, and yellow hues spilled over onto the dark blue, star-speckled sky above, drowning out the light of the ever-so-distant stars and effectively blinding the eyes of the night crew who were just finishing their watch.

Forced by the bright rays of the sun to turn their gaze to the east, they noticed a low hanging, wispy deck of morning fog clinging to the surface of the sea. Breathtakingly beautiful, it reflected the bright gold of the morning sunlight, and temporarily mesmerized them. They marveled at the splendor of the sight, initially missing the danger that lurked within the cover of the regal fog deck. However, as the tips of the many masts became visible to the lead watchman aboard the La Gina, the threat became obvious to all; directly to the north and east of their convoy was an armada of Omentian warships.

Though the fog obscured the Omentian warships, their flags displayed the unmistakable pagan markings of the enemy. The Omentians had changed the markings of their standard to the gold quarter moon and star on a black background to signify their worship of the celestial. They had turned their back on their Creator, choosing instead to worship the created.

Captain PJ realized the seriousness of the situation. His convoy was not prepared to fight a naval battle, especially not against a fleet of such size. PJ searched for answers, the fate of so many crewmen in his hands.

Lord, what do I do?

He briefly entertained trying to outrun the Omentians, but quickly realized the odds of such a maneuver were minimal at best, given they were behind the power curve.

PJ struggled for an option, and just then, God gave him one. PJ remembered how bright the sun was to the west, and he realized that this was precisely where his convoy was, relative to the Omentians.

The sun is blinding them! They don't see us yet. They are still in the fog.

This gave PJ hope.

How can I take advantage of this?

PJ's mind raced.

Meanwhile, throughout the convoy, the men panicked. The many alternatives for action flooded their minds. All the ships' captains wanted to take immediate action. Left to their own devises, this would certainly have resulted in the chaotic dispersal of the convoy as each attempted to evade capture in his own way. Instead, to the last, all eyes looked to the La Gina for guidance.

Captain PJ had discussed this scenario with the captains of his convoy frequently. "We must stay together. We must maneuver as one. Look to me for the plan and follow suit. There can be no exceptions. Discipline, to the last man, is critical."

Captain PJ continued to search for the answer.

If we can't outrun them, then we must remain hidden by the light; invisible. At the very least, it will buy us time.

Captain PJ gave the order to turn directly into the Omentian ships and then to drop the sails. This would give them the smallest visible signature on the water and hopefully they would remain unspotted by the Omentians, at least for a few minutes.

"What is he doing?" Mikole wondered aloud.

At first, it seemed Captain PJ had turned to fight the Omentian fleet. This both energized and terrified the men at the same time. The fight-or-flight response had kicked in with every man in the convoy. Not knowing themselves what to do, they were happy to not be in Captain PJ's shoes. None of them wanted to be making the no-notice, life-and-death decisions currently being asked of Captain PJ; none of them but Mikole, perhaps.

The crew of every ship held their breath as they turned toward the Omentians. The men prayed quietly to God that he give them the courage to stand before the invaders — that they not let their shipmates down if the time came for them to fight.

Then Captain PJ dropped the sails of the La Gina.

How does this make any sense?

To follow suit would leave them defenseless; they could not maneuver at the merge.

"He is getting skinny." Mikole commanded the lowering of the sails of the Sirenian and the preparing of the men for a fight.

As soon as he had given the order, Captain PJ began doubting himself.

What have I done? Please God, let this be the right decision. Please help us? Thy will be done.

As the last sails dropped in the convoy, the men stood ready to fight. Their eyes remained fixed on the Omentian armada, just now emerging from the cloud deck to their northeast. Mikole estimated the Omentians were about ten miles away from the La Gina; twelve or thirteen miles from the Sirenian. On the enemy's present course, they might pass five miles off the bow of the La Gina.

Captain PJ hoped the Omentians would not see his convoy until they had passed to the north of him. If the Omentians remained out of archer range, he and the convoy would raise sail and extend away from the Omentian fleet. The Omentians would have to turn almost one hundred and eighty degrees to chase them down. Captain PJ hoped his convoy was not worth the effort to the Omentian commander.

It was a good plan — the best afforded Captain PJ at this point — but in the end; it was not to be. As the Omentian fleet closed to approximately eight miles off the bow of the La Gina, the Omentians spotted the Adonian convoy and changed course, directly toward it.

Captain PJ and the Adonian crews froze. They had taken a shot at avoiding a fight, but it appeared a fight was now inevitable. It was well-known that the Omentians did not take prisoners on the open seas. In fact, the Omentians preferred their archers to do most of their dirty work for them before they ever board a ship. Out-manned, out-equipped, and ill-prepared, the outlook for the convoy was not good.

Captain PJ got down on his knees and prayed. Every Adonian followed his example. This must have looked comical to the Omentians as they drew close enough to see the defensive positions the Adonians were mounting. What the Omentians did not yet realize was that this was the greatest defense the Adonians had at their disposal. They were strongest when they were on their knees.

Your will be done, Lord. Whether we live or die, we are yours.

The Omentian archers took positions and fired their first volley high into the air. The arrows were strangely beautiful as they rose on a steep arc into the light-blue morning sky.

Your will be done.

Still out of range of the La Gina, the first volley of death from above fell short, splashing harmlessly into the sea. The Omentian archers readied their next volley, but as they prepared to fire, something unexpected happened. The winds shifted. Initially from the south, the winds suddenly shifted from the north.

I remember my father telling me when I was a child to beware when the winds shift abruptly.

As PJ looked up, he could see that the golden fog bank that had drifted through the Omentian fleet and spread out to the north was now turning back to the south. As it headed back, directly towards them, it had partially broken up.

It seemed crazy to think it, but Captain PJ thought the cloud deck now looked like a giant hand. As the fog headed directly toward them, the Omentians remained unaware of its presence as they focused on their next prize. Slivers of fog extended like fingers from the cloud deck and raced toward the Omentian ships.

"It's the hand of God," Captain PJ said out-loud.

"The hand of God" — his words echoed back among the crew of the La Gina. Every soul then turned its attention from the Omentian archers to the mysterious fog as the sailors watched it in awe and wonder.

The Omentians soon noticed the winds had shifted abruptly and raced about, adjusting their sails to the optimum settings for the dash toward the defenseless Adonians.

"Our gods assist us with a tailwind in our conquest of the Adonians!" The Omentian commander's voice rang out in recognition of the meteorological event that had put the winds at his back. His crew cheered in agreement, still unaware of the supernatural event that was taking place at their stern.

As the fingers of fog, approaching from behind, swiftly swept across the Omentian ships, a powerful twenty-five foot wave accompanied them. The wave slammed into the Omentian ships with a fury, throwing all the Omentians to the deck and many overboard.

The fingers of fog then turned, circling to the east, north, and south to hit the Omentian Armada repeatedly. Moments later, a giant, golden waterspout formed over the Omentian fleet, tearing at their ships' masts with hurricane-force winds and hammering their hulls with mighty waves.

Sails, masts, and men rose from the Omentian ships and ascended into the heavens, only to be torn apart within the golden waterspout. Despite their best efforts to resist, the power of the winds violently tore the large timbers that formed the very hulls of the Omentian ships in half. They joined the rest of the Omentian fleet, hurled high into the sky. Then they rained down from the heavens as worthless debris.

The Adonians could not believe what was happening. As surely as this incredible force was devastating the Omentian fleet before their eyes, it was leaving their convoy untouched. The winds and waves that swept across their enemy turned back to the north before ever reaching their ships, leaving them completely unscathed. To further stress the point, the seas around the Adonian convoy remained perfectly calm.

"The Lord God fights for us today!" Mikole could not take his eyes off of the swirling, golden column of fury tearing the Omentian fleet apart.

As the Omentian ships disintegrated and sunk under the unstoppable force of the elements unleashed upon them, the swirling, golden funnel slowed and serenely dispersed into thin air. The sea, having awakened to devour its quarry, slept again — its unforgiving waves returning to the deep from where they had arisen.

Already on their knees, the men of Adonia bowed their heads again and thanked the God of the heavens and of the seas for their deliverance.

These men would never again let the temptation to doubt their God go unrestrained. Though some in Adonia would doubt the truthfulness of their story — as doubters always do — the object of their faith had revealed both his power and his will to intervene in protecting his people. They knew their God was faithful, and they would desperately need this assurance in the days to come.

As the Adonian ships raised sails and headed for home to report all they had seen, a sole survivor clung to a small piece of wreckage drifting west on the current. He remained unobserved by the Adonian crews searching the seas for survivors.

Kala Azar, senses dulled and filled with hate, could only think of his revenge.

If I can reach Adonia, I can still strike a blow against the Adonians.

In fact, he could still accomplish his primary mission.

Chapter 28

The Knights

†††

The news had been disturbing. Omentia had fallen, and her venom was spreading throughout the east. Parlantis had fallen, and the Omentian fleet was fixing its gaze on Adonia. Truin and Abner decided, after much prayer, that they must form an Adonian Guard.

Truin called a meeting of all the leaders of Adonia. Many were Truin's truest friends and closest advisors. Among them were Jonn, Khory, Gladsel, Melkione, Willieim, Phillip, and Kristof. Some were old friends, and some were new; but all were some of the finest men Truin had ever known.

Kristof had been a trusted friend of Truin for decades. His faithfulness and loyalty were unquestioned. Kristof had heard the amazing stories Toro and Weiphal had told of the Strange Lands, and he had accompanied the brothers back to the southernmost territories of Adonia to witness them and report directly back to Truin on what he observed. Kristof had learned that Toro and Weiphal had not exaggerated when they had described the lands and the creatures that lived there. The knowledge and science of the time could not explain much about the strange beasts that roamed these time-forgotten lands. Though Kristof and Truin were unsure of the impact these lands and creatures would have on Adonia's future, they were confident the Lord had a plan for them. They felt they should be as prepared as possible when that plan became apparent. Therefore, Truin had assigned Kristof as a full-time ambassador to the Strange Lands and as such, Kristof had done an outstanding job.

Truin sent messengers to gather his seven sons. Geoff, Skottie, Daniel, Bigaulf, Gareth, Cusintomas, and Moesheh had all grown strong in the Lord, and remained men of unquestionable honor. They prospered in the land. Because of the Lord's blessing, the brothers had all established themselves as leaders in the seven provinces, resulting in the prosperous growth of their lands. Everyone respected the sons of Truin; the men of the provinces would follow them through the gates of death itself.

Truin was sure not to forget PJ and Mikole. As Master Captains, they knew the seas better than anyone in Adonia. Together, they had the naval resources to form an Adonian Sea Guard that could patrol the coasts of Adonia and provide Adonia its first line of defense against any attack.

Finally, Truin called for Ka'el and his sons, Toro and Weiphal, to join them; though he didn't think Ka'el could be easily located. Ka'el was usually very hard to find, as he avidly enjoyed hunting and was often on a safari somewhere in the wild. Truin had equal doubts about locating Toro and Weiphal in the mysterious Strange Lands, but he had to find them. Adonia needed all the help it could get if it were to survive the Omentian threat.

The Adonians knew they could not stand against the enemy that approached — not if standing depended on their own strength. The fall of neighboring Parlantis had made this perfectly clear. In all the known world, the Parlantian Guard was and had always been second to none. If any mortal army could have defended their land, the Parlantians could and would have. Though the brave warriors of Parlantis stood their ground, they fell because the ground beneath them was shifting sand.

Once the word went out that Adonia was forming an Adonian Guard, volunteers came dutifully from all corners of the land. Some men who volunteered were big and strong — some of them were not. In the end, the selection of volunteers was not determined by their size, strength, and fighting skills; though these characteristics were all valuable. Some men were in their thirties—some had barely reached manhood. Young and old came to join, but again, it was not their age that determined their selection.

There was one attribute and one attribute alone that qualified the men of Adonia for service in the Adonian Guard. There was only one quality that could equip them with the strength to risk everything, the courage to stand in front of the ominous storm that approached, and the eternal reassurance to not fear the sting of death. This attribute, the only factor in their selection, was their faith. The faithful ones, with their spiritual vision intact, could discern the illusions of the Omentian magicians and withstand the influence of the demonic hosts that accompanied them. Only the faithful would have the certain knowledge that — he that was with them — was greater than all those that were with the Omentian. Only the faithful could stand firm when face-to-face with certain death — and yet know certain death was nothing to fear.

The chosen were already individuals of well-known reputation. There was no test — no feat of strength, skill, or intelligence for these men. Rather, each had stood out in his community as a pillar of love, joy, peace, patience, kindness, goodness, faithfulness, gentleness and self-control; the fruits of the Spirit.

The chosen individuals fought against the temptations of immorality, jealousy, hatred, discord, selfish ambition, envy, and drunkenness. Their strength was in the Lord, and they were instruments of his will. They were the hands of the potter to execute the Master's will in the land. They put their trust in the Lord — not in the strength of their own hands, the speed of their own feet, or the brilliance of their own feeble plans. The very purpose of their life or of their death was to give the Master glory. Indeed, the Lord had chosen them long before this day. Still, it would have been a considerable miscalculation to think that those the Lord chose lacked tangible skills. The faithful God had chosen and blessed those individuals, equipping them in advance with the skills to serve and accomplish their deeds.

Many of these faithful men were from the family of Truin; these faithful sons and grandsons would soon face a test of their mettle.

Gareth and the mountain men, skilled in surviving the harshest of climates, came down from the mountains of Chastain. They were physically the strongest of the men in Adonia, unparalleled in climbing ability. Hard and rugged, they would form the backbone of Adonia's heavy infantry.

Cusintomas soon arrived from western Adonian, bringing with him the most skilled riders from Tanshire. Together with their wild ponies, known affectionately as mustangs, their skills surpassed those of the renowned Parlantians. Swift and agile, these men would form the cadre of Adonia's cavalry.

Geoff and the men of Tobar answered the call by adding to the mix the finest archers to be found anywhere. Proficient in hunting all forms of game and expert in using the bow, their skills became invaluable for dropping any threat — man or beast — at a great distance. In addition, they brought with them the many animal calls they used to signal each other across the forests of Tobar. Adonia swiftly adopted this collection of calls as their first set of signals for short-range clandestine communications.

Skottie and the men of Kandish brought an assortment of materials and skills from the diverse landscape of the Kandish countryside. Experienced in hill, valley, lake, and cave — the men of Kandish were adept in any terrain that might confront them. They brought clear crystals, found deep within the caves of Kandish. They could cut and assemble these crystals in such a way that they could use them to see great distances. In addition, they brought the practice of using the beat of the drum to signal each other beyond visual range.

Daniel and his wise men from Plattos were next to arrive. Accustomed to the vast flatlands and prairies of Plattos, they were the fastest of runners and became the foundation of Adonia's light infantry.

Moesheh brought many fighting men from the red lands of Rothing. They did not travel by land, but by ship around Tanshire and into the

Northern Sea. Joining with Captain PJ, Mikole, and the growing armada that accompanied them, they rounded out the First Adonian Fleet.

Bigaulf arrived with ample men and supplies from the fertile lands of Delvia. "There is plenty more where this came from!" His men, also very large and burly like he, filled out the rest of Adonia's heavy infantry.

Toro and Weiphal arrived with the sons of Truin, sharing many new and amazing stories of the Strange Lands to the south and the legendary creatures that still lived there. Like Kristof, Weiphal believed that their discoveries in these lands served a purpose—although no one could yet determine what that purpose was.

Truin's closest advisors took the faithful and made them a fighting force to be reckoned with. Jonn and Gladsel were critically important in organizing and equipping the various elements of the Adonian Guard.

Melkione, Khory, and Daeve tackled the tremendous challenge of training these very independent and diverse units. They taught them to work together and fight together as a unit — as a team. Melkione started by spreading the survivors from the earlier convoy attack — those who had seen firsthand the power of their God in the defense of Adonia — throughout the newly formed Adonian Guard, also known as the "777." Melkione felt these survivors knew the power of the Lord personally, and their faith would anchor the 777 in any future time of desperation. Khory and Daeve organized and supervised training exercises between diverse units of the Adonian Guard, preparing them for the challenges that would soon come.

As Truin had expected, they couldn't find Ka'el. According to Tala, Ka'el had been spending much of his time hunting, leaving Tala alone to her own devises. Truin knew it was not good for a husband and wife to spend so much time apart from each other, and he feared for their marriage. But right now, he had other matters that demanded his attention.

They chose seven hundred and seventy-seven men for the Adonian Guard. They divided these men into seven equal divisions of 111, with each division led by a commander, vice commander, and flag bearer. Truin chose each of his seven sons to lead one of the seven divisions of the 777. The divisions were further divided into three flights of thirty-three, each led by a commander, vice commander, and flag bearer. Likewise, they divided these flights of thirty-three into three squads of eleven, with each squad led by a squad leader and comprising ten fighting men.

In addition, they chose 333 men to guard the castle of Aanot. They built the outer perimeter wall of the castle as a great triangle. They assigned 111 men to each wall of Aanot — each side of the triangle. These were further divided into three equal partitions of flights and squads as that of the Adonian Guard. They chose Jonn, Gladsel, and Melkione to lead these three divisions and report directly to Truin or Khory if Truin could no longer lead.

All together, the divisions of the 777 and the 333 formed ten divisions. Each division had a flight of infantry, cavalry, and archers — referred to as air cavalry. The specific composition of the infantry varied based on the region of Adonia in which it was located. For instance, the infantry flight of Chastain was primarily light infantry, because of the likely need for maneuver in the mountainous terrain — while the infantry flight of Plattos was primarily heavy infantry, because of its predominantly flat terrain.

Adonia's divisions were numbered based on the province they protected. The First, Second, and Third Divisions protected Aanot, so they comprised the First, Second, and Third Infantry, Cavalry, and Air Cavalry. The Fourth through the Tenth Divisions guarded Delvia, Chastain, Kandish, Plattos, Tanshire, Tobar, and Rothing, in that order.

Though some relocation was necessary as personnel moved to the provinces they were to defend, all were happy to do their part in establishing Adonia's Provincial Guard. A new sense of cohesion, solidarity, and organization settled over Adonia as recruits flowed from their home provinces to their newly assigned divisions — intermingling with their Adonian brethren for the first time in a truly meaningful way. This cohesion increased Adonia's sense of unity. Led primarily by the formation of the Adonian Guard, the inhabitants of the provinces began to see and refer to themselves, more and more, as Adonians.

Truin and the other leaders of the Adonian Guard knew the newly formed army was growing very capable, rapidly. However, in the back of their minds, they also knew that left to Adonia's strength alone, the Adonian Guard would be no match for the growing horde approaching from the east.

This would be as much a spiritual battle as a physical one. They trusted the God of their fathers for guidance and help in any future confrontation they might face. Their God was their shield, their sword, and any hope they had of being and staying free. Everything depended on God and God alone. They wished only to be used as their God saw fit to use them.

And so, they established the 777. Thousands volunteered, but only these 777 knights comprised the final Adonian Guard. The Lord did not need great numbers; he desired the faithful.

CHAPTER 29

ENEMY WITHIN

✝✝✝

He did not know.

She watched Ka'el from afar as he worked in the fields — her dark green eyes cutting through the morning fog like those of a snake, eyeing its prey.

She had kept the secret from him all of these years. Though Ka'el thought he knew all that had happened before he and Tala had left Omentia, he certainly did not — not even close.

She became his wife, bore his children, and at least initially, pretended to love him. Over time, she had grown to love him — her husband — but the secret still haunted her, and uncertainty still plagued her regarding her true loyalties.

For long periods of time, Tala had fooled herself into thinking those days in the forests of Omentia were far behind her; that the ones she had left behind — her secret family — had long since forgotten about her and her mission.

Tala fell into a trance; her eyes locked onto Ka'el as she allowed her mind to remember that time, seemingly a lifetime ago. It was the night they had first seen Ka'el and Truin in the forest; the night Potentus revealed himself to them in the fire. That is where her journey — her mission — had begun. After their leader, Pete, had received his new name of Karyan, he had directed Tala and the others to keep a close eye on the brothers. This was easy for Tala to do, for Ka'el was truly pleasing to look upon.

Truin had never returned to their altar in the forest, but Ka'el had returned often. He had always kept his distance, of course — secretly observing their rituals beneath the full moon. He obviously thought they were unaware of his presence, but thanks to their master, Karyan, they knew when he was watching. They showed Ka'el just enough to keep him curious — just enough to keep him coming back for more. Their identities concealed beneath their hooded cloaks, they revealed just enough of the dark mysteries to awe their curious visitor. Karyan became convinced that Ka'el would one day join with the darkness.

To indeed seal the deal, Karyan gave Tala a secret mission. "Look Tala, Potentus brings you a man." Tala's green eyes had longed for Ka'el, and from the very beginning, she had been more than willing to give herself over to him — to seduce the stranger. Ever since she had first laid eyes on him that night by the light of the blazing fire, she knew she had to have him. His chiseled form and long, blond hair were just what she was looking for in a man.

It had been easy for Tala to catch him. Even against the urging of his family, Ka'el had rushed into marriage with Tala; her charms were too much for him to resist.

For a while, Ka'el was content, basking in Tala's potent elixir of carnal pleasure, but the marriage had driven a wedge between Ka'el and his family. Soon the vapors of physical satisfaction had dissipated and the icy chill of reality once again returned to remind Ka'el of his impetuous blunder. He had separated himself from his family, his beliefs, and his traditions, for the sake of a passionate and lustful escapade. Embarrassed by what he had done and yet too proud to admit it to his family, he slipped further and further away from all he knew to be true. He struggled continuously with how to undo what he had done, only to find himself without answers.

One day, Ka'el discovered Tala sneaking out after dark into the forest to practice the dark arts, and he confronted her about it. Tala told Ka'el that a friend had asked her to experience something "incredible," and not knowing if Ka'el would approve, she had temporarily kept it from him — planning to tell him as soon as she had discovered what all the hype was about. Then, tempering his anger with her feminine charms — a technique that always worked on her husband — she convinced Ka'el that she was sorry for keeping the secret from him. Knowing Ka'el's curiosity about the dark arts and his passion for acquiring power, she enticed Ka'el with the lure of the arts; placing him on the defensive. Though he could resist her pleas to join her in actively learning the dark arts, he was unsuccessful in keeping Tala from disappearing into the forest to hone her own skills on moonlit nights

As time went by, Ka'el's resistance waned. He periodically broke down, following Tala into the forest to watch the strange assembly do their mystifying deeds beneath the eerie light of a full moon. Ka'el knew it was wrong, and he tried very hard to resist the temptation. His sinful curiosity routinely got the best of him, and he found himself in the deep forest, watching things he knew he should not see.

Tala continued to work on Ka'el. She urged him to use the magic words and to mark his body — as was the custom of the forest people. Ka'el knew God had instructed them not to mark their bodies like the unbelievers did. They were to resist this custom to remain separate from them. Yet, one night after drinking too much wine, Tala persuaded Ka'el to do the forbidden. He awoke the next morning to find himself marked and pierced like the heathens. Realizing what he had done, he tore at his clothes and screamed in agony over his lack of self-control. The marks upon his body would forever remind him of the failures that dominated his life. Ka'el continued to be tossed back and forth; grieving the Lord God and suffering the consequences of his hedonistic actions.

More and more resentful over time, Ka'el had failed to love Tala, as he should have loved his wife. Instead of insisting he be the moral compass for their family, Ka'el had instead blamed Tala for his own weaknesses. Tala had returned the favor — constantly reminding Ka'el of his many failures, shortcomings, and secret sins. Their marriage had suffered, and they never became as close as husband and wife should have been.

As Tala watched Ka'el from the window of their home, Ka'el too was thinking of all that had transpired over the years with Tala. He reflected on his failures and thought of how he hadn't served the Lord, been a good husband, or been a good father. He thought of how his father must surely despise him for all he had done and what he became. It was his fault that Truin had sustained his injuries in the forest. Against his family's wishes, he had married an unbeliever. He had dabbled in the dark arts and could feel the dark shadows resting upon him — bidding their time, waiting for the day they would totally consume him. He had been a terrible son, brother, husband, and father. Truin, who was but half a man, had done infinitely better than he.

I have wasted my life!

Ka'el collapsed to his knees and, planting his face in his hands, cried bitterly over his sins as he had done so many times before.

"Father in heaven, forgive me for failing you."

A soft breeze blew across the field of grain where Ka'el knelt. For but a moment, the breeze left Ka'el with the comforting feeling that there was still hope.

Tala could not hear Ka'el's words, but she knew his heart was breaking as he fell to the dirt. The part of her that felt love for him wanted to run out and console him. But there was another part of her, a prideful and distant part that had been growing unchecked for many years; that part felt joy at the sight of Ka'el — broken.

A tear ran down her smooth cheek as she stood motionless, unable to move. A moment later, the edges of her lips curled ever so slightly as a faint smile found its place upon her face.

"Now he is mine." She didn't know where the words came from or stop to consider why she had spoken them.

†††

The accuser of the saints laughed in the darkness of his world of hate as he observed Ka'el's misery and weakness. "I have destroyed one brother, and he is no longer a threat to my plans; he is under my control, and he cannot go back."

†††

Unknown to Ka'el, Abner and Evelin continued to pray earnestly for both Ka'el and Tala. They knew that both their son and their daughter-in-law were under attack from invisible forces, and that the outcome of their spiritual struggle would affect much in this world and in the next.

†††

Ka'el's protector in the heavenly realm, yet always near to him, continued to comfort Ka'el and give him strength. "Be strong Ka'el. Do not give up. The Lord does not promise the faithful absence of suffering, but that he will use it all for good. There is still hope."

CHAPTER 30

EViL Intentions

✝✝✝

The fog poured in from the Northern Sea, creeping its way over the low hills to the east like death itself — engulfing all before it and settling into the many valleys in its path. It anchored itself to the low-lands, sinking its cold tentacles into every nook and cranny to prepare for the coming siege. As the fog swallowed up everything in its path, the songs of the birds, caught unaware by its stealthy approach, were permanently silenced. Ethereal, wraithlike sounds emanating from within the sinister cloud replaced all the normal signs of life.

Kieron, a twenty-four-year-old father of two young sons, stood with the other men of his village before this ungodly manifestation.

What am I doing here?

His eyes stung as the sweat poured from his brow and ran down his face.

"Hold the line!"

The command rippled through the Heathian formations along the ridgeline as the mid-level officers echoed the words of their commander through the chain-of-command.

Kieron and his countrymen held the line, though they nervously looked up and down the formation for encouragement — drawing strength from the false bravado that each man could summon up.

Kieron gripped a pitchfork in his right hand and a rudimentary shield in his left. He had never fought in a battle or even been involved in much of a fight. He was a farmer and fisherman, like his father before him, and he knew little of warfare. All of his friends from the village, like their fathers, were farmers and fishermen, too. Trade had long been their land's livelihood, and in their long history they had never needed to raise the sword — or the pitchfork, in this case — in anger against another person to resolve a dispute. Yet, here they stood, a makeshift militia attempting to stop an army of battle-tested warriors. Hopefully, their show of force would be enough to deter those meaning to do them harm.

It had only been two days since the cloaked messenger had arrived at their village and delivered the unacceptable ultimatum to Kieron's people.

"Surrender your lands, your homes, and your children to us. Become our slaves, and we will allow you to live."

Our children?

The men of the village had initially laughed at the threatening courier, ridiculing him and sending him away with disdain. By that evening, things happened that chilled their hearts and filled them with fear. Without warning, a fiery tempest simultaneously set ablaze the fields of their village, lighting up the night sky for miles and miles. Though the men of the village fought through the night to save what they could, their efforts were of little use. The next morning, messengers arrived with news that the waters of their harbor — the center of trade, fishing and livelihood for their people — had turned to blood. Everything within the waters of the harbor had died.

Fear and hysteria filled the land as the people of Heath wondered what evil had befallen them. They were at a complete loss for what to do next or who to call upon for help.

That evening, the hooded messenger of death returned to their village. This time, the villagers met him with hatred and fear. Echoing his ultimatum, the dark one now demanded unconditional surrender or the dark forces would destroy their village.

Some wanted to give in to their fear, to surrender to the invaders; that is until the courier stipulated the vilest of his demands. He demanded the sacrifice of six of their children; that they throw the children from the cliffs as a sign of the village's agreement on his master's terms. If they did not make the sacrifices at dawn the next day, the enemy force would take their village, obliterate their homes, and exterminate all the inhabitants.

The dark one faded away into the shadows of the night, leaving the people of the Heath speechless. Though they had little hope of defeating a trained army, none could fathom the thought of sacrificing their children to the invaders. Every man to the last joined the line at dawn on the hills of the eastern shore to face whatever menace approached them from the sea.

"Hold the line!" The command sent shivers down the backs of the farmers, fishermen, and their sons as they stood in the early morning mist — the sun failing to break through the gray overcast above.

Kieron reached up below his crude armor to grasp the necklace around his neck. The metal figure that hung there was the physical representation of Granus, the Heathian god of the harvest that Kieron worshiped.

"Help us Granus, protect us from this evil."

Most Heathians put their faith in one of the diverse group of Heathian gods and goddesses that represented the various aspects of their society. The Heathians had recognized that their world had not come to be on its own and that they should give homage to the maker and provider of all; whether it was the god of fishing or agriculture or trade. Not knowing which god was the true God, the Heathians had fashioned several gods to cover all the bases. Kieron's family, coming from a long line of farmers, worshipped Granus.

As Kieron called upon Granus for help, it quietly occurred to him that the god of the harvest might not be powerful enough to help in a situation like this. Hopefully, one of his companions in the line prayed to a god more able to serve them here on the plain.

The Heathians grew more and more agitated, apprehensive of the darkness that now crept across the plain towards them. As the dark menace moved ever closer, the cries and moaning from within the cloud grew in volume and regularity. Soon the skin of each Heathian was crawling. They fidgeted nervously and their eyes danced about fretfully as they searched for a source of courage, strength, or hope. They found none.

With every passing moment, their beliefs seemed more and more empty — that their gods were powerless to help them. Soon, fear overtook the battle-line of the Heathians. As the darkness approached them, the clouds above thickened, strangling out the little light that had been snaking its way through the low cloud deck above them. It was as if a giant hand was reaching out to take them, and there was nothing they could do to stop it.

As the darkness deliberately enclosed their positions, they observed countless creatures darting through the fog all around them. Some were big, some small, some with red eyes, some with green; the creatures took the form of whatever the men feared the most. The Heathians panicked. Their line broke.

"Hold the line! We must hold the line!" The command rang out again, alarm and uncertainty now flooding the voice of the one giving it and those echoing it.

Kieron felt like he was going to go insane.

What is happening?

He joined his companions in shouting out warnings to those around him as he saw movement here — then there.

The dark fog reached the Heathian line, and the many voices and sounds emanating from within the fog joined the panicked outbursts of the Heathian defenses. They mingled into one horrific symphony of terror, then madness, and then death.

†††

Unseen by men, the dark demons descended on the Heathians in waves. Led by Metus, Terrus, Sollicitus, Doldrus, Scire, and Viscere; the merciless messengers of death and destruction completely engulfed the mortals below like a spiritual tidal wave, overwhelming their souls with devastating fear and dread — until insanity reigned.

The Heathians had filled their minds with the useless imaginations of their time, rather than what was good and true. Their houses were empty, and evil made itself at home. Scire entered the minds of the men, seeking their innermost thoughts, and perverting all that they held as true. Many of the Heathians soon wondered what they believed in and why they stood on the plain at all. They doubted their convictions, their courage, and their cause. Terrus and Sollicitus followed close behind Scire, finding and feeding on each man's greatest worries and anxieties. They whipped the Heathians into an uncontrollable frenzy of emotion and confusion. Having discovered each man's weakness, Viscere immediately followed, distorting the Heathians' visual perceptions and manifesting their anxieties before them, until they saw every terror their perplexed minds could imagine. They became unsure of the surrounding reality. Many had fleeting glimpses of what was truly happening, but they were powerless to control their thoughts and willfully gave in, once again, to the uncertainty of their surroundings. Overwhelmed by the madness that consumed them, their hearts and souls were putty in Doldrus' talons; his polluted powers crushed their spirits and sent them into the pit of hopelessness and despair. In this environment, Metus reigned supreme. He released his cloak of fear and dread upon the Heathian line, wrapping up the souls of Heath in a common blanket of madness.

Kieron could not believe his eyes! All his friends screamed in terror at the creatures surrounding them in the fog. Some pleaded for their lives, while others fell to their knees, crying out to their loved ones.

Kieron too was overwhelmed with fear and regret. Surely, there was no hope against this enemy. They would all die on this field! His thoughts turned to his wife, Sasha, and his two children — Tamron and Kylar.

What will they do without me? How will they survive? What will these monsters do to them?

Kieron fell to his knees and pleaded, "Granus, Granus, help us!"

Granus did not hear.

As the Heathian line disbanded and crumbled before the Omentians, the Omentian infantry swept across the field of battle, beheading all within their path. Few of the Heathians put up any resistance at all, most having fallen to their knees before the invaders.

The cloud dissipated behind the Omentian onslaught, and the fields of Heath surrendered its fallen to the birds of the air, which gathered to feed upon the spoils of the battle.

Among the headless corpses was a twenty-four-year-old father of two young sons, whose family, like so many others, would never see their father or husband again.

With the fall of Heath, evil tightened its grip on the world.

†††

The living beings watched in righteous anger as the dark ones devastated the defenseless Heathians and gave them over to the Omentian horde.

"Heath has fallen," said one great being with large, ivory wings.

"Heath was dead long before today. Their time of grace has passed. They dismissed the light of truth that was once brought here. Heath chose other gods, and the light departed to shine in another land. It gave birth to many lights there," replied a living being with golden wings. "The Master works in ways that are far above and unknown to us. Who can know his ways? Blessed be the name of the Lord!"

And as soon as they had arrived, they were gone.

CHAPTER 31

LEGION

†††

Behind the cloak of mystery that shadowed the vast and unpopulated Strange Lands, Bestia worked his spell among the creatures that still lurked in secrecy there. Soon the Omentians would enslave these creatures; it was Bestia's mission to prepare their simple minds for the taking.

Hussein had not been alone in his mission to recruit the beasts of the land to help the dark prince Karyan in the conquest of Adonia. Karyan had also sent two other agents of darkness, Mansen and Sanger, to entice the powerful beasts that still roamed this mysterious land to join the cause. These magnificent beasts had not died off after the Great Deluge as so many others had. They had, however, restricted themselves to roam within the confines of the Strange Lands. For this reason, very few knew about them, and the vast majority of humans in the current age considered them legendary.

Many legends told of hideous creatures with enormous wings and long, razor-sharp tails dominating the skies. Legends claimed that these magnificent beasts possessed armor and could breathe fire. The legends also spoke of giant cats with large fangs that hunted by moonlight, catching unsuspecting travelers unaware and devouring them. And the legends told of other creatures too, creatures that lurked in the shadows; menacing monsters that controlled the grasslands of the Strange Lands.

Still, the prevailing belief was that all these creatures became extinct, if they had ever even existed in the first place. After all, it had been many years since anyone reported this type of story, let alone corroborated it with multiple witnesses. Truth had a way of becoming legend, simply with the passage of time.

Still, darkness knew of the beasts, and it was determined to seek them out.

CHAPTER 32

RISE OF THE LEADER

✝✝✝

Truin enjoyed his runs through the countryside. The rolling hills that surrounded Blue Lake were simply the most beautiful that he had ever seen. Everywhere he looked, the hillsides displayed an endless diversity of multicolored flowers. Blues and greens dominated the countryside. A carpet of green grass, green trees and green bushes was perfectly mixed with blue flowers, highlighted by a blue sky, and punctuated by Blue Lake. Of course, perfectly blended in with the blues and the greens were the bountiful reds, yellows, oranges, and violets that masterfully completed the harmony of this wonderful place. The Lord had blessed them greatly.

As Truin ran, he thought about anything and everything. He found that the physical act of running seemed to open up his mind and give him access to thoughts and ideas that he rarely thought about at other times. Or it could have been that just getting away from all the other chores and duties of life allowed his mind to rest, to wander to the places it so longed to go. Either way, the daily run was a peaceful time — a time when Truin's heart routinely turned to the Lord.

Truin communed with God, thanking and praising him for his majesty, his creation, his love, and his faithfulness. Truin was continuously in awe of the complexity and beauty of the creation that surrounded him. Even the sight of a tree astounded Truin.

Who tells it how to grow? How does it know how and when to produce its fruit? It is so wonderful to have a God that provides!

Many of his Omentian neighbors, before they had journeyed to Adonia, had believed that everything in creation had come to be without a Creator. They believed that the beauty, complexity, and orchestration of nature — her laws, her creatures, and even mankind itself with his reason and abilities — had simply advanced from a string of lower life forms, which had originally found life through some accidental mixture of elementary components.

This was absolutely ludicrous to Truin.

And where did this random mix of elementary components come from? The true believers in nature must be blind to everything around them. How sad a life they must live not knowing the God that has created such wonder, and loved it so immensely! Why do they work so hard to reject him? Why the elaborate imaginations to deny him the glory that is so rightfully his?

After Truin had praised his maker for all he was and all he had done, Truin brought intercessions to the King for his family, his loved ones, and his friends. He prayed for his mother and father, for his wife, for his sister, for his sons, their families, and especially for his brother — for he knew Ka'el was under attack to turn his back on the God of their fathers and worship instead the false god of the Omentians.

Truin also found that while running, he listened better for the Lord's voice than at other times when the many distractions of daily life competed with the Lord for his attention. Truin could more clearly hear the Lord's guidance when he was away from the distractions of the world.

On this day, Truin concentrated his focus on how best to protect Adonia. Though the provinces hadn't asked him to lead the defense of Adonia, Truin felt that this responsibility would soon land squarely upon his shoulders. Therefore, he had been instrumental in the formation of the 777 Knights of the Adonian Guard; he had ordered the deployment of the Aanot Guard, and he had asked his sons to prepare for the coming storm.

Karyan had advanced on Omentia, Parlantis, and Heath; he had taken all these lands with ease. Their defenses had relied completely upon the strength of men, and all three had fallen swiftly in the face of evil. The strength of men had proven to be completely insufficient for the task.

Truin knew Adonia could not, by muscle or iron, stand against Karyan. Only God could win the battle against the evil that was coming to their shores, and only through faith in the one true God could Adonia hope to stand.

Truin pondered on the Word as he ran, considering his life and realizing how small he was; how insignificant compared to the mountains that towered around him or the breeze that blew through the trees — how fleeting his life was in the ongoing story that continued to unfold moment by moment. He considered his several brushes with death and how each had affected him. He realized that when a man focuses on his own small existence and his few, fleeting days, he destines himself to a life of insignificance.

Where is there time or thought for bold service to God or others when one lives in constant fear of injury or death?

However, as a man opens up the aperture of his vision to consider those around him and how to live a life of service to them, the impact of his few days of existence increases exponentially. He realizes he has very little time to make a difference; indeed, very little time to serve. Urgency now dominates his life as he realizes he must get to work and work well!

There is so much to do and so little time!

Finally, as he considers his maker and the very purpose of his life from the maker of the universe's perspective, he can then see the intended course of his life. Only by accomplishing that which the Lord intends for his life does a man reach his true potential. Without the Lord, a man's short time on earth is ultimately worthless.

What does God want me to do? What is my purpose here? These are the questions a man should ask. As long as a man hangs on tightly to his own life, thinking only of himself, his own selfish pleasure and his accu-mulation of ultimately worthless material things; he is afraid to act for fear of losing that which he has already gained. His possessions are his god, and his life exists to protect his god of things. He allows greed and fear to enslave him; they shackle his feet and restrict his vision.

However, once he realizes that his life is but a whisper in the wind, and his time like the grass and flowers of the field, whose glory lasts for a season and then quickly crumbles; his vision widens to consider a greater viewpoint. When he realizes God gave him life for action and for pur-pose, then he is no longer paralyzed by the fear of movement, its risks and its corresponding change; he has no choice but to act. Action is the very purpose of his existence! What is it that this whisper — my life — means to shout from the rooftops? What is the greatest impact this whisper can have on the world?

After all that Truin had heard and seen in his life, it became apparent to him that there was no greater impact a whisper could have than to proclaim the glory of the God of the heavens.

For what is man next to God, and what are a man's accomplish-ments next to God's creation? Who could ever fashion an accomplishment from their own life to compare with the beauty and majesty that I see all around me as I run through these forests and meadows? How well a man proclaims the maker and furthers the maker's purpose — this is indeed the greatest measure of a man's brief and transitory life.

Without God's protection, help, and guidance, a man's life is nothing but a drop in an ocean of time that quickly dissipates and fades from memory. Even from birth, death is alive in a man's bones, leading him to the grave.

But with God directing a man's footsteps, a man's time can accomplish great things in service to the Maker of the Universe. His life can be a pillar in the temple of God's truth and a trumpet to the people of the lands — announcing that there is but one God in the heavens and that all men exist to worship him and him alone! With this worldview, a man is free! No longer bound by fear of loss; a man can live each moment in peace, comfort and courage; knowing he serves at the pleasure of the King of the Universe. He serves at the pleasure of the one who sets all men's days, the only one who can give as well as take away. He is free to serve, free to love, and free from worry — for all his days are in the hands of the Almighty God. This is true freedom!

Truin knew this was good and true, a noble purpose, a meaningful life. To this calling, he devoted his life, and on this day, he became a leader.

As his heart pounded and his legs carried him over the hills and through the valleys, he asked God to strengthen his body and spirit, to give him courage, and to prepare him for what was ahead. He knew the day was fast approaching when he would be called to serve. With that service would come commitment and sacrifice.

Create in me a clean heart, Oh my God, and renew a right spirit within me.

✝✝✝

As Truin approached his home in the foothills, Christina caught sight of him from the porch overlooking Blue Lake. She had taken a break from her daily chores and was quietly reminiscing.

So much had happened since that day, so long ago, when they forcibly took her from her home and sold her into slavery. From the slave ship, the shipwreck, and certain death; to rescue, a new land, a new people, and a new family; God had been faithful. Many times, she felt tempted to see only with her eyes, giving in to her feelings of hopelessness and depression. Many times, she felt tempted to doubt God's faithfulness and his promises. But God had never left her side, and he had never let her down. He had comforted her with his Word, sent protectors to help her, and strengthened her spirit. Every time she had walked through the fire, she emerged on the other side stronger and more certain of the beauty in God's plan for her life. Now, after all these years, God had blessed her with a god-fearing husband, seven wonderful sons, over thirty grandsons, a beautiful home, and every reason to never doubt her God again.

With tears in her eyes, she watched her husband approach, and she thanked God for him and all her blessings.

How great is our God!

Chapter 33

Adonia Prepares for War

†††

Truin called his sons to Aanot. There by the campfire, as they had done on that special night so many years earlier, they joined him once again.

So much had transpired since that night, the night they had presented him with the golden timepiece. Omentia, Parlantis, and Heath had all fallen to the dark prince, Karyan, and the powers of evil. When they saw the dark clouds gathering to the north and east, the people of Adonia had formed the Adonian Guard to protect the land from the evil spreading throughout the world. The Omentians had sent a fleet against Adonia, but it had fallen into the hand of God and delivered to the depths of the Dark Sea.

Truin knew evil would not rest, and though God could fully protect Adonia without the help of the Adonian Guard, Truin held they should all be ready to be the hands and feet of their God when called upon. They should be ready to serve, ready to stand in the path of evil, and ready to do the bidding of the one, true God — to his glory. For this calling, they existed; to this end, they must endeavor.

As they sat around the fire, below a sky of a trillion stars, two things were remarkably different from that time years earlier. The circle of men had grown in number. No longer was Truin alone with his seven sons. Now, dozens of Truin's grandsons joined the ranks, sitting with their fathers — broadening and strengthening the family circle. Further, fine-tuned by years of training and preparation, each of the men in the gathering brought with him full body armor, shield, and sword. The swords of Truin's seven sons, each representing a province of Adonia, held the respective symbolic stone of their leader: the emerald stone for Tobar; sapphire for Kandish; topaz for Chastain; amethyst for Plattos; beryl for Delvia; sardonyx for Tanshire; and finally, the jasper stone for Rothing. Then, following in their fathers' footsteps, Truin's grandsons also had their swords fitted with their province's stone. The myriad of precious gems sparkled brilliantly in the fire's reflective light, echoing to the majestic flicker of the stars above.

Foremost on all of their minds was the defense of their land — their home. Adonia was a place of truth and peace; a land where all worshipped and loved the true God. It was a land where families grew and prospered by working hard and helping each other. It was a land ordained by God, blessed by God, and protected by God.

Truin knew that he, his sons, and his sons' sons would all face evil in the coming days and weeks. Evil and its followers were many and their strength, both in the spiritual world and the physical world, was formidable. Though undoubtedly fit and ready for the challenge, Truin saw a hint of anxiety in the faces of his grandsons, still very young men. No doubt, their anxiety originated out of concern for their loved ones. These young men knew the coming confrontation with the enemies of Adonia would place each of them front and center in the wall of flesh and blood that would stand in evil's path as it assaulted the front gates of their homeland. These young men did not fear for their own safety. Being young, idealistic, and indestructible, they welcomed the opportunity to stand for what was right and true. They did, however, wonder what their families would do if they were to fall in battle; how their families would make-do without them. If only there was a way to spare their loved ones the sorrow of loss that would surely accompany the war to come. But some things were simply out of their control.

Truin began with prayer and a reading of Psalm 118 from God's Word to remind the men not only of what God had done to protect them in the past, but also of his promises and what they could expect of God in the future.

"Give thanks to the Lord, for he is good; his love endures forever… In my anguish I cried to the Lord, and he answered by setting me free. The Lord is with me and I will not be afraid. What can man do to me? The Lord is with me; he is my helper. I will look in triumph on my enemies.

"It is better to take refuge in the Lord than to trust any man. It is better to take refuge in the Lord than to trust in princes. All the nations surrounded me, but in the name of the Lord I cut them off. They surrounded me on every side, but in the name of the Lord I cut them off.

"I was pushed back and about to fall, but the Lord helped me. The Lord is my strength and my song; he has become my salvation. Shouts of joy and victory resound in the tents of the righteous: The Lord's right hand has done mighty things! The Lord's right hand is lifted high; the Lord's right hand has done mighty things!

"I will not die but live, and will proclaim what the Lord has done… The stone the builders rejected has become the capstone; the Lord has done this, and it is marvelous in our eyes. This is the day the Lord has made; let us rejoice and be glad in it.

"O Lord, save us; O Lord, grant us success. Blessed is he, who comes in the name of the Lord, from the house of the Lord we bless you.

"The Lord is God, and he has made his light shine upon us… You are my God and I will give you thanks; you are my God and I will exalt you. Give thanks to the Lord, for he is good; his love endures forever."

God had always kept his promises, and there was no reason for the men of Adonia to doubt him, to fear anyone or anything. Truin reassured his sons of God's love and faithfulness, much as he had done many times before during their childhood around this same fire pit.

His boys remembered those nights with their father with great longing, wishing again for the simple days of their past; being young and naïve, they didn't have to face the dangers of the world around them, let alone prepare to meet those dangers head-on in battle. Back then, their father had been their defense, and their greatest concern was that of their chores.

At the time of this gathering around the fire, most of the grandsons had families of their own, and they were the defenders. Some had ample time to prepare for this responsibility. For others, they had to assume responsibility hastily. Either way, all were ready for the challenge. They possessed powerful spirits, fueled by the faith given to them by God; they were determined to honor him, protect their loved ones, and survive — in that order.

Truin stood and spoke. "My sons, it is time to stand and meet the challenge before us. Omentia, Parlantis and Heath have fallen, and soon evil will make its way to our shores. You must prepare your divisions with haste."

They discussed the defense of Adonia. The men decided that their defense must remain flexible — in an alert status — for the time being. Since there was no way of knowing when, where, or in how many places the Omentians would make landfall; they decided that each of Adonia's divisions should remain in their own province but be ready at a moment's notice to converge as directed to meet the enemy where required. In the meantime, they would continue to train as they had been training since the formation of the Adonian Guard; honing their skills in the art of battle and maximizing their abilities to work together as a team. They must be an army of men moving as one organism; one body with many parts, able to work in unison or as independent units as dictated by the flow of battle.

The faintest glimmer of the coming sunrise showed itself on the western horizon of Adonia, and Truin chose his last words to the men of his family — the chosen commanders of Adonia's newly formed Adonian Guard.

"Remember, our struggle is not foremost with the men of Omentia, Parlantis and Heath, but with those spiritual forces of evil that have taken them prisoner and made them slaves to evil's plans. The flesh is the puppet, and the spiritual forces the puppet masters.

"My sons, trust the words and promises of God, those you know to be true — not what the deceiver tells you to see and the doubts he attempts to plant in your hearts! Trust God and his words, regardless of what your eyes, ears, and senses tell you! Do not trust your reason. Do not trust your emotions. The devil will try to use these to deceive you!

"Be resolute and stand firm before the enemy. Do not fear! In quiet expectation, wait on the Lord. Put your faith in God, the only rock on which to stand. He is faithful, and he will not be moved!

"Let us make our whisper a shout to all the lands! Let the world know that there is a God in Adonia, and there is no other! We will wait on the Lord. Let us ensure our whisper reaches the ends of the world and that we stand with the Lord for all time!"

With few additional words, the men left the place of safety and warmth. Resolute to do their duty, they departed to their stations around Adonia. They did not know when, or if, they would ever meet again.

CHAPTER 34

THE PROTECTORS

†††

Guardians of light, one for each of the Adonians, surrounded the men in the dim light of the starlit night as they gathered around the campfire by Blue Lake and prayed for God's help.

The living beings, protectors of the faithful, were not all-knowing like their master. Though they often played a part in serving, ministering, delivering messages to, and protecting the faithful as the Master willed and directed, they could not see the future. They knew their master was faithful by his very nature and that he always kept his promises, but for the specifics — the how — the protectors were very often as surprised to see matters unfold as the sons of men who lived below. Thus, they watched events develop with great curiosity, living in awe of both the Creator and his creation.

The Chief Being conversed with those who would serve as the protectors of the faithful for the great battle of this age within time. The brilliant eyes of the protectors sparkled as wings of gold, jasper, sapphire, emerald, topaz, and amethyst opened and closed; synchronized to perfection. They traversed both the dimensions of the mortals and of the timeless — seamlessly.

There was no need for them to speak as mortals did. The Beings communicated amongst themselves instantly and effortlessly in ways far too marvelous for the limited understanding of men to fathom. Like men, they were created beings — but what majestic created beings they were.

"Evil will soon launch its attack on the sons of the Most High," one of them flashed. "How will they stand against its onslaught?"

Spectacular beams of multicolored light flashed around them as their eyes darted about purposefully; meticulously keeping watch on the events unfolding below.

"Watch the Spirit move among the sons of man. They are more important than they realize. The Master loves them all, and he has plans for each one of them. It is the Master's will that these creatures of flesh and blood be used to defeat the dark forces below and those in the heavenly realms. Men are weak and frail, and we have all seen them fail — so very often. Yet, through these weak vessels, the Master shows both his mercy and his power."

Wonders, yet unseen by men, indeed unexplainable by human expression, enveloped the living beings, dancing around them gloriously as they moved between dimensions, across the boundaries of time and space; faithfully doing the Master's bidding.

"Soon, the Master will once again show his power over the creation — over the elements and the creatures below."

Together they responded, "And we will be ready."

CHAPTER 35

OmenTia Prepares

†††

The demons stirred the hearts and the minds of the Omentians to ever-increasing lusts, immorality, self-deprivation, cruelty, hatred, and destruction. Decadence reached feverish levels, and the downward spiral of debauchery continued unabated. The only allegiance that now remained among the Omentians was that of fearful faithfulness to Karyan, the giver of the dark arts. Through these arts, the people of the east enjoyed a self-proclaimed, new freedom — taking pride in the new ways they had at their disposal to express the evil that had lived within their hearts. They called it the "Great Awakening." In actuality, they had not chosen freedom but enslavement.

Led by Karyan's growing number of lieutenants, the most intellectual in their midst, the practice of magic and sorcery became commonplace, and Omentia slid deeper into the pit of darkness. The Omentians perfected the skills they would soon use in warfare against Karyan's enemies by turning their hexes against the weakest in their communities and against those few witnesses who still resisted the rise of the dark lord. The conjurers of magic, having given their souls over to evil, surrendered all of their reason to darkness. They no longer saw the willful harming of their fellow countryman as wrong or even detrimental to their cause. Immorality spread throughout the population, and they replaced Omentia's laws with anarchy and violence. The innocent recipients of the pervasive cruelty became the first witnesses, the first martyrs of the Great Struggle. When these martyrs were gone, only the fallen Omentians remained, and the demons in their midst, being all too willing to accommodate the insatiable thirst for bloodshed, drove Omentian against Omentian in frenzied displays of callousness and brutality.

Men became like animals. All social structures broke down. The family unit deteriorated as men and women abandoned their vows made to one another, carousing freely with whomever they wished. The consciences of the Omentians become more and more seared, and the unspeakable became routine. They abandoned their children and left them to fend for themselves. Homelessness and starvation became commonplace.

Even the animals of the land and the birds of the air fled the evil that descended upon Omentia. Their most basic instincts now telling them to flee the vile stench of death. God's creatures, both big and small, were driven relentlessly in mass for the western shore. And yet, the Omentians, ever more blinded to their wickedness by the demons that dwelt within, continued their rebellion, sinking deeper and deeper to hell on earth.

When the time was right, Karyan tested the commitment of his people to their new master, ordering them to worship him by sacrificing their infants. He promised them they would receive double or triple the magical powers they had already received if they did so.

Having given up all semblance of decency, the Omentians chose selfish desire over love. No more vile thing could a people do then sacrifice their children on the altar of self-interest, but the Omentians were past any concern over decency or justice. They chose a course that would guarantee their ultimate destruction; they sacrificed the inno-cent on the altar of evil.

††

The demons erupted in celebration as Doldrus, Terrus, Sollicitus, and Metus tore at the strings of human emotion, further crushing the Omentians' spirits with sadness, guilt, anxiety, and fear. Thus, they drove the Omentians further into the dungeons of madness.

CHAPTER 36

FEAR AND COMFORT

†††

The sons returned to their provinces and set about their duties to prepare for the coming storm. They met biweekly with their respective divisions to hone their fighting skills. Well understanding that their abilities would soon put to use against an evil invader determined to destroy their culture, way of life, and their families; the various fighting units rapidly improved both their killing effectiveness and efficiency.

While the men of Adonia waited for the inevitable, they tried to live their lives in peace, going about their daily duties of taking care of their families and tending to their homesteads. This, however, proved to be very difficult.

Only a small fraction of the population of the territories of Adonia had been faithful enough to be chosen to man the Adonian Guard. Some had wondered at the wisdom of this decision to limit the Adonian Guard's numbers, thinking it better to man it with as many men as possible. However, it soon became apparent why they chose not to select all the men of Adonia.

Across Adonia, in the wake of the rumors of impending Omentian attack, a wave of fear washed over those with little or no faith. These faithless Adonians moved from village to village, spreading gloom, despair, and their fickle philosophies throughout the population. Bands of disgruntled men — men born not of courage but of cowardly divisiveness — riled up the people. "We should form our own militias. These men of the Adonian Guard will not protect us. They will only protect their own."

Others took it further. "We should surrender to the Omentians. No one can stand against them. Parlantis couldn't. Heath couldn't. Maybe Karyan isn't so bad after all. Most of us were once Omentians. Maybe we still should be. They will not harm us if we do what they want us to do."

These men did not realize the part they were playing in the enemy's game plan. As planters of the seeds of fear, weakness, and surrender, their capitulation embodied Karyan's first wave of attack. The Dark Lord knew all too well that toppling a population's resolve to resist would eventually cripple its army and lead to submission.

Initially, most could see the pathetic senselessness of surrendering to Omentia without a fight. Karyan had proven to be a harsh ruler over the lands he had taken, and Adonia would surely suffer the same fate if they surrendered to him. Yet, as the naysayers continued their barrage on Adonia day after day, their relentless assault gnawed at the faith of even the strongest in Adonia. Though the men of the Adonian Guard had the utmost faith and confidence that God had a plan for their land and that he would protect them from the scourge that had so completely subjected Omentia, Parlantis, and Heath; their faith came under heavy assault.

The assault began in the families of the guardsmen. Though these women and children were true believers in the God of their fathers, the Creator of the World, the Sovereign Spirit of Truth that had promised mankind a Savior from sin, and the forgiveness that would flow to them all through a Savior; the women and children of Adonia feared. This fear made its way, like a poisonous snake slithering through the tall grass of human emotions, to the psyche of the faithful men of the Adonian Guard.

The guardsmen met together as often as they could to reassure each other, but as the sun set each night and the darkness crept to their individual doorsteps, they were each reminded of the painful reality that death and destruction would soon visit their land, and that they would be the only thing standing between the evil horde and the families they so loved. Focusing on themselves and their own strengths, the men of the Adonian Guard slipped; they doubted. Once they doubted, their doubt gave birth to its firstborn child — fear.

Fear wrapped its long tentacles around the guardsmen's hearts and sank its claws into their reason, their courage, and their resolve. Fear relentlessly assaulted them as they worried about their loved ones; wives and children who depended on them for protection. They feared losing their homes, their livestock, and all the possessions they had accumulated. They were afraid they hadn't sufficiently prepared and doubted the ability of the Adonian Guard to stand against the powerful arm of Omentia.

Even the sons of Truin felt the continuous volley of invisible arrows, poison arrows of doubt and fear that now rained down upon them. It had been easy to talk of defending the homeland, while they had rested in the strength and encouragement of their father's words; while renewing the strength of their family bonds, basking in the spiritual peace and comfort of Aanot. But as the distance and time from Aanot had increased, an overwhelming cloud of foreboding had settled upon the sons, and dark specters had emerged from every shadow to assail them. They could sense the darkness spreading around them, and even they wondered what tomorrow might bring.

And so, the noose tightened around the spirits of the sons of Adonia.

†††

A living being spoke. "They falter."

Another replied. "They are weak, and they are under heavy attack by the evil one."

"How will they stand?"

"Alone they will not."

"The Faithful and True does not will that fear should cripple his faithful. They have received a spirit of power, not of fear."

"He will work his will."

And together they echoed, "Thy will be done."

†††

It was at this time that a man with one eye came out of the mountains of Kandish. The man spoke from the Word of Truth. "Strengthen the feeble hands, steady the knees that give way; say to those with fearful hearts, Be strong, do not fear; your God will come, he will come with a vengeance; with divine retribution, he will come to save you."

The words of this man were so different from the prevailing thoughts and fears overtaking

Adonia at this time, that news of this stranger from the hills spread across the territories.

Those who put their faith in God listened to his words. "Blessed is the man who trusts in the Lord, whose confidence is in him. He will be like a tree planted by the water that sends out its roots by the stream. It does not fear when heat comes; its leaves are always green. It has no worries in a year of drought and never fails to bear fruit."

And the man moved throughout Adonia, sharing the news, uniting the believers of the provinces, and strengthening them through the Word. "He who dwells in the shelter of the most high will rest in the shadow of the Almighty. I will say of the Lord, He is my refuge and my fortress, my God, in whom I trust. Surely he will save you from the fowler's snare and from the deadly pestilence. He will cover you with his feathers and under his wings you will find refuge; his faithfulness will be your shield and rampart.

"You will not fear the terror of night, or the arrow that flies by day, nor the pestilence that stalks in the darkness, nor the plague that destroys at midday. A thousand may fall at your side, ten thousand at your right hand, but it will not come near you.

"You will only observe with your eyes and see the punishment of the wicked. If you make the most high your dwelling — even the Lord, who is my refuge — then no harm will befall you, no disaster will come near your tent... You will tread upon the lion and the cobra; you will trample the great lion and the serpent.

"'Because he loves me,' says the Lord, 'I will rescue him; I will protect him, for he acknowledges my name. He will call upon me and I will answer him; I will be with him in trouble, I will deliver him and honor him. With long life I will satisfy him and show him my salvation.'"

The man's name was Donstup. He had lost the sight in one of his eyes many years earlier as a small child. Though it would seem to most that life would be more difficult for a man with but one eye, Donstup had adapted very well. A Nomen's son, his parents brought him up in truth, teaching him to trust in God. They taught him not to trust in the temporary abilities that might come through his physical skills or intellect, but in the one who was always faithful and true and would never let him down. This training had served him well as he had matured into manhood.

Only able to see from but one of his two eyes had proven to be a tremendous blessing to Donstup in several ways. Through the loss of an eye, God had shown Donstup that no two men on earth saw their surroundings or the events of their life in the same way; that we all saw things differently. This helped Donstup relate to others with differing perspectives, to empathize with various points of view, to reconcile diverse viewpoints, and to settle disagreements among the people he encountered. In addition, his disability had taught him to see not only with the physical eye but also with the spiritual eye, the spiritual sight that God had given him through the Word and through quiet time in prayer with God.

Though the learning of these things had been difficult, Donstup would not have traded these insights, these gifts, from God for any temporary or perishable possessions. They had proven much more useful in life than, say, another eye would have been. The wisdom he had gained from his infirmity had drawn him much closer to his maker and equipped him with precious talents with which to serve God. His relationship with God was everything to him, and he thanked God daily for his many blessings, including the ways God had used the loss of his eye for good.

Donstup ministered to the people, and they put their trust in God. The faithful turned their eyes from the created things of the earth, those that are seen through physical eyes, and put their trust instead in the Creator. Through faith, they could clearly see the hands of the Creator at work, exhibiting his invisible qualities, his eternal power, and his divine nature. Through spiritual eyes, the faithful could see so much more than the limited vision provided by physical eyes; flawed eyes that so often blind men with trivial pursuits.

The men of the Adonian Guard focused their vision once again on their true strength, not the power in their own arms, but the might of the God in whom they placed their trust — the God of the heavens who feared no army. They trusted, once again, in God's strength, his omnipotence, and his faithfulness. Through the Word, the Spirit moved over the men and their families, restoring their peace.

Donstup blessed the people of God. "The Lord bless you and keep you; the Lord make his face shine upon you and be gracious to you; the Lord turn his face toward you and give you peace."

Thus, it was at this time that fear assaulted the shores of Adonia. But fear did not reign in Adonia, for God repelled it with the promises of his Word and the strength of his Spirit. Comfort, reassurance, and peace settled once again on Adonia.

"They will target him," the sapphire living being said.

Bolts of lightning and flashes of color streaked across the ethereal backdrop in which the living beings themselves came and went — there one moment and gone the next.

"Send him helpers that will assist him in his ministry to the faithful and protect his life."

A great struggle was about to ensue; one that would test the Adonians' beliefs, convictions, and loyalties as they stood against those who, not so long ago, were their friends and neighbors to the east; neighbors who had since turned to the dark ways and submitted to a dark master.

Without delay, the protectors flashed through time and space, ministering to the faithful and strengthening them for what was soon to come.

CHAPTER 37

Magic, Ruthlessness and the Hunters

†††

No sound. No movement. Ready.

A pair of golden eyes pierced through the darkness of the rocky grassland. Only the occasional glimmer of moonlight slicing through the low, fast moving cloud deck provided any clue as to his presence among the shadows.

Tall grass, large black rocks, and the occasional cluster of bare-limbed trees covered the terrain in this place. In the night's stillness, where everything appeared as shades of black and gray, the greatest hazards to movement were the tar pits.

Indistinguishable in the black of night from the solid ground that surrounded them, countless creatures had met their demise there, struggling hopelessly to free themselves from the black death. Once caught in its grip, resistance was futile. Any attempt to escape the pools of death hastened the victim's inevitable descent to the mass grave that waited deep below in the dark bowels of the earth.

If a creature traveled at night, attempting to navigate the eerie shadows by the pale moonlight, the tar pits were arguably its greatest threat to a successful journey. But the tar pits were not the only danger, and tonight, in this place, they were not the greatest.

A pair of bison made their way through the high grass of the meadow between two large rocky ridges. Separated earlier in the day from their herd, the bison wandered blindly, unprotected by the usual great numbers present in their group. In the vain attempt to find their way back to safety, they highlighted themselves precariously against the moonlit rocks.

A fleeting silhouette flashed across one of the rocky crests. It provided the bison with but a brief warning that something in their immediate environment had just changed. Something lethal lurked in the darkness, and that something was about to emerge from hiding.

As the bison turned to look to the ridge, where now only stars flickered in the night sky, six hundred pounds of bone and muscle struck the larger of the two bison, sinking its seven-inch fangs into its victim's throat and knocking the hairy beast to the ground with enough force to crush most of its ribcage. The bison's massive muscles quaked uncontrollably as its mighty heart sorrowfully surrendered to the inevitable, and it gave up the struggle to survive. The bison died almost instantly under the attack of the stealthy killing machine, its eyes screaming silently in horror as the life faded from its eyes.

Sheer panic instantly overcame the second bison. It charged off into the darkness and ran full steam into a nearby tar pit. Howling in terror, it struggled wildly. Its unforgiving foe mercilessly enveloped it, and it sank helplessly into the murky tomb below.

Daytona, an exquisitely cunning, orange and white lion, voraciously tore at the flesh of its kill. His golden eyes and rounded ears scanned the horizon vigilantly for any scavengers that might look for an easy meal. It would be wise for them to look elsewhere.

Though the lion often lived together in a pride, they always hunted alone. It had been three days since Daytona had left the pride to hunt for food, three days locating the prize.

††††

Across the valley from where Daytona was feeding, Smilodon was leading a hunting party. Unlike Daytona, these lions set their sights on ambushing an entire bison herd.

Typically alone on the hunt, the lion-kind, driven by instinct, would attack only one of their prey, only enough to satisfy their immediate need for food. This night, however, under the leadership of Smilodon and filled with some insatiable rage, they had united to hunt together as a group.

Something had changed. Killing for killing's sake was not a sign of the Creator's creation, but a telltale of evil. Their instincts now told them to work together to kill all the bison, whether or not they needed them for food.

Mansen, Bestia's shadowy ambassador from Omentia, had always taken joy in causing chaos, death, and destruction. He had followed evil's bidding and successfully sought and summoned the pack of lions, successfully culling them to the side of darkness.

The demons' plans for the lions did not end with the bison, but the time for that purpose had not yet come. Overwhelmed with blood lust, the demons that possessed these killing machines could not contain themselves. They drove the pride of thirty-plus lions, led by Smilodon, the biggest and strongest cat, into a killing frenzy.

When it was done, the carnage on the plain was appallingly clear. The sun rose to reveal that the lion pride had mercilessly slaughtered the entire herd of bison. The bloodthirsty puppets, controlled by their new evil hosts, had torn young and old alike to pieces.

Temporarily pacified by the decimation of the bison herd, the demons within reveled in their power over the beasts. However, they soon realized, after the fact, that they had wasted much of the life sustaining meat that the bison could have provided the lions. Most of it lay rotting on the grassy plains before them. Panic among the demons set in as they recognized their blunder in destroying the lion's primary food source. "How will we sustain our fanged pawns? What will be their alternative food source?"

Bestia answered their questions. "Do not be afraid, my dark comrades," his voice hissing in the never world. "Soon we will eat tastier meat. Soon we will dine on the flesh of men!"

Pleased with his success thus far, Mansen watched the powerful creatures from a secluded place. Karyan had equipped him well with the dark words of control, and these beasts would assist in the conquest of Adonia. The next component of his mission would soon begin.

Once finished gorging on their victims, the lion pride slept amidst the blood and gore of their kill. Mansen rested, and the demons plotted their next move.

†††

For thousands of years, they ruled the Strange Lands. Since the fall of man, the curse of sin, and the birth of the carnivores, no beast struck as much fear in the hearts of the creatures that roamed upon the earth as they did. The most menacing predator of all God's created creatures still in existence; this predator knew no threat but that of man. Men had not seen its colony for so long that man thought of them as legend only. Man was wrong.

With unequaled cunning but for that of man, they had hidden themselves from those who would hunt them down, concealing themselves deep within the rocks below the earth during the day and exposing themselves to the light of the moon alone. They carried the carcasses of their victims below the earth for consumption, leaving no trace of their presence but the transient and piercing screams of their victims as they ferried them away into the darkness of the night — snuffing out their lives like candles in the wind.

No indigenous predators threatened them in the cold dungeons below the earth in which they dwelled. The ancient raptor had once been their truest rival. The great raptors, hunting in mighty congregations, had devoured a similar prey, contending with them daily for food. Not anymore. The great raptors, like so many other carnivorous species that had survived the great deluge by the grace of God alone, had never regained the strength of their original numbers. They, like so many other ancient predators, had subsequently neared extinction.

And so it was initially for the giant, flying lizards. Hunters had hunted down and killed most of the remnant of their species after the great deluge, before their numbers could truly thrive. Hounded relentlessly and starving, the great flying lizards had nearly vanished — nearly.

A couple of their species, formidable enough to deter potential predators and subsisting on the plentiful foliage of the planet, had survived and even flourished. By taking refuge deep below the earth, they avoided the fate of their fellows who stayed on the surface. Uncontested, the endless caverns below the Strange Lands provided the precious seclusion needed to hide the existence of their kind, as well as the ample storage space to store their nocturnal culling. Over the centuries, their numbers continued to grow larger and larger.

They dwelled deep below the rocks by day. The caverns provided the moist, chilly environment required to keep their dense, scaly skin flexible; their enormous bodies cool; and their oversized and light sensitive eyes, keenly optimized for nocturnal hunting, protected from the harsh, direct rays of the daytime sunlight. The many layers of rock between the surface and their pitch-black lodges below also provided quiet solace from the day-to-day bustle of life on the exterior of their rocky fortress. In the cold still of the caves they slept, only the sound and caustic smell of their breathing and the occasional burst of fire from a dreaming tannin disturbed the lethal tranquility of the lightless chambers in which they rested, marking this place as unwelcome to any visitor that might consider otherwise or accidentally stumble within.

A mature tannin, standing on its hindquarters, could easily reach twelve feet in height. In flight, its stature became even more foreboding, with both a wingspan and a total length of well over twenty feet. Its razor-sharp claws, jagged teeth, and powerful tail were as formidable a threat as that of any remaining in all the creation, but its fire-breath truly gave it an edge over any adversary. Able to propel a biochemically produced flame from its mouth, the tannin could strike an enemy before most foes could bring their weapons to bear.

At dusk each evening they awoke from their deep sleep to rise as one from the secluded entrance of their den and search the countryside for food, taking what they needed from the surface dwellers above.

Sanger had spent weeks searching the Strange Lands for any sign of the ancient beast. Guided by the whispers of demons and the stories of wanderers who had reported sightings of strange lights in the night sky and occasional fires caused by 'lightning' on cloudless nights, Sanger had tracked them down to this place, the entrance to their hidden burrow.

Sanger targeted her attack on their leader, the first and most powerful tannin to emerge from the caverns. She spoke the words of darkness and cast the spell on the creature.

I shall call you Draken in honor of my master of darkness.

"Master, these are truly magnificent beasts and will do well to annihilate the weak and inferior Adonians. The Adonians refuse to bend their knee to us, the superior race upon the earth. We will rid the planet of those worthless and wretched ones and rule over it forever!"

Sanger had been told that the others, driven by instinct, would follow the example set by this dominant one. As Sanger watched, she saw it was true.

Draken broke off from his previous course and circled around, momentarily blocking the moon's rays as he passed over Sanger and landed on a nearby ridge overlooking a swampy bog. The other tannins followed until they all came to rest alongside Draken on the ridge, forming an eerie silhouette against the moonlit clouds in the sky far behind them.

†††

Though the prideful demons truly believed that the Master of all time and space did not know their schemes, the protectors of the faithful observed all that was taking place below them in the dark filled fog of the Strange Lands.

"The great dragon summons his kind to emerge from the deep and do his bidding."

"Surely the day rapidly approaches for which the Master kept these creatures alive upon the earth. Though they are no doubt terrifying to his children below, the Master will glorify himself through them."

"Indeed."

The reply echoed through the dimensions as the living beings moved from one place to another and to the next.

"Indeed."

CHAPTER 38

WEIPHAL AND TORO

✝✝✝

Amidst the chaos that was their parents' marriage, Toro and Weiphal had spent much of their childhood with Truin, Christina, and their seven cousins. In their Uncle Truin's house, they had learned about the true God. They had grown strong in the knowledge of the Lord, and the Lord was with them.

When the time had come for them to set out on their own, the sons of Ka'el had settled in the Strange Lands of South Adonia. They, like their father, had grown big and strong, and having heard of their father's many exploits as a young man, were eager to find adventures in the wild and untamed lands to the south. Adventure they had found.

Toro and Weiphal had witnessed so many amazing creatures during their exploration of the Strange Lands. They had both learned to enter each new experience with their eyes wide open, awed and amazed at the diversity in God's creation, searching for God's purpose in their lives, and eagerly expecting the unexpected.

Though they had both experienced many amazing things in southern Adonia, their experiences with the gorn and the wolf had stood out as the most special. The bonds Weiphal and Toro had formed with these two species of creature were phenomenal. And yet, right from the beginning, these bizarre experiences had seemed destined to be.

Their Uncle Truin had always said that there were no accidents. This had led Toro and Weiphal to wonder.

Perhaps Uncle Truin is right. Maybe our bonds with these creatures are not by accident at all. What if God has meant for them to happen, actually directed that they happen? What if there is a special purpose that will come from these bonds?

It was not much of a stretch to think that God had intended them to have a special relationship with the gorn and the wolf that inhabited these lands. Perhaps God would use these relationships for his purpose and glory in the future.

They, like every other young man that has ever walked the planet, wished they had some superhuman power or ability. The ability to communicate and control such magnificent beasts would have been an awesome ability to have!

Weiphal and Toro each embarked on a journey to test their ability to communicate with the special creatures that had crossed their paths, aiming to establish stronger relationships with them. They sought the wolf and the graptor and on various occasions tried communicating with them in a variety of ways. They tried to influence them, direct their behavior, and get them to accomplish certain tasks. However, no matter what they tried, they could not make the creatures do their bidding.

Initially, their inability to control the actions of these magnificent beasts and harness the power that lived with them caused them great frustration. But soon, both Toro and Weiphal could understand these things properly.

Certainly, these creatures had helped them in their time of need. It was not, however, something they had done that had brought about the interventions. True, it was a superhuman act that had transpired. Indeed, even a supernatural act. God himself had intervened superhumanly and supernaturally to work his will.

Any desire to exploit these creatures for their own benefit, for their own plan, would simply be wrong. Instead, the Creator alone should use these creatures to influence the events and outcomes desired for his created world and the execution of his omniscient plan, rather than for any individual human's flawed vision of how things should be.

Toro and Weiphal realized they did not have the wisdom to direct these creatures. It would be better for the power to remain in God's hands, for his glory and for the completion of his plans, rather than for those with limited understanding to unwisely use it for their own personal glory.

Further, Toro and Weiphal realized they had true superhuman powers at their disposal, powers greater than any they could think of acquiring — faith and prayer. Truly, with their faith firmly rooted in an all-powerful God who heard and answered their prayers, a God who loved them dearly, nothing could threaten them or affect them without his permission. And if their loving God willed it, they willed it too.

Toro and Weiphal shared their wisdom with Truin and his sons. Though readily accepting the truth that the creatures of the land were not under their control, they remembered how God had used them to protect the faithful, and they remained open to the signs and signals that these creatures might send them. Always watchful, they observed the creatures and gained knowledge from their observations.

"Our God works in mysterious ways."

††††

The living beings watched and were pleased.

"Their eyes are open."

"Unlike the Omentians who believe they control the beasts, the faithful understand that God's creation belongs to him and that it acts under his will."

"They add wisdom to their knowledge."

"Yes, unlike the others who thirst for power and fall victim to the deceiver's lies, these thirst for service and understanding. They see the truth."

Chapter 39

Always My Son

†††

As was his habit, Truin rose as the sun was just breaking over the mountains and sat in the early morning rays of sunlight as they warmed the porch overlooking Blue Lake. Beginning his morning devotions, he echoed the words from the book of Psalms.

In the morning, O Lord, you hear my voice; in the morning I lay my requests before you and wait in expectation.

When Truin was a young man, he had often wondered if the Lord was listening to his prayers. Many times, Truin just could not see how the Lord was working in his life. At other times, like when he had suffered the devastating injuries in the forest, Truin had not only felt like God wasn't listening, but even as if God had abandoned him entirely.

But now, having lived long enough to see the Lord answer so many of his prayers, it was easy for Truin to be sure that the Lord was not only listening, but that he cared deeply and interceded directly in the lives of his children. God didn't always answer every prayer exactly the way Truin would have desired, but the way the Lord worked things out, always turned out to be much better and much grander than Truin could ever have planned or imagined.

For example, through the most traumatic event of Truin's life thus far, the tragedy of the forest accident, God had blessed Truin's life in several ways. Truin had learned to trust in God for all things and to depend totally on God. After all, it was only through God's miraculous intervention that Truin had survived, recovered, and been able to live a healthy life. In addition, Truin had grown much closer to his sister, Elin, during his long recovery. He thanked God daily for his sister and all that she now meant to him.

Truin had matured spiritually through his accident and recovery. This maturity had positively affected Truin's character. Christina had made it well known that it was Truin's qualities of humility, empathy, and fervent trust in God that had drawn her to him. In retrospect, God had turned a terrible tragedy into a series of tremendous blessings, and a much wiser Truin was now the first to admit that he would not trade the past, not even the devastating accident in the forest, for anything.

Truin prayed earnestly, knowing a loving and all powerful God heard his prayers, cared for him, and was more than willing to shower him with blessings. Truin waited in eager anticipation for these blessings to be revealed.

However, one unfortunate outcome of the forest event remained; the broken relationship between Truin and Ka'el had never mended. Ka'el continued, after all the years that had passed, to blame himself for Truin's handicap and deformity. Despite Truin's repetitive claims that he no longer saw his injuries as handicaps and his passionate pleas for Ka'el to forget it, Ka'el could not get past his feeling of responsibility for the accident. Every time Ka'el saw Truin, he saw Truin's loss. Ka'el continuously relived the accident in his mind, able to see nothing but his own failures. The passage of time only made the unresolved feelings after the accident worse, and now, the memories had taken on a life of their own, forming an impenetrable wall that might separate the brothers forever.

Even with all of Adonia being imperiled by the impending Omentian invasion, Ka'el remained secluded, purposefully cutting himself off from the family and from his duties to serve in the defense of Adonia. There was no doubt in Truin's mind that Tala had something to do with Ka'el's resistance to serve in the Adonian Guard, as well as Ka'el's feelings that he had let the family down in his choice of a wife.

This day, as Truin sat on his porch overlooking the rolling hills of the countryside and the families of geese gliding over the still, blue waters of the lake, Truin could not help but remember his childhood days with Ka'el, his best friend.

How did everything get so messed up? How did it come this far? Oh, how I miss my brother!

As he had done so many times before, he brought his heartfelt pleas to the Lord in prayer.

"Please almighty God, save my brother? Bring him back to us? Use him for your service? You, Oh Lord, are faithful!"

And then, as he sat quietly, listening for God's reply, a still, small voice spoke to his heart. "You need to go to your brother. He needs you."

Alone at dawn, on her knees at the window of the tallest tower of Castle Armon, Evelin prayed to the Lord God Almighty.

Eve had been remembering her son Ka'el and what he used to say to her and Truin every night when they put him to bed. "Sleep tight, don't let the bedbugs bite. God bless you, say your prayers, don't forget, pleasant dreams, kiss me two times, and tell me when you're in bed."

Ka'el, her little boy, always needed so much love.

All that guilt he is holding inside now, for so many things. It must be eating him up, and he must be starving for love.

Her heart was breaking for him. As she prayed, God set it on her heart that she needed to go visit Ka'el, and as she rose to her feet, Truin arrived.

"Mother, Ka'el needs us."

"Yes, he does. We leave immediately."

Within the hour, Evelin and Truin were on their way to see Ka'el

†††

Evelin and Truin arrived at Ka'el's cottage, surprising Tala with their unannounced visit. Tala had been taking advantage of Ka'el's absence, as she so often did, by working on some secret words she should surely not have been toying with. Tala, expressing clear dissatisfaction at the interruption of her session, greeted the two coldly at the cottage door.

"Ka'el is working in the fields," Tala informed them, not too happy about the untimely visit and hoping the added trouble of needing to track down Ka'el would give the two cause to abandon their quest and return home.

"No trouble, I'll go find him?" Truin took off his cloak, laid it on the table, and headed out the door.

"Do you mind if I wait here with you, Tala?" Evelin was very uncomfortable.

Tala replied, poorly feigning an interest in visiting with Evelin. "No, not at all."

Evelin stayed with Tala and made small talk while Truin rode his stallion, Ashwin, into the fields to find Ka'el.

Soon after, Truin found Ka'el working the crops under a midday sun.

"Brother!" He cried, when he saw Ka'el.

He startled Ka'el — but once he saw who was approaching, Ka'el was both elated and apprehensive. He didn't know what to make of his brother's visit.

Truin dismounted Ashwin. "Brother, it is so good to see you!"

"And you. Is everything alright?"

"As alright as it can be with Omentia threatening to invade us at any moment." Truin offered Ka'el some fresh water, and Ka'el accepted it gratefully. "Mother and I wanted to come and see you. We both felt we needed to, so here we are."

"Mother is here?"

"Yes, she is waiting at the cottage with Tala."

The idea of Evelin and Tala chatting alone did not give Ka'el a warm, cozy feeling, and his demeanor showed it.

"We had better get back there then." Ka'el was a bit agitated as he dropped his shovel and headed toward his horse.

"It will be alright, Ka'el. I just want to talk with you a few minutes alone, if that would be acceptable."

"Well, alright."

The two brothers sat down beneath a large oak tree on a hill over-looking southeastern Chastain and the Dark Sea far in the distance. They talked. Actually, Truin did most of the talking, while Ka'el listened quietly.

"No one can know the limits or mysteries of God. They are higher than the heavens and deeper than the grave. What can we know of his plans? What could our puny minds fathom?"

Ka'el gazed out over the fields. Ka'el was listening to his brother, but didn't really want to show it; his pride had a problem with his younger brother lecturing him about anything.

Truin knew he had few opportunities to bridge the divide that had grown so large between them, so he went right to the point.

"Ever since that day in the forest, our relationship, our friendship, has not been the same. Everything changed that day. We are no longer like brothers, but like strangers."

Ka'el's gaze moved to his feet.

"It wasn't your fault. There was nothing you could have done. In fact, if it weren't for you, I wouldn't have survived. You carried me all the way back home in time to save me. You saved me!"

Ka'el's countenance became very rigid, like stone. He had thought about this countless times over the years and had always come to the same conclusion. It was his fault. And the guilt had built a mighty wall, strong and high, that would not easily fall.

"Who knows the mind of God? Who is his counselor? Look at all the good that has come to me out of this tragedy. There is no reason for you to feel any guilt over that day."

Ka'el accepted Truin's words, but the truth of the matter was that the forest tragedy was not the entire reason for the division between them.

The breach had begun that day in the forest, but it had grown substantially wider with the family's non-acceptance of Tala.

For years, Ka'el had listened to Tala express her feelings and perceptions of how Truin and his family had rejected her, how they had wronged both of them. At first Ka'el had tried to convince Tala it wasn't true, that it was just a misunderstanding. But over the years, hearing the words repeatedly, they eventually rang true. With no counter argument available, Ka'el accepted Tala's point of view, and soon after, he bought in to it hook, line, and sinker.

As Truin laid bare his heart to Ka'el, he could not know that Ka'el's heart remained deeply secured behind a fortress of steel within a mountain of rock. Ka'el's now perverted view of how cruelly the family had treated Tala and in contrast, how readily they had accepted Christina, blocked any progress Truin's pleas might have made to reach the inner dungeon where Ka'el's heart now dwelled. And Ka'el was not ready to admit his anger or his jealousy to Truin. He just wanted Truin to go away and leave him in his misery.

"I miss you Ka'el."

Tears formed in both men's eyes. Part of Ka'el wanted to give in to Truin's appeal for reconciliation. He wanted to, but there were too many locked doors between his cell and the outer courts where Truin stood. He just couldn't get there. There was so much anger, pride, jealousy, and time between them now. Part of him wanted to give in, but a greater part of him refused.

"And God still has great things planned for you. I know he does. Let God take away your guilt, give you peace, and show you what his plan is for you."

Truin's words struck a sour chord with Ka'el.

Still has great things planned for me? What does that mean? Have I not been doing great things? Is my little brother lecturing me on greatness?

Where moments before a gentle softness had showed in Ka'el's eyes, heaviness like a fresh foot of wet snow now fell over Ka'el's face, his eyebrows furled, and his face turned, once again, to stone.

"I never gave up on you, brother. I pray for you every day and —"

Before Truin could finish, Ka'el interrupted. "Maybe we should get back. Mother is probably running out of things to talk about."

The bitter harshness in Ka'el's voice caught Truin by surprise.

"Ok, but —" Truin tried once again, but before he could finish —

"Really, we need to go." Ka'el looked straight into Truin's eyes. "We are done here." He got up and mounted his horse. "Are you coming?"

"Yes, I'm coming." Truin said, noticeably saddened by the obvious setback to what, for a moment, looked like it might be a warming in the years of ice that had accumulated on their friendship.

Truin mounted Ashwin, and the two brothers rode swiftly back to Ka'el's cabin.

†††

The visit between Evelin and Tala had not gone well. Evelin had given her best effort to opening up a dialogue with Tala, but the years of silence between them had created a very limited number of topics that were open for discussion. By the time Ka'el and Truin arrived, they were no longer speaking.

When Ka'el came through the door of the cottage, Evelin rose immediately to her feet and rushed to him.

"Ka'el!" she exclaimed, her mind flashing back to a time and place when Ka'el was still her little boy, not a grown man with a family of his own.

"Ka'el, my son!"

Evelin hugged her first-born son.

Tala grimaced at the sight and mumbled something under her breath.

Ka'el, cold at first to his mother's touch, gradually softened and returned her hug.

"Mother."

After all too brief a moment of reconnecting, of sharing again the warmth and love that is forever unique to a mother and her son,

Ka'el looked up and caught the demeaning scowl of his wife. Knowing nothing much good could come from a prolonged visit, he said softly but firmly, "Thanks for coming to see me, mother." Ka'el looked at Truin. "But I think it is best if you are getting back to Armon. The sun will soon set, and there is much danger on the roads these days."

Truin took his mother by the arm and gently pulled her from Ka'el. "Come along, Mother, Ka'el is right. We should go now."

Evelin looked up longingly and lovingly into Ka'el's eyes as she followed Truin to the door. Her heart was breaking, and it was now clear to her that Ka'el's imprisoned heart was breaking, too. She could see it in his eyes.

"See you soon, Mother."

"God bless you and keep you, my son."

As Ka'el watched Truin and Evelin leave his home, Tala secretively covered Truin's cloak with a blanket.

How opportune.

CHAPTER 40

THE GREAT STRUGGLE

†††

"The Great Struggle continues."

Lights of every color imaginable and unimaginable flashed through and across dimensions that men would never see.

"A time of testing for the elect is at hand."

Their blurred shapes streaked across the horizonless heavens, temporarily sharpening only as they passed near each other. Their lightning speed slowed just long enough for them to commune with one another. They communicated through a language of light — unspoken, yet clearly understood, instead of using words as commonly recognized.

"The enemy advances."

Light emanated gloriously in all directions from their multicolor wings, as if beamed through thousands of invisible prisms.

"And the Master reigns! The Omnipotent One will show his power."

The images blurred into a mix of color, then sharpened once again as the paths between the created universe and the heavens converged.

"What of those below? What of the light?"

The eyes of the brightest living being flashed fiery gold as he answered.

"The chosen will stand. Light will endure. Light will remain in the created world until the end of time."

†††

In the depths of the demon-dominated dungeons of darkness, the devil and his demonic doers of depravity and destruction further devised their depraved delusions and devilish designs to complete their conquest of the creation.

"It is almost all ours, master!" One of the lesser demons did not realize his given place in the pecking order of the demonic host.

"It is almost mine!" Belial lashed out, latching onto the inferior beast with his powerful claws. Mercilessly tearing at the careless demon, Belial ripped the wings from its body and thrust it asunder. The frayed fiend shrieked in agony in the backdrop as Satan turned away from the pitiful creature and spoke to his lieutenants, those awaiting his instructions, now quite quiet in the shadows.

"My ultimate conquest of the created world is almost complete. Soon, the entire world will be mine, and darkness will rule the land forever. I will reign over it all!"

The ghastly ghouls, only their beady, red eyes clearly visible in the dim light of the forsaken pit in which they met, smirked and cackled in delight. Sulfuric fumes in the pit blended hideously with their repugnant stenches to produce a noxious odor so repulsive that the demons themselves noted it and were summarily distressed.

"In their minds, the corporeal fools who do our bidding believe themselves to be powerful and in control of their spoils. They think the material world of sight is all there is to be concerned with, all that they need to fear. I will use their lust for power against them and the spoils of their forays to further enslave them to my desires, all to the furtherance of my dominion. And soon, they will discover the meaning of genuine fear. They will rot with me in the bowels of hell!"

The dark one smoldered as an intense shade of crimson. Centuries of combat with the warriors of light had grossly disfigured his massive body and enormous wings. Covered with rotting sores, oozing putrid pus, he pulsated wildly, as if convulsing. Huge varicose veins that covered his torso and legs swelled until they looked as if they might burst. His mammoth wings fully extended and then crashed closed, sending a powerful reverberation through the decayed air in the chamber that blasted many of the smaller demons against the slimy walls of the pit.

"Finish it now, my fiendish friends," the father of lies shrieked, "and I will make you princes of my kingdom forever!" The bloodied and torn carcass of the demon he had so savagely discharged moments before roasted behind him on the cavern floor. Its venomous juices oozed from its body into puddles of bitter fluids already pooled there, the noxious vapors of which rose steadily to fill the expanse of the hellish chamber to the depraved delight of the pit's master.

At his command, a horde of demons took to flight to do their master's bidding and enslave an unsuspecting world.

CHAPTER 41

ASSAULT FROM THE SEA

†††

As the sun set over the eastern horizon of the Dark Sea, countless warships sailed from a growing shadow that stretched its long tentacles westward. The shadow's destination was Adonia, a land still blessed by the presence of the light.

Karyan had fully used Heath's almost limitless supply of ships; Parlantis' historic knowledge and expertise in land battle; and Omentia's newfound power in the dark arts to assemble and direct an attack force like that unparalleled in history.

No man, no country had stood against him, since he had discovered the dark ways. Soon, he would crush Adonia and end forever any threat to his rule over the lands. He would establish a global empire and force it to pay homage; homage to the ones who even now directed his thoughts and orchestrated his actions.

His multi-pronged attack from Heath, Omentia, and Parlantis would hit Adonia simultaneously in the north, east, and south. Even if the Adonians had prepared for the upcoming assault, his dark horde would vastly outnumber them and outflank them on all sides.

Karyan himself commanded the Omentian armada, though few knew for sure if he was actually present with the fleet or if he had remained in Omentia, choosing instead to direct the invasion through some dark magic. He sailed at the rear of the formation, seeing no need to endanger the brains of this operation by leading from the front and exposing himself to untold dangers; dangers from Adonia and from within his own army. Indeed, the less his minions knew of his plans, the better. He had given his commanders explicit instructions on how to proceed, and further, he had placed several of his closest disciples with them to aid in carrying out his intent.

His dark army knew all too well who ultimately directed this fight, whether in person or through his appointed commanders, and if ever he heard that any man had hesitated in following one of his orders, he would deal with it immediately and mercilessly. He ensured immediate and merciless consequences for anyone who hesitated to follow his orders, as evidenced by the severed and decaying heads of three of his lieutenants perched upon spikes on the deck of his ship. His was not a democracy, and if any man were to forget it, even momentarily, it would be the last thing that man ever did. Compassion and understanding were for the weak.

Karyan's fleet sailed on through the darkness of the night. The dark storm clouds to the east blocked out all the light from the stars in the night sky behind them, but to the west, the starlight shone magnificently, guiding the menacing fleet onward toward their target.

Karyan had composed the fleet of men from all the lands he had conquered thus far. Though most Omentians would say that they followed Karyan by choice; he, of course, knew better. The Heathians, Parlantians, and Omentians intermingled aboard the ships, with each class having its own responsibilities to perform. The Heathian men performed the sailing operations as they were used to sailing for a living. It wasn't much of a problem being aboard the ship for those who were previous sailors, though the Heathians who had predominately farmed for a living were getting more than a bit stir-crazy aboard the vessels.

The Parlantian men of the fleet were even more stir-crazy and aching for a fight. They were used to being free to roam the land. The compressed conditions aboard the ship were horrifying to them. There was little food to eat, little but wine to drink, and the demon-infested spirits of the dark warriors drove them tirelessly to steal from, to fight with, and even to kill one another. Crazy, bloodthirsty men, hell-bent on committing every dastardly act possible, packed the transports — shoulder-to-shoulder. They could not wait to get off the floating caskets and meet the Adonians on the battle line; the sooner the better.

The Omentians, though not at all used to life aboard a ship, eased their burdens and entertained one another at the same time. They conjured up spells on the Parlantians and Heathians, practicing their dark arts and fanning the flames of division. The demons within them were all too eager to oblige their every whim in this endeavor.

Overall, the Heathians were at the bottom of the social order, with the Parlantian warriors and the Omentian warlocks holding the middle and highest levels of prestige. Unknown to all the men aboard the warships, the demons within them mirrored this hierarchy, holding similar levels of authority and using it to harass those of lesser stature.

Though Karyan's fighting horde was not as unified a fighting machine as he would have liked, it was an army of killers without conscious. To him, this was a military's most important attribute. Karyan knew that once his force hit the shores of resource rich Adonia and swept across its countryside, pillaging the land of all they desired, the infighting among the men would cease.

As they sailed through the darkness, Karyan stood high above his men on a platform to the rear of the ship, gazing out over the dark expanse ahead. His long, black hair and dark crimson robe fluttered behind him in the wind. Deep in thought, a smile crept across his face.

Soon I will rule the world, and my power will grow exponentially. I will never have to fear anyone or anything again.

†††

Over the horizon, the Sirenian cut through the shallows just off the northeast tip of Delvia. Captain Mikole was used to this mission, patrolling the coast of Adonia and looking for any sign of impending attack, while precariously dodging the treacherous rocks that sporadically lie just below the waves.

Any mistake in piloting the Sirenian in these waters could and would spell disaster for her crew as hitting the rocks was sure to split the hull of any craft wide open and toss the inhabitants into the shallow and tumultuous surf, where they too would slam against the rocks like fragile Heathian china — bludgeoned, and torn to pieces.

Mikole loved the challenge of navigating these waters as well as providing the first line of defense to the Adonian Guard. Though she was a small craft, the Sirenian was sure to outmaneuver most anything the Omentians could muster, and with Mikole at the helm, who could hope to keep up with her?

Mikole's crew was similarly confident in its abilities. The crew had been together for seven years, and performed like none other in the newborn Adonian fleet. Captain PJ, appointed as the Adonian Fleet Commander, recognized the crew's distinction and placed the utmost trust in Mikole and his crew. Captain PJ had given Mikole and his crew the responsibility of ensuring the Omentians did not surprise Adonia. Mikole and his crew took this responsibility seriously.

At any sign of Omentian aggression, the Sirenian was to fire a volley of flaming arrows into the sky, signaling watchmen on shore of the danger. A chain of watchmen, spread across the ridgelines and various other higher elevations about Adonia, would then light a series of signal fires alerting the Adonian Guard that the Omentian invasion was underway.

As Mikole and the crew of the Sirenian honed their maneuvering skills in the early morning rays of a rising sun, the lookouts scanned the shadows of the eastern horizon, ever vigilant of the imminent threat that lurked there. The steady stream of birds radiating out from the lands to the east continued its massive migration, but there were no other visual signs of trouble. Though, in the back of their minds, the lookouts knew the Omentians would someday come, wishful thinking ruled the day. Each man hoped, for the sake of his family and his comrades, that the invasion would somehow never arrive.

Completely unaware that their worst nightmare was just over the horizon, the crew of the Sirenian enjoyed their last patrol.

Chapter 42

Fog of War

†††

"Land!"

The Omentian scout cried out from his eagle nest position high above the mast of the lead ship in the Omentian first wave of fast attack vessels.

"Land ahead!"

The eastern hills of Delvia had just come into view; behind them and to the north, the faintest outline of the mountains of Chastain.

"Land ahead, Commander," the relieved lieutenant, second in command, echoed to the grizzly Omentian Commander.

Crastis the Cruel, the Omentian Fleet Commander, found satisfaction in their timing, which was good because any dissatisfaction would have resulted in significant pain for his crew.

It was Crastis' responsibility to get the Omentian attack force to Adonia on time. Of this, his lord, Karyan, had been very clear. Crastis habitually transferred this heavy responsibility to his crew. He held them responsible for any failure, whether or not they controlled the circumstances of that failure. Had the winds, the currents, or the enemy hindered their progress, he would have directed the full magnitude of his displeasure upon them. None of them wanted Crastis' displeasure directed in their direction; Crastis was merciless.

The lieutenant was feeling unusually relaxed by their successful journey thus far. "It is such a clear day. Won't they see us coming?"

Crastis glared at the lieutenant in response to the question. "That won't be a problem!"

The lieutenant, having insinuated that he could somehow offer any thought or idea useful to his battle-seasoned commander, instantly realized his error. At once, his demeanor turned from relaxation to fear. Staggering backwards, he imprisoned his gaze on the deck of the ship to show that he recognized the seriousness of his unforgivable error.

"Yes commander, of course, I didn't mean to —"

"Do you think there are any sharks in these waters?" Crastis casually questioned another lieutenant who was standing with them on deck.

The second lieutenant, eager for any opportunity to rise further in rank and authority, was quick to answer. "Yes Commander Crastis, I am sure there are."

Crastis considered showing his crew, yet again, the unpredictability of his ruthlessness, but decided against it at the last moment. There were more important matters at hand, and he didn't want the crew being handicapped by another brutal, yet enjoyable, incident.

Instead, Crastis had another duty to perform, one he neither savored nor looked forward to performing. Karyan had instructed Crastis that at the first sight of land, he must call Karyan's onboard minion to the helm.

Crastis, previously a notorious pirate, did not appreciate ever being told that he had to do anything. This especially was true with being told what to do on his own ship. However, though no doubt still a threatening figure to his crew, Karyan had become more influential than Crastis. His instinct for self-preservation guided him to comply with the order he had received.

Crastis gave the command. "Summon the witch!"

Four of Crastis' men, after a brief hesitation, rushed as one to beckon the evil-one that had been more than happy to remain in dark seclusion below deck, until her time had come.

Moments later, the four emerged, escorting the hooded sorceress to their captain.

There was no need for Crastis to explain to Karyan's dark disciple why she had beckoned her. The invasion of Adonia was about to begin, and her job was to delay the invasion force's detection and give the Omentians the advantage.

Her beauty immediately overwhelmed the men present when they removed the hood that had so well veiled her womanly features. Crastis saw her long, dark hair fall over her thin pale shoulders and reveal just enough skin to fuel his passions. Her narrow facial features, full red lips, high cheekbones, and dark green eyes mesmerized him, instantly rendering him and all the crew-members present dumbstruck.

A master at deception, the men had no inkling that she appeared to them each exactly as they most wanted her to appear, different to each man, according to his innermost desire. None of them saw her as she truly was. This was her spell upon them.

In reality, the evil that had taken control of her had terribly disfigured her ever since she had first surrendered herself to the ancient fire. Once a lovely girl to the eyes, she had so envied the most beautiful in her midst that she had sold her soul to be just like them. The fire-beast had assisted her in acquiring the ability to appear as she did through the casting of spells on all those around her. However, when not engaged in conjuring up the enchantment, she stayed covered; her burned flesh and most revolting appearance, making her a pariah to all. She, therefore, needed to hide in darkness whenever the enchantment was not in play.

This was not the witch's only power. Demons had further empowered her with the ability to influence not only her appearance, but also the appearance of extensive areas of her surroundings. She had used this ability to aid Karyan's armies in their recent campaigns in Parlantis and Heath. Again, she spoke the words of her dark master's deception.

As she spoke, Crastis' ship and the rest of the invasion force following it became cloaked in a thin fog, indiscernible at a distance from the sea on which they sailed.

Crastis and the others were dumbstruck. They had heard stories of such things, but had doubted their veracity. Who could stand against the mighty arm of Omentia's strike forces and the dark forces that assisted them in this campaign of conquest? Surely, a small band of refugees that, but a handful of years prior, had fled Omentia to a land of refuge in the west could not hope to repel them. Surely not!

The fog settled over the waters in their path, and Mirare, once again, carefully replaced the heavy hood over her head, shrouding her dreadful visage with a cloak impenetrable to the eyes of those around her. Convinced by the dark demons that controlled her she must maintain, by her own power, the cloak of fog that covered the Omentian fleet, she immediately withdrew to the dark chamber below where she spoke the words of enchantment repeatedly, praying to the dark angels of death that ravenously gnawed upon her soul.

Crastis could barely see the ships in his own flotilla. Though they followed but a mere thousand feet behind them, they had all but disappeared from his view. There was no way the Adonians could see the threat that approached.

This is good. This is very good.

As the warships stormed westward, their crews prepared to go ashore and meet the unsuspecting Adonians.

✝✝✝

There was no warning.

As if lulled into a daze by the soothing songs of mythical sirens, the crew of the Sirenian was suddenly and completely disoriented. Where once a clear and bright morning had allowed the Sirenian and its crew a steady and brisk clip through the jagged rocks that dotted one of the narrowest passages off Delvia's eastern shore, a sudden blanket of thick mist and fog encapsulated the ship, instantly turning the relaxed sentiment of the crew into one of panicked desperation; the ordinary patrol into the challenge of a lifetime.

Unexpectedly, unable to see what threats lay in the water in front of them, Mikole immediately ordered a full stop, but it was too late. Directly off the bow, lying in wait for the fast attack vessel, like a great shark stalking its prey, was the serrated sea stone that spelled the end of the Sirenian's days.

The Sirenian had wantonly violated these treacherous waters one too many times and now it would feel the unforgiving sea passage's full wrath. The ragged edges of the stealthy guardian of the waters sliced through the hull of the unwelcome trespasser, and the Sirenian disintegrated beneath its crew. Its deck crumbled like a house of cards and its towering masts snapped like twigs in a mighty wind. One by one, the stealthy sentinel cohorts broke Mikole's men like fragile marionettes.

It all happened so fast! Mikole had no time to prepare his crew, men he considered like brothers, for their abrupt ends. Amidst the thunderous crashes of splintering oak, Mikole heard the panicked cries of his brothers being swallowed up by the surf, and the roaring of the waves as they ruthlessly disassembled his greatest passion. The force of the surrounding waters thrust him to the bottom of the sea and pinned him against its floor. Here, in a place and time he could never have foreseen, he fought against all hope for his life. In this moment, a torrent of emotions and thoughts overwhelmed Mikole.

Pamela! My men! Who will keep watch for Adonia? Why is this happening? I have so much more to do. Is this how it was all meant to end? Help!

Pinned beneath a mountain of water, unable to reach the surface for a life-saving gasp of air, powerless to help himself or the men under his command and no longer able to continue the fight by his own strength, Mikole conceded.

God, help me?

Three days later, Mikole washed up on a Delvian beach.

As the sun rose over the distant mountains of Chastain, sending its life force far across the countryside, the warmth of its golden rays reached Mikole's face, and he opened his eyes.

CHAPTER 43

La Gina

†††

"Parlantian!"

The designation of the ships just sighted to the west of the La Gina rang out from the spotter in the crow's nest high above.

"Parlantian, I'm sure of it!"

The entire world knew where Parlantis' allegiance rested. The once great nation of freemen and warriors had fallen to Omentian sorcery and had joined in her mission of siege and conquest to the detriment of all mankind.

Captain PJ and his task force of Adonian Defense ships had taken a position on the eastern side of Adonia, prepared to defend the eastern coast from attack, whether it came from Omentia or Parlantis. They had posted patrols off both the northern and southern coasts to alert him of any attack. In the meantime, PJ had continued to sail up and down the east coast, running drills, and preparing for that inevitable moment when everything would change.

Until that moment, Captain PJ had heard nothing from either the northern or southern patrols, and his spotters had seen absolutely nothing out of the ordinary. With the arrival of the enormous armada of enemy ships, the moment he had been dreading abruptly arrived; change had come, and the change would be brutal.

Captain PJ wasted no time in directing his men.

"Battle stations!"

The men of the La Gina sprang into action, manning the positions and signaling the other ships under Captain PJ's command to do the same.

Since bidding their loved ones farewell and leaving port in Delvia three weeks earlier, the men of the La Gina had been eager for action. Defending Adonia from the Omentian scourge was a noble calling, and each of them, to the last man, considered it an honor to answer the call. The ignorance of battle was bliss.

The call to battle positions filled the men with both excitement and apprehension. They were happy to meet the enemy and do their duty to protect their loved ones and serve their God. However, they knew that doing so could mean that they would never see their wives and children again, at least not in this life.

The men of the La Gina were not afraid to die. They rested securely, knowing that God loved them and would be with them, in life, as well as in death. Death was not the end of their existence any more than leaving the womb of their mother had been the end to their lives. They knew that both transitions — from womb to life and life to God's arms — were beautiful and necessary phases of existence. Death was simply a door, a door to another state of being where they would live forever with a loving God and with those believers in him who had passed faithfully through the door before them. For the faithful, the view of this door posed no threat or cause for fear. Still, none of the men felt the need to rush the last steps through the door of death.

Their lifetime, their time of grace, was in the hands of their God. The timing was not theirs to decide. They hoped they would survive the coming battle and return to their loved ones, to their homes, and too many years of living out their lives in peace and service; there was so much for each of them left to do. But God would decide this day who he would call home, and who he would have remain behind to continue the struggle and accomplish the unforeseen acts of service planned out for them, before the beginning of time, in God's glorious plan; his-story.

The men surrendered the weight of all anxiety about the outcome of the coming struggle to their faithful God, and with it, they shed the weight of hesitation that accompanies unbelieving men into battle.

The men were ready; not through false bravado, but through the trust that accompanied their assurance that a power much greater than themselves, the battle, or even nature itself, was present with them and would direct the fight for their ultimate good. As they readied themselves for war, they were at peace.

The fleet turned to the east to engage the Parlantian armada. Just then, an unexpected turn of events occurred. The enemy ships, along with the entire eastern horizon, disappeared before their very eyes. They were simply gone!

"All stop!" Captain PJ commanded.

The Adonian fleet came to a full stop; ten ships, facing east, line-abreast, with approximately one-mile spacing, dead in the water.

An eerie silence fell over the sea.

Captain PJ looked down the line of Adonian ships, but he could barely see the ship immediately to his south — the ship his deputy, Captain Mellon, commanded. The rest of the ships in the fleet had disappeared entirely from sight, along with everything else in all directions. A heavy fog surrounded the fleet, giving the sensation of being thrust into a fishbowl.

It was indeed a perplexing dilemma, winning a naval battle against a vastly superior force they could not see; but deciding what to do next was easy. Captain PJ had been clear to all the other ship captains that the number one priority, should they learn of an Omentian attack, was to get a warning to the Adonian forces on the mainland.

"Signal torch ready!"

"Ready!" The quick response came from the stern of Captain PJ's ship.

"Fire!"

With his command, one of PJ's archers fired a flaming arrow straight up through the dense fog and high into the sky overhead. The torch remained in view for but a second before disappearing into the fog above them.

PJ and all aboard the La Gina shared the same hope as they quietly watched the light of the signal arrow vanish amidst the cloud that blanketed the fleet;

Please Lord, let the watchers see it.

Perched high on a rocky ridgeline overlooking the eastern plains of Kandish, a lone spotter, covered in heavy furs from head to toe, faithfully watched the coastline for any sign of trouble. A member of Adonia's newly formed signal corps, Mathias, an honorable Chastainian, known by all of his clan as "Caveman" for his strikingly boorish personality, was used to the bitter cold and low levels of breathable air present at the higher mountain elevations.

The Adonian Guard had recruited several mountain men to fill the critical job of warning Adonia of impending attack. Maintaining posts on towering mountain peaks and ridges across Adonia, these men patiently watched and waited for the sign.

Caveman's moment had come. As he deliberately and methodically scanned the eastern horizon, he saw a flaming arrow rise out of a dense fog that had appeared only moments earlier. Almost simultaneously, nine other fiery arrows rose alongside it to form a line of fire across the hazy horizon.

Caveman shot to his feet in nervous excitement, instantly shaking off the sluggishness of the cold-induced lethargy. There was no mistaking the sight. The fleet had sent the signal; the invasion had begun!

Caveman ran to the fifty foot wide pile of wood he had prepared weeks before. He lit his torch and threw it into the pile. It erupted instantly into flames. Within seconds, the fire's long, crimson arms reached up ferociously into the morning sky.

Upon the lofty ridgeline, the warning fire shared its warning for forty-plus miles in all directions. It didn't take long before similar signal fires appeared on both the northern horizon and the south-western horizon. Dozens of others followed them, rapidly spreading the warning across the expanse of Adonia.

The signal made its way to the northern and southern coasts of Adonia within a minute. Soon, all of Adonia would know that the Omentians had launched their offensive. Adonia would respond. The war had begun.

†††

The sky showered arrows of fire.

A moment before, they had fired their warning arrows high into the sky from the Adonian ships of the line, the only physical impediment standing between the Parlantian attack force and the Adonian home-land. PJ and his crew had just watched the flaming arrow from their signaler disappear into the thick cloud above them, when innumerable arrows sliced through the all-encompassing cloud to the east, riddling the La Gina with a fiery hailstorm of destruction. The flaming comets of death skewered themselves into the La Gina, lighting various por-tions of the La Gina's sails and deck aflame.

Captain PJ wasted no time in retaliating. He couldn't see through the thick gray soup all around them, but he could strike back, none-theless. Even though he couldn't see through the thick gray soup all around them, Captain PJ could estimate the distance and direction of the enemy by observing the trajectory of their arrows and making an educated guess. PJ's archers reciprocated in-kind and magnitude. Launching a cluster of deadly arrows back into the cloud, they hoped the arrows would find a fitting destination upon a Parlantian ship.

They did.

PJ could now see a host of faint, red flashes to the south of them. He knew the other ships of the guard were also taking and delivering fire in the same way the La Gina was, though he couldn't tell in any detail how well they were faring.

Aboard the La Gina, the crew was performing valiantly. Men were racing both above and below deck, putting out fires, tending to the injured and dying, resupplying arrows to the archers, and preparing to board any enemy vessel that should emerge from the fog. However, the casualties were mounting, and Captain PJ wasn't sure how long the men could keep up this pace, or how long he could ask them to.

It was like fighting ghosts. Javelins of death emerged from the gray cover that blanketed them, multiple volleys every minute. Although they fought back with everything they had, they could not be certain they were even hitting the Parlantian ships.

Without warning, the Adonian vessel to their south erupted in flames, burning brilliantly through the fog. Like a dying campfire raging against its inevitable demise, the dying ship fed the spark and flame until it was totally consumed. As pieces of the ship disintegrated and fell into the Dark Sea, the distant cries of her crew combined into a heartbreaking wail of pain and sorrow.

The La Gina's crew fought fearlessly for another hour, but by then they had suffered substantial casualties, their sails were ablaze, and they could no longer continue the fight.

Captain PJ was about to give the command to abandon ship when he spotted a Parlantian warship breaking through the fog a thousand feet off the starboard bow. In one last act of defiance and defense of the homeland, Captain PJ gave the order to ram the oncoming enemy ship before it could break through the defensive perimeter of the Adonian Fleet, a perimeter that had now essentially become a barrier of fire.

To the Parlantians' surprise, the La Gina had just enough rudder authority left to bring her around, and more than enough to deliver a lethal punch to the enemy. The two ships fused together; the force of the impact sending everything and everyone aboard both ships into the air and into the sea. As the great ships exploded, burned, and sunk into the depths, they took with them many of those who had survived the initial impact.

Captain PJ, beaten and battered, clung to a large piece of floating debris. He stubbornly held on to a hope that this battle, apparently lost, did not mean overall defeat for Adonia. As the icy waters of the Dark Sea chilled him to the bone, he couldn't help but think of all the men who had just given their lives in Adonia's defense; he worried that their contribution had not proven to be as valuable as Truin and his sons had hoped.

What contribution did we make? Did the fleet even dent the Parlantian attack force? What if all these men have given their lives in vain?

Unknown to Captain PJ, many of the Adonian arrows had indeed found their mark, and the Parlantian force had suffered at the hands of the Adonian Fleet. The Parlantian attack force in the south had lost one-third of their assault vessels, and twenty percent of its fighting force.

As the remaining Parlantian vessels passed eerily through the burning wreckage and thick fog that surrounded Captain PJ and the remaining survivors of the Adonian fleet, Parlantian archers mercilessly took potshots at any Adonian sailors they found still afloat in the deadly waters.

"Take no prisoners!" Lord Crastis' command passed to all the ships in the armada.

"None of the dogs shall live! Kill them all!"

CHAPTER 44

FIRE AND RAIN

†††

The flames rose high into the starry sky.

What had, just moments before, been a clear, cool, and calm summer night had abruptly become a raging inferno. Within seconds, fifty miles of Delvian grain fields were in flames. The smoke was rising hundreds of feet into the night sky, blanketing the stars in fiery red.

The frantic cries and screams for help that echoed relentlessly up and down the agrarian countryside shattered Bigaulf's peaceful sleep.

"Fire! Father, the fields are burning!"

Bigaulf's eyes snapped open like those of a dead man abruptly shocked back to life, and the mountain of a man shot out of his bed like a boulder fired from a catapult. In what seemed like no time, he was running alongside his two sons toward the blazing fields.

"What happened? How could this happen?" As far as the eye could see, the horizon was in flames. They ran to the river for water.

"I saw it, father." Abrahm, his youngest son said as he searched for an ever-diminishing source of air. "It happened instantly. It didn't start and move along the horizon, it started — everywhere! All at once!"

"That is impossible!" Andru, Bigaulf's oldest, replied as they reached the river and filled their buckets. "How could that be?"

In an act of desperation and futility, the men raced with their buckets back towards their home. For a moment, their home was clear of the savage advance of the flames. However, the moment would not last long.

Delvia, the breadbasket of Adonia, was ablaze. Why and how were the key questions. The answers to those questions would have to wait. For now, saving what they could was all that the men could focus on. Up and down the coast, the situation was the same — desperate.

Though the men instinctively knew their efforts were hopeless, they had to save their home. They never even considered their grain fields; it was a foregone conclusion that they were gone.

Unbeknownst to the men of Delvia, the fire was being controlled by a demon via a wizard, and any attempt to evade the fire's terror would prove pointless. As Bigaulf and his sons ran across the open fields toward their home, the winds suddenly changed, redirecting the long talons of blistering fiery flame directly at them.

"Father!" Abrahm fell, hitting the ground hard.

As Bigaulf stopped and turned to see Abrahm's predicament, a large branch hit Andru. Torn from its home by the wind and sent like a lethal projectile through the air, the limb knocked Andru from his feet and instantly unconscious.

Bigaulf stood in the fiery inferno, frozen in time between his two sons, both laying on the ground in desperate need of his help.

Without hesitation, with no thought of his own safety, Bigaulf threw Andru, not a small man himself, over his shoulder and headed back for Abrahm. Reaching Abrahm, Bigaulf hoisted him over his other shoulder.

Then, standing with his two sons in his arms, Bigaulf's priorities changed from saving his home to saving his family. He was instantly thankful that his wife Lydia had gone to Aanot to visit Evelin, saving him the impossible predicament that her still being in their home would have presented.

Bigaulf's choices had evaporated. There was nowhere left to run and nowhere left to turn. The fire had surrounded the men, and the field on which he stood was a tinderbox, ready to go up in flames any second.

Bigaulf recognized the inevitable, but unlike a man defeated, Bigaulf stood tall, his back straight and his head high. Though the heat of the fire and the acrid sting of the thick smoke mercilessly assaulted his senses, he opened his eyes and looked to the sky.

High above him, the fire and black smoke circled, funneling through the caustic air in a deadly torrent sent straight from hell, but through the smoke and the fire, through the sure signs of death that raged against the heavens above him, he saw the bright stars in the night sky, and as he had done so many times before, he praised the God of the heavens.

"Oh Lord, my God, the God of the heavens and the Earth, to you, Oh God, I lift my praise!"

The fire, now moving in to engulf the ground on which Bigaulf stood, would soon consume them in excruciating pain and burn their bodies beyond any recognition.

Bigaulf continued. "My God, I love you, and I thank you for all you have blessed me with. Thank you for my life, for my wife and for my sons. Most of all, thank you for your love."

The heat of the flames burned at his skin. "Take us, Oh God, your humble servants, to be with you in your loving presence or save us from these flames, as only you are able. It matters not to us. We belong to you, and we are yours to do with as you please. Thy will be forever done!"

As the fire engulfed their position, Bigaulf and his sons disappeared in the brilliant light of a thousand flames. The fire swept across the land and consumed their home in but an instant.

For a time, the flame reigned supreme.

†††

Commander Crastis sent him with the landing force to "shock and awe" the enemy, and he used his special talent to do so well — very well indeed.

The Omentian wizard watched with delight and a sense of power as the flames he had birthed across the land of Delvia consumed the men and their home mercilessly. He considered himself to be a god.

However, within an instant, his delusion shattered. As he looked back on the place where he had just watched a farmer and his sons overrun by the flames — his flames — the Omentian wizard could not process what his eyes were telling him.

Within the flames, the three men stood. Yet, the flames did not consume them. They didn't appear to be on fire. They didn't even seem in distress.

He spoke to the Omentian soldiers accompanying him. "How are they not consumed by the fire? How is it they stand?"

The Omentian soldiers beside him saw the men within the fire. They stood like dead men in complete disbelief, terrified at what they were witnessing.

As they watched the three men stand within the flames, they saw what appeared to be others there with them in the fire. Only the outline of the others was visible, and they did not look like human men. They shined in brilliant light, even more radiant than that of the fire that surrounded them, and they spread their multicolored wings over and around the farmer and his sons, protecting them from the burning heat of the flames.

"What matter of magic is this?" Never had the Omentians seen anything like this before. It simply was beyond human reason's ability to grasp.

"This cannot be!"

And yet it was.

Within the fire, Bigaulf and his sons stood in equal amazement at what their God was doing. Instead of feeling fear, like the Omentians were feeling, they felt awe and wonder. The fire was everywhere, all around them, above them, and below them — if that were possible. And yet, they lived. They were not even uncomfortably warm. In fact, the realization of the awesome thing they were experiencing gave them the chills!

They knew God could do great things, though they never expected he would choose to intervene in this manner. What was happening amazed them, but unlike the Omentians, they had no problem believing it.

They watched their home go up in flames, and the men were surprisingly indifferent. All that they knew before, all that they concerned themselves with prior to this event, paled in significance to what was happening to them now. This was just unbelievable!

As the Omentians watched the flames burn up and down the countryside, enormous flashes of light across the crimson sky joined the billows of smoke from the fire. The sound of ten thousand angry drums rumbled with them.

The Omentians wisely withdrew to the cover of the forests of western Delvia. As they did, the sky opened up and released its waters upon the earth below, extinguishing the fires raging beneath it.

The walls of flame soon settled around Bigaulf, Andrew, and Abram, and they were again free to walk through the ashes that were once their home, their fields, and their very livelihood. It was all gone: the house, the barn, the equipment, and the livestock.

Where normally such a tragic event might have psychologically broken them, they emerged as changed men, still astounded by the impossible thing that had just happened to them. Despite the hopeless devastation around them, their spirits filled with warmth and hope.

God had chosen not to spare Delvia completely of this calamity, but God had not stood by passively either. He had limited the extent of the damage by bringing cool rains from a clear night, and he had shown his power by miraculously sparing many lives!

Bigaulf and his sons mournfully grabbed what they could from the charred remains of their home. Then, they hastily set out to help those of their neighbors who they could help and assemble what remained of the Delvian Division as efficiently as possible.

Bigaulf knew his father had to be informed of what had happened here right away and the rest of Adonia had to be alerted that the Omentians had landed in Delvia and were advancing to the west.

As the men headed north and west, toward Aanot, they knew they would never again be the same. The experience had forever reset their concept of reality. A God who not only answered their prayers, but did so undeniably shattered their once superficial, academic, and limited notion of God and how he might intervene in the lives of men. Who would ever believe their account of how God had delivered them?

The Omentians had moved on, thinking the burning of Delvia was complete, and with its destruction, Adonia's critical supply of grain. The knowledge of their presence in Adonia would soon spread across the land. This was acceptable; better than acceptable, it was as the Omentians preferred it.

"Let the Adonians know we are here. Let them hear how the flames consumed Delvia, how they will burn their lands, and how we will bring destruction to all those who resist Lord Karyan! They will beg for mercy, but they will have none."

The Omentians rallied to their commander's triumphant proclamation of victory and future glory as they headed inland, eager for the next encounter with the Adonians.

But one Omentian wizard and his guards remembered what they had seen, keeping secret what they instinctively knew about the coming battle to take Adonia and the God that stood in their way. They knew the coming fight would not be as easy as the previous campaigns in Parlantis and Heath had been. And though the wizard ordered his guards to keep quiet about what they had seen within the fire, the story passed swiftly and quietly through the Omentian ranks.

CHAPTER 45

Mountains and Deserts

✝✝✝

As Crastis' major landing force departed Delvia and pushed into northern Kandish, the northern arm of the invasion, launched from Heath, landed in northern Chastain. Like Crastis' attack from the east, the northern prong of the attack pushed inland, uncontested.

The Heathian force, under the command of a brigand named Wendal, immediately encountered the majestic mountains of northern Adonia and had no choice but to divert their path, either to the southeast or the southwest. The Heathians were flatlanders; climbing and fighting in the highlands of Adonia was not a realistic option for these warriors. Since Crastis attacked from the east, the Heathian force surged southwest through Chastain and toward eastern Tanshire.

The Chastainians were well aware of the invasion. Still, the speed at which the enemy was pushing ashore surprised them. They knew the Omentians, Parlantians, and Heathian forces could attack at any time, and they had seen the warning fires spread across Adonia. The great fire that had erupted to the east in what many thought to be the Delvian wheat fields punctuated the reality of the events taking place. Undoubtedly, the enemy was on the move.

The Chastainians, along with all of Adonia, had their peaceful and pleasant life suddenly and ruthlessly taken away from them. In its place, as promised, was the scourge of war and the stench of death.

No one had yet tested the fledgling country of Adonia in combat. Adonia had always lived in peace with its neighbors, solving disputes rationally. This was different. An enemy had decided the Adonian way of life, her beliefs, and her very existence had to be eliminated. There was no way around the struggle that was coming, and none would be immune from its testing.

Gareth and the people of northern Chastain were unaffected by the Heathian assault, at least initially. They were a hearty people that inhabited the beautiful and rugged mountains above five thousand feet in altitude, and the Heathian invaders confined themselves to the valleys and lowlands well below that.

Though Gareth carefully monitored the Heathian advance to the south, prudence dictated he pick a better time to commit his division to the fight. Vastly outnumbered by the Heathian army, it was wiser to dictate the time and place to engage the heathens than to allow them to lure the Adonians into a suicidal assault.

Gareth knew his people were safe in the mountains, but it still drove him crazy that the infidel invaders moved about at will inside Adonia. He also feared for Cusintomas and the people of Tanshire, who did not enjoy the natural defense of the high mountains.

Gareth ordered the Chastainian Fifth Division readied for combat and organized to march at a moment's notice. He knew the division would be called up soon enough, either in the west to support Cusintomas and Tanshire, or to the south to assist in the defense of Aanot, should the enemy decide to circle the mountains and attack Castle Armon and the great city from the southern mountain passes.

Gareth and the Fifth Division watched and waited. It was the Heathians' move.

†††

Cusintomas loved and respected his brother greatly, but he didn't share Gareth's apparent nonchalance regarding the Heathian invasion.

All of Adonia was marshaling their forces to repel the invaders that had evidently landed in several locations around Adonia.

Cusintomas understood Gareth's point of view and his tactic of waiting on the enemy's next move, but he didn't agree with it. First, Tanshire didn't share in the convenience of having the majestic mountains to protect them. Second, the thought of the enemy holding just one square foot of Adonia was absolutely intolerable to Cusintomas, even if only for a short time. And finally, Cusintomas had remembered well his father's words. "If men stand by and do nothing, evil will have its way." He had internalized these words, and they had altered him to the very core of his being.

Act first, and sort it out later. Often a seemingly directionless vector, Cusintomas' abundance of sheer energy mandated movement. From youth, Cusintomas would charge into a fight, many times without thinking. His people knew him as "Surge" because of his seemingly inexhaustible energy and passion for fighting evil. Surge was a man of action, and if ever there was a time for action, this was it!

This is one man that will not stand idly by while evil has its way!

The Mighty Eighth Tanshire Division mobilized and headed for southern Chastain to meet the enemy. Surge, like his brother, knew he should not engage the Heathians directly; their numbers were too great. Instead, he used the strengths of the men of Tanshire to their advantage.

He scouted out the enemy formations from the mountains, and found the Heathians had fundamentally misunderstood the lack of resistance they had encountered, thus far, as either a lack of ability on the part of the Adonians to defend their land or a lack of commitment to do so. Either way, they had made a terrible miscalculation. On their brief visit to the Adonian homeland, the Heathians had grown very careless in defending the fringes of their formations.

Surge gave them a lesson on the dangers of such negligence and lack of discipline. He directed the squads of the Mighty Eighth to deplete the enemy's periphery, using the indirect tactics of guerilla warfare.

273

Surge reorganized the Mighty Eighth, comprising light infantry, archers, and cavalry flights. He directed the cavalry flight to stay concealed at a safe distance to the southwest in order to intercept and eliminate any Heathian scouts that might attempt to reconnoiter Tanshire. Expertly trained and capable in the art of concealment, climbing, and hand-to-hand combat, he directed the light infantry to attrite the enemy at every available moment and in every available way. He directed the archers to provide standoff support to the stealthy infantry, working with them to ensure successful ingress and egress operations.

The tactic worked brilliantly! The rangers of Tanshire left no signs of their coming or going. Following Surge's explicit commands, they even concealed the lifeless bodies of the unfortunate Heathians they had so stealthily liberated from this life, and had put the fear of God into the entire Heathian army.

Like a cold shiver passes down your spine when you find you are suddenly alone in the dark and think someone is watching you, so a wave of fear passed through the Heathian ranks, consuming their every waking moment and prohibiting even the thought of a peaceful sleep.

As their numbers rapidly decreased without explanation, the Heathians struggled to explain the unexplainable. Stories of ghosts, sorcery, and the supernatural sprung up among them, infecting the invading army with dread and panic. Their only solace came in congregating in large formations. Instead of seeing themselves as the invaders, the Heathian army soon took on a persona of defensiveness, wondering who would be present when the sun rose the next day and who would be taken.

Though the Heathian commanders tried their best to contain the fear that was sweeping through the ranks, the apprehension they all felt regarding the ghosts in their midst was all too apparent; their voices impersonated that of courage, but their eyes told the actual story. The subtle crack in the Heathian commanders' voices and the darting about of their eyes belied any attempts they made to convey strength and fearlessness to their troops.

The longer the Heathians encamped in the foothills of Chastain, the more their numbers depleted and their courage eroded. They soon realized they had to move, and move they did. The Heathians split into two large attack forces, marching south toward Plattos and west toward Tanshire.

Gareth responded immediately, dispatching half his division to pursue the Heathians marching on Plattos, while his brother Surge and the Mighty Eighth continued to attrite the Heathians headed toward Tanshire.

Both the Fifth and the Eighth Divisions were still greatly outnumbered and any thought of a direct attack on the Heathian forces was completely out of the question. Only in a dire emergency would the Adonian Guard take on such a superior force in a frontal assault. Truin and his sons felt that their best chances for victory lay in using their vast knowledge of Adonia to their advantage and in massing at just the right time and just the right place to inflict strategic injury on the invading forces. The big questions remained about when and where this right time and place might be, but they hoped God would show them the answers.

Surge's Eighth Division felt a new sense of urgency as the enemy entered Tanshire. Surge directed his infantry and air cavalry flights to continue to pursue and attrite the Heathians as best they were able. He frantically rode ahead of the infantry and air cavalry flights to rejoin with his calvary flight to the west before they met the superiorly numbered Heathians; he needed to be there to lead them into battle.

Surge had appointed his most trusted lieutenant, Travish, to command the cavalry, and Surge knew Travish would not sit idly and allow the enemy to overrun Tanshire. Travish would die before he would let that happen. Surge needed to be with Travish and the cavalry when they clashed with the heathens.

As Surge pushed his steed to the limits of its endurance to join up with Travish and the Eighth Cavalry, he wondered what he would do when he rejoined with them.

Should I continue to run raids against the Heathian force, slowly depleting their numbers, or should I boldly attack the invaders in force and trust God to win the day?

His father had seen this impetuous streak in Surge many years earlier when Surge was but a boy, and he had taught Surge that there was but a fine line between boldness and stupidity. Surge had always been bold, almost to a fault, pushing closer and closer to that fine line. The responsibility of command and of so many other lives under his direct control, he took his decisions far more seriously. The consequences of any mistake in judgment he might have in this campaign would be much more far-reaching — affecting the futures of hundreds of men, their families, and perhaps the fate of Adonia itself.

On the other hand, God had put him in this position of leadership for a reason. Maybe God wanted him to step forward boldly in faith and do God's will. Perhaps direct confrontation was the answer he was searching for.

Better an army of sheep led by a lion than an army of lions led by a sheep.

Surge understood he had an army of lions.

Do they not expect me to be a lion? Surely my father expects me to be a lion.

As Surge charged across the open plain to the cluster of trees where he knew the Eighth Cavalry was waiting, the answer came to him.

Be a lion, but be a wise lion.

†††

The ferocious beasts swooped down on the small villages, attacking all with impunity and showing no mercy. Granting safe harbor to none, the scaly creatures did not distinguish between the men of a village and the frail and innocent. The women and children of the mountain valley screamed in fear as they ran for their lives.

After the rapid Heathian withdrawal from the area, the winged serpents had appeared without warning across the mountain valleys of Chastain, leaving death and destruction in their wake. The fire-breaths mercilessly torched villages as they spread across the region. Their blood-curdling, high-pitched screech announcing their arrival, the thick-skinned monsters appeared in the heat of the day, seemingly from nowhere. They shot javelins of flame from their mouths and tore the flesh from the bones of their victims with their razor-sharp claws. They were the perfect killing machines. Village after village fell to the fire-breaths' fury. Those spared apprehensively watched the skies, knowing the creatures would soon return, and that they would be next.

Gareth had to thwart this new enemy that mercilessly continued to rain disaster upon his land. The refugees from the many decimated villages were steadily growing to startling proportions and fear was taking control of his beautiful and once peaceful, land. Gareth meditated on the Word, prayed, and took his troubles to the God of the universe.

The fearsome creatures had attacked throughout Chastain, showing no sign of weakness. They were tremendously formidable killing machines, and any attempt to stand before them in battle had proven futile. Many brave men had courageously attempted to stand and fight the beasts in defense of their families and their homes. These men had fallen, giving their lives as a love offering. They had passed with honor to their eternal home in glory.

But the more Gareth thought about it, the more certain truths stood out. Gareth hoped these truths, taken all together, were the answer to the fire-breath's weakness. The fire-breath always showed itself in the heat of the day, when the valleys had warmed and the sun was high in the sky. Additionally, the fire-breath had attacked none of the villages in the highlands.

Could it be that the cold somehow limited the fire-breath?

Gareth hoped beyond hope that this was its weakness. If so, with God's help, they could defeat the creatures and end their reign of terror on Chastain.

First, Gareth had to give evil a target, a prize it could not refuse.

Short of a glorious prize for the enemy, I could restrict the availability of other enticement; take away the plethora of targets the fire-breaths currently enjoy and give them only one target of opportunity. Thus, I will dictate the place they will next attack and be ready for them when they arrive.

Gareth gathered the division and informed them of the plan. Wasting no time, he gave the order for all the refugees of Chastain to congregate in one area. In addition, he asked all the inhabitants of the lower-valley villages to travel to the highlands and mass with the refugees there.

Certainly this was a huge undertaking, both psychologically and logistically, for a people that had been so ravaged by this hellish plague of destruction. Many members of the Adonian Guard itself doubted the wisdom of such a move. But Gareth believed that this was the answer, and out of loyalty to Gareth — and ultimately his position of leadership in the Adonian Guard as sanctioned by Truin himself — the members of the guard followed Gareth's directives, praying he indeed knew what he was doing.

The refugees and villagers moved higher into the mountains, and the fire-breaths continued to attack. The Fifth Division did their best to protect the travelers, but there was little they could do against the deadly, airborne creatures. Though any loss of life was truly tragic, a day of but a few casualties became widely known as a good day.

After two intense weeks of moonlit retreats from the valleys of death and the hastily assembled, makeshift defenses during the day, most of Chastain's remaining inhabitants, numbering approximately one-thousand souls, progressed through the narrow mountain pass and packed into the ice-covered highland plateau known by all of Chastain as the frozen tundra of the Lambeanian Fields. On this home turf, the people of the highlands had never known defeat. Here, the Chastainian refugees set up camp and rested their weary bodies, unsure of how long they would stay or when the fire-breaths might find them.

Gareth, or Koldas as the Chastainians knew him, and the Fifth Division mounted their defenses around the narrow pass. They knew it was just a matter of time before the fire-breaths would arrive. The creatures had attacked every day during the long journey to the Fields, so this place would not remain hidden from them for long. In addition, more and more of the monsters had shown up each day, so the guard expected nothing but the worst.

All too soon, the sun rose high into the sky, and Koldas grew anxious — waiting and wondering what would happen next.

Koldas hoped that in fighting the enemy here, the guard might hold an advantage, and finally end the fire-breaths' scourge once and for all. The fire-breaths had been unstoppable. But here, high above the mountain valleys of Chastain, the altitude made the air thin and freezing. Even in the heat of the day, the temperature rose only slightly, and Koldas hoped this would prove to be a decisive factor in their struggle with the flying reptilian devils.

The Chastainians did not have to wait for long. As the sun approached its apex, blazing in the sky overhead, the lookouts on the peaks on either side of the pass signaled that trouble was approaching. Koldas ran to the center of the pass and looked out to the south. From the center of the pass, Koldas could see a distance of more than one hundred miles, since the terrain dropped off sharply and nothing obstructed the nearly God's-eye view of the valleys below.

Approximately three miles away and perhaps five thousand feet below them was a dark cloud in an otherwise clear sky. It moved toward them at an unnatural rate of speed, and its consistency was much denser than that of any cloud Koldas had ever seen before.

Koldas knew this was not a cloud. It was them.

"Battle stations!"

"Battle stations!" The command echoed across the snow and ice that covered the mountain.

The men watched the living cloud approach. They could soon see the individual beasts of the formation break out, and they were awe-struck at the sheer number of the creatures approaching. Their huge wings were waving up and down, their massive tails swinging back and forth, while their powerful arms and razor-sharp talons remained flexed below their enormous torsos — ready to strike at anything that stood in their way.

The approaching formation mesmerized Gareth and all the men with him. It had to contain over fifty of the giant, gargoyle-like fire-breaths.

The men prayed what they thought to be their last prayers to the God who had always been faithful in keeping his promises. They hoped it was God's will that they should defeat these monsters from hell, though they were still unsure how such a thing could be done. Before any one of them was ready for the conflict to arrive, the wave of ferocious killers poured through the mountain pass.

Though the Fifth Division's archers had landed three separate volleys of arrows into the beasts as they approached the pass, none of their arrows had made an impact. Rather, the arrows had simply deflected off the thick armor plating of the creatures' torsos.

The guard light infantry scattered to engage the monsters that had already landed within the pass, futilely striking at the creatures with sword and javelin. The fire-breaths tossed the men of the guard around like dolls; like the light fabric dolls stuffed with straw that Chastainian women gave to their young daughters to play with.

With powerful talons and mighty tails, the fire-breaths lashed out at the men of the guard, slashing their flesh and breaking their bones. In rage, the fire-breaths unleashed their flames on the defenseless soldiers. The men attempted in vain to block the fiery inferno with their wooden shields. As more and more of the beasts flew through the pass and onto the frigid battlefield, it seemed more and more useless for the Adonians to continue to resist.

Koldas watched in disbelief as his men contacted the enemy, and his plan failed. All around him his men were falling, and soon the beasts would be free to feed on the defenseless women and children huddled together behind their floundering defensive lines — the same women and children that had arduously followed him to this place, hoping that the guard could protect them.

But it was never really about the guard, was it?

Koldas looked up into the heavens, the bright rays of the sun blinding him as he closed his eyes.

"Father, help us? Save us, Oh God, from thy enemies."

One of the mighty creatures landed near Koldas and swung its enormous tail, striking Koldas across the back and sending him through the air and face first into an ice wall. His sword flew from his hands as he ricocheted off the wall and landed flat on his back in the snow, looking skyward. Unsure of whether he was still conscious, or perhaps dreaming, the sounds of the battle, though still audible, faded, and darkness clouded his vision. Koldas' faculties slipped away.

"Save us, Oh God. You alone are the Almighty One." Koldas' prayer was a humble request, but a request anchored in an ironclad faith that God would indeed act.

As he laid there in the snow, the sounds of the battle returned once again to full volume, and his lieutenant yanked on his arm. "Koldas, are you alive? Stand up, look, something is happening!"

Koldas, with the help of his number one, stood. He now realized that the fading light that he had mistaken earlier as his life slipping away was, in fact, the sudden clouding up of the skies above them. Angry clouds had encircled the mountain peaks all around the plateau. Further, the clouds had sprung leaks, sending tentacles rapidly down the surrounding mountain slopes toward the icy fields below. Even their flying foes seemed to notice the atmospheric changes and had taken to flight, joining up into formations of six and flying in large circles overhead.

The soldiers of the guard took advantage of the brief reprieve and scrambled to help their fallen comrades and drag them to cover.

Koldas and his men watched the rolling peaks around them and hoped that somehow this was the help they had prayed for — help coming from the clouds.

Their hope was not in vain.

Along with the heavy, swirling clouds proceeding down the mountain slopes above the pass came the roar of mighty waters. No one knew what to make out of what their senses were telling them.

Is this an avalanche? If so, we are all lost!

The fire-breaths, now taking the approaching thunder clouds as a threat, darted toward the south to flee the impending disaster, but their efforts were too little, too late. The clouds of thunder swept across the fields and through the pass, their frigid currents of air reaching hundreds of feet into the sky.

Koldas had witnessed nothing like it. In but a second, the air surrounding them fogged up, crystallizing all about them. In the tidal wave of frost, visibility fell to nearly zero. The thundering cloud reached them and then overtook them. There was neither sound nor wind. The surrounding air remained peaceful, with no sensation of a breeze at all. It was as if time stood still.

Within another second, the temperature of the air plummeted. Though the already frigid air temperatures fell even further in temperature, the change posed no significant threat to the Adonians, who were used to conditions much colder. They were a hardy people and well prepared for such temperatures. The beasts flying above them, however, were not as fortunate.

As the air cleared, Koldas and his guardsmen watched the flying monsters' wings stiffen. Those fire-breaths not already grounded plummeted to the frozen turf. Some glided there clumsily. Most, however, controlled by demons that refused to let them follow their natural instincts and return to the ground, agonizingly succumbed to the oppressive weight of the ice forming on their massive bodies. Dropping like rocks through the ice-filled air, their wings trailing helplessly behind as they plunged to the surface, they hit the frozen plateau with such a force as to send the snow and ice all around the point of impact exploding high into the air.

The guardsmen charged the felled beasts, first attacking the creatures that had hit the ground the hardest. The vulnerable areas of the winged demons now critically exposed, the guard wasted no time in running their long javelins through the hearts of the hellish creatures; creatures that only moments before seemed invincible.

The other mighty beasts, those not yet permanently dispatched back to hell, continued to fight. Their cold-blooded bodies grew more and more sluggish in battle with every passing moment. They were still quite a formidable opponent. But they were no longer a match for the valiant warriors of the Adonian Guard, who, now renewed in strength and resolve, were eager to snatch victory from the jaws of defeat. The guardsmen dropped one beast after another until there was only one creature remaining.

The last of the winged serpents seemed to realize that its end was near. It laboriously attempted to flap its wings as it struggled to drag its battered body along the ice toward the entrance to the mountain pass.

The men of the guard gathered around and watched the beast as it pulled itself along the ground. It was still attempting to make the fire it had used so effectively against the Adonians moments earlier, but the air was now too cold. None of the men made a sound as they watched the monster take its last few breaths. The air was so quiet that they could even hear the magnificent beast's heart thumping the last few beats of its long life.

And then its heart stopped, and the battle ended.

The grisly and bloodied beast's last position as it made its dying attempt to reach sanctuary would remain in place, frozen for all of time, a perpetual warning to all who would dare to fight against the Almighty One and his faithful.

From that day on, the fighting men of the Adonian Fifth gave Gareth, the fifth son of Truin, the foreigner known as Koldas, a new name. He became known as Koldas Ice.

Surge stood in the open desert with Travish, his most trusted friend, a brother like no other. Together, they stood, alone, against the entire western arm of the Heathian Army.

The route through eastern Tanshire, one that any invading army would have to take in order to reach, let alone defeat, western Adonia, led through the desert. The natural pathway for anyone wanting to transverse this desolate wasteland known as the Great Desert of Tanshire led directly through this exact spot, through Mobjack Mound. Alone, on Mobjack Mound, stood two warriors intent on defending their homeland to the death if required.

The common convention of the time dictated that Surge and the Tanshire Guard, highly outnumbered no matter how one looked at it, choose a location more helpful for a smaller force, hoping to defeat a vastly superior one; perhaps a narrow pass to unleash an ambush, or maybe a series of unpredictable locations in which to employ hit-and-run tactics. At the very least, if Surge chose a high-risk operation, he should have broken company with his second-in-command to avoid an entire loss of division leadership should things not go as planned.

Surge and Travish stood on Mobjack Mound, alone, facing three thousand Heathian warriors, who had followed the all too predictable path and arrived at their exact location.

Over the last few days, Surge and the Mighty Eighth had fought and killed over two hundred of the Heathians, who were part of advance scouting parties. The two Adonians now stood back-to-back, swords and shields in hand, facing the entire Heathian assault force, the largest army to ever enter Tanshire uninvited.

"Well, this definitely fits the bill of being a lion." Travish had a slight smirk appear on his face. Travish was a daring warrior and loved the idea of fighting a numerically impossible battle — and of course of winning said battle.

"Yeah, but I am wondering about the wise part." Surge had the same gallant expression crossing his face.

Across the sand, the Heathian commander, Gorus, assigned the task of taking Tanshire, wondered what matter of insanity he and his army were observing. True, these two men had apparently been responsible for the deaths of some of his sharpest soldiers, but what could they now hope to accomplish? These men were either fools with a death wish or the bravest men he had ever seen.

The Heathian soldiers that now surrounded Surge and Travish lavished the two with scorn and ridicule. One Heathian announced, "Behold, the defenders of Tanshire have arrived to repel us!" Another screamed, "We have summoned the men of Tanshire to defend her, and two have answered the call! Apparently, there are only two actual men in all of Tanshire."

Surge and Travish were unaffected by the taunting. The Heathians were ignorant of what they were saying, controlled by the principalities of darkness, and their ignorance would be their undoing. Surge and Travish wished these men no ill; they pitied them, both for their eternal fate and what was now about to befall them.

Surge and Travish had discussed their plan fully before deciding upon it, and they were both in complete agreement. No matter what the plan might be, they knew there was no way to defend Tanshire against such great numbers unless the Lord fought for them, and if the Lord fought for them, it mattered not if they stood with a hundred, a thousand, or alone; they would be victorious.

Travish quoted the Word. "The fear of the Lord is the beginning of wisdom. They are foolish and have no fear of the true God."

"Indeed. Today we shall put our faith in the Lord's Word into practice." Surge added. "Today we will put our trust in the one who can do all things. If it is the Lord's will, we will not fall."

At Surge's command, the rest of the Mighty Eighth had taken defensive positions throughout Tanshire. Surge and Travish had boldly stepped out in faith and relied on a plan that could only succeed if God acted to save them, and in so doing, they prayed God would show his glory marvelously.

Commander Gorus could have used his archers to drop these two Adonians in the sand where they stood, but he had decided instead that his troops needed some entertainment to take their minds off the long march through the desert. In addition, his greener infantry soldiers needed more experience fighting the enemy; many of the Heathian conscripts had never stood against enemy infantry face-to-face.

So, in consideration of his men and in some small way out of respect to these two enemy soldiers who had survived this long against his scouts, Gorus had surrounded the two men with his entire fighting force. This had the additional benefit of boosting morale for the Heathian soldiers; surely, if this was the best Tanshire could do, the campaign would be a breeze.

After a short time, Gorus gave the order to attack, and the Heathian Army advanced. The circle of troops surrounding the Adonian guardsmen constricted. In no time at all, his troops would crush this small but symbolic Adonian force, as they would surely crush all who stood in their way.

"Surge, are you sure this is the place?" Travish watched the Heathians advance.

"This is it. This is where we stand."

As Surge thrust his sword deep into the sands before him, he dropped to a knee and bowed his head. "Our faith is built on the rock."

Travish followed suit, surrendering his sword deep into the golden sands at his feet and bowing his head.

There on the golden sands of Tanshire, under the bright, midday sun, the two guardsmen kneeled in prayer to the God of their fathers, to the maker of the universe. And when they prayed, they prayed fully expecting the one who loved them to act.

Unknown to the Heathians, Surge and Travish now stood on the only rocky formation that existed in the deep, three hundred foot layer of sand that had covered this part of Tanshire for the past, one thousand years; on the only solid foundation in the entire Great Desert of Tanshire. The Adonian men had literally built their defense on a rock. The Heathians, in contrast, stood on shifting sand. And without warning or reason, the sands shifted.

The Heathians' confidence faltered and completely eroded amidst the disbelief of what was happening. The very ground on which they stood disintegrated as if it was dematerializing before their eyes. Unknown to both the Heathians and the Adonians, much was at work below the shifting surface of these desert sands. Far below the surface, thousands of sand creatures, known only in ancient legend, obediently performed the task for which the Master of the Universe had summoned them to perform.

Beneath the sands of the Great Desert, a colony of underground burrowers had thrived for a hundred years — a colony of sand dwellers. Their instincts had abruptly told them it was time to rearrange the tunnel system in which they had worked and dwelled for so long. Unfortunately for the Heathians, above this tunnel system was not the place to be when the furniture was being rearranged.

The once solid ground on which the Heathian force stood became completely unstable, rapidly approaching the consistency of a fluid. Amidst the turmoil of the mixing currents and eruptions of sand all around them, the Heathian men lost their footing and sank into the sands below them.

Thousands of men, abandoning their weapons and all concern for their mission, clawed unsuccessfully at the ever-changing surface in a horrifying scene. They screamed for deliverance as they sunk into the depths below. Occasionally, giant mandibles gnawed at the arms and legs of the doomed Heathian warriors as the sands engulfed them.

Surge and Travish watched the incredible event in awe of God's power and in pity for the men perishing before them. The evil one had deceived these men, enslaved them to fallen spirits, and now they had fallen into the almighty hands of the Living God; hands that are both mighty to save and mighty to destroy.

Within minutes, only a few remnants of the entire Heathian Army remained upon the sand. A helmet here and a spear there is all that existed of the once powerful army.

Surge and Travish bowed their heads once again. This time the prayers were prayers of thanks. They prayed the words of 1st Samuel. "There is no one holy like the Lord; there is no one besides you; there is no rock like our God."

Once again, the surrounding sands froze into place as a cool wind made its way down from the distant mountains of Chastain and blew across the Great Desert.

CHAPTER 46

PLEA FOR MERCY

✝✝✝

The news was bittersweet. On the one hand, the great grain fields of Delvia had burned; the enemy had invaded Chastain and Tanshire; the armies of unbelievers had poured across Adonia; and Truin's scouts now reported that elements of the enemy's army were marching on Aanot from both the east and the west. But the God of their fathers, the only true God, had remained faithful to his children. Using both the forces of nature and the creatures below the sands, he had fought for his faithful against the invaders; and he had used his supernatural powers to spare Bigaulf, his sons, and countless others from being consumed by the fires of the devil's sorcery.

After the miracles in the frigid mountains of Chastain and the arid desert of Tanshire, Gareth and Surge assumed the enemy would attempt to attack Aanot, and Castle Armon — the pride of Adonia and the nucleus of her leadership. They assembled their guard divisions and united with Bigaulf and what remained of the Fearless, Fighting Fourth Division.

Hearing the news of what had transpired in northern Adonia, Truin ordered all the inhabitants of Aanot to take refuge within the walls of the grand castle. There, at Castle Armon, Truin would protect them, with the help of six Adonian Guard Divisions.

Truin's thoughts wandered to Ka'el.

Where is Ka'el? He should be here, standing with us against the horde.

Truin had not spoken to Ka'el since the day he and Evelin had visited him at his home. He had hoped that Ka'el would make the next move at reconciliation, but he had not. Truin tried again. He went to Ka'el's cottage a few weeks after his first visit. Tala was there alone and told Truin that Ka'el had gone hunting by himself. Ka'el had supposedly been gone for three days, and Tala did not know when he would return. Truin told Tala of the coming storm and asked her to return with him to the safety of the castle, but she had declined. "I have just never fit in, and I don't think I am welcomed there; I'll be alright here."

Truin had tried at length to convince Tala to change her mind, but she wouldn't budge. Tala demanded Truin return to the castle without her.

Where is Ka'el? With everything that is going on, Ka'el should be here in the Castle, with his family. What will Mother think when she finds out that the Omentians and Heathians are about to attack Aanot — attack the castle — and we don't know where Ka'el is?

Though troubled that he did not know his brother was safe, Truin continued to function, drawing up defense plans with the Jonn, Gladsel, Melkione, Bigaulf, Gareth, and Surge. Still, the whereabouts of his one and only brother weighed heavily on his mind.

Night and day, during his quiet time, and at every available opportunity, Truin pleaded with God in prayer for his brother's safety — many times in tears. Truin was just as concerned for Ka'el's spiritual wellbeing as he was for his physical safety. So many years of bitterness, unresolved anger, jealously, guilt, and separation — separation from his family and his brothers in the faith — had undoubtedly taken their toll. In addition, there was no telling the influence Tala and her pagan beliefs might have had on Ka'el's faith. Faith needed to be fed, and from all indications, Ka'el was being spiritually starved to death.

Truin knew the time to reach Ka'el was rapidly slipping away, even more so considering recent events. So Truin prayed ceaselessly for his brother's soul with a sense of the utmost urgency.

As he lay in bed with Christina inside their warm cabin, the chilly wind blowing briskly through the trees around Blue Lake, they prayed together as they did every night. Truin included a prayer, as always, for Ka'el.

"Please Father, send your Spirit to my brother, your servant, Ka'el. Revive and strengthen his faith in you. Stir the fire and rake the spiritual coals of his heart. Purify my brother's soul. Cast out the evil that has been assailing his body and his spirit. Work in ways that only you can know and only you can do."

Ever since the accident, Truin had tried to live his life in a way that left nothing undone and left nothing unsaid. He had learned through experience that it was not wise for a man to take even another hour of life for granted. No man knew when his time of grace would be up, so as much as possible, it was best for a man to live a life without regrets.

Truin, however, like all men, had regrets, but he had done his best to right the wrongs, put into practice what he believed, and say what he knew needed to be said.

He held his wife close and whispered his love for her in her ear. She returned his love affectionately.

The warmth and love they had always shared, ever since the day the Lord had made them one, continued to burn intensely. They had taken every opportunity to nurture it, never taking it for granted, but seeing it for the great blessing that it was. It had strengthened their relationship and warmed their home. Though time had aged their bodies, time had also fused their souls, accomplishing the work begun when they had made their vows. Once they were two individuals wanting not to be alone in an inhospitable world. They had grown together, becoming one; little by little, day by day. Through the blessings, the trials, and the heartaches, the two had truly become one in spirit — two halves joined to make a whole. Truin and Christina completed each other, and the thought of ever again being alone was a thought too unthinkable — too unbearable — to entertain for long.

The soft moonlight caressed their faces as they snuggled close to one another and drifted off to a peaceful sleep, resting in the peace and protection of their loving God, who never sleeps.

†††

As the Adonians slept, red eyes burned in the darkness, carefully directing and watching evil's plan unfold. It was all going exactly as designed, and all the pieces were nearly in place for the ultimate defeat and subjugation of Adonia.

The demons delicately pulled the strings of the human marionettes that had so easily given themselves over to evil's ways. These men, these puppets, while pretentiously presenting themselves to each other as the enlightened men of the world — men liberated from long-established, childlike beliefs in the supernatural, in the invisible powers, and in the dominions that inhabit the spirit world — were themselves the fools, overcome by the very forces they pompously denied.

The demons squealed in laughter as they directed the sinister script; the strength of Adonia was about to be cut down by the feebleminded, Omentian slaves, slaves who thought themselves to be masters.

"Truly, our master is the authority of deception," One demon quipped.

The demons screeched even louder as he stated the obvious.

However, the demons suddenly grew serious as they considered how their master's noteworthy abilities of deception could ultimately mislead them as well.

Could it be that the master's promises of power and glory for his followers are also less than sincere?

They had followed him since the rebellion. Now, as he had done then, Belial had promised them he would be victorious, that he was the one to follow. But their rejection of the Holy One had brought them only pain and torment thus far.

The sudden reminder of their master's history of disloyalty and treachery overwhelmed them with anxiety. They were anxious both because of the uncertain outcome of their current plan and the ancient curse that warned of their ultimate demise in the dungeons of hell.

Powerless to change the nature or their course, they refocused on the temporary pleasure of steering others to a similar destruction; as if this would somehow ease their own horror regarding their inevitable doom. They covered themselves in a shroud of self-deception, assuring themselves they could turn it all around, just as their master, the Devil, continued to promise them.

"Soon they will join us, and we will feast on the sons of Truin!" squealed one of the many.

"How sweet their blood will taste!"

Far behind them in the darkness, Abaddon and his chief demon watched the others.

"The flies grow restless, master."

"They are of no concern. They are already mine. There is no turning back for them. They will do as directed. But those still in time, they belong to the Holy One. These are the ones I want for my own. These are the ones we must take away from Him."

They turned their attention to a small farmhouse cottage in the rolling foothills of Chastain.

"Is she still ours?" the chief demon inquired of his master.

Abaddon focused his gaze on the lonely woman. "The timing is perfect. The plan unfolds."

Tala sat alone in her cottage with the dark stranger. He had shown up at her door moments earlier, as the sun was just beginning to set.

It had been so long since she had seen her old friend, since the early days in the forests of Omentia. It took her a moment to realize who he was, but once she recognized him, she threw her arms around him and gave him a big, long hug, which he was all too eager to return.

Kala Azar and the others from the forest were once like family to Tala, the only actual family she had ever remembered having as a child. They gave her something she desperately needed at the time; acceptance, belonging, and something greater than herself to believe in.

But Kala Azar was more than an old friend, more than family to Tala. For a time, before the day in the forest when Karyan had directed Tala to pursue Ka'el, Tala had dreamed of spending her days with Kala Azar.

But it wasn't meant to be. Or was it?

Tala tingled from head to toe when she saw Kala at her door, and she more than allowed him to enter her home — she welcomed him in.

It was good Ka'el had gone on an extended hunting trip to think things through. Tala was sure he would not understand Kala's visit. Plus, it would bring up so many other uncomfortable questions that Tala didn't want to answer. But then Tala knew Kala Azar would not show up while Ka'el was there. The message she had received from him a month earlier had told her so.

The message had made a strange request of Tala, one she didn't truly understand or feel very comfortable in complying with. Yet, for her dear old friend, she had complied, and seeing Kala face-to-face, she was glad she did.

The emotions she felt for Kala Azar came flooding back over her like a warm bath, and she was once again completely smitten. Almost stumbling over herself to make him comfortable, Tala scurried around the cottage, getting Kala refreshment and preparing him a meal.

Kala Azar, however, had not dropped by for a social visit. He was there on a mission, and seeing the prize he sought lying on a table beside the door, he seized it, and slipped out into the darkness without so much as a goodbye.

Tala, returning to the front room of the cottage with the meal she had just prepared for Kala Azar, found the room empty, the door ajar. As she struggled to understand the meaning of Kala's brief appearance, her eyes wandered about the room, settling on the empty table where Truin's cloak had rested.

A flood of thoughts and feelings poured through Tala's mind. She felt embarrassed that she had so ignorantly assumed Kala Azar had sought her out, emerging from the depths of a past life, because he still cared for her. She felt angry that this had obviously not been the case, and angry at herself for so readily believing it had been so.

Anxiety slowly but steadily overcame Tala as she sat wondering what part she was playing in the still unfolding struggle that had befallen Adonia.

What have I done?

Will they find out it was me?

What will happen if they find out?

Tala sat alone in the dimly lit room of the cottage. The walls closed in on her as the small flame flickered from the solitary candle lighting the room.

What have I done?

†††

Kala Azar followed the instructions and dropped the cloak, then backed away from it. As he did, they emerged from the darkness of the forest. The sleek beasts eyed him carefully as they approached, their golden eyes reflecting in the moonlight.

They stopped when they reached the cloak lying on the forest floor. Their taunt shoulder muscles flexed as they stooped to breathe in the target's scent, its odor still lingering upon and within the garment's fabric. As each beast sniffed the cloak, its disposition changed from calm stealth to open aggression. Instantly agitated, the creatures snarled and let out ferocious growls. Instantly turning, they dashed off into the dark forest, keenly intent on fulfilling their mission.

CHAPTER 47

Castle Armon

†††

"Raise the drawbridge!"

The order echoed through the early morning fog as the last of Koldas Ice's forces crossed the moat at Castle Armon. Huge chains clanked as they arduously lifted the wooden planks that bridged the deep chasm surrounding the Castle. Truin watched closely as Koldas and his warriors arrived, the Heathian army right on their tail.

"Archers at the ready!" Khory ordered.

Adonian archers, under Khory's command, lined the southern facing wall of the castle.

Khory waited until the Heathians came well within range. The height of the castle and its position on the top of the hill gave the Adonians a vast ballistic advantage regarding the range of their arrows. There was nothing without wings that could challenge the Adonians for the space around the castle so masterfully built in the foothills of the Great Mountains of Chastain.

"Fire!"

The sound of a vast flurry of arrows whizzing through the air caught the attention of all within the castle, a deadly herald of the battle to ensue.

"Will they hit their mark?" Truin waited anxiously to see if the cloud of death that stealthily made its way down the mountainside, concealed within the morning mist, would find its target.

"Do birds fly?" Khory replied, confident in the Adonian Guard's abilities and exhilarated by the opportunity to attrite the invaders at a distance.

"Unfortunately, I am afraid their numbers are so many that our arrows cannot miss," Khory added, bleakly.

As the guard raised the drawbridge, the first of the Heathians arrived at the edge of the moat. The startled enemy, seeing they had nowhere to go, reversed direction. Confusion abounded in the early morning light as the soldiers directly behind those reversing their course were momentarily unaware of the sea change in progress; they collided with the front line of their own countrymen. To make matters worse, it was at this moment that the airborne harbingers of death, completing their flight down the mountainside, found their marks, instantly dropping dozens of the Heathians in their tracks. Those around the fallen retreated in panic as their optimistic fortunes abruptly reversed.

There was no celebration or elation by the Adonian archers or those watching as the arrows hit their targets. The sight of those poor, deceived souls departing this world to meet their maker, so ill prepared, gave none of the Adonians joy; only relief that their battlements had held, at least for the moment.

Koldas arrived at the wall and briefed his father on the events that had transpired the week prior, high in the mountains of Chastain, and how God had miraculously delivered so many of their people from the fire-breath kind. After their victory on the mountain, the elated people of Chastain had cautiously returned to some of their most hidden and sheltered villages. Koldas had assembled what remained of the Fifth Division and made haste to Castle Armon, because Chastainian scouts had reported spotting previously unknown enemy forces headed south toward the castle. Koldas believed these forces would soon attack the castle, intending to destroy the bulk of the Adonian leadership.

Truin carefully considered all his son had told him and then gathered with the rest of the leadership in the Great Hall to discuss the castle's defenses, recent events that had transpired since the multi-pronged invasion had begun, and the defense of Adonia as a whole.

Before they began, Truin asked Donstup to lead the gathering in devotion from the Word and a prayer to God for guidance. Donstup chose verses from Psalm 20: "Now I know that the Lord saves his anointed. He answers him from his holy heaven with the saving power of his right hand. Some trust in chariots and some in horses, but we trust in the name of the Lord our God."

Donstup reminded the men to trust in their God no matter what their eyes told them, no matter what their ears told them, and no matter what their reason or emotions told them.

"We have been given a spirit of power, not a spirit of fear. Do not fear men, monsters, or demons! The Lord is with us, and none can stand against the Lord! Not man, not monster, and not demon! His Word has promised this to you. This is true. Believe it!"

"Be strong in the Lord!"

"Be faithful!"

"Stand!"

The men then bowed their heads as Donstup, their spiritual shepherd, led them in a prayer of praise and a prayer for guidance. As Donstup concluded the prayers, Truin added a silent prayer of intercession to God for his brother Ka'el, whose whereabouts were still unknown.

Truin then instructed Koldas to open the discussion by providing a detailed account of the battle with the fire-breaths and how God had defeated the creatures. Those who heard the story for the first time listened intently to what had happened in the icy heights of the mountains and to the descriptions Koldas gave of the flying beasts; beasts they had never seen with their own eyes. Until that moment, they had believed these beasts to be legend only. Even having heard the account from a trusted source, they had a hard time accepting that such things could have transpired.

While Koldas was telling his account of the great ice battle, Truin noticed Weiphal seemed distracted and distant, deep in thought.

"Weiphal. You have discovered and studied more of the beast species in this new land than any of us in this hall. What do you make of all this?"

Weiphal stood. "I have never encountered this creature in my journeys. However, having seen the monsters that live in the Strange Lands of southern Adonia, it is of little surprise to me that creatures such as this exist. Whereas most of the creatures we have discovered remain neutral in the struggles of men, it would seem that these demons have risen from the depths of hell itself to fight against us."

"Indeed it would seem so," Gladsel replied.

"Then again, I have discovered that the titans of God's creation, like the sons of men, can intervene in the great struggle, though maybe not in the same fashion as men. What exactly possesses a creature to do what it does can vary. Sometimes it is hunger, sometimes protection of its own, and sometime rage. But we have always held that it is primarily instinct."

Everyone listened intently as Weiphal thought aloud, struggling to come to terms with his thoughts on the matter.

"Still, in these later times, here in this land, something beyond instinct appears to be in play. What would prompt these creatures, so long hidden from the eyes of men, to awaken and travel so far from their dark dens to attack the sons of Adonia? Someone or something directs them. This is not their instinct."

"Karyan." Someone whispered the name below their breath, clearly not intending to say it aloud. Everyone in the room visibly reacted.

"No!" Truin responded to the slip of the tongue. "It is not Karyan. Even his dark magic is not this powerful."

All eyes turned to Truin as he composed himself.

"His master's perhaps. As we have all seen, more is at work here than the ways of men. You have all seen and heard how the Lord our God has delivered us time and time again from the sea, from the fire, from the hands of men, and from the beast."

All nodded and agreed.

"There is more at work here than the ways of men, and there is more at stake here than physical gain or loss — more than life or death. There is a greater spiritual battle in play. Our God has shown his presence, and our enemies in the spiritual realm have also shown theirs."

A new sense of awe and astonishment settled on the men in the hall. They saw the events of the recent past, indeed the events all the way back to their fathers' exodus from Omentia, as more than merely that of human decision and human preference.

Indeed, much more was happening here than that which met the eye. A new kind of sight was necessary to understand and interpret the sights, sounds, and signs of these times. They were only beginning to see with their fresh eyes, eyes that saw what human eyes could not see; eyes of faith.

"From here on out, we should expect the unexpected."

"About that," Weiphal said, "I had a dream."

All eyes turned back to Weiphal.

"I wasn't sure if I should say anything about it; I'm still not."

Everyone waited patiently as Weiphal decided.

"Overall, the dream was fuzzy, like most dreams, but some things were very clear. It is like I knew about the fire-breaths before today, though not really. In my dream, there were beasts, beasts that were threatening us with mortal danger, like the fire-breaths. The beasts were coming to the castle, and we knew it. And we wondered how we could defend against them."

There was a mix of facial expressions as the men in the hall listened to Weiphal speak of his dreams. They were not used to sharing their dreams with each other, and the discomfort it brought to some showed readily.

"This is where it gets, well, strange." Weiphal paused, took a deep breath, and continued, occasionally closing his eyes to better "see" the dream again.

"Ok, we knew the fire-breaths were coming, and we had a plan."

Everyone listened more intently at this point.

"I know it sounds strange, but I think we surrounded the castle with archers, and when given the sign, our archers fired their arrows straight up into the sky."

They all waited for Weiphal to tell them the rest of the plan.

Truin was silent for a moment. "What was the sign for firing the arrows, and what would firing the arrows into the air accomplish?"

"It gets stranger," Weiphal added before continuing. "In my dream, I saw an eagle, an orn, to be exact. It flew to the castle from the south and landed on my arm. This, I think, was the sign — the sign to fire the arrows."

Everyone in the hall whispered to one another. Even Koldas, who had just witnessed an incredible intervention of the supernatural variety, couldn't disguise his skepticism.

"An orn lands on your arm and you fire a ring of arrows into the air?" Koldas looked bewildered.

"I told you it sounded strange," Weiphal replied. He got it all out while he had the nerve. "Remember the gorn I told you about, the giant orn of the Strange Lands? They were in the dream too, but I can't remember much about them."

Everyone around the table, and those that had gathered in the hall, discussed what Weiphal had told them.

"What should we do with this information?" Truin asked his division leaders and closest confidants. "Do we act on this dream or not?"

Kristof joined in. "Are we to act on our dreams now? And if so, what are we to do with this one? Does it make sense for us to circle the castle with archers and fire our arrows up into the sky? It would require our men to venture out beyond the moat, beyond our defenses, leaving them terribly exposed to the enemy. To what end? Would this not be ludicrous?"

Jonn, however, had a different view. "Have we not just determined that there is more at work here than what we see with our eyes? Has Truin not just said that we should expect the unexpected? If this is a sign from God — a message, maybe even a directive — should we not follow it in faith that God can and will bring his plan to completion? And if it is not a sign from God, can God not still protect us, or use this act of faith to our good? Surely, it is wiser to follow in faith what may be God's direction, even if it seems extraordinary, and trust him for deliverance if it is not his direction — than to choose to disregard his direction out of a lack of faith in his power to protect us."

All pondered carefully the thought Jonn had laid before them.

Then Jonn said, "As for me, I will join the archers outside the fortifications."

Kristof responded. "It is a hard thing, you ask."

"Often, doing the right thing is very difficult until you have the right focus. Where is your focus? Are your eyes on the enemy, or on the deliverer?"

There was silence in the hall. After a moment of thought, Truin smiled.

"Our God works in mysterious ways. I cannot say whether or not God has directed us to do this. And yet, God has laid down the decision before us. Do we step outside our earthly shelters and trust God in faith, or do we put our trust in our physical protections, our moat, and our castle?"

"Seems pretty clear when you put it like that," Gladsel said. "We have seen the Lord at work. I, for one, do not think he is through with this fight."

Melkione boldly suggested, "I think we should ready some arrows, amaze the Heathians with our audacity, stand back, and watch what the Lord plans on showing us next!" Melkione said boldly.

"Amen to that!" Bigaulf added.

"I'm in," Kristof agreed.

"We will take a hidden vote, just to be sure," Truin announced.

Donstup prayed again to the Lord for his guidance in the decision they were about to make — a decision that could decide the fate of all of those within the walls of Armon, and ultimately the people of Adonia.

Following his prayer, the men voted, each voting their conscience on what the Lord would have them do. Sunlight flooded the hall as they tallied the results — reassuring the men that the Lord was present. To the last man, all had voted to accept Weiphal's dream as direction from the Lord and to obey it.

As the men left the now golden hall, Donstup's words seemed to still echo from the stone walls. "Be strong in the Lord, have faith — stand."

And the angels ministered to each of them as they prepared in their own way for deliverance from the storm that was coming.

†††

Talon circled thousands of feet above the mountain range below, riding the warm air currents to ever-higher altitudes. From this height, he could see for many miles and spot prey long before it perceived him as a threat.

It was now midmorning; the sun was baking the countryside with its life-giving rays. Talon glided through the sky effortlessly, content with the sweet scent of the high forest stimulating his senses and the fresh air blowing coolly through his feathers.

As Talon searched the countryside far below for items of interest, his eagle eyes focused in on the men and their fortress home, a home made of many rocks. His senses told him that the men below had been hunting each other; man-carcasses still littered the open area, encircling the rock walls, and the stench of fresh meat still permeated the clear, fresh air like an invisible cloud.

This did not cause Talon much concern. All the creatures of the forest hunted, and as long as the men were not a threat to the orn, which the men of Adonia had not yet been, the orn had little interest in what they hunted — even if they hunted each other.

However, this occasion stood out in one other way. The manhunt was on a much larger scale than that which he was used to observing. This level was like what the orn had witnessed in Omentia prior to their exodus, and for this reason alone, it caused Talon elevated interest.

His instincts directed him to investigate the matter further. He tucked his wings and darted for the massive, rock structure far below him, streaking through the sky at lightning speed, while weaving acrobatically through the puffy, white clouds just now beginning to build around the mountain peaks that surrounded the man-made nest.

As he descended, his senses flashed momentarily to a great, white cloud high above him and then to a large, ominous cloud approaching from the south. Neither held his attention more than a moment as his focus returned to the man-rocks speedily approaching him from below and, more specifically, to a man standing high upon one of them.

†††

They had risen from the bowels of their earthen caves before the sun rose. It was not the way of the tannin to awaken so early in the day, while the air was still so cool. Yet, this morning their blood had come to a boil, early.

They had held their rage long enough. Their rage had been building up for days as their sister brood failed to return from the frozen land to the north, and now they had been called upon to complete the task of destroying the men of Adonia.

They moved across the countryside as one dark formation, following the valleys and riverbeds that flowed to the north, hugging the earth at the lowest possible altitude to avoid detection and achieve maximum surprise. Among the shadowed trees of the forest, which still eluded the early morning rays of the sun; only the startled creatures they unexpectedly passed over knew of their presence. The creatures of Adonia scattered before them as the cloud of hatred and death moved north, looking for a fight.

Weiphal stood high upon a steeple balcony, looking towards the sun now rising in the west and lifting his hands in praise to the Lord.

His dream had led to the daring deployment of most of the Adonian Guard's remaining archers from the First, Second, Third, Fifth, and Eight Air Cavalry to positions outside the wall and in easy reach of enemy infantry. Available elements of the Adonian light infantry, under the command of Sir Adrian the Bold, deployed as hunter-killer squads to protect the Air Cavalry by keeping the enemy occupied. This was a very dangerous gamble in that it required Truin to split his forces, exposing all of his remaining and essential air power to a potential disaster. In addition, Truin left the castle defenses depleted, and no one knew for sure the enemy's strength or how much force they would bring to bear upon the castle.

The weight of his decisions weighed heavily on Weiphal's conscience, and in his prayer, he gave his burden to the Lord.

"Oh my God, how awesome you are on all the earth! Hear my prayer, for only you reign in the heavens. Forgive us for all the times we have failed to walk in your ways and to follow your precepts. Have mercy on us, Oh God, for we are weak. Save us from our enemies, protect us from all evil, and use us to bring glory to your name, the name of the one and only true God."

Weiphal struggled with his doubts.

What if the dream meant nothing, if men would soon die because of my pride and my over willingness to think my dreams of some importance in this struggle? What if —

"Oh my God, forgive me for my doubts. Forgive me for my weaknesses. Remember that I am nothing more than dust. If this is your plan, bring it to completion. Bring it to the end that you want, for we are your servants. And if this is not your plan, if I was wrong to think it so, please use your mighty hand to bring good of it. Have mercy on us, Oh my God."

Beside him stood an archer at the ready; he could signal the other archers to fire at a moment's notice. And in the open, surrounding the castle walls, stood the archers; bows in hand, ready to launch their arrows high into the morning sky — the exact purpose of which remained unknown.

Far outside the castle, standing watch on the deep defensive perimeter with his father, a young man stood amidst the early morning shadows of the magnificent castle. The shadows reached deep into his soul as he contemplated his youth and voiced his heartfelt concern. "We are defenseless, father."

His father replied with a bright smile that instantly warmed his anxious son's heart. "We are never defenseless, son. The Lord is always with us, and he will defend us. What more defense could we ever need or want?"

The lad knew his father was right, but he lacked the experience to truly feel the comfort that this knowledge brought to his father. That was all about to change.

†††

As the heavy Heathian infantry clashed with Sir Adrian and the Adonian light infantry in skirmishes about the hills surrounding the castle's foundation, the airborne horde approaching from the south split into several menacing elements, preparing to attack the castle from all directions simultaneously and overpower its now meager defenses. An unnatural hate filled the beasts' bitter hearts as their bloodlust overwhelmed their instincts; the bloodlust told the creatures that they had remained undetected. As they began their assault on the rocky nest of men, they unwisely dismissed their crosscheck of the skies for air threats, fixating all of their senses on their ground targets.

Talon's gods-eye view informed him of the threat that had encircled him as he continued his rapid descent into the center of the coming storm. Some unseen force overcame his instinct to investigate the threat, and the sudden warning of danger did not deter him from his task. He was now being guided directly to the man standing high amidst the man-rocks.

Weiphal's spirit skyrocketed as he saw the large eagle approaching him from high above.

Could it be true?

Through eyes of faith, he had believed his vision was truly a sign of what God wanted him to do, but seeing the events unfold with his physical eyes elevated the hope that he had not been mistaken — that he had correctly followed God's will.

As the great eagle glided towards him, Weiphal made a fist with his left arm and lowered his arm to horizontal. Time seemed to stand still as the eagle flared its wings, instantaneously bringing its descent to a halt, extending its talons, and landing on Weiphal's arm, gripping it firmly. Its large golden eyes now inches away from his, Weiphal could feel the load of the majestic bird weighing heavily upon his arm, threatening to throw him off balance.

Time slowed. Weiphal stared into the great eagle's eyes. He could see his reflection and that of the bowman, undaunted by the fantastic event, dutifully following his instructions and launching the flaming arrow from his bow. Weiphal followed the red flame of the arrow in the great eagle's eyes as it left the bow and rocketed skyward.

As the flaming arrow left the platform of the tower, the eagle also left its perch on Weiphal's arm and vaulted itself out over the castle's walls, gaining airspeed as it glided down toward the countryside. Weiphal followed the eagle's flight as it departed, mesmerized by its motion and still coming to grips with what was happening.

Weiphal watched the great bird fly into the distance, and his eyes focused out over the surrounding hills. As if still caught up in a dream, the surreal experience abruptly turned dreadful. Scores of winged monsters unexpectedly appeared out of nowhere. The horrendous procession, approaching from the valley below, would be upon the castle before the Guard could react.

About the time Weiphal realized the full meaning of everything that was happening, he noticed the explosion of innumerable projectiles erupting along the entire perimeter of the castle, soaring up from their cloaked positions within the trees to intercept the evil intruders.

The Adonian archers in response to the signal sent just moments earlier from the tower had fired hundreds of flaming arrows skyward, totally unaware of the flying menace that approached. Screaming skyward and guided by a force invisible to men, many of these missiles now found their mark in the soft tissue of a fire-breath's lower neck, surgically striking the only vulnerable weakness the great dragons had in their armor; ironically, the same area that protected the massive hearts of the beasts.

Weiphal watched in amazement as many of the enormous dragons froze midair and dropped lifelessly from the sky, crashing into the walls and ramparts of the castle below. He could hear the horns of the Adonian Guard alerting the castle to the attack and summoning all available guardsmen to the castle's defense.

Though the perimeter defenses had cut down roughly half of the attacking tannin, many of the monsters survived the onslaught of supernaturally guided arrows. These tannin continued their assault on the castle, many of them clawing away at the castle's fortifications as others flew in circles above the castle, diving on the guardsmen at synchronized intervals while unleashing the flames of hell on all who attempted to engage them.

Several areas of the castle erupted in flame as men and beast clashed. All the able-bodied men, who were big enough to wield a weapon, rushed to fight the beasts while women and children remained below cover.

Jonn and his oldest son Isaak emerged from the inner halls of the castle armory to join the battle, both carrying sword and shield in hand. One of the largest and most menacing of the tannins immediately met them. The creature spotted them; its massive tail whipping about wildly, sweeping across the ground to down the two Adonians. Jonn saw the attack coming. As he dove over the top of the spiked tail, he yelled out a warning to Isaak. Isaak heard his father's warning, but he couldn't react fast enough and the tail struck him, propelling him through the air and into a nearby wall. The monster reared up on its hind legs and breathed fire toward Isaak. Jonn sprung to his feet and intercepted the flaming death ray. Holding out his shield just in time to disperse the fire and heat into a funnel that surrounded but did not touch him or Isaak. The flaming attack harmlessly scorched a circular pattern on the wall behind them.

The hideous beast prepared to lunge forward and throw all of its mass against the now seared shield and the men huddled behind it. As it did, many long spears pierced its armor-plated hide as several guard, heavy-infantry flanked the beast and attacked — attempting to distract it. Their efforts were not in vain as the beast defensively swung around to answer their aggression, giving Jonn the time he needed to carry Isaak to safety.

Castle Armon became a battlefield as the Adonian archers and light infantry surrounding the perimeter of the castle fought with Heathian forces intent on entering the castle's walls, and Adonian heavy infantry clashed with the fire-breaths within. Those outside the castle, realizing they needed to join the fight against the monsters that had breached the castle's outer defenses, attempted to fall back and assist. However, the relentless Heathian onslaught prevented them from making much progress. The heavy infantry within the castle fought valiantly against the monsters that had breached the walls, but it rapidly became apparent that the Adonians would soon fall to the much stronger adversary. They needed help from above, and help from above came.

The battle below raged on as a white cloud hanging high above the castle settled, gradually at first, and then more rapidly as it poured down directly above the castle like a giant funnel cloud reaching down from the heavens. As the sound of loud shrieks drew closer and closer, even the fire-breaths took notice. First the monstrous creatures became distracted by the shrieks, allowing the Adonian Guard to land critical strikes against them. Then, as the cloud dispersed directly over the castle, the tannin broke off their assaults entirely, flapping their enormous, scaly wings and rising laboriously into the air to once again join in dark formations.

Given the reprieve from battle, Truin, Jonn, and the others took time to more closely observe what was happening high above them. The white cloud drew closer, and the shrieks became louder. The Adonians could see that what they had previously perceived to be a cloud was, in fact, something much more spectacular. An enormous flock of the giant raptors, or giant orn that Weiphal had spoken of while describing his adventures in the Strange Lands, approached from high above them. The gorn had joined the Battle of Armon.

A massive air battle ensued. Where the fire-breaths had the advantage of a thick hide of armor and devastating weapons, the gorn had the advantage of speed and agility. Much lighter than the fire-breaths, the gorn could speed up much faster and turn much tighter than the heavy, flying reptiles. Thus, the gorn enjoyed the ability to change altitude effortlessly and to turn in horizontal or vertical circles around the monsters.

Besides its speed and agility, the gorn possessed formidable weapons of its own. True, its weapons could not compare with the razor-sharp claws and powerful tail of the fire-breath, but the gorn's sharp claws and jagged beak, combined with its high agility and attack speed, made it a lethal opponent for the tannin.

And there was another advantage for the gorn. They, unlike the reptilian fire-breaths, were warm-blooded. This became a tremendous advantage for the gorn as the freezing temperatures of the northern mountains of Chastain made the tannin sluggish and slower to respond. Already at a disadvantage in intelligence and cunning, the cold-blooded creatures responded even more sluggishly in the frigid air. In addition, the tannin could not climb to the altitudes that the gorn could or their blood would freeze and they would fall from the sky like hail in a thunderstorm; their insides smashing to pieces as they hit the ground. The orn instinctively used the high altitude to their tactical advantage, climbing above the fire-breaths' ceiling when they needed to rest, only to dive from high above moments later at tremendous speeds to take the tannin by surprise and pierce their armor with beak and claw.

The air battle raged high above the castle. Streams of contrails marked the flight of tannin and orn as they fought savagely to reassert their ancient dominance over the land. The orn outnumbered the superiorly armored tannin two-to-one, but even as such, the outcome of the clash was too close to call.

As Truin, Jonn, and the Adonians watched from the relative safety of Castle Armon, orn and tannin fell from above, powerfully crashing about the castle and the countryside below. Outside the castle, the Adonian Guard continued to clash with Heathian infantry.

The women and children, huddled in tight clusters within the relative safety of the darkest and most secluded areas of the underground tunnels of the castle, prayed for their fathers, husbands, and brothers engaged in mortal conflict on the other side of the thick, rock walls. They carried the pain of knowing that some of their loved ones would not return to them that night, and it weighed heavily on their hearts. Their voices clearly reflected this as they prayed.

Yet, these women and children were Adonian. They were strong in faith and determined to survive, both for their posterity and for the future of Adonia. Painful as it might be to lose the men of the family, they knew they were all part of a bigger family of believers and that family must survive. So they prayed for each other and for all the men who would lie down their lives in the great struggle that had ensued. "May they fight bravely, dear Lord, in your name and for your kingdom. Whether they live or die, may they valiantly present their lives to you, to be used in whatever way gives glory to your name. Let them be your hand upon the earth, an instrument of truth, justice, and freedom for all those who fear the one true God. In your name and for your glory, we pray. Amen."

As the sun sank behind the eastern peaks and the ice fog crept down the snowy cliffs behind Castle Armon, the air high above the castle glistened in the many colors of the impending sunset. The many overlapping contrails covered the sky in a spectrum of colors, as if finger-painted by a young child using all the colors of the palette. Even considering the gravity of the situation, the sight was one of incredible beauty, one that those who now observed it would never forget for as long as they lived. Indeed, even those whose life now ebbed from their bodies could see the masterpiece unfolding in the vivid spectrum of twilight colors.

One young man, barely the age of twenty, gazed up into the sky to see the radiant picture of the air battle above. He fell mortally wounded in the fray and was living his last moments upon the earth. He still resisted the invitations of the dark gremlins that scurried about as the battle continued to rage all around him. As a gentle smile broke across his face and a tear ran down his cheek, he thought of his childhood, his mother's face, and how, even in the grip of death, he could see God's beauty — everywhere.

As his eyes slowly closed, and his last tears ran down his young cheeks, falling to the bloody battlefield on which he lie, so the last of the tannin fell through the freezing air above the foothills to impact and shatter on a distant cliff.

The remaining gorn, barely visible and now appearing as dark specters in the fading light, flew low and fast over the castle. Weiphal, still standing upon the tower from which he had signaled the arrow barrage that had started the battle, waved in thanks to the noble birds that had helped to defend the castle from the ancient reptilian beasts.

Outside the castle, the Adonian air cavalry and light infantry had turned the battle and routed the Heathian infantry. Sir Adrian's light infantry now swept the area for any remaining Heathian forces as the draw-bridge lowered and their loved ones welcomed Armon's defenders back into the castle.

And so the Battle of Armon concluded. Though the Adonians had held the castle with a little help from their large avian friends, the battle had cost Adonia much. The defenders of Adonia, her greatest sons, had paid dearly for the victory with their blood.

Truin ordered that all Adonians honor her fallen sons as heroes and lay them to rest in a special place within the castle's walls; a place set aside for Adonia's greatest defenders. In keeping with his command, Gladsel officially designated a special burial ground in clear view of the northern gate of the castle.

The next morning, they held a memorial ceremony. All the survivors of the battle were in attendance, along with the women and children that had gathered to mourn their fallen fathers, sons, and brothers. Though there was tremendous sorrow for the fallen, there was also tremendous pride and love for these men who willingly made the ultimate sacrifice and gave their lives in defense of their loved ones and their homeland. They had laid down their lives willingly, courageously, and in loyal obedience to their calling from God. And now, they rested in his loving arms.

When they had honored and mourned their dead, Truin and his makeshift council strategically decided that all available forces should deploy south to reinforce Plattos, since the enemy, repelled at Armon, would undoubtedly continue its offensive by attempting to overwhelm the province of Plattos in a pincer attack; the remaining Heathian forces attacking from the north and the main Omentian attack force striking from the west.

Truin sent Khory, Kristof, Jhim and Wristo; his sons Bigaulf, Koldas, and Surge; and what remained of their respective divisions to assist Daniel in defense of Plattos. Khory did not want to leave Truin's side, but Truin convinced him he must look after the safety of his sons. After much prodding, Khory reluctantly agreed.

Truin stayed at the castle and oversaw defensive preparations in case the enemy should decide to re-attack the castle. He chose Jonn, Gladsel, and Melkione to stay behind with him. Once Truin was sure that Armon was safe from attack, he planned to place the castle under Gladsel's command and join the Adonian forces in the south. Jonn's younger brother Gladsel had proven himself a very capable military leader and a skilled diplomat, earning Truin's utmost confidence.

After a brief goodbye with loved ones, Adonia's warriors and their divisions departed with haste to reinforce the southern provinces, directly on the heels of the Heathians.

As they had so many times before, the women and children prayed for their defenders as they watched them disappear over the horizon. Not knowing if they would ever see them again, they placed them in the Maker's hands, knowing full well he would watch over them.

Truin, watching from the southern tower of the castle as his sons passed from view, couldn't help but wonder —

Where is Ka'el?

CHAPTER 48

SHADOWS

†††

Skottie sat on the southern ridge of Crystal Valley, watching the sea fog roll into the valley below him from the east. Beside him was a young mariner named Mikole. Mikole had joined Skottie and the Adonian Sixth a week earlier. He had miraculously survived a shipwreck while patrolling the eastern shore. Having lost his vessel, Mikole had vowed to fight with the men of Kandish. "I have already given up my life once; my life is no longer my own. It belongs to my God, who saved me." Mikole's pledge was good enough for Skottie, and Skottie had instated Mikole as one of his advisors.

Skottie had received reports that the Omentians had landed in Delvia and were advancing on northern Plattos by way of northern Kandish. Skottie could not be sure, but if he were new to Adonia, like the Omentians, he would march his invasion force through the Crystal Valley.

The Crystal Valley received its name from the many colored crystals that covered the surface of the valley floor and its surrounding ridges. This characteristic made the valley unique indeed. Although people commonly found the crystals deep within the caves of southern Kandish, they rarely discovered them on the surface. People believed that some kind of underground quake had brought the crystals to the surface of the valley many years earlier when the valley itself formed.

Skottie sat with his junior lieutenants on the ridge. "Yep, this is the way I would enter the heart of Adonia — if I were them."

Lieutenant Jacobin smiled as he heard the words, for both he and Skottie knew something that the Omentians did not know.

Their attention turned to the eastern end of the valley, where a strange fog had appeared. The fog had deliberately made its way unnaturally through the valley, heading west toward their position. Skottie and his men instantly recognized how rare it was for the fog to be moving inland, with the sun as it rose, instead of receding. As a matter of fact, in their recollection, it had never happened before.

"It appears we have visitors for breakfast. Ready the men."

Jacobin used a palm-sized crystal and reflector to refract the morning sun's rays into a bright red signal, which he fired to the northern side of the valley. Different crystals from the valley refracted the sun's rays into various colors which the Kandish Guard used to communicate across great distances. Seconds later, a fiery green flash shot back to his location, signaling that the Adonian Sixth Division was in position, as instructed.

The strange behavior of the fog might have gone unnoticed or possibly considered an innocent aberration if not for the intelligence Skottie had received earlier from Phillip, the Parlantian. Phillip had revealed to the Adonians the methods the Omentians had utilized to use the fog to their advantage — conjuring up dark illusions to give the appearance that their ground forces were much larger than they actually were. This form of deception had served the Omentians well in the earlier siege of Parlantis.

Phillip had told them, "Do not let your fears overpower you. The enemy uses illusion to deceive. They multiply their forces unnaturally. Remember, men without shadow are no men at all." This had initially confused those listening to the Parlantian that day, but Phillip had explained. "Don't you see? This is why the Omentian uses fog to blind the eye and arouse fear. Men fear what they cannot see, but with the light comes truth." Phillip had then spoken the words that would be worth more than gold to Skottie in the battle that was about to unfold. "Only the enemy forces with shadows are real. The rest are but phantom."

The Omentian wizards used the fog and cloud to conceal their force strength and to blind their adversaries as to which of their forces were real and which were illusion. Before the Omentians ever contacted their adversaries, the fog perpetuated and magnified the anxieties of their enemies, clouding their minds and using their own worst fears against them.

The targeting of the Omentian forces was much more difficult when trying to discern which was human and which was chimera. The key to this problem, Skottie had concluded, was to dispel the fog and let the light bring the truth to the battlefield. In addition, perhaps the Sixth Division could give the Omentians a little of their own medicine by blinding them, not with the darkness but with the light.

Skottie had rallied the division a day earlier, directing the heavy infantry to ready their positions behind the countless large boulders in the center of the valley, and the light infantry to dig-in to the rocky sides of both the northern and southern faces of the valley. Then he had stood on the northern ridge and addressed his men. "The Omentian has used devilish deception to drive their enemies mad, to cause them to abandon their positions, and to flee like mice before their army. They will try to unnerve you also by using your fears against you. But the Omentian has never confronted the Adonian Sixth! They cannot use our fears to overwhelm us if we have no fear!"

Skottie had continued. "The Sixth will not turn tail and run if hell itself stands against us! Those that will stand against you and against your home, they are nothing more than mortal men, trying to use illusory tricks to deceive you; they do not have the courage to fight you one on one, man to man!"

"Regardless of what your eyes, ears, and senses tell you is happening, regardless of what deceptions and fears their demons try to plant in your hearts, do not give them a passing thought. They are but feeble attempts to lure you into despair. Deny their power! Trust in your God and your God alone! He alone rules in your hearts; there is no room there for any other! The enemy has no power over you! Our God rules and he will uncover all the deceptions of the enemy, dismissing their darkness with his light!"

The men had listened intently to the golden words of their commander. They knew he cared for them and their safety more than anything; more than anything but the security of the land they had all sworn to defend. His words sunk deep into their souls, strengthening their will, setting their resolve, and focusing their minds. The battle would be the Lord's. They believed that the Lord, their God, would guide the battle and show them the way to victory.

"See with spiritual eyes! The enemy deceives the physical senses, but cannot deceive the spiritual sight our God gives us. Let the light shine through the darkness and expose them. Then you will know them. Then you will see them. Choose your targets carefully."

That was yesterday. Today, Skottie knew his men were ready, and now he waited on the Lord.

Skottie watched the fog move inland through the valley. Like a dark blanket of death enveloping everything in its path, it moved forward — creeping purposefully.

And though I walk through the valley of the shadow of death, I will fear no evil, for though art with me.

The sun's light now showered down upon the countryside, and the thousands of stars that previously lit up the dark blue sky above them faded. Taking their place, the thousands of crystals lining the valley's walls glowed ever so faintly in the early morning light.

The churning cloud of darkness continued to roll westward through the valley, approaching the eastern-most positions of the Adonian Sixth. Skottie's signal lieutenant grew restless, eager to give the signal for attack.

"Wait for it," Skottie whispered, "it is not yet time."

Far below them and throughout the valley, the men of the Adonian Sixth held their breath, remaining as motionless as possible so as not to give away their positions. To the last man, the men thought the

Omentians would surely hear the beating of their hearts, like that of thunder echoing through the valley. And yet, the valley remained unnaturally still and quiet; so still and quiet that perhaps the Omentians should have known that something was wrong — the quiet before the storm.

The cloud moved forward, ever so leisurely, clawing its way through the silence of the tranquil valley. To the men of the Adonian Sixth, there was still no visible sign of the menacing army that moved within it, along the rocks, and through the crevices of the valley floor.

But Skottie knew.

"Wait for it."

The foreboding cloud advanced, reaching the outermost perimeter of the division. In a matter of seconds, the foreboding cloud would expose the Adonians' positions.

The swirling dark cloud came within yards of the Adonian Sixth, and the sounds of men and beasts emerged from within it. The eerie sounds grew steadily until they soon echoed down the valley and up the cliffs to the ridgelines high above. Normal men would have felt tempted to abandon their positions and flee from the sinister forces that concealed themselves behind the dark cloak of evil, invading the valley. But these men stood firm.

As the sounds of the cloud reached his position, Jacobin nervously watched his commander, ready at a moment's notice to signal the attack. This was it; any second now. He could not help but wonder.

What if the Lord did not reveal the enemy to them? What would happen to all the men below? His brothers and his friends — they were running out of time!

Jacobin's pulse raced!

Still a young lad, he believed with his mind that the Lord would be faithful, but he had not yet experienced that he could always trust the Lord. Jacobin simply did not know if the Lord would show.

But Skottie knew.

"Wait for it."

The sun had just crested the rolling hills to the west. Its sharp rays of golden light shot over the ridgelines and continued on a straight vector, directly into the thousands of crystals lining the northern and southern ridges of the valley, powerfully reflecting a full spectrum of light in all directions. The light rays majestically illuminated the fog-filled valley of darkness to the east with a vast array of colors, decisively cutting through the fog and exposing the Omentian army below.

"Now!" Skottie commanded!

Jacobin sent the signal for attack and instantly the sky filled with hundreds of Adonian arrows, promising to rain down death from above on the invading army. Adonian archers from the northern and southern ridges, their targets now clearly delineated in the reflections of multi-hued, crystalline light, fired mercilessly on second echelon Omentian targets — those that clearly cast shadows. They bypassed those many phantoms in the enemy's midst, casting no shadow. Simultaneously, the heavy Adonian infantry emerged from behind the large boulders in the center of the valley and cut off the enemy advance, while light Adonian infantry collapsed upon the Omentians from the northern and southern ridge lines.

The rising sun shattered the darkness of the night, taking the Omentians completely by surprise. Normally accustomed to over-whelming their enemies through guile and deception, they entered the battle completely exposed and blinded by the intense rays of light besieging them from every direction. The tables turned on them, and the intense rays of light destroyed their battle plan.

The Omentians panicked, frantically conjuring up illusions as they tried desperately to seek shelter and regroup. But the men of the Sexy Sixth, as they called themselves, did not give in to their delusions, and there was no shelter to be found in the valley of light for the Omentian. In the open, the Adonian archers mercilessly cut them down. Behind every rock formation in which they attempted to seek shelter, they found an Adonian heavy infantry soldier ready to dispatch them to their hellish masters.

The Omentians struggled in vain to retreat. On the earlier campaigns with the Parlantians and the Heathians, the Omentians had showed that there would be no reprieve in this epic struggle between the light and the darkness. The most ancient of forces were clashing. This was total war.

†††

As the great orn made its way south, it flew over the sparkling valley below.

Just seconds before, the sun had spread its light into the valley of darkness and shadow, transforming it instantly into a sea of motion — a scene of interest and curiosity to the majestic bird of prey.

The great orn looked down upon the valley and the battle that raged there. It could perceive more than any human eye could see. What would stun a human to observe had all but grown commonplace to many of the creatures of Adonia. Besides the clash of the two human armies, the gorn could see countless dark specters traversing the valley below, fleeing the assault of thousands of multicolored angels of light. As the specters left their human hosts to perish before the arrow and sword of the Adonians, the mighty cherubs hunted them down and dispensed with them.

The gorn had seen this before, in, around, and over the great, rocky man-nest to the north. There, too, the angels of light had forced the phantoms of darkness to retreat.

The gorn did not know why, but it knew this was good and right, the way it should be.

†††

The hand-to-hand combat raged for over an hour, up close and personal — dreadfully personal. When it was over, the carnage, overwhelmingly Omentian, covered the valley.

321

The swirling cloud of anger and hate that had invaded the valley less than two hours earlier had hastily retreated before the light of the rising sun. Now, only the many colored rays of light, light still reflecting off the thousands of exposed crystals in the valley, covered the battlefield, giving the dreadful sight of carnage a more surreal quality as Skottie and his commanders walked the length of the valley, tending to the Adonian wounded.

Skottie surveyed the thousands of Omentian corpses, still fitted in the various coats of armor that they had taken from the peoples they had conquered and pillaged. The overwhelming loss of life before him pierced his soul. True, these men had been the enemy and had invaded their land, but now, spread across the valley floor in front of him, all he could think about was how every one of these men was someone's son, brother, or maybe father.

What evil had overtaken these men in these last days to inspire them to rape, pillage, and steal from those living in the surrounding lands? How could men's hearts be so clouded by anger, bloodlust, and the thirst for power that their consciences would allow them to perform such deeds?

"But for the grace of God, go I." Skottie said the words aloud.

"But for the grace of God." Jacobin and Mikole repeated.

Skottie dropped to one knee, and beneath the wonder of thousands of different rays of crystal light, he and his son Jacobin prayed for the souls of the lifeless men sprawled out before them on the valley floor. The men of the Adonian Sixth, to the very last man, did the same. They lifted their petitions for the fallen, along with their individual thanks for their deliverance; and they acknowledged the Lord of the heavens and the earth as both the keeper of their souls and their deliverer from death.

When they had finished with their prayers, they gathered the bodies of the Omentian soldiers and piled them all together in a circular pit in the center of the valley. They covered the pit with hyssop branches and set it ablaze, sending a cloud of acrid smoke high into the blue skies above as a testimony to all of Adonia's enemies that the true God of the heavens was watching over Adonia. The fire burned for five days straight, and people could see its cloud as far away as Eastern Omentia.

To this day Crystal Valley, the Valley of Light, is called the Valley of Death by all who would do Adonia harm.

CHAPTER 49

SEEN AND UNSEEN

SEDUCTION

†††

The Adonian divisions from Castle Armon continued their pursuit of the Heathian attack force, relentlessly advancing south toward Plattos. As they pursued the invaders, it soon became quite obvious that the size of the remaining Heathian army was much larger than what they had previously thought.

The Heathians were practicing a scorched earth policy of destroying anything useful to any would be pursuers as they passed through the countryside, making it very difficult on the Adonian divisions in their wake to get the needed food and supplies.

Khory had believed that the Heathian attack force had directed the major thrust of their attack towards Aanot and Castle Armon. It now seemed to be the case that the Heathians had deceived the Adonians into thinking Castle Armon was the "northern prize" when, in fact, the city of Pax in central Plattos was to be the primary aim of the Heathian northern offensive.

This was very troubling news as it seemed unlikely that Daniel and the Seventh Division could stand against this large of a force without help.

Khory pushed ever harder to catch up with the Heathian attack force while struggling to understand their importance in God's unfolding plan.

If the Lord could defend Adonia without our help, as he had shown several times within the last few months, why do we rush so to defend Plattos? Does Daniel really need us to assist in its defense? Not really. And yet, what should we do, stand by and do nothing? Surely not!

So Khory and the others pushed on, trusting that the Lord would show them what he wanted them to accomplish, if anything, and trusting that God would take care of the rest.

The Lord's will be done.

†††

"There is much that we can offer you," the Omentian ambassador said seductively, as she tried to entice Daniel to see things her way. All Adonia, as far as you can see, can be yours. My master will give it to you. You will be second to no one here but the master himself. In addition, all the pleasures of this world can be yours for the taking. My master has learned much of the secret ways. He has shown them to me, and I will teach them to you."

Daniel focused intently on her words, doing his best to avoid falling prey to her non-verbal advances.

Aside from Daniel's chief advisor, Benhjami, who stood watch by the entrance of the room, the two of them sat alone in the dark chamber, discussing Plattos' options, as the Omentian Ambassador, Mirare, had so delicately put it. As a matter of policy, Daniel, who was most wise in these matters, always had at least one other person accompany him when meeting with any woman besides his wife, Karena. This was especially true when entertaining young envoys like Mirare after sunset.

Mirare wore a long, red-velvet robe that tightly clung to her well-rounded body. She sat across from Daniel in the shadows of the chamber; her long, black hair flowed elegantly from the hood she still wore.

Her ruby-red lips spoke the words of seduction to Daniel, and she delicately repositioned in her chair, crossing her long, slender legs and brazenly showing Daniel much more than any woman should.

"We can make your rule of Adonia most pleasurable." The words flowed off her soft, full lips like a gentle stream of chocolate.

For a moment, Daniel felt tempted to hear more. Although aware that this woman and her master were determined to destroy him and that he couldn't trust anything she said, Daniel couldn't resist the temptation to hear more from her. Daniel froze, momentarily basking in her words and the delight her appearance brought.

When she thought she had Daniel under her spell, Mirare turned her gaze to Benhjami. "We can bring beneficial change to your land. We can make everyone here very happy."

Benhjami returned her gaze. He couldn't help but feel enchanted by the allure of all that this mysterious woman represented. She was fascinating and beautiful. Her long, blonde hair and seductive mannerisms differed from those of the Plattosian women.

Could all Omentian women be like this?

As the men allowed their desires to take control of their senses, the light in the room suddenly and dramatically changed. Once illuminated by only the dim golden glow of but a few candles, the room unexpectedly erupted in an explosion of bright, white light as a single bolt of lightning flashed across a cloudless night, illuminating the summit chamber with the light of thousands of candles. A deafening clap of thunder immediately followed the intense light, hammering the senses of all within the chamber and jolting Daniel and Benhjami back to their senses.

Daniel regained his sight, but a faint image remained in his vision. The image was that of a ghastly creature, not that of the woman he thought he had been entertaining. After a moment, this image faded, and as his sight returned to normal, he could once again see the beautiful woman sitting across from him.

Daniel noticed the woman was quite shaken by the unexpected bolt of lightning.

"It is alright, it was just lightning."

Mirare had curled up into a ball on the chair and had pulled her hood down over her face. As she heard his words and gradually regained her composure, she lowered her legs and again sat upon the chair as she had before.

Daniel and Benhjami saw the beautiful and sensuous woman before them as she repositioned in her chair, but the ghastly image from a moment before remained clear in their mind's eye.

Then, from nowhere, Daniel's *sight* returned. "Is it not true that your master has forcible taken both Parlantis and Heath?"

Mirare's hood shadowed most of her face. Only her beautiful ruby lips remained visible to Daniel, and the lips said nothing.

"Is it not true that even now your armies attack our land, burning our fields and killing all those who stand in your way?"

The temptress responded seductively. "Some do not know what is good for them, and they resist. Only those who refuse the enlightening and fundamental change my master brings have anything to fear. My master knows what is best for you. Embrace his wisdom. Be thankful he is here to take care of you."

"Here to take care of us like he took care of the Parlantians? The Heathians?"

Mirare removed her scarlet hood, carefully revealing the rest of her face. The soft hood slid smoothly down her long dark hair, coming to rest on her shoulders. Her eyes seductively rose to meet Daniel's.

"I will take care of you, Daniel. Everything you want can be yours."

Daniel resisted her charms. "Answer my question."

"Those poor, dumb peasants who clung to their ancient beliefs and resisted the change; they got what they deserved. You, however, are much wiser that they are. You will reap the rewards from my master as you accept this change, as you and your people accept the new and better way."

"This change you speak of, why should we believe it is for the better and not just an empty promise?" Benhjami joined his father in questioning her.

"Our people have power and everything that they desire. They are not bound to any of the old rules, nor prisoners to any of the old ideas. They are free to do as they please, when they please. This is the way of true freedom. This freedom is what we offer you."

Daniel forcefully addressed her again, no longer seeing the beautiful shell of the woman she used to disguise her true identity. He now saw her inner being, the decayed and deceptive creature that lived within. "This freedom you offer is no freedom at all. It is rebellion against the one, true God, against all that is good and right. You offer us nothing but slavery to your dark master."

With this, Mirare's demeanor changed. A sinister grimace covered her face, and her words lost the soft and inviting qualities they possessed a moment before. In a hard and threatening tone, she fired back. "If you do not submit, you will die like all the others! And for what? Your ancient beliefs? Your dead brothers? Your dead god?"

And with that, Mirare crossed the line.

Daniel stared intensely into the beast's eyes. "Guards!"

Two Adonian guardsmen entered the chamber, awaiting instruction.

"Get her out of our sight."

"Yes sir! "The men did as instructed, escorting the woman from the chamber, while marveling at her beauty.

She passed by Daniel, sneering, and declared, "No one can stand before my master! Kneel or my master will destroy you! Your souls are ours!" Daniel and Benhjami listened to the evil envoy's cackles as they echoed off the cold stone walls of the corridor leading away from the meeting chamber.

After a few minutes of quiet thought, Daniel looked at his good friend Benjhamin. "We will bow before no man, or woman, for that matter. We cannot do this great wickedness and sin against our God!

If it is the Lord's will for our bodies to be destroyed, then so be it, but they will not take our souls."

As he spoke the words, a solitary hooded figure, having used her enchantments and successfully slipping away from the guards by changing her appearance yet again, faded into the shadows. Disappearing into the darkness of the night, she returned to her kind. Metus, her demonic master, the spirit of fear, remained behind, searching for those he might still find open to his influence.

Unknown to Daniel, an enormous army approached Plattos from the north. A storm was on its way.

†††

Throughout Plattos, Mirare's minions had been busy spreading fear and apprehension about the invasion of Adonia and what it might mean to its inhabitants. A large segment of the population, having not descended from the house of Abner, was especially susceptible to their persuasive efforts. "Why should we not do what they ask of us?" they said to one another. Not having the spirit of the one true God, they considered only their temporal lives. "What can be the harm in doing what they ask? Is it not better to accept the change? Is it not better to bow to the invader than to die resisting? Does not the Omentian promise a better life?"

These were the weak of Adonia; those who for so long had been the fellow recipients of God's exceedingly gracious gifts; gifts given to Adonia for the sake of the faithful who lived in the land. Never truly understanding these gifts, these native peoples, many of whom still clung to their pagan beliefs, were naively ready to trade away the gifts and protection they had received for the empty promise of change. They cared for nothing more than their own personal safety. There was nothing they considered worth risking their lives. They were morally corrupt in their thinking and steadfast only in making decisions based on immediate comfort and collective cowardice. Indeed, they unwisely fell prey to the lie that they would prosper when the fundamental transformation came. All they needed to do was betray Plattos' current, benevolent leadership by encouraging dissent within the Plattosian citizenry.

And so, the magic tricks of the sorcerers easily impressed these unbelieving feeble souls, and so the sorcerers believed that Omentian magic would also easily overwhelm Plattosian defenses.

Daniel was keenly aware of this self-destructive movement within Plattos, even within the capital city of Pax itself. It was human nature to fear, and the fear-mongers amongst them never rested. They planted their poisonous ideas at every turn and in every shadow. Retreat, betrayal, submission, survival; these were the offerings of the intellectuals in their midst — reason and logic over faith and truth.

But Daniel remained steadfast in his faith in God. He prayed for wisdom and strength. He received both. Despite growing increasingly anxious over the moral poverty that grew within the citizenry of Plattos and being tempted to fear that this corruption would eventually destroy the land from within, Daniel refused to question God.

Daniel realized all Plattosians were being asked to make a choice; put their faith in man and magic, or put their faith in God. A line was being drawn, and men were lining up on both sides of this line, confident that their choice was the best — that their faith was true. One faith was born of God. The other was born of a demon. In the end, it did not matter which faith was the strongest, but rather, which object of faith was the strongest. To Daniel, God was stronger than man and God was stronger than demon. In fact, God was stronger than all men and all demons combined.

Daniel knew God would prevail. He was certain of it. No amount of sorcery or magic tricks would persuade Daniel to turn his back on God. But how many of his countrymen would fall to the lure of the Omentian? How many would accept the change, not realizing, until it was too late, what that change would really mean and how bad that change would truly be? This he did not know, and this concern for his neighbors caused him the greatest consternation.

††††

The bulk of the Heathian Army, minus the diversionary units sent to skirmish with and preoccupy the Adonians at Armon in the east and Tanshire in the west, emerged unscathed and at full force in the northern plains of Plattos, twenty miles from the city of Pax. Accompanied by several Omentian witches to aid in battlefield deception and two high priests of Karyan to ensure the commanders followed his directives to the letter, the number of Heathian warriors stood at just over ten thousand. Surely the jewel of Plattos could mount no defense capable of repelling such a force, and Karyan would have a stronghold in the heart of Adonia from which to spread his venom throughout the land.

It was Baldrus' strategy to feint the major thrust of their attack on Chastain and Tanshire while pouring into the heart of Adonia and taking Plattos, before the Adonians ever knew what happened. The northern arm of the Omentian army, which was simultaneously driving in from various positions on the east coast of Adonia, would join his force in Plattos.

Baldrus smiled as he observed the thousands of Adonians approaching his position from the south. The Omentian emissaries, sent by Karyan to Plattos ahead of the attacks, had successfully deceived these Plattosians and were leading them to Baldrus to embrace the change in governance.

History had shown that a certain segment of every population believed that hostile invaders of their country would respect nonresistance and even surrender. These, albeit peace-loving people, were at best — overly idealistic and naïve; at worst — completely pacifist and cowardice. Though invaders appreciated the willful reduction in the indigenous fighting strength that surrender by some portion of the defending population offered, no self-respecting invader would choose to keep worthless cowards around following their conquest of the land. They simply represented no value added; they were bad seed — a negative contribution to the gene pool and trash to be disposed of at the earliest opportunity.

The so-called "peace-loving Plattosians" approached the Heathian army singing songs of greeting and friendship. Meanwhile, Karyan's witches ensured these naïve and idealistic sheep saw nothing ahead of them but the serene and familiar grasslands of their homeland; it was better that way. By the time the Plattosians knew what waited for them over the hill, it was too late for them to run. They found themselves in the midst of the Heathian killing fields. They had come out to meet the invaders with nothing but the best of intentions. These men, women, and children fell mercilessly — first to the bow and then to the blade. The Heathian warriors, blinded by the venom that had taken root and overcome their souls, passed through the peaceful Plattosians effortlessly. They did so without blinking an eye and as if only exercising for the main event; the upcoming clash with the best Plattos offered.

The Heathians confiscated the peace offerings the group had brought them, reclaiming their blood-soaked arrows and anything else of value to be found on the slain. Then they continued on the move toward the city of Pax, leaving the remains of Plattos' meekest to the carrion-eating vultures that circled overhead.

As the sun set in the east, the Heathians made camp fifteen miles from Pax, beside the river Placid. The numbers of man and beast were so great that they all but emptied the river of its life-sustaining water.

Daniel awoke.

It had been a rough night. All his attempts to sleep were to no avail. He could not get the previous day's events out of his mind. He wondered what had happened to all those who had left the city the day before — all those he had been powerless to convince not to leave.

Daniel quietly rose from the bed, walked across the stone floor of the room, and kneeled before the large window to pray, as was his habit every morning as the sun rose. He tried to clear the nighttime cobwebs from his mind. Daniel gazed out the window that overlooked the city of Pax. He was astonished and unsettled by what he saw. Normally, he could see for many miles to the east of the city from this perch high in the central tower of Pax. He and Kharin had witnessed many beautiful sunsets together from this vantage point. Today, like most mornings, he could see everything as clear as crystal. Unlike most mornings, he could only see as far as the city boundary; beyond the city gates, a wall of cloud and fog completely encompassed the city.

He ran to the large window facing to the west. From here, the bright orange sun would enter their room every morning, bringing with its golden rays the warmth that both he and Kharin both found so soothing and invigorating. But not today; today, there was no sun to see. Only a faint impression of its radiance penetrated a foggy wall of gray.

Cloud and fog covered the city of Pax, but not any ordinary cloud or fog. The gray beast seemed to stop at the boundary of the city in every direction.

"What is it, Daniel?" Kharin struggled to awaken.

"Something is wrong, very wrong."

Kharin joined Daniel at the window, and they stood in awe, speechless, as they watched the wall of cloud rotate precariously around the city.

Khory ordered a full halt.

The Adonians had followed the Heathian horde out of Chastain onto the plains of Plattos. They had been closing in, catching up gradually, but surely. They had overtaken several of the Heathian guards protecting the Heathian army's flank, and by Khory's best estimates, they could soon see the enemy in strength.

As they looked to the south, several large funnel clouds sprung to life beneath a cloudless sky, growing right before them from the ground up. As the funnels formed, they lit up the sky with flashes of light and peels of thunder.

Such menaces were notorious in these flatlands. They would typically rise amidst the worst of storms and wreak havoc on unsuspecting towns and villages, usually in the darkness of the night. The Plattosians called the clouds "tearing winds" for the damage they so often caused.

But these tearing winds were different. The monsters that now formed before the Adonians formed in the middle of the day with no storms in sight. In addition, multiple funnels formed simultaneously, constructing a would-be wall between them and the Heathians.

Khory assembled the Adonian Division Commanders and spoke with them about what they were witnessing.

"The Lord is speaking to us. I do not think he wants us to pursue the Heathians onto the plains," Wristo offered.

"We have all seen the mighty hand of the Lord in recent days. We are here to serve him and to fight for him; but he does not need us to fight this invader." Jhim added.

Kristof, having been a fighter for most of his life and perhaps the most battle-hardened warrior of them all, did not readily agree. "Whether we live or die this day, we are the Lord's! These clouds are no threat to us. We are here for a reason. We must proceed!"

Bigaulf addressed his fellow commanders. "Kristof is correct. We have nothing to fear. Nothing of man or nature can harm us if it's not the Master's will to allow it. We know this to be true. I have stood in the fire, and yet I did not burn, for our God sent his protectors to shield me."

Bigaulf had their undivided attention. Even though they had all seen God's amazing acts, Bigaulf's story of how God had delivered him and his sons from the fire amazed them as much or more than any of the events that they had witnessed.

He continued. "But I did not choose to stand in the fire. Nor would I choose to do so again. Though we trust God to protect us, I do not think we should throw ourselves recklessly into harm's way to prove it."

Surge entered the discussion. "Normally, as you all know, I would not hesitate to charge into the storm. For better or for worse, it would not matter to me; thus has been my habit. However, there is much at work here, both above us and below us, and I believe we should use the wisdom and experience our God has given us to decide the most prudent course of action." Everyone's eyebrows rose when Surge said the word "prudent."

Koldas said, "I have seen the winds change the course of the battle. I am convinced that these winds are from the Lord and that they will do the Master's bidding. We should wait on the Lord but be at the ready to strike if need be."

They all pondered the words spoken. After a few moments, Khory said, "The Lord is speaking, and we will listen. Tell your divisions to make camp, but to be ready to move out on an hour's notice. We will pray and wait on the Lord."

Bigaulf, Koldas, Surge, Jhim, Wristo, and even Kristof agreed. Though each of them was eager to reach Pax as soon as possible to help Daniel, something much greater was at work on the plains of Plattos. They had witnessed extraordinary events in the past weeks. The Lord their God had delivered each of them in the most wonderful ways, ways they never would have expected, and their eyes were now wide open to that which was admittedly still well beyond their understanding.

Baldrus ordered the Omentian witch to be brought to his tent at once.

"Why have you proceeded with preparing the battlefield when I have not yet ordered it?" he thundered! Baldrus was an enormous man. His many battle scars and physical deformities made him even that much more intimidating.

The Omentian witch, however, knowing she could at will use her black magic to twist his already evil-enslaved mind into knots and tear out any senses he still commanded, was not flustered. She stood before him, covered in her dark, hooded robe that all the witches of Karyan wore, and calmly answered the Heathian commander. "I have done nothing."

He abruptly opened the entrance of the tent, startling the entrance guards. He extended his arm and pointed outside of the tent. "Then why can I not see beyond the river? Why can I not see Pax?"

"It was not I, my liege," she replied, her sarcasm openly deriding him before his guards, which could now hear every word. "I have only summoned the clouds around us — as was your command."

"Watch your tone, witch, or I will —"

"You will what?"

Baldrus' mind filled with terror as he found himself overwhelmed with images of his own death, images that were no doubt conjured up by the witch standing before him, but still real to him.

The witch saw Baldrus had learned his lesson; she removed the spell.

Baldrus regained his composure and began again, more respect-fully. "What, then, am I to do? Do I cross the river and advance in the blind, not knowing what the Plattosians have planned for us? This is unacceptable! You must fix it."

"I cannot," the witch replied. "I have already tried. It is not my doing and not within my power to undo."

"Then what good are you?" As the words left his mouth, Baldrus tried to pull them back. Beads of sweat instantly formed on his brow as he realized he had gone there again.

Before the witch could teach him a harsher lesson in respect for the witches of Karyan, their attention turned elsewhere.

Out of the blue, the Placid River, known for its peaceful current, became enraged. Energized by a deluge of rain a day earlier far upstream, its waters suddenly began to rise and churn. This immediately captured the attention of the soldiers and their horses camped on the river's edge. The turmoil rapidly spread throughout the camp as the Heathians awoke to the sounds of growing confusion. Bewildered soldiers exited their tents to find that things were not as they had expected them to be.

Besides the raging river and the foggy nothingness beyond it, a horrific sight soon caught their attention. Terror seized their souls as they turned to find that the thunderous sounds they were hearing were not coming from the river before them, but from the skies behind them.

To the north, south, and east, monstrous funnel clouds formed out of nowhere, sucking up the cloud and fog that was the Heathians' normal camouflage and turning it instead into a terrible and unexpected threat. The immense torrents of wind and earth grew at lightning speed before their eyes; each of the monsters of nature complete with dark swirling clouds, emanating long tentacles of lightning and thunderous bursts from within.

The Heathians were terrified. They stood like dead men before the awesome sight. Both Baldrus in full body armor and the witch in her crimson robe exited the tent to behold the spectacle. Baldrus' jaw dropped. "What manner of magic is this?"

The witch had no reply, standing in awe of the unbelievable sight.

The Heathian soldiers, awaking from their stupor, gathered their battle-dress and looked about frantically for cover as they awaited orders from their commanders.

Baldrus ordered his commanders to assemble. As soon as had he given the order the fiery funnel clouds moved towards them, collapsing on the Heathian positions in such a way and at such a speed that it soon became clear to all that the Heathian army could not move fast enough to outrun the flaming pillars of death that now approached.

"Take cover!" The cry came out of nowhere as commanders struggled to make sense of the situation that had so suddenly come upon them.

Sensing the danger, no one could console the horses. They broke loose from their stables by the hundreds, running through the camp and trampling everything in their path.

Soldiers, some half-dressed, ran blindly in every direction, trying to figure out what to do and where to go, but there was nowhere in the flatlands to take cover.

The entire camp was soon in a state of panic. Baldrus and his commanders tried in vain to gain control of the soldiers, but it was no use. Fear had taken them and fear now controlled them.

The towering torrents moved on the Heathian camp. The angry clouds grew darker and more ominous. They hung over the spinning torrents, feeding the funnels with energy and directing their fury at the invading army.

In a swift realization that their only refuge must lie beyond the river, the masses surged as one to the west, making their way towards the tumultuous river. Those farthest away from the river trampled over those that got in their way. A stampede of men and beast moved like a wave across the camp, emptying itself into the raging river. The river had grown massive in just moments, tearing mercilessly at the collapsing banks, which struggled futilely to hold the raging waters in place.

The Heathians attempted to navigate her turbulent waves safely, but the River Placid opposed them, violently yanking them under water with her vicious currents and mercilessly sweeping them away.

Thousands, realizing the river was no longer a viable refuge, stopped at her shores, searching frantically for any hope of sanctuary.

The funnels converged.

Many soldiers attempted to run the gauntlet between the funnels, only for the funnels to catch them in their grasp and swallow them up. The torrents catapulted them through the air and devoured them in immense meat grinders that callously consumed everything in their path.

As the rest of the once massive army huddled together on the shore of the once peaceful river that now meant certain death, the tearing winds bore down on them. Many, overwhelmed by the ferocity of their impending doom, chose certain death amidst the waves rather than being swept away by the winds. They threw themselves into the river and descended into the quiet depths below.

Those that remained and faced the tempests that approached prepared as best they could to resist the clouds of fury. They clung to one another, attempting to form a unified, immovable body that could withstand the force of the wind. Those with shields held them high above their heads to form a shell of armor to repel the force of the wind.

They had almost convinced themselves there was hope, but abruptly, their mission became even more daunting. While they waited on the inevitable impact of the twisters, yet another unexpected turn of events fell their spirits. Gigantic shadows moved along the ground toward the Heathian formation, telegraphing yet another unforeseen enemy. From beneath their shields, the Heathian remnants glimpsed a new level of terror.

Enormous hailstones emerged from the funnel clouds, dropping in waves upon the Heathians. Massive chunks of ice, larger than the boulders found along the river's shore, fell on them from above. There was no refuge on the plain. The boulders of ice impacted the ground with tremendous velocity, smashing the armored Heathians into the soft plains on which they stood, creating man-sized craters of metal, earth and flesh. Armor ripped from the bodies of the soldiers became deadly instruments of wrath within the tearing winds, filleting and dicing those who remained. The winds forcibly ripped the men's shields from their grasp and used them to decapitate those around them. Soon, the ground became covered in a sea of blood and the pulverized remains of men.

Baldrus, surrounded by the devastated remains of his once invincible army, stood helpless and alone on the field, raising his fists in defiance to the power that encircled him. A moment later, he too was gone. The clouds, crimson red with the blood of the invaders, carried their decimated bodies high into the sky, where they then disappeared forever from the sight of men.

†††

Khory and the Adonians watched the tearing winds turn red and then disperse before them in the distance. When they had completed their prayers of intercession for Plattos, they rose from their knees.

†††

As the Adonian army moved south, a peace fell over the River Placid, and a gentle breeze dissipated the fog that had surrounded the city of Pax. The sun shined down on the city, and there was no sign that the Heathian Army had ever set foot in Plattos.

CHAPTER 50

FOREST FRIENDS

†††

E vil has many faces. While the fires burned in Delvia and seduction tested her charms in Plattos, a different evil lurked in the shadows of the forests of Tobar.

The Omentians had sent raiding parties, composed of the worst spirits Omentia offered, ahead of their main attack forces. Murderers, rapists, and assassins, all endowed by their new master with varying degrees of magical power, covertly infiltrated Adonia and settled into the thick undercover of Tobar. These groups disappeared amidst the dense forest until it was once again time for them to commit their abhorrent acts.

With ever-increasing frequency, incidences of unthinkable malice and brutality began occurring throughout the forests, events unlike that which had ever occurred before on this side of the Dark Sea.

Soon, the unknown evil lurking in the shadows haunted all of Tobar.

Geoff had been the first of Truin's sons to leave home; the first to set out and make his place in the bountiful new land the Lord had given him and his family.

Arriving in the forests, Geoff had made a very unorthodox decision. Geoff had observed that the forest floor, thick with vegetation and wildlife, was a great repository of all the nourishment that he and his future family would need. However, a dwelling on the forest floor offered little regarding security. For security, his eyes turned to the strength and majesty of the forest; his eyes turned to the trees.

High above the threats that lurked in the dense underbrush of the forest, high in the solid branches of the mighty oak trees, that is where Geoff lived. First perfecting the one-person dwelling, then expanding it to a more elaborate home, Geoff had systematically perfected the best practice of building the tree dwelling, becoming a well renowned arboreal architect.

Soon, others wanting to make their homestead in the forest followed his lead, and before long, many villages sprung up high in the trees of Tobar.

Geoff had prospered in Tobar and had begun a family of his own. He and Ahnettia, his wife, became the proud parents of several sons and daughters, who had then given Geoff many grandchildren.

The Tobarians, or tree people as they became known, were a proud and strong people with a unique affinity for dwelling with the birds. As a community, they excelled with the bow, surpassing any other in Adonia, using the tool for both hunting and defense.

The Tobarians hated violence. Rather, they were bound by their love, service to one another, and their shared faith — a faith which was firmly anchored high in the skies above Tobar.

Though the Tobarians made their homes in the trees, they spent much of their time on the forest floor hunting, hiking, and playing. Parents taught children how to shoot their bows long before they could go unaccompanied into the forest. Once a child became proficient with their bow, their parents taught them to never leave the safety of the trees without it.

Tobarian children, though quite comfortable on the ground, developed a sixth sense that alerted them to predators that hid in the forest's thick foliage. From an early age, their elders taught them to seek refuge in the trees at the first sign of danger, as most of the forest's predators could not follow them there. Then, from their high vantage point above the danger, they could effectively eliminate the menace with the bow, if need be, or wait until the threat went on its merry way.

More often than not, it was clear to all when a stranger entered the forest. There were many telltale signs that would instantly give an outsider away. First, the stranger might not carry a bow, which was simply unheard of for the tree dwellers. Perhaps he might not know the forest like the back of his hand. But the surest sign that a traveler was alien to the forest would undoubtedly be the shackles that held him to the forest floor; incapacity to move through the trees was the mark of an outsider.

The trees were life to the Tobarian, but to the stranger in the forest, the trees meant mystery by day and terror by night.

††††

His green eyes searched the darkness.

He had followed the two-leg, known as Toro, from the Strange Lands to these forests. This land was rich in prey and scant in predators. He and his kind had then settled here, prospered here, and grown very large in number here.

They could have gone to war with the two-legs, had the two-legs pursued them. But the two-legs seemed to be completely unaware of their presence in the forest. Farkus and his kind had kept to the shadows of the forest; they didn't compete with the two-legs for food or violate their living areas. The wolves kept to themselves, living in peace with the two-legs. Thus the family of wolf became second only to the two-legs in the forests of Tobar.

Then the strangers came.

Though also of two legs, the strangers were not the same as those that lived peacefully with the wolves in the forest. The wolves sensed it immediately, even before the *happening*.

Several of Farkus' pack witnessed the happening while they were hunting one night beneath a full moon. Several of the strangers to the forest had abducted two Tobarian children from a nearby village; they had carried them bound and gagged into the darkness. The pack had overheard the commotion and had closed in. Then the unthinkable happened.

The wolves had never witnessed the brutality and butchery of two-legs upon the young of their own kind. Wolves of a pack would never turn on their young like this, simply for the joy of killing. Only a very diseased wolf could do such a thing. If this were to happen within the pack at any point, the pack would immediately turn on the sick wolf and end its life. This was the way of the wolf, but not so with these two-legs.

When word of this *happening*, and that of others like it, reached Farkus' ears, his blood, like that of all the wolves who heard the report, boiled in rage.

Farkus had grown to respect the two-legs, perhaps even more than respect them. Since the day in the cave, when he had kept a two-leg from cold-death, he had felt a special closeness to them all. That sense of closeness with Tobarian two-legs had passed on to all the wolf kind that had journeyed to Tobar from the Strange Lands.

Now, it was obvious to the wolf that not all two-legs were the same. How these stranger two-legs could have done what they did to these innocent ones was beyond the ability of the wolf to fathom. Further, if these strangers to the forest would do this evil to their own kind, did not they pose a dire threat to the wolf? Someone had to protect the forest, indeed, to protect not only the home of the Tobarian, but also the new home of the wolf.

Though until now the wolves had predominantly stayed in the deep forest, making sure they remained unseen by the two-legs, the wolves made a bold decision. The Tobarian wolves, through instinct or perhaps guidance from a higher power, supported Farkus' decision to seek out and rid the forest of the strangers. They would do this even though this action would make their widespread presence in the forest known to all. In addition, their action against the stranger two-legs might be seen as blood-lust against all the two-leg kind, inviting retaliation from the very ones they were acting to protect. It needed to be done. They would do this at their own peril. They would do this at all costs.

For whatever reason, the fate of the Tobarian wolf and the Tobarian two-leg became entwined. They were all Tobarian now. The evil invaders were not.

†††

Two men, one very young and one old, sat high above the earth at the top of the forest canopy. The canopy stretched from their position for a hundred miles in every direction.

"It has happened again, Father. What can we do?"

Samuell, now a strong and knowledgeable young man, had never faced this situation before. For as long as he could remember, they had lived without threat in the forest. Now, something wicked had found their sanctuary in the trees, and the Tobarians searched for the wisdom to deal with the crisis.

It had all started a week before, when two young children had disappeared, vanishing from the spot where just moments before their mother had watched them playing together in the midday sunshine. The search party began searching for them right away and discovered their remains that evening, buried in a mound of leaves some two miles away. Someone had done unspeakable things to them.

Soon, all across the forest, children of all ages went missing. One by one, they found the missing children. In ever-increasing brutality and gore, the perpetrators of these hideous acts, whether man or beast, displayed their slain victims in vile ways, as if now to revel in their ability to commit these crimes unabated and to taunt the tree people into action.

Geoff, like all the peace-loving people of the forest, anguished over the loss of the children and their inability to find the perpetrators of these savage crimes. Though the Tobarians had searched high and low for any sign of the evildoers, they could not track the killers. It was as if the strangers to the forest were ghosts, materializing to commit their deeds and then vanishing again into thin air once the evil deeds were done.

Deep in thought and staring far into the distance, Geoff replied. "Indeed, Samuell, what can we do?"

Geoff bowed his head and prayed to God for the wisdom, the thoughts, and the words to pass on to his son. Then, when he finished, Geoff looked deep into his son's eyes, just as he had done many times before, and he taught him.

"We must not despair, and we must not fear. Those without hope, those without God, they fear and despair. They live in darkness; lost. They know no love, no hope, no justice, and no honor. Their only motivation is carnal, and their drive is a selfish pursuit of immediate pleasure. Like the animals, they live only for the wordly and the temporal.

However, we know that the Maker of the Universe, the designer of the amazing world around us and of all its creatures, loves us. We know our God can use all for good, even the evil that, through sin, has infected the perfect world He made."

Geoff continued. "Years ago, my grandfather, Abner, saw evil gaining a stronghold in the land he loved across the waters, and he trusted our God to bring him and his family across the Dark Sea to this land. We evaded the evil for a time, but it now appears the ugliness of sin and death has made its way to the shores of Adonia and to our home. Perhaps we were foolish to think we could leave the evil in that land totally behind — that we could hide from it."

"But our home, the forest, what will become of it? Will our home, the forest, also fall victim to evil?" Samuell asked.

"Remember, Samuell, we are not home yet. This is a temporary home. The longer you live, the more you will understand this. Someday we will be in our eternal home, the home our God has promised us in heaven — but we are not there yet.

"While we are here in this place, there will be trials and tribulations because of sin. Evil is alive and well. It has been growing in strength across the sea, and now, it has come here, to our land, hoping to unseat peace and justice, to rule over us with fear and despair."

Geoff paused, and then he repeated Samuell's question. "What can we do?"

"We can do several things. First, we must not fear. Our Father has promised us he will be with us. We must continue to have faith in him and his promises, never losing sight of the sure hope that we have a champion in heaven that has promised to keep us forever. The land may fall, but our God will ensure that we do not.

"We must continue to love and take care of each other, building each other up in the faith and reminding each other of God's Word and his promises to us.

"But we must also act. We must contest evil wherever it lives, and now it has made its way to our land. It now falls on us to stand against it."

Geoff's eyes turned to the outstretched forest before them. "Put out the word. The people of the trees will search out and rid the forest of the evil that now makes its home amongst us. Evil wants our land, but we will not flee. The light will not leave the forest. If evil wants our home, it will have to go through us."

†††

Geoff and the Tobar Division, now comprised almost entirely of archers, split up into flights of eleven and combed the forest for any sign of the intruders.

Samuell, due only to his young age, had not yet become a member of the Adonian Guard. Geoff convinced Samuell to stay behind and take care of the family while the men of the Adonian Guard embarked on a hunting party.

For seven days, the Tobar Guard searched for any sign of the trespassers in their forest, but they searched in vain. Whoever or whatever had infiltrated the forest and had caused such grievous harm to the tree people simply left no sign of their whereabouts. Whoever they were, they were dead set on staying hidden, and it soon became very obvious to Geoff that they were good at it.

Geoff and his flight began their journey home on the seventh day of their search, as all the search parties had agreed to do before they left. The plan was to report to each other what they had found during their hunt and decide as a group what to do next.

Geoff took little solace that they had found no sign of the evil that had invaded their home. Though he tried to convince himself that this might mean the villains had moved on, maybe even left the forest, he was having little success.

He feared going back to the families of his village empty-handed, unable to offer them any news, any reassurance they had avenged their loved ones, that justice had been served, or that they no longer had to fear the strangers hiding in the shadows of the forests below. He wondered how he would convince them to go on with their lives, to not live in the grip of fear and the trap of hatred for the unknown assailants.

As Geoff's hunting party entered his forest village, Geoff soon knew the situation had taken another turn for the worse in their absence. The first sign that something was wrong was that the village sentries, those posted at all the entry points to the village ever since the events of ten days earlier, were nowhere to be found. Geoff and his flight entered the village unchecked; security had totally broken down.

Though Geoff tried to pretend that this was simply a breakdown of discipline that would need to be dealt with immediately, he couldn't help but feel that the situation was much, much more grim. The solemn faces of his neighbors, followed soon after by the tears running down his Ahnettia's face, confirmed his worst fears.

Geoff later found Ahnettia sitting alone in their home, silently staring out a window into the forest below. He knew there was nothing he could say that would take away the grief, the sorrow, and the fear she was feeling for her youngest son, Samuell.

"It was like they knew you and the other guardsmen had left," she said to him, without turning to face him. "How did they know?"

Geoff's heart was breaking. He couldn't help but feel he and the other men of the village had done the unforgivable. They had let the enemy walk right into their homes, uncontested, and take not their gold, not their food, but their most precious gift — their future, their children!

Geoff walked to where Ahnettia was sitting, still facing out the window, and gently placed his hand on her shoulder.

The grief was unbearable.

"I am sorry," Geoff whispered. He bowed his head, large pools of water forming in his eyes. "I am so sorry." The words left his lips like stone, falling to the floor and echoing through the empty room.

Ahnettia continued to stare out the window, another stream of tears flowing down her cheeks. She lifted her trembling left hand from her lap where it lay idly, and laid it upon his hand, their wedding bands now in contact with each other.

"Find them."

Geoff did not know if Ahnettia meant he should find the children or their captors. It did not matter. Finding one meant finding the other.

The attackers took seventeen children, killing four and leaving them behind for the Tobarians to find. The others were still out there, somewhere. One of them was their son, Samuell.

A righteous anger swelled up within Geoff; it was anger like none he had ever felt before. He would search the land until he had no more breath, if that was what it took. He would find his son and the monsters that had violated his home, so wounding the heart of the one that he so deeply loved.

Geoff turned, leaving Ahnettia alone in her prison cell of worry and grief.

"I will, if it is the last thing I ever do."

Darkness.
Silence.

Cold.

Samuel regained consciousness. As his faculties returned, he wondered if he was dead.

He opened his eyes to find the darkness blinding, the silence deafening, and the cold of this place burning through his ability to focus. He felt disoriented, his senses were confused, and he had no awareness of his location.

Taught from childhood that his bow meant life, Samuell's first inclination was to reach for his bow, but as soon as he did, his senses reported to his mind that he could not reach; he was both badly injured and bound. He couldn't feel his legs at all. With searing pain in his arms, back, and head from the first attempt, he was unsure if he wanted to move again.

Samuell barely broke the silence with a scream of pain that was mostly muffled by whatever his captors had put in his mouth to keep him silent.

He once again gained his composure, and realized he was lying on his stomach, his hands and feet bound behind his back, and the right side of his face was resting against a cold, rocky surface. He was sure they had broken his left arm. His left shoulder was out of its socket, and the rest of his body had taken a severe beating.

Samuell felt completely out of his element. He was no longer high in the trees of the forest, basking in the sun's warmth and listening to the songs of the forest birds with his father. He was now, from everything his senses told him, trapped deep underground in a cold, dark, and silent tomb in which someone had thrown him.

Who has done this to me? Why?

Samuell's mind drifted in the darkness. Ever so slowly, brief glimpses of memory returned. He remembered leaving the security of the trees with the others to explore, as they liked to call it. Yes, their parents had warned them that the times were especially dangerous, with the various killings that had been taking place and the mysterious strangers that were supposedly wandering about the forest. But all that seemed such a distant threat right then, with the birds singing and the soft wind blowing through the trees. Surely, whatever danger lurked in the forest was far away.

After all, what are the odds?

In a flash, everything had changed. From nowhere, the ugly men had surrounded the children as they played. Instinctively, the older children, like Samuell, had prepared their bows for defense, but before they could mount an effective defense, the brutes were upon them.

The strangers had concentrated on the older and stronger of the children first, knowing full well the younger children would freeze if the older children went down. At worst, they thought, the young would scatter helplessly. To their attackers' surprise, the younger children had done neither, but had bravely stood their ground as they had they learned to do, and fired on the aggressors with their bows. Though initially surprising their attackers, the archers' defense had been too little, too late to make a difference, and the attackers captured all the children.

Samuell and the others fought fiercely while bound, gagged, and hoisted onto carrying poles for rapid transport to some secret location. Some of them had eventually succumbed as their strength gave way to shock. Samuell and several of the older children had continued to make trouble for their captors, who had mercilessly responded with the club. He remembered seeing his good friend Devon wrestling wildly against the ropes that bound him. That is when the lights had gone out for Samuell and everything had gone black.

Screams pierced the silence, tearing Samuell away from his dark memories of the past and slamming him into the terrible reality of the present. The distant screams echoed through the rocky passageways around him, making it impossible for him to judge from which direction they had originated.

Still bound, still gagged, lying in the darkness on the cold, rocky floor, the doubts and fears that had crept up on Samuell in the darkness now made no pretense of subtlety, but launched their full frontal assault on his sanity.

All at once, Samuell's thoughts accused him of not obeying his mother's directives to stay in the trees or to protect the younger children in his care. Samuell's conscience sentenced him guilty of being responsible for the pain being inflicted upon the one whose horrible screams now filled the dark caves around him. Samuell's fear told him his turn would come soon.

Why didn't I listen! I am so sorry! Father in heaven, forgive me? Help me?

Samuell pulled hard against the straps that bound his hands and feet, frantically trying to break free and help the children get away. His muscles screamed in pain as he struggled in vain upon the rock floor of the cave.

Almost immediately, Samuell's energy completely dissipated. Samuell was motionless, helpless.

Father, help me.

The screams continued — terrible, high-pitched screams — then silence.

Samuell didn't know how long he had been there, staring into the darkness, watching, wondering when they would come for him.

That is when Samuell first noticed the eyes burning ever so faintly through the darkness of the cave. From the end of a long, dark tunnel, they watched him.

What evil is this that watches me in the darkness of this cold cave? Has this evil creature come to devour me in my helplessness? Lord, help me?

Samuell remained motionless. Knowing that any attempt to struggle against his bonds would be futile, he stared motionless at the eyes as they approached him through the darkness. He was totally defenseless against this creature, and he knew it.

As he felt the cold blood trickling down his arms from the wounds on his back, he concluded the creature must have followed the scent of his blood, which was now forming a pool on the rocky ground.

What torture awaits me from this creature? Perhaps it will be more merciful to me than the monsters that have stolen us away and brought us to this place.

The dilemma paralyzed Samuell's mind, unable to decide which fate would bring him the kinder death, the jaws of the beast, or the tortuous death at the hands of his kidnappers.

The glowing eyes were upon him now — green eyes.

They towered over him in the darkness, and Samuell could feel the weighty presence of the enormous creature; the coarse hair of its coat brushing against his body. The faint outline of the magnificent beast was barely visible in the dim light as it bent down over Samuell.

Samuell felt the breath of the beast on his face, and he asked God to take his spirit, pleading for a swift and painless death at the jaws of the creature.

†††

It hadn't taken long to find the place.

Their highlighted sense of smell was such that they could practically see the prey that had left its scent behind, hours after it had departed the area. This made them as effective at tracking their prey as they were at killing it.

Two-legs were like any other prey, only easier to track and easier to catch. The stench they left behind lasted for hours. It was very particular to each individual two-leg, and they could smell it at great distances. It was an effortless task to trace the footsteps of the strangers to the place where they hid, though it would soon be painfully obvious to the strangers that, hiding from the wolf, they could not.

Most two-legs did not know of this place. How the strangers had found it was a mystery. Perhaps by chance they had stumbled upon it. Maybe it drew their empty souls to its dark, cold, and damp caverns to hide their evil deeds from the light.

The cave was very difficult to locate — few two-legs had ever known of its existence. The wolves could sense things other creatures could not see and thus the cave's secret entrance was easy to locate for the wolves.

Sealed from within, the entrance to the underground cave was not accessible to the wolves, but the wolves found other entrances to the caverns — entrances unknown to the two-legs that had so recently taken up residence there.

The pack entered the caverns in silence. Dozens of its members entered, all following the lead of its largest and most powerful alpha male. Their mission was to rid the diseased two-legs from the forest, and this was the secret lair of the sick ones. To the wolf, the stench of the corrupted flesh of these two-legs was almost too much to bear. Normally, the wolf hunted to eat. This night they hunted to kill.

†††

The bloodcurdling scream echoed through the torture chambers of the underground dungeon. Samuell had closed his eyes to prepare for the worst. Upon hearing the screams, he thought he was hearing his own death cries as his spirit left his body. But it was not so.

Samuell open his eyes just in time to see the bright, green eyes of the beast standing over him snap to the right. Almost simultaneously, the creature darted off into the darkness. Samuell could see many other similarly sized shadows dash off after him in the dim light.

Samuell didn't know what to think. The trauma of his physical beating and the terror of what he thought to be his imminent death at the jaws of the shadow beast had overwhelmed his senses. He was pretty much incapable of putting two rational thoughts together.

Mentally paralyzed, physically bound, and bleeding from multiple wounds, he lay on the cold cave floor in a trance. His body shook as it struggled to keep warm.

The last thing he sensed before losing consciousness was the warmth emanating from the coat of the magnificent beast that had laid itself down beside him in the darkness. He didn't know what to make of it, but felt thankful as he drifted off. He did so, not knowing what would await him if he should again regain consciousness. In his weakened state, he didn't care.

†††

Balok and the others had retreated to their hiding place deep underground. There, by the light of the torch alone, they worshipped the demons that they so fervently served; performing their rites and rituals, chanting their dark words, and planning out their next strike against the tree people that lived above in the light.

The plan was simple, and it had proven successful before. First, they would attack the inhabitants of the light with fear and intimidation, threatening their most basic concerns over their safety and preservation. The people, exhausted by the tragedies unleashed upon them by the veiled assassins and unable to release their anger on the perpetrators of these crimes, would turn their frustration on their teachers, on their protectors, and on their governors. Realizing the old ways were not working, they would entertain proposals for change. Considering the proposals, they would be vulnerable to the traps laid out so masterfully before them.

Karyan would present the glories of the new order to them; freedom from moral laws and behavior; an anything-goes lifestyle; and the unfettered pleasures that this new way promised to provide. And of course, fealty to the new way included the safety and protection of Karyan; no more worry for their children's safety.

Blinded by the glitter of their immediate, carnal gratification, and empty promises of security, they would walk the wide road in mass and freely slide down the slippery slope to slavery and destruction. Soon, the inhabitants of the forest would forget the ways of their fathers and remember only the ways of the decadent. Soon they would join Balok and his minions in the total embrace of unbridled indulgence, shameless pleasures, and the darkness which so freely offered it all. Those who didn't blindly follow the glitter of their immediate, carnal gratification would hear the warnings of the perceptive few who could still see the light amidst this expanding cloud of darkness, as well as the pleading cries of those who had not abandoned all that is good, right, and just. But their numbers would be too few to matter.

Darkness and its servants would rule the forest and spread throughout the land. Until then, it was Balok's job and perverse pleasure to seed the oats of fear through the most despicable acts imaginable. He had assembled and led this band of evildoers into the heart of Adonia, taken the children of the tree-people, assembled with his fellow worshippers in the caves, and prepared to sacrifice the offerings. It was time to get down to business.

"Raise them!"

Across the torch-lit dungeon, many of the captured Tobarian children, those deemed still well enough, had been prepared for the black ritual. The captors bound their hands behind their backs, doused them with flammable liquids, and hooked them to long chains hanging freely from the ceiling of the cave. At Balok's command, his followers hoisted them up into the air, elevating them six feet above the ground.

Until this time, they had silenced the children by gagging them. This prevented them from screaming and giving away their position during the transport to the secret underground prison. However, now considering their hideout quite secure, Balok ordered they remove the prisoners' gags. It was time to make some noise.

Balok's followers took pride in the pain they caused others during torture, feeding off the cries for mercy from their victims. They fully expected the terror these children were undoubtedly feeling to provide them with an acoustic ecstasy of unforeseen proportions. They had attempted to heighten the fear of the children by torturing one of the strangers' very own, a volunteer, just moments before; his terrible cries of pain echoed through the tunnels of the caverns, serving as an appetizer for the delicious banquet to come.

The children hung in a large circle; their silent tears reflected the flames that burned throughout the cave, the same flames that illuminated the bronze statue of the crowned bull Molech that dominated the center of the assembly.

Their captors surrounded the defenseless children, each holding their weapon of choice to participate in the orgy of torture that would soon follow.

The plan was to inflict horrific pain upon the children and then set them ablaze, the whole time deriving the maximum pleasure from the ordeal, a pleasure only the followers of Molech could fully understand or appreciate. Once they sacrificed and subsequently prepared the children with fire, they would consume their flesh.

Balok began the chanting, and the rest of his followers soon joined in. They chanted in unintelligible words; beating their swords, chains, and clubs to the monstrous beat; working each other into a demonic frenzy.

There was a time when Balok would have felt some empathy for those given in sacrifice to their king, but not anymore. His mind had grown callous to the predicaments of others, especially those he deemed as his enemies. These children were like cattle to him, merely meat sacrificed to their god-king.

The agitation of his followers grew, and the shouts of bloodthirsty rage thundered throughout the cave.

To the frustration of the Omentians, the Tobarian children showed no sign of the terror the situation dictated they should show. Instead, they sang, their young, pure voices breaking through the smoky cloud of the deep, sinister chant of their captors and highlighting with a stark contrast the diversity of the ways and the respective gods they each followed.

"Abide with me; fast falls the eventide. The darkness deepens; Lord, with me, abide. When other helpers fail and comforts flee, help of the helpless, oh, abide with me."

Their words and their reverence to the God of the heavens drove the Omentians into even more of an uncontrollable fury. Balok was nearly unable to hold back his followers from tearing the hanging sacrifices before them to shreds.

Balok tingled from head to foot. He longed for the culmination of the sacrifice. He yearned for the feeling night and day. It was a drug that he couldn't get enough of, and he wanted the exhilaration to last for as long as possible.

The children continued. "I fear no foe with thee at hand to bless; ills have no weight and tears, no bitterness. Where is death's sting? Where grave thy victory? I triumph still if thou abide with me."

Balok's anger grew to the point of madness.

How can these children not cry out in terror?

The more he heard the cherub like voices singing out in peaceful harmony, the more his rage grew. He knew it wouldn't last much longer, and this knowing made it all the more exhilarating.

And Balok was right — it wouldn't last much longer.

In the twinkling of an eye, the exhilaration he felt ended. Like a bolt of lightning slashes through the night sky, changing the very makeup of the air it passes through and altering the very reality of everything it touches, a presence made itself known within and throughout the cave — suddenly, overwhelmingly, and completely.

Unknown to Balok and his followers, his hiding place was no longer secure. Something had infiltrated it — many somethings. Quietly stalking through the tunnels, sniffing out its prey, coordinating its attack, and now swarming its enemy, an unobserved threat had unleashed itself upon the Omentian strangers, overrunning their positions from all sides.

Until that moment, Balok had noticed nothing unusual; there was no alert from his sentries posted at the cave entrances, no cries of warning from the others within the cave, and no unexpected sounds. But in the briefest moment of time, Balok's reality, everything he knew and felt, changed. As if awoken from a long dream, his senses became crystal clear, and he entered his worst nightmare.

Instantly, he could see many of the creatures streaking across the underground sanctuary; their large, powerful bodies colliding with his followers around him, smashing into them with bone-crunching force. He could see, as if in slow motion, the faces of his men as they cried out in agony under the awesome wrath of their attackers. He could see the limbs being torn from their bodies as the powerful claws and teeth of the beasts ripped them to shreds.

In this, his most terrifying of all moments, Balok knew what it had been like for the many innocent victims of his ruthlessness. The faces of those he had tortured, both young and old, even those of the many unborn that had died at his command, flashed before his eyes.

In that moment, as his mind tried to absorb all the sights and sounds around him, Balok's senses reported the shocking truth that he too would feel the lightning's heat. With a speed and strength previously unimaginable to him, the lightning struck his existence, the spear pierced his being, and the unseen blade made the fatal cut. Pain shot through every nerve in his body as they struck Balok simultaneously from three different directions. The creatures hit him at full speed. As one beast took off his right leg, preventing him from escaping judgment, another sunk its fangs deep within the left side of his heart, tearing his ribcage open and permanently separating his still beating heart from its body. The third beast, one with blazing green eyes, hit Balok head-on, instantly decapitating him. For a moment longer, his one leg would hold his body in a vertical position — his body minus his head and much of the left side of his torso, that is.

The last thing Balok saw as his severed head hit the cave floor was his now lifeless body falling to the ground amidst the carnage that surrounded it, testifying to the fact that all his followers shared in his fate.

In this last fleeting moment of his life, Balok understood justice. He understood that there was a price to be paid for the crimes committed against others, and that this price was high, very high indeed. Judgment day was upon him, and all he could hope for was that there was no afterlife, no judgment. Unfortunately for Balok, there was an afterlife, and his situation would soon get much, much worse.

The wolf took no joy in the fall of these two-legs. However, once the course of action had begun, the wolf showed no mercy on its enemy. Mercy would only unnecessarily endanger members of the pack. It was necessary to eradicate this evil, this sickness, from the forest, so the wolf did it quickly and decisively. In the end, the wolf completely exterminated the carriers of the sickness; those hiding throughout the cave complex and in the forest surrounding it.

†††

Before that morning, the wolves had left virtually no trace of themselves in the forest. Before that morning, Geoff did not know of the wolves' presence there. Until that morning —

The sole gray wolf positioned itself on the main trail to Geoff's forest village, where someone from the village would notice it. Word of the wolf's presence passed swiftly through the village, reaching Geoff as the sun rose. Geoff and several of the Adonian Guard responded rapidly to check out the strange sighting.

The gray wolf made no movement as the Tobarians approached. It was careful not to give the two-legs any reason to consider it a threat or to signal hostile intent. This was a good thing, since Geoff had determined to drop the wolf where it stood, should it show that it was in any way a threat to his people.

As Geoff approached the wolf, he couldn't help but remember the stories that Toro had told of the wolf kind from his journeys in the Strange Lands of southern Adonia, stories of how the wolf kind had once saved his life. These memories tempered Geoff's tendency to consider the wolf as a threat. Instead, Geoff saw this unlikely encounter to be more of a curiosity than anything else.

Why has this sole wolf made its way to Tobar Forest, so far from its home in the Strange Lands? Why now? Could this have something to do with the missing children? Something to do with Samuell?

As the men of Tobar approached the wolf, it remained motionless. It sat in the open, watching and staring back at them. Geoff slowed his advance as he reached a range from the beast that was comfortable and made eye contact with the wolf. There they remained, staring at one another, fellow inhabitants of the vast forest, though of this Geoff was still unaware.

Deliberately, carefully, the wolf rose to all fours.

Several of Geoff's men, sensing the potential danger the wolf posed to Geoff at such close range, raised their bows to defend him, should the need arise. Geoff stilled them by raising his left hand calmly, instructing them to stand down.

The wolf paused, turned toward the dense forest, and then looked back over its left shoulder, once again making direct eye contact with Geoff. Geoff got it; the wolf wanted them to follow.

After a moment, the wolf moved at a brisk pace into the forest. Geoff had to decide hastily whether to follow. On the one hand, this could be a trap, and there was no time to go back to the village and get reinforcements. On the other hand, his son was missing, and if this was in any way related to Samuell and the other missing children, he couldn't pass up the invitation, no matter what risk might be involved.

Geoff addressed his men as he set off to follow the wolf into the forest. "If any of you wish to remain behind, I will find no fault with thee. This is an unprecedented, unplanned, and perhaps unwise decision, but it is one I must make. Let each of you decide for yourself what course to take."

Without hesitation, the nine guardsmen that accompanied him agreed; there was really no choice.

All of that day and through the night, they followed the wolf through the forest. As they did, a kinship formed between man and beast. With each moment that passed, trust increased. Trust brought about a greater desire for understanding. As understanding grew, a sense of cautious camaraderie developed.

As the sun rose in the west, man and wolf arrived at the entrance to a previously unknown cave. Geoff and his men, though tired from the journey, felt a quick surge of energy upon seeing the sight.

Why has the wolf brought us to this place? What secrets does this cave hold? Could this have anything to do with the missing children?

The questions brought with them an adrenaline surge that, when combined with the newfound hope that they might yet find their missing children, awoke all of their senses.

The men assembled makeshift torches and proceeded into the cave. It didn't take them long to realize that the cave was more of a series of complex caverns and tunnels.

The first cavern they found horrified them. Hung from the center of the small cave by a hook and chain was an adult man, a stranger to the forest. From all indications, someone had recently tortured him to death brutally. The men were terrified of what this find might suggest regarding their missing children. Their hopes of recovering the children unharmed all but vanished in the cold, dark silence of the caves.

They moved on, following the gray specter that led them somberly through the tunnels. They grew ever more fearful with each step of what they might find beyond the next turn?

What they found next shook them to their core. As they rounded a sharp turn in the tunnel, the cave abruptly opened into a large cavern room. Several fires still burned there, spreading their flickering red and orange light throughout the expanse. The first thing that hit them, like a punch in the face, was the smell. The stench was almost unbearable. It was the smell of death, the smell of rotting flesh.

For a moment, the men stood frozen in shock. Scattered on the rocky cave floor were many mounds of flesh and meat. Once men, as far as anyone could guess, they were now reduced to pieces of torn apart body parts, strewn through the room in a gruesome display of chaotic carnage. Someone or something had savagely butchered these men, slaughtering them in a bloodbath of primal rage.

The first thought that flashed through Geoff's mind was an ambush. He and his men had spent the last day learning to trust the gray wolf that so mysteriously appeared on their doorstep.

Has the wolf lured us here to suffer the same fate as these men? Is this a trap?

About the time Geoff entertained the thought of treachery by the wolf, his eyes made out the many shadows that hung throughout the room. The apparitions seemed to vacillate in the flickering light of the torches.

Could it be?

The surrounding men silently echoed his thoughts, glancing at each other in quiet disbelief. Then, as if they had all come to the same conclusion, the men darted to the children, pulling them down from their monstrous bindings and praying to God that they were still alive. Instantly, the dismal scene paradoxically changed to one of joy and celebration as the searchers realized the children were alive. The searchers revived the children and carried them from the nightmarish cavern of death to the safety of the light.

Geoff dashed about the cave, sharing in the joy of the men around him as they rescued child after child from the jaws of death. However, his excitement waned as he realized each child delivered was not his own. In fact, there had been no sign at all of Samuell.

Where is my son? God, please have mercy? Where is Samuell?

The flurry of emotions, from apprehension to fear, terror to elation, and hope to despair overcame Geoff as he dropped to his knees on the cave floor, covered his face with his hands, and broke down in tears — pleading with the only one who could help him now.

Please, Father, do not make me return to Ahnettia without our son. Please, Lord? Please?

As he prayed, Geoff felt the coarse hairs of the gray wolf's coat brush against his arm. He saw the wolf standing over him, its nose and jaws but inches from his face, its golden eyes reflecting the flames of the cave torches around them.

In that moment, Geoff thought again about the destructive power that had unleashed upon the men who had inhabited this cave. Surely, it had been the wolf-kind that had done this; wolves like the one that now stood over him.

Geoff didn't care what happened to him next. Emotionally, he had no more energy left. Perhaps it was better for him not to return to Ahnettia if he could not return with their son.

Then another thought flashed through Geoff's mind.

Didn't the wolves save our children? Didn't this wolf bring us to this place to find our missing children?

In a moment of desperation, frantic hope, and perhaps a bit of insanity, Geoff acted without thinking; his hands, still hanging motionless in front of him, thrust themselves forward and latched onto the thick coat of the wolf standing above him. Face to face, staring down certain death, Geoff pleaded with the wolf. "Where is my son?"

The wolf did not react; its eyes remained locked onto Geoff as if he was its only concern.

Again, he yelled into the face of the wolf. "Where is my son?" Instantly realizing what he had just done, Geoff's eyes doubled in size, and he released the wolf, falling back on the floor of the rocky, cold cave.

To Geoff's surprise, the wolf did not take off his face. It didn't shred him to pieces. Instead, for just a moment, the wolf remained motionless, eye-to-eye with Geoff, as if it could see into Geoff's soul and record all the thoughts, all the ways of the man that stood before it. Then, as it had done the day before, the wolf turned and led Geoff down yet another tunnel.

Geoff followed blindly, not thinking anymore — unable to put two rational thoughts together. Before long, the tunnel opened to another cavern, much smaller than the one he had just left. As he entered the room, he saw there was very little light besides that which emanated from his own torch. Still, in the dim light, he could make out something lying in the center of the cave.

As he approached the form, he saw it was not one, but two forms: one human, one wolf. On closer inspection, Geoff could not believe his eyes. The human form was Samuell! Huddled around his son was another wolf. Its green eyes were now looking directly at him through the darkness.

Without need of persuasion, the noble beast rose and joined the gray wolf at the side of the cave. Geoff rushed to his son. To his utter amazement and overwhelming joy, he found Samuell alive.

"Samuell, Samuell my son!"

Samuell mounted just enough energy to whisper. "Father, is that you?"

Geoff took off his shirt and wrapping it around Samuell, Geoff replied. "It's alright, Samuell, everything is going to be alright. I've come to take you home."

Geoff looked up to see the wolves departing. He made eye contact with each of the wolves one last time. "Thank you."

Others from Geoff's rescue party soon arrived to help free Samuell and tend to his injuries. Then, the men brought all the missing children safely home to the uncontainable joy and thankfulness of their mothers.

✝✝✝

The living beings instantly gathered from many faraway places in the spiritual realm. There, within time, and yet unaffected by it, they existed in several unseen dimensions simultaneously.

Combat with the demons of darkness had been especially fierce, relentless, and ever-increasing. Evil had been active, throwing its darkest warriors into the conflict to unleash madness over the entire world of men and propel it hopelessly into endless darkness.

The living beings took a brief reprieve to reflect on the battle, a timeless moment to ponder about all they had seen and heard.

A living being which appeared as that of clear topaz spoke. "The Master has thwarted the deeds of those who would further the cause of darkness, and yet, many have suffered and many have died."

A living being like that of a rainbow thundered in response. "Some things we know, other things we do not know yet. Those who are according to the purpose, those who love the Master, receive only blessing from all that transpires below. Physical eyes and physical faculties alone cannot see this, but those with spiritual eyes and understandings know it to be true."

A living being, which mirrored the first, except in a brilliant combination of amethyst and beryl, asked, "Will they then triumph against their enemies in this time?"

"The power of the Master will fulfill the faith of these little ones and their hope through love," thundered the response.

The voice then became still and quiet as that of a soft breeze or quiet brook reaching out from the distance. "Though for a short time, the faithful must traverse a veil of tears, they will ultimately be preserved."

The living being with golden wingtips phased into the time that they gathered and spoke. "We have accomplished much in this time. Yet, we must spare another of the children."

The Chief Being spoke. "Indeed. The Lord has plans for the sons of Moesheh."

"Darkness is again marshaling its forces. We are called."

As the many eyes of the living beings darted back and forth to meet those of the others in their presence, their countless wings flashed and, in a blur of color and light, they vanished.

CHAPTER 51

İRREGULAR WARFARE

†††

"Move!" the battle-hardened warrior thundered as he violently punched Moesheh in the back, pushing him closer to the edge.

Moesheh stumbled uncomfortably along the makeshift plank assembled just for this occasion. Jutting out from the protective railing that usually formed the boundary of the Parlantian attack vessel's deck, the plank beneath his feet now provided the only thing standing between life and death for Moesheh, at least as far as the vengeance-seeking, Parlantian crew members were concerned.

They bound Moesheh's hands and tied him to a large stone with a ten-foot rope. A second Parlantian executioner prepared to push the stone from the deck when commanded.

"For crimes against his Lordship, Karyan, and the people of the province of Parlantis, we the crew of the Serpentia sentence you to death! We will give you the same fate as our brothers received by your hand."

For Moesheh, this was all a bit too ironic. Many of the Parlantian invaders had already become intimately familiar with the predators swarming the seas below. His Parlantian captors were now determined for him to have the same introduction. They thought this would provide the storybook ending to their little invasion and unravel the will of the men fighting in the resistance against the Omentian-led occupation of Adonia.

Little do they know.

The Parlantians understood so little about the land they were attempting to conquer. Apparently, they cared little for researching the history, values, and fighting spirit of the peoples they attacked. No doubt the Parlantians, having been so easily overrun themselves, thought none could stand against Karyan's scourge, and therefore considered it a waste of time to gain intelligence on their enemies. Had the Parlantians bothered to scout out the land of Rothing, they would have discovered that the men of Rothing would fight to the last rather than surrender even one inch of their province, their homeland, to the heathen invaders. In addition, if the Parlantians could kill the Rothing Commander, it would only strengthen the resolve of those serving in the Adonian Guard to fight.

The Serpentia's Captain scowled. "Join the rest of the refuse at the bottom of your stinking sea!"

As earlier alluded to, intelligence was not the invading zombies' strong suit, and what this ill-suited commander of misfits failed to realize is that the refuse at the bottom of this — only recently odoriferous — bay was that of dismembered and decaying Parlantian corpses that Moesheh and his fellow Parlantian naval officers had so graciously donated to the cause of freedom.

Much to the Parlantians' chagrin, Moesheh returned the Parlantian's glare with a pleasant smile. "Roger that. I will say hi to all of your buddies down there when I see them."

"Cut him!" The furious Parlantian ordered the guard. "I doubt you will have eyes remaining by the time the stone brings you to the bottom."

I hate this part.

The Parlantian Guard drew a curved blade from his belt and carelessly slashed Moesheh across his upper left arm and right thigh. The all too happy guard obviously took pleasure in his performance. "We wouldn't want the red-tooth to have any trouble finding you."

From his earliest days in Rothing, Moesheh had loved the water. He had spent much of his early years fishing and swimming in the warm bays and rivers that formed so much of the western boundary of this southern province of Adonia. In his youth, Moesheh had faced death numerous times, but arguably, this predicament was being uncharacteristically intimidating.

The Province of Rothing was a land rich with red pastures, red rivers, and copious amounts of red vegetation. No one knew for sure what the cause of the predominance of the color red was, but its prevalence was incontestable. Indeed, even the many fish of the area, from the red bass to the red herring, shared in this distinction. So abundant was the color red across the countryside, that Moesheh had named the land Rothing, meaning red pasture.

However, when Moesheh's all too zealous guard had mentioned the red-tooth, he was not referring to the color of a tooth, or the preponderance of the color red in the great fish. Unfortunately, he referred to the color of the water that frequently surrounds this particularly aggressive fish.

For the most part of any year, the waters off the western shore of Rothing provided fishermen of the province a bountiful catch of delectable red fish; making the waters off the coast of Rothing the preeminent fishing lane in the region and the leading source of white meat for all of Adonia. The warm, tropical waters presented a paradise for fishermen and divers alike. Divers for clams and a plethora of various underwater vegetation would inundate the coastline, providing an active commercial industry and a rich livelihood for all.

However, as the year would draw to a close and the days would shorten, the currents of the Southern Sea would shift. Instead of originating in the south, the currents would flow from the north, bringing the cooler waters of the Northern Sea to the shores of Rothing and with them the menace of the deep, the red-tooth.

The red-tooth normally consumed seals and larger prey that could be found off the northern cliffs of Chastain or even those of southern Heath, but during this time of the year, the red-tooth couldn't ignore the plentiful bounties of chunky tropical fish that inhabited Rothing's waters, presenting the voracious predator with a smorgasbord of sorts.

Throughout the annual red-tooth migration, all the inhabitants of Rothing knew to stay out of the water in certain, shall we say, no swim zones. These areas would frequently run red with blood as shivers of red-tooth would swarm the region, consuming everything in their path.

The enormous killing machines, some twenty feet with row after row of razor-sharp teeth, had insatiable appetites, to where they gained the reputation of killing for the sake of killing. In other words, they were cold-blooded killers.

The Parlantian commanders did not know about the red-tooth migration a few weeks ago when they brought their fleet into Rothing's waters, but they knew about it now. Moesheh and his men had introduced the invaders to the red-tooth in a major way over the past few weeks, hence their particular testiness on the subject.

The red-tooth had proven to be quite the ally to the Adonian Guard. With their tactics and the red-tooth's ferocity, the Adonian Guard had successfully reduced the number of Parlantian invaders. With the use of a flammable, tar-like substance known as Khorygen or K-7 that his uncle Khory had discovered in the marshy areas of Ghurgania in the Strange Lands, Moesheh and the Rothing Guard had dealt a devastating blow to the Parlantian Armada.

Moesheh didn't have any moral reservations about striking at the invaders before they formally attacked Rothing. Though the Parlantian invaders had not yet set foot in Rothing, their intentions were obvious from their many violent incursions throughout Adonia. Thus, Moesheh authorized the preemptive attack and struck the Parlantian Fleet anchored off Rothing's shores.

The tactic was simple; a different type of red herring, if you will. Captain PJ, Captain Mikole, and Captain Mellon, who had just returned to the fight after previous encounters with the enemy in the north, took command of three of Rothing's most powerful fighting vessels: the La Gina II, the Sirenian II, and The Susanna. Together, they had already won a great sea battle in the south, which substantially reduced the enemy's number of escort ships. Together with several other vessels of the Rothing fleet, they funneled the Parlantian Armada into the prime feeding area of the red-tooth. There, using their tactical advantage of speed and maneuver, they kept the invaders distracted long enough for the Rothing Guard to give their unwelcomed guests a surprise they would not soon forget.

The Rothing divers had long since perfected an underwater breathing system, or UBS, composed of large sea shells they called "ox shells." Together with hollow tubing from an indigenous snorkeling plant, the divers had developed a technique which gave them the ability to stay under water over thirty minutes while diving for clams off the coast of Rothing.

Guardsmen divers, each equipped with a UBS, could thus covertly infiltrate the waters beneath the Parlantian fleet and attach under-water explosive devices, filled with K-7, to the hulls of many of the enemy ships.

Moesheh's men were unchallenged by the red-tooth, which com-pletely ignored their presence, because of another special attribute of the K-7 substance. One year earlier, a fisherman in these same waters had accidentally discovered that the smell of the K-7 was highly repug-nant to the olfactory senses of the red-tooth. This relatively new dis-covery provided the Rothing Guard with a defense against the red-tooth that they used to their advantage. Guard divers covered their exposed skin with the sticky K-7, hoping it would protect them from the jaws of the red-tooth. It did. The Parlantians, however, did not enjoy this knowledge or this protection.

The results were decisive, to say the least. This stunning sea battle sunk upwards of seventeen Parlantian warships, which were trans-porting many hundreds of Parlantian troops for the conquest of Rothing. The Parlantians never knew what hit them.

The innovative design of the weapons and the pressure of the sea water against the hulls of the invading ships caused the K-7's explosive force to violently direct inward, surprising the unsuspecting Parlantian crewmen. One moment, they were sleeping or peacefully preparing for the upcoming battle, and the next moment, a violent torrent of water caught them off guard, leading to their chaotic struggle for survival.

Those Parlantian invaders who escaped the large sinking coffins found themselves in the turbulent, red-tooth infested waters, as their massive transport vessels sank to the depths under the light of a pale moon. At first, in the eerie silence of the moonlit waters, they were thankful to be alive, but that soon changed.

Many, if not most, of the thousands of invading Parlantian warriors were in full battle dress when they hit the water. They had been preparing to disembark from the transports and begin their campaign on the southwestern shores of Adonia. Fully clad in breastplate and leg armor; and clinging to their shields, swords, and helmets for survival in the imminent battles to come; these unsuspecting men began a skirmish that they were completely unprepared to fight. It was a battle where their normal tools of survival became their greatest liabilities as gravity violently pulled them to the bottom of the sea and anchored there in their armor.

As the surprised warriors struggled to survive the unexpected environment they found themselves in, the situation became much, much worse. One moment, the dimly lit waters revealed only the somber and surreal scene of thousands of men walking upon the bottom of the sea, frantically pulling at their armor in a last ditch effort to free themselves from their lethal anchors before air ran out. The next moment revealed something far worse.

The luckiest of the men, those able to free themselves from their armor before their precious few moments of air were exhausted, attempted to reach the surface. That is when the dark phantoms of the sea arrived. At first they emerged from the gray waters discreetly, quietly, and peacefully appearing through the murky waters as only a glimpse of shadow here or there. Then, with the most horrific intensity imaginable, they announced themselves in mass, mercilessly striking the assembly of defenseless men in an awful display of hellish fury, overwhelming the senses of their victims, and creating a mass panic beneath the water.

Instantly, the sudden discharge of life's most precious fluid clouded the waters, as the red-tooth ripped and tore at the flesh of the defenseless men from every direction. The red-tooth, focusing on moving targets first, tore into those escaping their armor and attempting to reach the surface of the sea. The men who remained stuck within their lethal anchors at the bottom of the sea, those who ran out of air without knowing the bone-jarring shock of the red-tooth's attack and the searing pain of its menacing jaws, became the lucky ones; they died in relative peace.

Cold-blooded killers met Cold-blooded killers, and the Cold-blooded killers with the fins won — decisively. Within an hour, much of the Parlantian army had disappeared. The waters of the sea, like so many other things in the Province of Rothing, turned crimson.

That was then.

Now Moesheh stood before his judge and executioner. The judge and executioner announced the sentence, and it was time for Moesheh to "walk the plank."

It was at times like this, when his days are about to end, that a man thinks about his life. The thoughts come more in waves of feeling than they do in conscious thoughts; emotion rather than reason. There are waves of love for family and friends he will never see again in this world; uncertainty over whether his sacrifice has made a big enough difference in the causes for which he has fought; hope that all he has done — and all the reasons he has done what he has done — was right, just, and true; and optimism that his life was one of service and value, worthy of the time God gave him. In the end, this final judgment is the one he will live with for all of eternity.

These were Moesheh's feelings as the Parlantian guards forced him off the edge of the enemy vessel into the deadly waters below. Moesheh hit the water with a crash. The large millstone followed a split second later, violently jolting Moesheh to follow it as the rope connecting them immediately became taut. Like an ominous specter late for an appointment with its master, the millstone insistently escorted Moesheh deeper and deeper into the obscurity of the shadowy depths, to the gloomy gates of death itself.

Moesheh was sure that Sandrah and his two sons, both courageous flight commanders in the Rothing Guard, would know he had died with honor, though he now questioned the dignity of this demise. Surely it would have been better to die in battle, taking some of the enemy with him, than like this, as fish food.

Moesheh had lived his life well. He lived every day like it could be his last, especially now that they were at war. There was no doubt in his mind that Sandrah and his sons knew he loved them. Still, he wished he could have seen them one more time, just to say goodbye. This feeling weighed heavily on his heart as he unwillingly followed the millstone to the rocky floor of the sea, his precious few seconds of air quickly dissipating.

He wondered if his family would know what had happened to him, or if his disappearance would forever remain a mystery to them. Could Sandrah find closure when he did not return, or would she wonder for the rest of her days whether he was still alive, perhaps taken to Omentia as a prisoner of this war? Moesheh silently prayed for his wife and sons as the cold currents of the sea whooshed past him, carrying with them a long crimson tracer of blood from his wounds.

Lord, please bring them peace.

But as Moesheh reached the bottom of the sea, his thoughts wisely changed to more immediate pressures.

Moesheh had made the sea his second home over the years; fishing, diving, and exploring the sea floor became a dominant aspect of his existence. Though he had dove thousands of times, the rapid plunge and great depth to which he had just descended resulted in intense pain, pain that shot sharply through his ears and into the center of his head. The pain was nearly intolerable!

To make matters worse, much worse, Moesheh could now see the dark shadows of the red-tooth killers circling the waters above him. It was lunchtime, and he was the main course. Moesheh knew his time was rapidly running out. He used his last moments to thank his Master in heaven.

"Thank you, Father, for my life, for my wife, and my sons. Thank you for all the blessings you have given us and for the wonderful home you have prepared for us with you when our days in this place are through. Please be with Sandrah and our two wonderful boys. Please mend their hearts and bless their lives. Keep them and all our countrymen safe, and if it be your will, let them live in peace and freedom. Save them from our enemies, Oh God. Please forgive me for all the ways I have failed you, and accept me into your eternal kingdom."

As Moesheh finished his prayer, the tightness in his chest now capturing his undivided attention, he saw the sleek monster begin its deadly approach. Moesheh had hoped he would run out of air and lose consciousness long before the red-tooth found him, but thanks to the wounds he had recently incurred at the hand of his Parlantian friends, the red-tooth had experienced little trouble in finding him. It simply followed the stream of blood from the surface.

There it was then, death, approaching at high speed across the sea floor, directly for him. Its massive mouth now opened to reveal the several rows of razor-sharp teeth on a collision course with his flesh.

This won't take long. Either I run out of air, or I become intimately acquainted with ugly.

In that moment, Moesheh felt tempted to release his air and gulp the sea water, considering drowning to be a much more painless option for transitioning from this life to the next. But he didn't.

Moesheh knew that all his days, even his minutes and seconds, were in the hands of his God, the Creator. He knew it was not up to him to decide when it was time to walk through the door from this life to the next. True, his end might come at any second, but then again, maybe not. Only the Lord knew the course of events, and it was up to his Master in heaven to decide when his time of service was through.

If it is my time, nothing can keep me here, but if it is not my time, nothing can take me.

So he held his breath, and time seemed to stand still. Just as the massive red-tooth came all too clearly into sight, its enormous jaws stretching open to engulf Moesheh as it passed by, the Master altered what had seemed to be the inevitable fate of Moesheh. From nowhere, a sea dolphin arrived on the scene at a very high rate of speed on a collision course with the dominant predator. It continued its collision course, steered by an unseen director, until it impacted the red-tooth, altering the monster's track just enough for its jaws of death to miss Moesheh.

As the red-tooth passed by, its teeth caught the rope that held Moesheh anchored to the sea floor, momentarily jolting both Moesheh and the boulder from their resting places. A second later, its knife-like teeth sliced through the rope and permanently separated the two, freeing Moesheh from his underwater prison.

I'm free!

Hope once again abounded. A remarkable turn of events, no doubt, but still a myriad of problems presented themselves.

Now what?

Moesheh was out of air. If that wasn't enough of a dilemma, a hungry red-tooth surrounded him and the Parlantians still waited above the water for the expected telltale signs that he had met his intended fate.

Instinctively, Moesheh sank to the sandy floor below him. In retrospect, he did this for two reasons. First, he needed air. The thought of swimming through the red-tooth swarm above and surfacing amidst the Parlantians, who had put him in this predicament in the first place, did not fill Moesheh with warm fuzzies. Second, aligning himself with the sea floor reduced both the ability of the red-tooth to detect him and his exposure to their attack.

When he reached the sea floor, Moesheh began his search for the enormous sea shells the divers used to provide them with critical air while diving. As if by design, directly before him in the sand, Moesheh found what he needed. He forced the ox shell to his face and filled his lungs with lifesaving air from the shell. Color returned to Moesheh's face as he used the sharp edges of the shell to cut the ropes that still bound his hands. The red-tooth swarm still circling all around him, Moesheh struggled for ideas on how to escape.

Again, as if directed to his location, the sea dolphin, Moesheh's new, best friend, descended through the circling red-tooth swarm and swam a protective circle around him, forming a protective shield that dissuaded the agitated multitude of red-tooth from getting too close to Moesheh. It was amazing to Moesheh how the dolphin willingly exposed itself to danger in order to protect a man. He had heard stories of such sea dolphin behavior in the past, but seeing it firsthand was truly astounding.

Without warning, the dolphin broke off its defensive orbit and darted to Moesheh's location. Stationary in the water before him, it brushed its long nose under Moesheh's right arm and swam below it, almost forcing Moesheh to latch on to the dorsal fin on its back. Moesheh caught on, and not really knowing where this would lead, decided in an instant that anywhere the dolphin would take him was better than the place they were currently at.

As they moved along the sandy floor, Moesheh was once again astounded at the speed the dolphin could move through the water, especially with him in tow, as well as the ability the dolphin had to see where it was going. Whereas Moesheh was all but blinded by the turbulent waters around them, the dolphin appeared to have no problem in maneuvering over the underwater terrain and avoiding the predators all around that were actively hunting for them.

Before Moesheh's ox shell ran out of air, Moesheh found they were surfacing within an underwater cave. The elaborate system of underwater caves was another well-kept secret amongst the divers of Rothing. The system connected many underwater caves to a similar cave system on the mainland. Moesheh and the Guard had even entertained the possibility of evacuating women and children from Rothing using the cave system and hiding them within the offshore caves until Rothing had repelled the Parlantian invasion. That contingency had not yet become imperative, but was being reserved as a last resort.

The moment was exhilarating! More than the sharp sting of the salt water upon his wounds or the incredible beauty of the many glowing colors of phosphorescent <u>lichen</u> that glowed brilliantly within the luminescent cave; the realization that his time in this life was not yet over and that he would see his loved ones again was overwhelming!

Life! Life! Thank you Lord!

Moesheh had never considered using the cave system to move undetected from the sea to the mainland — that is, until now. Tearing off strips of cloth from what remained of his pants, Moesheh bandaged and tended to his injuries as best he could. Satisfied it was the best he could do under the circumstances, he bid a fond farewell to his new friend, and taking his cue from the natural flow of the cave current, he made his way through the underwater cavern back to shore.

✝✝✝

"How can this be? He is dead!"

Ormand, Captain of the Serpentia, and other top-ranking officers, especially those who were present when they fed Moesheh to the redtooth, couldn't believe their eyes as they witnessed him assume the position of command at the front of the Rothian battle line.

"He is a ghost!" one said.

"It must be one of his sons. Yeah, that's it, one of his sons," said another.

As word of Moesheh, the Rothing commander who came back from the dead, spread down the battle-line of the invaders, fear stole their courage. There he stood with the warriors of Rothing, this man whose body should now have been rotting at the bottom of the sea, battle-axe in one hand, Rothing shield in the other, shouting commands to the line.

The Parlantians had heard rumors of amazing things taking place across Adonia; amazing things that had resulted in stunning defeats for their coalition. All this despite their supposedly overwhelming numbers and the promised umbrella of protection Karyan was to provide via his unholy contract with the powers of darkness. And yet, here they stood. They had already suffered losses at sea, and now they encountered a formidable line of thousands of battle-ready Rothian warriors.

Colin watched as the vast Rothian line separated, dividing itself into two equal parts, each formidable in its own right. Moesheh and his handful of personal bodyguards maintained their position at the forefront of the Rothian force.

What are they doing?

Colin had once been a man of honor. He had served Parlantis for twenty-eight years, rising to the position of Supreme Land Commander in the Parlantian Guard. However, after the fall of Parlantis to the Omentians, Colin made a solemn oath to Karyan and the Omentian way, ensuring the safety of his family from death.

The Omentians, assuming all positions of leadership in the ranks, had demoted Colin to the position of a mere foot-soldier to ensure his obedience and minimize his influence with his former troops. This was hardly necessary, as his former troops now despised Colin. They hated him for the cowardly example he had given them in not dying in the defense of Parlantis and further for swearing allegiance to Karyan; though they themselves had made the same choice. Perhaps they hated him most because he was a visible reminder of their own weakness and perhaps even their cowardice.

Colin and the others had been told that as long as they continued to fight courageously in battle, their families could live, albeit as slaves to the Omentian lords now ruling Parlantis. To this hope, they had sold their allegiance, and with it their swords; they had no way of knowing whether the Parlantians would keep their end of the bargain.

They are splitting their formation — what are they doing? This can't be good.

379

Colin and the Parlantians had pursued the men of Rothing into the Red Valley, which sat just east of Cariba Marsh and just west of the Great Plains of Rothing. Following the trail of what appeared to be nothing more than a small band of Rothian Guard, the Parlantians had unwittingly maneuvered themselves into a very precarious position, though they didn't yet know it.

Colin knew from his vast military experience that surprise was an invaluable weapon. If you were using this weapon on your enemy, surprise was your friend, but if it was being used on you, it could be devastating. It appeared the Rothians had a surprise for them, and Colin was not looking forward to finding out what it was.

The Parlantian commander, not wishing to be outdone, directed a surprise of his own. On his command, his chief Omentian magicians spoke some of their incomprehensible words and threw their walking staffs to the ground. To the amazement of the Parlantians in the front lines, the Omentian staffs became slimy, black vipers, six to eight feet in length. The dozen Omentian vipers, directed by some invisible force, sped off together towards their target — Moesheh and his entourage. Unlike any vipers Colin had ever seen, these vipers had large, pointed heads and hissed menacingly as they slithered away. Every fifty feet, they would rear up like a desert cobra and lash out at the air with their seemingly oversized mouths of piercing teeth.

While the Rothing lines adjusted their formation, Moesheh, as if he had foreseen the Parlantian plan, instructed for seven Rothian staffs to be hurled down. Instantly, these staffs became man-sized, crimson vipers with glowing yellow eyes. The crimson vipers instantly sped off on a vector to intercept the black vipers crossing the grassy plain between the two military formations.

The red and black viper broods merged, and a furious battle began. Much to the embarrassment of the Parlantian commander, the outnumbered crimson serpents emerged victorious, entirely devouring all the black vipers.

Panic engulfed the Parlantian front lines as the crimson vipers, their insatiable hunger unquenched, continued across the plain directly for them. Terrified, the Parlantians struck at the vipers in vain. The slithering serpents singled out an unlucky few and tore off their hands, feet, and various other body parts. As the vipers penetrated deep into the Parlantian lines, the Parlantians fell into disarray, frantically moving about in a frenzied dance to keep from being the next victim. They struck hysterically at anything suspicious moving in the thick, red, knee-high grass.

Colin knew things were not looking good. He had heard about this phenomenon developing in the ranks of armies that he, while commanding the Parlantian Guard, had defeated. The men were descending into a state of hysteria. Fear was an incredible force multiplier, and left unchecked, it would be their undoing this day on the crimson fields of Rothing. Their superior fighting force was psychologically crumbling. If anything else were to happen before the army regained its collective composure, the results could be devastating.

During the serpent mayhem, the Rothian army completed its dividing maneuver. Moesheh and his personal guard joined the northern half of the formation, leaving the Rothians divided in two before the invaders. Even more puzzling, it appeared as if the two branches of the Rothian formation were spreading out, possibly to attack from both the north and the south.

Though dividing one's forces before the enemy was generally not a great idea, this tactic had merit if one successfully executed it. Here, it was almost as useful as a flanking maneuver in that it would now force the Parlantians to fight in two directions.

Ormand realized he had to do something. Despite the disarray of his army, he had to divide his forces to engage the two elements of the Rothian formation effectively. He was losing control and was upset at this turn of events. He had his own plans for destroying the Rothians, and was being forced to react instead of dictate the course of the battle.

What happened next made Ormand and the entire Parlantian host completely forget about Moesheh, the ever-shifting Rothian formation, and even the vipers causing havoc in their midst. As Ormand began the unplanned division of his formation, the winds blew. Not just one wind, from one direction, but multiple winds from every direction. The winds gathered up the clouds from the surrounding skies and pushed them toward the battlefield. From all directions, the gray clouds converged at a point over the Rothian army; more specifically, over the ground they had left between their two formations. Within a matter of a minute or two, the clouds then spun around at this point in the sky, and a funnel descended to the earth. As the funnel reached the plain below, it erupted into a swirling cone of flame, roaring as it churned, like the sound of a thousand winds.

Terror again gripped the hearts of the Parlantians as the enormous funnel cloud of wind and flame moved their way, seemingly in step with the progression of the Rothian elements. Even more alarming was the fact that the Rothians appeared unfazed by the sudden arrival of the flaming torrent, continuing their advance unabated from the north and the south.

"What is this?"

Ormand analyzed the situation and hastily recognized that he had no choice but to withdraw.

"Retreat! Back to the shore! Get back to the ships!"

But the Rothian elements that now strangled their formation from the north and the south cut off the Parlantians from their ships. Since the funnel of fire was advancing from the east, their only means of escape was to the west.

The men of the heavily laden Parlantian army retreated to the west and soon realized they were treading deeper and deeper into the marshlands. At first they were unfazed by the inconvenience, as it was much less a price to pay than facing the fiery inferno or bearing the fury of the Rothian battle-axe; all the Rothian warriors had stopped their advance when reaching the boundary of the marshes. In truth, the Parlantians were retreating and barely able to think more than a moment ahead of time. All they could think about was staying alive.

Colin withdrew with the rest of the invaders and couldn't help but second-guess his decision — for at least the thousandth time — of aligning himself with Karyan. In all his years as a military man, he had never retreated; never run from the enemy! Better to have died as a man in battle, fighting for what was right, than to sell his soul for his own security or that of his family!

What was I thinking? Now I will die not only as a traitor but also as a coward!

As Colin hit the marshes with the men who had once trusted him with their lives, the strangers to Adonia learned even more about the land they had foolishly surmised would be so easy to conquer. Now wading chest deep through the marshy water, it became very clear that they had made a very poor choice indeed! With every step they took, they sank deeper into the murky mud of the Cariba Marshes and one step closer to their eternal fate.

Awakened by all the commotion from their midday slumber in the warm water of the marshes, the red death instinctively responded. Thousands in number, yet moving as one, the crimson tide of the red death collided with the Parlantian army, now chest deep in the water and bogged down in the marsh's mud. Like a stampede of Parlantian horses, the ferocious school of predators, each equipped with a row of razor-sharp teeth, slammed into the unaware army, starting a feeding frenzy that made the marshy waters churn and boil with blood. Instantly, the waters turned crimson red as the screams erupted from the misguided followers of Karyan, each entering their own personal hell.

In a matter of minutes, minutes that surely seemed an eternity to the Parlantians, their last melee was over, and their once powerful army was no more. Shredded and torn to pieces, nothing remained but bones, armor, and memories — lost in the murky shadows of the crimson marsh.

†††

Moesheh watched in awe as the pillar of fire pushed the Parlantian army into the marshes.

"The Lord fights for us today," Moesheh exclaimed as the red fury erupted within Cariba Marsh, engulfing the invaders and giving Rothing the victory.

In astonishment, the men of Rothing witnessed their victory in the battle with no losses to their friends and brothers-in-arms. They kneeled and gave thanks to their God, their Savior, for the wondrous thing he had done.

CHAPTER 52

DARK KNIGHTS

✝✝✝

P rior to circumnavigating the southern tip of Adonia, the Parlantian fleet had put ashore a substantial number of Dark Knights, hoping to catch the Rothians off guard by attacking their eastern flank prior to, or simultaneous with, their main landing party coming "feet dry" on the western shore. Unknown to these backdoor, party crashers, they would need to journey through the western region of the Strange Lands, a narrow piece of grassland notorious to the inhabitants of southern Adonian for the, shall we say, hazards.

The Dark Knights consisted of the toughest fighting men that the invaders fielded from Karyan's evil coalition. These were the elite infantry of Omentia, Heath, and Parlantis — the best of the best. They traveled light and fast, moving with precision and stealth. They had perfected their skills to a sharp edge and became very efficient at killing. Their number was two thousand strong.

The leader of the Dark Knights was Hanjian. Hanjian, a former Parlantian commander, had betrayed his loyalty and received a generous reward for his actions. He had served in the Parlantian Infantry, and had long been bitter of his subordinate position to the Elite Parlantian Cavalry. One of Karyan's spies had contacted Hanjian and secretly brokered a deal. Hanjian swore his allegiance to Karyan and informed the Omentians of Parlantis' much sought after battlefield strategy and tactics. If there are levels of treason, Hanjian was not only a traitor, but the worst of traitors.

Hanjian was there the day Karyan's forces butchered the Parlantian Guard. He exposed his true colors when led the Omentian monsters to all the Parlantian hiding places within his village, where he not only watched but mercilessly took part in the butchering of his own people.

When Karyan heard of Hanjian's faithfulness to the darkness and his unrivaled brutality, he gave Hanjian a fitting reward — command of the Dark Knights. Hanjian not only became feared, but his ruthless command of the Dark Knights earned him the power he had sought after for so long.

Hanjian was not without his faults, and one of Hanjian's greatest faults was his persistent lust for power. Determination can be a great asset if measured with ability and good sense, but Hanjian was driven by his own delusional sense of reality, a reality that dictated that he would, he must, always succeed, no matter the cost to those around him. In this sense, he was very much like the men he led; being the best of the best, they all felt that failure was not an option.

He differed from the others, however, in that he believed he was special, even more special than Karyan himself. He knew his exploits would one day fill the pages of history. The stunning defeat of Rothing would be the first of many brilliant victories that would both elevate his stature among Karyan's inner circle and bring him even more of the power he longed to exercise. No one would stop him from achieving this goal; nothing would stand in his way.

Anak was Hanjian's second-in-command. He and fifty other Anakim earned the reputation as the greatest of the knights — giants among men. Standing an arm's length taller than the others, they towered over all the inhabitants of this or any other known land. They wore heavy gold and silver necklaces, flaunting the bountiful spoils they had taken in battle or pillaged afterwards from the many distant lands that they had conquered. The weapons they wielded — the swords, battleaxes, and scythes — would be a challenge for any other man to lift, let alone use in combat.

The Anakim surrounded Hanjian, providing an impenetrable circle of defense. For this reason alone, everyone knew that no man was safer than the commander of the knights.

Though the Anakim did not agree with Karyan's vision of conquest and dominion, their tribe had long grown used to their special status, being in control of everything and most everyone around them. Since they could not contend with Karyan's secret knowledge and dark magic, they thought it more prudent to continue with him instead of suffering the potential consequences of open resistance against him, at least for the time being.

Hanjian treated all the Dark Knights, including Anak, with the cold brutality they expected from their Omentian masters. If Lord Karyan had not ordered obedience to Hanjian, Anak wouldn't have hesitated to kill him. It would have been easy. Anak loathed taking orders from such an inferior man, but he endured it; waiting for the right time to both deal with Hanjian and reassert the Anakim's rightful place in the order of things.

Hanjian knew that in order to claim the victory over Rothing, he and the Dark Knights had to defeat Rothing's forces prior to Commander Ormand engaging them from the west. Ormand had put the knights ashore on the southern cliffs, where they faced an unexpectedly tough climb, significantly delaying them. Now they were well behind their planned schedule.

Obviously Ormand planned this, hoping to take all the credit for the victory!

Hanjian could not, would not, accept this. He would overcome Ormand's plan and win the victory over Rothing! The knights just needed to make up for the lost time.

Hanjian drove his men north, through the flat grasslands. Surely, if the Dark Knights were going to make up the time they had already lost, they had to cut through the grasslands. This seemed more logical than the route Ormand had directed, which would bring the knights to the fight even later.

A full moon rose, and Hanjian was thankful for the light with which to navigate. Insistent on making the best time possible, Hanjian needed to push the Dark Knights forward through the night.

When the moon had risen just above the distant tree line, the sounds of the grasslands and nearby forests erupted into a small roar of nocturnal activity or *night music*, as the Anakim liked to call it. Unfortunately, the night music jammed the warning sounds of would be enemies or predators that lurked ahead of them in the darkness. Fortunately, little could pose a threat to the knights, so it really didn't matter.

The Dark Knights forged on through the tall, wavy grass. The already cool temperatures plummeted once again, chilling even the burliest of the knights to the bone. Soon, a light fog swept across the top of the grass, and the pale moonlight, providing only a poor semblance of its daily master, played tricks on the weary warriors. They heard sounds — unidentifiable sounds — coming first from the left and then from the right. Shadows appeared; fleeting phantoms darting across the vague horizon. They feared.

Then, silence.

The silence was deafening. The knights had grown accustomed to the background sounds of the night creatures around them, so when the night music abruptly stopped, it was instantly apparent to all.

Anak stopped in his tracks, obviously concerned by the cessation of sounds. "Something is not right. This is not good," he whispered to himself. He was not alone. All the Anakim had the same thought the moment the night music stopped.

The newer knights, those surrounding the inner circle of Anakim, simply looked puzzled. Theirs was bewilderment, an ignorant fear. They knew something was amiss, but that was all.

The Anakim, much more experienced in combat and educated in all the threats of the known world, were more anxious than puzzled. Their anxiety was not from ignorance, but from experience. They knew few threats would intimidate the night enough to silence the night music. They had heard stories, stories of ancient creatures that moved through the night like the wind, stealing the souls of men from their bodies without ever being seen. Most of the Anakim had regarded the stories of the whispering death as mere myth and the substance of legend; until now.

Now, the Anakim hoped the situation was not as it seemed; not as they feared. Had they blindly walked into the plains of the whispering death? They did not have to wonder for long.

The bloodcurdling screams of falling knights bombarded their senses. All around the perimeter, men were being taken, disappearing into the tall grass in the eerie moonlight. The night fog danced about erratically in circular vortices as indiscernible shapes moved through the grass, devouring the knights one by one.

"What is it?" Hanjian demanded of Anak. "What is happening? What is out there?"

Anak, unwilling to take the time to explain his darkest fears to Hanjian, shot only an angry glare at the man who had led them into this disastrous ambush. More knights continued to fall throughout the formation. The outer ranks endured the brunt of the attack as the invisible night demons maneuvered at will through the formation.

"Collapse, diamond formation, battle-line drawn around the commander!" Anak commanded the knights.

But it was too late; the demons of death had already penetrated the perimeter of the formation as it collapsed, and the knights soon fought an enemy within as well as without. As the formation folded in on Hanjian, his army disintegrated. He did not know what to do, what to order, whether to retreat, or where to retreat to. The invisible specter was assaulting them from all sides. Overcome with confusion and fear, he simply fell to his knees, shaking uncontrollably, and blurted out contradictory commands like that of a madman.

Anak, the true commander of the knights, steadied his men — the tribe, the Anakim — with one brief, quiet order. "Stand firm! Ready your weapons! Nothing can defeat us!"

Under his leadership, his men had experienced nothing but victory, and their faith in him was unwavering. But, in this instance, he was dead wrong. The knights had trespassed on the territory of the claw-tooth, and the Anakim would pay for the mistake with their blood — all their blood.

Those men remaining in the outer ring of the formation as it collapsed around the commander had no hope of surviving. They cried out to their gods for help — the gods of thunder and the stars. But help did not come.

One by one, the knights fell, most not knowing what manner of beast was taking them from this life to the next. Without warning, teeth and claws would emerge from the darkness, gripping and tearing their flesh to shreds. The darkness pulled them away as they screamed in terror.

For a moment that became an eternity, men knew the fear and pain of hell. In just a few minutes, only a few of the Anakim remained of the knights. They stood stubbornly beside Anak, their commander, defiantly keeping their oaths to protect Hanjian — the cowardly vestige of a man who now huddled on his knees behind Anak like a terrified child.

Then there was silence. A light breeze softly blew through the carnage from the north, clearing the air of the heat of battle and the stench of blood. As the surrounding fog momentarily cleared, the Anakim, still standing, could see innumerable sets of eyes all around them, eerily reflecting the pale blue moonlight. The eyes watched and waited.

The Anakim and their commander stood in a tight circle at the center of the grassy plain, a field of blood and death where they had met their first and last defeat. Here they would soon fall, forever gone.

One of Anak's men asked, "What are they waiting for?"

Anak did not reply. What could he say?

The handful of remaining Anakim searched the darkness, waiting for the attack that was sure to come. They focused their gaze on the glowing eyes in the distance, searching for any signs of movement.

Anak's mind raced as he struggled for a way out of this predicament, as improbable as it seemed. Remorse over the men he had lost plagued his thoughts.

How could I have allowed Hanjian to lead us into this trap?

He and his men kept their eyes locked on the horizon and all the ghostly eyes that floated there, weightless in the fog. It wasn't until he heard the grass in front of him rustle ever so slightly, ever so faintly, that his eyes broke their fix on the horizon.

Anak lowered his eyes, and terror instantly gripped his soul. Anak found himself face to face with a claw-tooth. It had held its body, head to tail, not over two feet above the ground, and had stealthily approached their position through the tall grass. But now, slowly raising its scaly, reptilian head, it fixed its cold eyes on Anak, and Anak returned its stare.

Anak could not move a muscle. His eyes locked with the creature's eyes as if in a trance. He could feel the hot breath of the monster as it exhaled through its nostrils. He could smell the raw scent of the beast's leathery hide and its repulsive breath. Fresh flesh still hung from the creature's jagged and razor-sharp teeth.

The claw-tooth stretched its body to full height, directly in front of Anak. It stood eye to eye with Anak. Its long tail now whipped wildly behind it, lashing the tall grass it had used moments before for cover.

Anak's body remained frozen as most of his mind reeled, attempting to grasp the totality of the experience. Still, a small part of his mind, the warrior center of his consciousness, resigned itself to fight, to deal a crushing blow to the creature before it could move. Just as the claw-tooth was about to strike, it was this small spark that took control.

Proud and defiant to the last moment, Anak raised his sword with lightning speed, but lightning speed was not fast enough. The claw-tooth's hunting instincts were much more finely tuned than those of Anak. Sensing Anak's intent, the claw-tooth lunged forward before he could even begin his attack, seizing Anak's neck and instantly crushing his throat in its jaws. A stream of blood jetted out from Anak's neck into the moonlight like a Chastainian geyser. Anak's immense body, initially convulsing in the final pangs of death, became motionless a moment later.

Hanjian watched in horror as Anak hung lifelessly in the claw-tooth's jaws like a child's rag-doll. The sword that Anak would no more employ in the service of his earthly masters fell to the ground beneath him. Hanjian screamed in terror as a dozen of the claw-tooth young, young that had followed their mother in for the kill, dove into the remaining Anakim and their petrified leader. Their end was much slower and unmerciful than the Anak's had been, especially that of Hanjian. The young claw-tooths made special sport of the one with the incessant screaming, playing with their food at length before devouring it.

✝✝✝

The demons were stunned!

"How could this happen?" thundered Bestia! "Who controls these monsters that have torn through Hanjian's Black Knights?"

He knew very well. Though the demons often feigned ignorance when the protectors or their surrogates stunned them in battle, they knew who held the edge in all of their clashes with the Holy One and his forces of light. Unlike the angels of light, the demons served a master fatally ignorant of all future events, which put the evil ones at quite the strategic disadvantage.

The demons gathered around Bestia. In vile contempt and familiar misery, they lashed out at one another to dispel their overwhelming defeat at the hands of the mighty ones — those who served the Faithful and True.

They squealed in torment and frustration. Such was their eternal existence.

CHAPTER 53

Lions

†††

After the defeat of the Omentians at Chrystal Valley, Skottie had thought, or rather hoped, that the worst was behind them. He hoped that they, with the help of their omnipotent and merciful God, had swiftly defeated the invaders and no further trial or spiritual growth would be necessary. This was his hope, but it was not to so.

In the east, the beasts of the land now made their presence known. Allied with the invaders through the dark arts, the lion, whose bloodlust was no longer satisfied by the buffalo, acquired a new appetite for men.

Reclusive and distant until now, the lion migrated east in search of its new prey. Uncontested through the eastern plains of central Kandish, Smilodon and his lion pack devastated the indigenous livestock and attacked the peaceful villages in their path, killing for no other reason than for the sake of the hatred that drove them forward. They attacked at night, making use of their superior senses of sight and smell to devour the vulnerable, withdrawing to secret dens during the day to conceal their whereabouts.

Skottie and the Sixth Division did their best to track down the savage beasts, but their efforts had been unsuccessful. They were merely being reactive to the lion attacks, arriving well after the last of the killer cats had done its wicked deed. It was a deadly and seemingly never-ending game of cat and mouse, and the Adonians were the mice.

After the miraculous events that had taken place in Plattos, Daniel, Benhjami, and most of the Seventh Division had traveled east into Kandish to aid in the neighboring province's defense. They joined up with Skottie and the Adonia Sixth, and split into squads to track the lions, occasionally encountering small packs or prides of lions running together after dark. Though they aimed to track down the lions, they hardly rejoiced in achieving their goal. The men were all too aware of the ferocity and lethality of the lion. The village reports of their encounters with the beasts were both sobering and disheartening. None really looked forward to meeting them in combat — only a fool would.

It took a minimum of five heavily armed men to defeat one lion. Operating in squads of eleven, the Adonian Guardsmen could realistically plan to engage two of the lions and expect to have a chance of defeating them. If a squad clashed with over two lions, they could expect heavy, or possibly total, losses.

Unfortunately, there was really no way to set the conditions for engagement. If a squad encountered a lion clan operating at night, the guardsmen would instantly be at a disadvantage. The same was true if a squad stumbled upon a lion den by day, where they would find themselves face-to-face with a vastly superior force and in extreme peril.

†††

Daniel's squad had been operating in Eastern Kandish for three days. Skottie had briefed him and Benjhami on everything they knew about the lions' movements, and Daniel, Benjhami, and the Seventh Division had divided up into squads to help eradicate Kandish of the menacing creatures.

Daniel's squad, like most of the Seventh Division, consisted of men he had known for years; men he loved as brothers. He trusted them with his life, and likewise, they trusted him with theirs.

Daniel's squad searched the rolling hills in the darkness for any sign of the deadly beasts that had been ravaging the land. In a long, line-abreast formation, twenty feet between each man, they moved quietly through the thick shrubbery and trees that spotted the hilly countryside. Though it would have been prudent, defensively, for the men to carry torches and stick close together in their search, they instead experimented with a new tactic of moving abeam each other without the flaming torches. They hoped that by letting their eyes adjust to the darkness, they could reduce the lion's night vision advantage. They also thought that by abandoning their torches, they could gain the advantage of surprise that they otherwise would not have had if they had broadcasted their presence for miles in advance with the flaming torches. Finally, by traveling in a long line-abreast formation, they hoped to better net a lion. Though this was inherently more dangerous than traveling in a group, safety was not the reason they had taken to this venture, and therefore, they decided safety should not drive their tactics. They were on a seek-and-destroy mission, and it made little sense to employ a tactic, like carrying torches through the night in a large formation, that guaranteed they would never find a lion. Better to have some chance of success, even if it involved an elevated level of risk, than to have no chance of success at all, thus making the entire effort futile.

This tactic seemed like a great idea, right until it wasn't such a great idea. One moment Daniel was leading his squad quietly through the darkness, and the next he was lying on his back at the bottom of a fifteen foot hole, unable to move or even breathe. He had unknowingly crossed over a weak patch of earth that had — until that time — covered a large and hidden underground enclosure. Crumbling under his weight, the ground had given way and pulled with it Daniel's unsuspecting body through the small cavity and down to the bottom of the pit. The fall instantly knocked the air out of Daniel, leaving him unable to call out for help or even take in a breath.

As Daniel lie on the earthen floor of the pit, writhing in pain and trying to breathe, his senses told him what his mind did not want to accept; the game had changed. In addition, Daniel was instantly aware of several facts.

By the time I can breathe again, the men will have moved on. They will no longer hear my cries for help. It will be hours before they will even discover my absence and the morning before they can begin a search for me.

He was also aware of another fact; he was in terrible, terrible trouble.

✝✝✝

Flash!

Boom!

Flash! Flash!

Boom! BOOM!

The living beings darted in, with, and through all that is, was, and will be. Their infinitely colored wings flashed countless colors of light in all directions, both within and without as they passed between times and spaces to accomplish the Master's will.

A voice thundered. "Daniel is in danger!"

"I am there!" echoed another as a flash of emerald shimmered in, between, and through the multiple dimensions.

The lights twinkled and flashed in perfect cadence. An endless symphony of voices, powerful voices, rang in unison and harmony.

✝✝✝

As the unsettled dirt in the air above him settled, Daniel, still lying on his back, could see the stars in the night sky through the small opening high in the darkness above him. He wondered if he should move, or if by moving, he would further alert any other creatures that might be in this pit with him as to his exact location.

The minutes passed. Daniel quietly checked his body for injury and found none other than his back, which still felt like a bull had hit from behind him.

I can't just lie here. If I am not alone down here, surely my companions already know of my presence. After all, I made quite a stunning entrance.

Daniel rose to his feet and attempted to see through the darkness of the pit. The light of the stars that shone through the small hole above him, though they emanated from an unimaginable distance away, was the only luminescence Daniel had to reveal clues to the contents of the dark enclosure in which he now stood. Fear knocked at the door of Daniel's heart, but Daniel refused to answer. Daniel bowed his head and kneeled on the earth where he just moments before lied. He prayed to his helper in every trouble.

"Father, help me. I find myself in yet again, another bad situation. I will not fear, because I know you are with me, as you are always with me — no matter where I am. There is a way to give you glory in this place. Show me the way to give you that glory. Help me honor you with my life, whether it lasts for fifty more years or perhaps only fifty more seconds. I love you Father."

A quiet peace came over Daniel as he gave his trouble to God, raised his eyes and watched the stars twinkling through the small opening above him.

We are so small, so small compared to the immensity of the heavens. How great is our God that he could create all the stars up above and still hear our prayers? What an honor to serve such a king.

After a few more moments of thought and praise to the God of the Heavens, Daniel turned his attention to the immediate problem at hand.

Daniel had just spent the last two hours in the dark, searching the forest for any sign of lions, and his eyes had well adjusted to the night. Unfortunately, it seemed he may have found more of a lion sign than he intended, and if this was indeed a lion den, the hunter may have just become the hunted — or worse yet, dinner.

Though his eyes had adjusted as well as possible to the lack of light, human eyes still needed some light to see shades of gray, and there wasn't much light to be had in the underground pit. It amazed Daniel that he could see anything at all.

Even a tiny light makes a big difference in total darkness.

Daniel's thoughts then returned to his childhood, when he and two of his brothers, Skottie and Geoff, along with his cousin, Toro, had explored the hills and forests of Chastain together as teenagers. They had so much fun together before the age of maturity and the seasons of life had forced them to depart and make their own way separately in the many unsettled territories of Adonia. Each age of life had its advantages and, likewise, its disadvantages. The goodbye to such adolescent activities was, unfortunately, the cost of turning the pages of time. Though now separated by great distances, they would remain brothers forever, bound by their history, their memories, and their love for one another. They were eternal family, both here in the now and there in the forever with their Lord.

Daniel found great strength in knowing his family thought and prayed for him often, as he did for them. He knew that the actual words spoken in prayer held no special power, no magical control over events, as those who practiced the dark arts believed their dark words and chants to have. Indeed, the great power of prayer resided in the intended recipient of the prayer. Likewise, it was not the faith of the faithful that held the power to shake the foundations of the world, but the object of that faith — the God in whom that faith rested and in whom the faithful trusted.

There was but one God, the Creator of the heavens and the earth; a God of love, justice, and power. The prayers of his faithful found his ear and had an effect because of God's person; his love, his promises, his will, and his omnipotence.

A low, guttural growl interrupted Daniel's thoughts. Daniel froze. Piercing the darkness, Daniel could now see the dim glow of the eyes upon him; one set, two sets, then three sets of eyes. As Daniel looked around him, he soon realized several massive beasts surrounded him. They stood equal to his height. He could not distinctly make out their shapes, only their shadows, standing in the dark pit with him, watching.

Realistically, there was little Daniel could do. He could see very little beyond his immediate surroundings. Only a small circle of the pit was lit, and ever so dimly. Beyond that circle, he had only a little clue of what was there. Even if he knew where to run, it was doubtful he could make it before being cut down.

There was a certain comfort in not having any options. It brought clarity to the situation. *There is no use in panic. There is no use in running. If it is your will, Lord, I will live. If not, I will be with you. Whether I live or die, I belong to you.*

Daniel raised his eyes to the light high above him. Tears ran down his cheeks. They were not tears of fear. He wasn't afraid of what was about to happen to him. He trusted God and knew whatever happened would be for his ultimate good. God's understanding was much greater than his — or any man's understanding. Created man could not expect to even begin to understand the Creator's ways, except for that which the Creator had revealed through his prophets and his Word. His tears were for his family and for the separation from them he could already feel.

"Please take care of them, Father."

Daniel dropped to his knees. He raised his hands in prayer, and gave thanks to God for his life, his family, and all the blessings he had known. In a peace beyond all human understanding, Daniel surrendered his will to his Lord and King, fearlessly placing his life in the gracious hands of the giver and keeper of days.

†††

The six adult lions circled the man in near darkness. Their keen eyesight exceeded the eye-sense of the man-flesh, who appeared to have little ability to see them in the shadows; he neither attempted to flee from them or fight them.

The scent of the man-flesh instantly drove them into a feeding frenzy, as they craved to devour the defenseless prey that had violated their lair, literally falling into their den from the ground above. What the lions would soon find out was that this man-flesh was far from defenseless.

Just as they prepared to attack the man-flesh and tear him to pieces in a ferocious display of their newfound bloodlust, the underground enclosure exploded in blinding light, and an invisible shockwave knocked all the lions, first, to the ground and then against the den walls. The intense burst of radiance and the powerful impact of the shockwave went unnoticed by the man-flesh now kneeling on the ground before them, but it hit the lions like a bolt of lightning.

The light emanated from a living being that suddenly appeared to the lions within the enclosure. Glowing in indefinable radiance, the glorious living being's six enormous wings waved threateningly over the heads of the startled beasts, as beams of brilliant emerald light burst forth in all directions from its countless eyes. It held a flaming sword high above its head, giving further warning to the lions that it was ready and willing to strike dead any creature that might threaten the man under its watch.

The lions were stunned, and having no conscious thought, they instinctively flattened out against the walls of the lair. Recovering, they cowered low to the ground, looking for any reprieve from the dominant presence that had so unexpectedly appeared and interrupted their kill. A moment earlier, determined to tear the man-flesh to pieces, they were now interested only in self-preservation; searching for the quickest means of escape.

But just as quickly as the lions' plans had changed, the tables turned again; evil was determined to have its way. Only the briefest of moments had passed since the glorious living being had so powerfully appeared in the pit to defend the man; a man who remained completely oblivious to the spiritual events transpiring around him. Without warning, six other spiritual beings entered the fight, bursting into the pit in a blaze of crimson.

Sent by Potentus, these demons — Desolote, Temptis, Anxetichis, Angara, Furomis, Hatia, and Despondus, along with the rest of the condemned — were among the foulest and most ancient of all creatures. Jagged and tattered from millennia of battle, their wings cracked the air as they arrived. Their ghastly bodies, dreadfully diseased by eons of service to evil, defiled everything in their presence.

Satan's servants wasted no time. In an instance they attacked the glorious being from all sides with flaming swords of crimson fire. Though not a third the size of the glorious being, they had waged war with the living beings from soon after the beginning, making them experienced and formidable opponents in their own right. As the condemned fiends rushed the glorious living being's perimeter, the emerald beams of light emanating from its many eyes focused predominantly on the six gruesome attackers. Five of them instantly slowed down; their advance repelled by the living being's power. The sixth demon proceeded unimpeded to its target, launching itself forcefully into the air with its sword held out in front of it like a spear, attempting to impale the glorious living being through its center. But the demon was not fast enough. The glorious being's mighty sword flashed and in a blur abruptly thwarted the demon's assault, landing a quick succession of strikes that first sliced the demon's sword in half and then immediately after did the same to its owner.

The demons' onslaught continued. Still believing they were executing their plan to overwhelm the mighty being by hitting it from all sides simultaneously, they drove forward, unleashing everything they had on the heavenly warrior. However, because of the living being's divinely enabled gift to phase through time, the demons were really attacking the much more powerful creature sequentially and being handily discharged one at a time.

As swords collided with a thunderous crash and a blinding burst of light, the last of the hellish demons fell to the glorious living being. The threat to the man no longer imminent, the living being's scan once again widened to cover the entire perimeter around it and the man under its protection. Still standing guard over Daniel, the living being showed no sign of weakness from the combat that had just taken place. If anything, its radiance shone even more brilliantly.

The lions — their eyes having seen a glimpse of the spiritual combat taking place in the pit — had retreated to the far walls of the enclosure, and at the dispatch of the last demon, made haste to the nearest exit of the pit, never to return.

✝✝✝

Daniel continued to pray.

When he had first realized that he had fallen into the pit, he became very lonely. This loneliness had opened the door of his heart and mind to anger, rage, and even hate for the ones who had placed him there. Left alone to his own thoughts, Daniel might have easily drifted into despair.

But God had not left Daniel alone in the pit. The Lord of the heavens was, as always, with him.

Daniel stood in the darkness of the pit, his hands still raised to the tiny glimmer of light shining through the hole in the underground's enclosure, and he remembered something his father Truin had told him and his brothers when they were children. "The darkness has no choice before the dawn."

How true it is! Only in the absence of light is darkness dominant. Darkness flees at the arrival of the light.

Daniel continued to pray, and as he did, God lifted Daniel's spirit. Time seemed to stand still as Daniel communed peacefully with his maker.

When Daniel opened his eyes, bright rays of morning sunlight were shining through the opening in the roof above him, lighting the interior of the pit that had imprisoned him. He could clearly see that he was now alone. The evil that had surrounded him earlier in the darkness had fled before the dawn.

Soon, Daniel heard his friends calling out to him, and moments later, his companions dropped him a rope and pulled him out of the pit.

✝✝✝

The lions remained a fluid and illusive quarry. They attacked more and more often in the mist and fog, making a true estimation of their numbers impossible.

Skottie directed his hunting parties to use drums to drive the lions before them.

Since we aren't having any luck finding and killing the vermin, we might as well scare them a bit!

The tactic seemed to work, since none of the hunting parties using drums ever encountered any of the lions. Then again, they might not have run into the lions either way. Still, it became a nightly tradition for the villages of southern Kandish to beat the drum in the evening, hoping to keep any lions in the area away. In addition, a town crier announced the hour and state of the village for four hours after sunset. His call would sound something like, "Seven O'clock and all is well." And thus, the townships became accustomed to hearing the "news" every evening.

Soon, the lion attacks seemed to taper off in frequency. Though the people of Kandish were very relieved, thanking the Lord with happy hearts, they knew the attacks against their homeland were far from over.

Truin's latest intelligence was that a major Omentian invasion through southeastern Adonia was now imminent. Khory, Bigaulf, Koldas, Surge, Weiphal, Gareth, Cusintomas, Geoff, Toro, Moesheh, Kristof, Jhim, and Wristo, along with their Adonian Guard divisions, moved south to join Daniel and Skottie in southern Kandish.

Evil did not sleep, and evil was not done with Adonia.

CHAPTER 54

AWE AND COMFORT

†††

Toro sat alone in the chilly room, reading the Word by the glow of one small, flickering candle. Anxious and unable to sleep, he had spent some quiet time with his Lord.

Much had happened over the last few weeks. The Omentian invasion, led by the dark disciples of Karyan, had been extensive and well dispersed across Adonia. Though all the provinces had come under considerable pressure to capitulate in the face of the attack, they had all held, thanks alone to the supernatural power of God.

The attacks on Adonia were not just physical. Toro and the others had each had their own doubts and fears to contend with. Even after having heard the incredible reports of the mysterious and awesome works of the Lord and having observed many of them with their own eyes, they, being the weak human beings that they were, often drifted into worry and a sense of dread over what might still be on the horizon. Such was man's fallen condition.

How long will we have to live in fear of attack? Will the coming battles hurt our sons and daughters? When will these attacks end and peace return to our land?

No one could answer these questions, and they incessantly gnawed at the hearts and minds of the people of Adonia. Even the young men, projecting their typical fearless bravado, held in their hearts the same unspoken concerns as their sisters, mothers, fathers, and grandparents.

How many more must give their lives before this ends?

Toro prayed for his uncle Truin, his brother Weiphal, his cousins, and the men they led. Rumor had it Truin had ordered the Adonian Guard to assemble in southern Kandish to prepare for repelling a massive Omentian invasion there. Truin himself was traveling from Aanot to lead them in the fight. Toro prayed God would bring them all safely to the marshaling area, and that in the end, they would not have to engage the enemy again; for if they did, more of his loved ones might have to give up their lives.

At times like this, Toro knew the best thing he could do was to turn to the Word, meditate on the promises of his God, remember the Master's faithfulness, and pray. Leaving all his worries, cares, and fears at the throne of the Almighty, the only one capable and faithful to deal with them, brought peace and joy back to his heart.

Toro prayed by the dim orange glow of the candlelight and heard the faint sound of a wolf in the distance, howling in the frigid winter night. Toro smiled. The wolf, once feared by men as a ferocious predator, now brought comfort to the hearts of the faithful.

It had been years since the gray wolf had saved Toro's life in the frozen tundra of the Strange Lands. Since then, many people had reported sightings of wolves throughout southern Adonia. The gray wolf and its descendants appeared to have followed Toro north, settling throughout Rothing, Tobar, and Kandish. They had not threatened the livestock or the human population of the provinces. Quite the contrary; they had recently shown themselves to be a considerable ally in the fight against the lions.

It was not only the Adonian Guard who had gone on the offensive against the deadly lions that had infiltrated Adonia, but also the wolf. The wolf packs had successfully sought and killed several; their torn and dismantled carcasses being found on the outskirts of towns by traveling villagers. The wolf packs also patrolled the perimeters of villages at night, prepared to prevent any potential lion attacks.

How can this beast of the land now be our friend?

Toro questioned whether the wolf had migrated north because of some threat to its food source, his peculiar encounter with them in the Strange Lands, or because of divine intervention. No one knew for sure; maybe all three or for some other reason altogether. No matter the cause, the dynamic of the land had changed, and as far as Toro was concerned, the change was for the better.

It was not only the dynamic of the land that had changed, but also the dynamic of the air. Weiphal had reported the common occurrence of graptors flying defensive caps over Adonian villages. Frequently, these graptors had intercepted flights of tannin bound to destroy the otherwise defenseless villages. How these graptors knew of the imminent tannin attacks was unknown, but the people of Adonia, standing far below the aerial dogfights, were very thankful to have the giant raptors around.

How odd, Toro reflected, that creatures which once would have struck fear in the hearts of men, now invoke comfort.

The Lord works in very mysterious ways. Truly, our God is the master of his creation, and it should not surprise us a bit when his creation follows his will.

Another distant howl of a wolf again interrupted Toro's thoughts, coming this time from the north, apparently answering the cry of the first.

What are they telling each other?

Like many things, Toro did not know the answer to these questions. Bottom line, he didn't need to. His God knew the answers, and his Father in heaven would use all things in heaven and on earth to protect his faithful; this God had promised.

Toro smiled again. The anxiety of the night and the chill of the unknown had dissipated. In their place was the assurance of an ever-watchful God, using his creation to protect his own and accomplish his will.

I am definitely alright with that, Father. Thy will be done.

Freed from the attacks of fear and worry, Toro quietly blew out the candle and fell into a peaceful sleep. How awesome it was to know the truth.

CHAPTER 55

THE LIGHT

†††

"I know that my Redeemer lives, and that in the end he will stand upon the earth. And after my skin has been destroyed, yet in my flesh I will see God; I myself will see him with my own eyes — I, and not another. How my heart yearns within me!" (Job 19:25-27)

The message was critical and had to reach its destination. The falcon flew with blistering speed across the plains of Plattos, over the forests of Tobar, and through the valleys of Kandish to deliver the time-sensitive message it held firmly in its talons.

High above the falcon, a large bald eagle flew Close Air Patrol over the more agile messenger, keeping a vigilant watch for any distant enemy approach, while the falcon used its superior speed and maneuverability to transverse the contested territory, hoping to remain undetected by the sinister eyes of the dark watchers.

But the watchers were many. Their clandestine presence within the provinces became quite extensive, and soon the falcon caught their attention. While shadowing the falcon, several large ravens pursued the infiltrator as it approached Aanot, plotting an intercept course and signaling ahead to the others that lied in wait.

The perfect moment to launch the ambush was at hand, and they attacked as one. Though the attacking ravens' speed was no match for the falcon's, the sheer numbers of the dark birds in pursuit of her, as well as those that had emerged simultaneously in ambush, could overwhelm the falcon's defensive response and reduce her avenues of escape. As a last ditch maneuver, she streaked into the vertical, heading skyward for the unrestrictive blue sky above — above, where an ally waited.

The eagle, already alerted to the falcon's plight, had started a steep dive on the falcon's position. The ravens, target-fixated on the falcon they had besieged, did not observe the eagle's rapid approach from the sun until it was too late. As the falcon bolted skyward, the eagle plummeted past her, fatally slashing open three of her closest pursuers. The rest of those shadowing her scattered as they saw their fellows fall from the sky, mortally wounded.

The remaining ravens' focus desperately switched from targeting the falcon to surviving their clash with the great raptor. But their efforts were in vain. The eagle dominated the fight, littering the countryside with remnants of raven.

Swiftly extending away from the aerial dogfight, the messenger falcon plunged for the forests below, seeking safety in the cluttered terrain. The falcon reached the southernmost boundary of Chastain and approached its final destination.

But this was one message, one warning, that evil did not want reaching its intended audience. While the victorious eagle used the warm air currents to return triumphantly to the cool, blue skies high over the mountains of Chastain, the valiant falcon met its sudden and merciless end far below, at the hands of an expert archer and servant of Karyan. The powers of darkness alerted Rahm to the falcon's approach, and he fired the deadly dart that instantly killed the falcon and sent its lifeless body crashing to the earth below.

The Omentian spy pried open the rigid talons of the dead falcon, and tore free the warning message. Reading it aloud, he smiled pompously at the bird. "Little one, little one, we couldn't have you ruining the surprise, now can we?"

†††

The six traveled with stealth and speed. No one could detect them until they reached their target; they had to hasten. The scent on the cloak was strong; they had no problem tracking the two-leg.

†††

Truin's latest intelligence report stated that a major Omentian invasion force, the largest ever assembled, would attack southeast Adonia within days. His sons were assembling what remained of Adonia's divisions to stand directly in front of this ominous onslaught. Though Christina urged him to reconsider, no force on this side of heaven would stop him from being there with them. He was not about to miss this fight. Neither was Christina.

When Christina, who became a formidable warrior in her own right, announced her intentions to go with Truin and join their sons in southern Kandish, Truin had insisted that she stay at Castle Armon, where it was safe. His insistence, however, had only strengthened Christina's resolve to accompany him on the journey.

Likewise, Jonn was adamant that he too accompany Truin on the trek. Gladsel had learned the administrative affairs of Adonia well from Jonn and had all but taken over the management of day-to-day activities, which left Jonn free to accompany Truin. Though Truin wanted Jonn to stay in Aanot and continue to oversee the affairs of Adonia, Gladsel could fill in for Jonn. Truin realized he was fighting, yet again, another losing battle.

So, Truin, Christina, Jonn, and a small security team of the Adonian Guard made haste to join the main Adonian Defense Force in the south. Within two days, they had progressed to the forests of Tobar. Though they didn't want to stop, wisdom dictated that Ashwin and the other horses must rest or they would not last the journey.

Ashwin had served Truin a great deal longer than expected, and they had built a relationship much greater than horse and master. The animals, like Ashwin, that God had placed in the lives of men became more than pets, or servants, but like members of the family. This was the way of men and the way of love.

Truin's household had cherished both Ashwin and Hammer, who was from the offspring of Thor. Christina had cared for them in Truin's many absences. They had cared for her in their own special way, and their loyalty to the house of Truin was without question.

Once the travelers had stopped, Jonn and the soldiers made camp and set up a defensive perimeter, while Truin and Christina spent some quality time together. Recent events had necessitated most of Truin's attention, and he didn't want things to get too out of balance; his relationship with Christina was very important to him. As Truin and Christina strolled away from the others, hand in hand, Hammer, who had grown to be larger and more powerful than Thor had been in his prime, assumed his dutiful position at their side.

It was a crisp, sunny day. Countless patches of sunlight danced on the ground around them as the bright burgundy and gold leaves performed their annual ballet with the fall breeze high above their heads.

Truin and Christina walked through the forest, and the burdens of the day gradually lifted. It was a special moment in time; they renewed their love and felt young once again.

They reflected on their life together. How swiftly, it now seemed, the years had gone by. So much had happened since they had pulled Christina from death's icy grip in the waters of the Northern Sea; the moment their eyes had first met. Together they had settled a God-given land, flowing with endless riches. God had blessed them with seven noble sons, now grown men, each leading god-fearing families of their own.

What a blessing to have found each other when neither of them had thought they had much of a future to look forward to. At the edge of despair, the Lord had unexpectedly brought them together, brought them to each other and made them one. First, he had given them hope. Then he had given them love. And ever since, he had blessed them beyond their wildest dreams. How faithful was their God!

The couple found a small, grassy clearing nestled between several large rock formations. So, enjoying each other's company and the opportunity to rest from the cares of the world, they nestled themselves down in the grass and enjoyed the beauty of nature that surrounded them. They left all their worries and cares behind, and reminisced peacefully about the past, reliving the many wonderful memories they had shared.

"Did I ever tell you about my earliest memory with my father?"

"No honey, I don't believe you have," replied Christina.

"It was a wonderful day; a day much like this one. It was just the two of us, taking a walk together, talking, and relaxing — which might be why I thought of it."

Christina snuggled close to Truin while he spoke. Smiles crossed both of their faces as they settled comfortably into their shared personal space, both of them longing for the familiar security and warmth of the other.

"It was a sunny summer day, and I was still a young boy. I loved taking walks with Dad, throwing stones in the river, and just sharing his company. He used to call it, sharing air. He would say, 'C'mon boy, let's go share some air!' I would drop whatever I was doing and off we would go to share some air. Truin stopped to chuckle.

"This particular day, we talked, laughed, and wondered about many things: why birds eat worms, why fish are always yawning, and why we don't have wings." Both Truin and Christina laughed. "Then he sat me on his knee and told me that what he was about to share with me was very important. He read me **Psalm 37**. He said I should always remember the words, live by them, and trust in God's promises. I have done my best to do so."

Truin said the words out loud from memory. "Do not fret because of evil men or be envious of those who do wrong; for like the grass they will soon wither, like green plants they will soon die away. Trust in the Lord and do good; dwell in the land and enjoy safe pasture. Delight yourself in the Lord and he will give you the desires of your heart. Commit your way to the Lord; trust in him and he will do this: He will make your righteousness shine like the dawn, the justice of your cause, like the noonday sun. Be still before the Lord and wait patiently before him; do not fret when men succeed in their ways, when they carry out their wicked schemes. Refrain from anger and turn from wrath; do not fret — it leads only to evil. For evil men will be cut off, but those who hope in the Lord will inherit the land. A little while, and the wicked will be no more; though you look for them, they will not be found. But the meek will inherit the land and enjoy great peace. The wicked plot against the righteous and gnash their teeth at them; but the Lord laughs at the wicked, for he knows their day is coming. The wicked draw the sword and bend the bow to bring down the poor and needy, to slay those whose ways are upright. But their swords will pierce their own hearts, and their bows will be broken. Better the little that the righteous have then the wealth of many wicked; for the power of the wicked will be broken, but the Lord upholds the righteous. The days of the blameless are known to the Lord, and their inheritance will endure forever. In times of disaster, they will not wither; in days of famine they will enjoy plenty. But the wicked will perish: The Lord's enemies will be like the beauty of the fields, they will vanish — vanish like smoke. The wicked borrow and do not repay, but the righteous give generously; those the Lord blesses will inherit the land, but those he curses will be cut off. The Lord delights in the way of the man whose steps he has made firm; though he stumble, he will not fall, for the Lord upholds him with his hand. I was young and now I am old, yet I have never seen the righteous forsaken or the children begging bread. They are always generous and lend freely; their children will be blessed. Turn from evil and do good; then you will always live securely. For the Lord loves the just and will not forsake the faithful ones. They will be protected forever, but the offspring of the wicked will be cut off; the righteous will inherit the land and dwell in it forever... The salvation of the righteous comes from the Lord; he is their stronghold in time of trouble. The Lord helps them and delivers them; he delivers them from the wicked and saves them, because they take refuge in him."

"I have thought often of these words through the years, and I have found them to be true, not lacking in any way. God has done wondrous things in our lives, truly miraculous things. Some are exceedingly obvious to all who have eyes; though some with eyes still choose to be blind.

"But I have also found that the Lord, the God of the heavens and the earth, very often reveals his awesome glory while speaking in a still, small voice. It is unquestionable that he has guided the major events of our lives, working them out for our eternal blessing. Still, the peace, love, and care that he gives on us daily — he does gently, quietly, and personally. He pierces our hearts, seeking our anxieties and calming them with his peace. With his promises of love and protection, he confronts our fears and dismisses them. He lovingly holds us in his almighty hand and guides us through our lives to our eternal home."

Christina, deep in thought, pondered on her own experiences and nodded slowly in agreement with Truin as he spoke. Christina still remembered how alone she had felt after being sold into slavery and then tossed into the sea. Though the experience was many years earlier, she remembered it like it had just happened. She had wanted to give up, but God had saved her. He had sent his angel to her to give her the strength to go on.

God had a plan for her life, for Truin's life, for the lives of their sons, and for Adonia. He was working it piece by piece through their daily lives. When looking at the pieces of the puzzle by themselves, the picture was incomplete and almost impossible to see; but once all the pieces were in their appropriate places, she could see the puzzle-maker's beautiful picture and the story it was telling.

Truin continued. "It has not always been easy for us, as you well know. Our vision as a man and a woman is so limited. Our thoughts are so basic, our understanding so simple, and our motives very often so predominantly selfish. The Lord's ways are so much higher — his plan so far-reaching. We cannot know all that is to come or how our lives will play out, but we can rest assured that the events will all work together for our eternal good, and for the Lord's glory."

A gentle peace fell on them like a warm blanket as they meditated on their Creator, their protector, their God.

"For those who deny him, those under the spell of the evil one, these promises do not apply. They are already alone in a world of fear, condemnation, and dread of what is coming. Their condemnation will come, and they know they will not escape it. They live their lives as a bitter, angry orgy of hate and destruction — a foreshadowing of what is coming to them in eternity."

Tears of pity formed in Christina's eyes as she thought of the poor souls still living in darkness; they neither knew nor wanted to know the love, mercy, and protection of the Lord.

"But we do not need to fear them. Their numbers are many, and their power is great, but he who is with us, the Mighty God, the Creator of all things, is so much greater. The dark powers, the puppet masters that even now pull the strings of the Omentian, the Heathian, and the Parlantian; God has already judged and condemned them. They have lost the eternal struggle and even now writhe in agony in fear of the Day of Judgment. Their eternal fate is sure."

Truin held Christina tight.

"Remember these words. We are already victors in this war, even if it might appear that we are losing the battle. Our God reigns supreme. His wisdom is far greater than ours could ever be, and his love for us endures forever! His will be done!"

"His will be done," Christina echoed.

✝✝✝

Streaks of color and light flashed across the spiritual domains, causing the dark ones to scatter like roaches to temporary safe havens of shadow, where they cowered in fear.

"They love each other," a powerful voice said — softly.

"They always have. Though for periods of time, the temporal events and trivial affairs of their lives have obscured that which is most important," a second voice said — quietly. "They forget how much love they have to give and how readily the Master told them to give it."

"Now they remember."

"Yes, and it is important that they remember, for they may soon deeply cherish these memories. Behold, darkness gathers at the door."

†††

They lurked in the shadows, unseen. They grew close now, closer by the hour. Long they had waited for the two-leg to be vulnerable, and now it was so. Soon it would be their time.

†††

Time stood still.

So much had happened over the last few months. There just hadn't been time to stop life's events long enough to decompress, connect, and share again the memories, thoughts, and dreams that a husband and wife should share with each other often, if not continuously. Both of them had bottled up so much inside. Once they started talking, however, the words continued to pour out.

"Oh, how I love this land," Truin said as he held Christina close. "We have built so much here; we have accomplished so much. This place is our home now, a place where we can worship God in freedom and peace."

"Unless the Omentian has his way," Christina said.

"The Omentian will never have his way." Truin showed noticeable agitation. "Not in this land. This land is the Lord's, and he has given it to us, the people who love him. As long as we love him and worship him, he will protect this land and its inhabitants from all who would oppose the truth. Like a city on a hill, the light will shine from this place, lighting up the darkest corners of the world, a beacon to all who would live in truth, freedom, and peace."

Christina continued. "And what if the people of the land someday forget the Lord? It is easy for them to look to him for help when the Omentian is at the door, easy to remember the Lord's deliverance when they see his hand at work before their very eyes. But what about later, long after they have experienced salvation? What about then? We have seen how unfaithful people can be — how soon they can forget. Both Heath and Omentia once had the light, but they took the light for granted, thinking it was not worth protecting. They let the light fade until it was gone. Then, they fell into the darkness."

Agreeing with Christina, but still unsure why she was taking the discussion in this direction, Truin spoke prophetic words. "If the people forget the Lord, if they are unfaithful, he will withdraw his protection from their land. But he will always be faithful to those who love him. He will never forget the faithful. This he has promised, and he always keeps his promises."

Truin looked into his beloved's eyes and realized her questions, during this entire discussion, were all about their boys. She was worried about them and their families.

"Honey, our boys have all been called. They believe the truth and have taught their families the truth. God loves them, and he will always protect them. We do not have to worry about them. The Lord holds all of them securely in his mighty hands."

Her anxiety melted away as she pondered his words. "The Lord holds them securely in his mighty hands."

For a moment, there was silence as they held each other tight in the warm sunlight. Christina knew what her husband was thinking, and she said the thought out loud so he could hear them from her lips. "The Lord holds Ka'el securely in his mighty hands, too."

Truin's eyes filled with tears as he gazed into his wife's soft, caring face. He let her words warm his heart like a wool blanket. For so long, he had prayed to the Lord on behalf of his brother Ka'el. For so long, he had waited for his brother to come home. He knew the Lord would not let Truin go, but he needed to hear the words from someone else.

A single tear rolled down Truin's cheek. "Ka'el is wandering. I've tried to bring him home, but I can't reach him."

Christina held Truin tenderly in her arms. "You have done all that you can do. The Lord will show him the way home."

She cupped his face in her hands, and repeated the words again, more slowly. "The Lord will show him the way. Trust the Lord."

"I love you so much Christina, so very much."

"And I love you. That will never, ever change."

They expressed their love for one another and left nothing unsaid. They expressed their love for one another, freezing it in time, for all of time; never ending, never fading, eternal. It would remain a cherished memory throughout the ages, both in the here and in the there. This is the way of love.

The birds of the forest danced in the bright sunshine, gathering around the lovers, and singing their melodious songs of joy. And all the heavens danced with them.

†††

Bestia could barely control himself.

"This will be a glorious victory for my master. Metus himself will certainly commend me for it!"

He floated through the moon-made shadows of the forest trees as he guided the beasts below.

"They will elevate me to the status of Metus, and they will give me even more power! Before long, I will sit in the company of Lucifer himself!"

He watched the slender and powerful creatures nimbly glide over and around the woodland obstacles in their path. He longed to be one of them, craving the experience of sinking long fangs into prey and tearing soft flesh from bone.

How exhilarating that would be!

418

Bestia's excitement dissipated as he nervously scanned the darkness ahead for protectors. His jowls curled wryly as his thoughts turned to the angels of light and the hatred he carried for them.

"The protectors will fail. Soon the mothers of Adonia will feel pain like never before. Soon their tears will flow like a river never-ending. They will scream through the night, and my master will be very pleased."

†††

Without noticing, the sky had become overcast, and a stiff wind now blew through the trees, sending a chill through their bones.

Those bright scarlet and gold leaves became drab and stale in the fading light and broke off their syncopated ballet with the once gentle breeze; the dance now became a burdensome struggle against an unwelcomed guest.

Birds that had gathered around them swiftly darted for their nests as the foreboding winds announced the presence of evil.

Truin looked around curiously, momentarily stunned by the unexpected change in the elements. He stood urgently and wrapped his heavy outer garment about Christina. Together, they turned and headed back for camp.

Hammer, still by their side, let out a guttural growl and shot out ahead of them.

"Hammer," Truin called out. "Hammer!"

There was no response from Hammer as he continued to storm ahead, turning the corner ahead of them and passing out of view. This was not his way.

"Hammer!"

"What is he doing?" Christina asked. "It is not like him to leave us like that."

"He would never leave us, unless —" Truin paused, hoping not to frighten Christina, and then realized he just had.

"Unless what?" Christina was growing very troubled.

Though Hammer's instincts had informed him of the threat much earlier, Truin was now catching up; something was very wrong.

"Unless he had to —" Truin answered under his breath, straining his neck to see his four-legged friend as they hurried after Hammer.

As they rounded the corner, things went from bad to horrific, and in the back of his mind, Truin instantly understood something his father, Abner, had taught him many years earlier. "Like a punch in the face, the events of life can change in an instant. Always be on your toes, because you don't know what lies beyond the next bend. Leave nothing unsaid."

Truin and Christina stood in shock, petrified by what they now saw in the clearing ahead. Only twenty yards ahead of them, Hammer stood in a low crouch as three lions circled him. The hair stood tall on the back of Hammer's neck, and almost all of his teeth were showing as he snarled ferociously at the beasts bent on doing him harm.

Truin drew his sword and Christina her bow; both thanking God that Hammer had so bravely alerted them to the threat; the lions had undoubtedly planned to ambush them moments later along the trail. As it stood, their circumstance was daunting enough, but had they wandered back to camp unaware of these beasts, their situation would have been much more precarious.

Though some would have run, running was not an option for Truin. First, running was not Truin's way; retreat was not in his vocabulary. Nor was it in Christina's, for that matter. Maybe at one time in their lives, they would have considered withdrawing, but no longer. They had seen too much of life, and too much of God's power. God was with them, and because he was the Creator, there was nothing in all the creation for them to fear. They met their challenges head on!

Even if withdrawing had been an option, it was not an option in this case; one of their own was in peril. Admittedly, Hammer was a dog, a pet. But anyone who has ever had a dog for a companion will tell you that a dog is more than just a pet; they are much more. A family dog is part of the family, and family does not leave family to die — not ever! Retreating and leaving Hammer to fight alone would leave deep regrets, a lifetime of second-guessing that would be worse than death. Truin and Christina both decided instantaneously that they would not retreat; they would stand and fight!

So long, having been as one, they knew without hesitation what the other would say and what the other would do. Though Truin would have preferred Christina to withdraw to a place of safety, he knew she would not have heard of it, so why should he spend the energy trying to convince her? Though Christina would have preferred they keep their distance and defend Hammer with the bow alone, she knew Truin would soon charge into the fray, so why spend the time trying to convince him? With but a brief glance, they instinctively compromised. Truin began the charge as Christina began the assault with her bow.

The lions noticed them an instant later. Simultaneously, the three lions stopped circling Hammer and ominously turned to face Truin, identifying him as the greatest threat and their high-priority target.

As Truin closed on the lions, they too began their charge toward him. As they did, Hammer, momentarily overlooked, lunged at one lion, sinking his teeth deep into its left hindquarters and bringing it painstakingly to the ground.

Still, Truin found himself in a dead sprint toward two giant carnivores that were likewise charging directly at him.

This cannot be a good thing!

As the thought crossed his consciousness, an arrow crossed his path, nearly grazing his ear as it accelerated from Christina's bow, past his position, to reach its final destination directly through the throat of one of the charging lions. As it continued its charge, blood sprayed out of the neck of the lion. A few seconds later, the lion lost power in its legs and tumbled.

Truin knew he had but seconds until he merged with the third lion, and he also knew he didn't have any experience with fighting lions. He had only heard a few nonspecific stories of the Adonian Guard's encounters with the lions in Kandish. Nothing he had heard would help him defeat the beast, but Truin hoped and prayed the lion would strike high, going for his head and neck.

Truin's plan was to dive for the ground while twisting his body to hit the ground on his back. As he slid below the charging lion, he would pull his sword vertical, hoping to slice the lion's underbelly in one fluid motion. If the lion went high, this might just work. If the lion stayed low, well, not so much.

Blindly exposing oneself during an attack and becoming vulnerable thereafter was not the conventional wisdom for a sword fight, but Truin knew he would only have one shot at this lion, and it had to be a great one if he wanted to survive. He was all in and fully committed.

As miraculous as Christina's archery shot had been, fatally felling the first feline, the outcome of Truin's drop-twist maneuver was perhaps even more amazing. As Truin and the lion closed at full speed to within ten feet of each other, the lion launched itself into the air with its front paws outstretched and deadly talons deployed for the kill. A split second later, Truin dove for the ground and, landing on his weak side, twisted his body, striking firmly into the air in a last-ditch maneuver to make the fatal cut.

The maneuver worked perfectly. As the lion passed over Truin at high speed, the tip of Truin's sword pierced the lion's belly, just below its chest. The lion's momentum continued to propel it forward as Truin's momentum continued to push his sword in the opposite direction. Truin's sword sliced the lion's belly wide open, exposing all its vital organs. It landed behind Truin, still on its feet, stunned, as its innards spilled out onto the ground. A moment later, dazed by a rapid loss of blood and stumbling over its own entrails, the lion collapsed lifeless to the earth. Truin watched in amazement as the lion fell.

His heart now racing and all his senses focused on the fight, Truin scanned his surroundings. Truin's first concern was Christina. As he looked back, he saw her still standing where he had left her moments before, her bow charged with an arrow, covering him. Their eyes met for but an instant, enough time to say, *I love you.*

Then Truin's eyes snapped to the place he had last observed Hammer take down the much larger lion. Truin fully expected Hammer to still have the upper hand. Instead, what he saw pierced him like an icy knife through the heart.

Hammer had indeed brought the first lion down, crippling it instantly by savagely tearing open its hind quarters and severing vital tendons and arteries. But the lion had quickly reacted to Hammer's attack, twisting awkwardly and lashing back at Hammer. However, it was no longer agile in its movements and failed to land a single hit because it could not adequately compensate for its injuries. Hammer had continued to circle the crippled lion, moving swiftly and fluidly to land several strikes on its back and neck. The lion's attempts to repel or defend against Hammer's attacks had proven futile, and the once nimble cat had grown weaker and slower in its attempts to fight Hammer off because of blood loss and fatigue. Finally, the opportunity had presented itself for Hammer to deal the lethal blow. Striking again from the lion's blind side, Hammer had pinned the lion's head to the ground and had torn out its throat.

This is how Truin now observed his loyal dog, standing triumphantly but exhausted over his kill. Truin had seen a variation of this picture many times before on the hunt, though the prey had been much different. Hammer, struggling to recover his depleted strength, instinctively looked towards Truin, ensuring there was no further harm threatening his master.

The feelings of nostalgia and pride flooded Truin's heart, but terror and fear soon overcame them. What Hammer could not observe was the threat that rapidly closed on him from behind. Time seemed to stand still as Truin watched yet another lion storm out from the cover of the bushes and attack Hammer from his blind side. His faithful companion was defenseless.

Christina, though equally surprised by yet another lion, had launched an arrow to intercept it. Unfortunately, because of the aspect angle of the intercept and the lack of time to get off a clean shot, her arrow narrowly missed the lion, passing just over its back.

Truin tried to call out to Hammer, but by the time his mouth formed the words, the lion hit Hammer like a bull at full charge.

Truin cried out in helplessness. "Hammer! No!"

Hammer never had a chance. Even if he had been at one-hundred percent, the much larger lion had caught Hammer unaware, ripping open Hammer's neck as it hit him and nearly severing his head from the rest of his body.

As Truin watched Hammer fall and the life ebb from his body, part of Truin died with him. Adequately describing the pain of losing a loyal friend — human or pet — to a sudden and brutal death is difficult. The love and friendship shared between Truin and Hammer was extensive, running deep indeed, and providing a testament to the reach and effect of the intangible emotions, loyalties, and memories that bind us all with those we love.

But this was no time to mourn. Truin felt the deepest sadness — a sadness that he would fully express later. The sadness instantly became a righteous anger, and the anger instantly became an absolute resolve that the lion must die!

Within seconds, Truin was again on the attack. Unlike the previous attack, the purpose of which was to help defend his friend, this attack was for honor. His friend was dead, and to the mortal souls that value nothing more than their own lives, and feel very little or nothing is worth putting their own lives at risk, this charge would make little sense. It would be downright ludicrous. But to Truin, it made perfect sense. This lion was a killer. It had killed his friend, and it posed an imminent threat to Christina. It was evil and had to be destroyed! Now!

Christina wished Truin would retreat to her side under the cover of her bow. She hoped it with all her heart.

Come back to me honey, come back!

But she knew Truin, and she knew the love he had for Hammer; she shared that love. She knew, right or wrong, Truin had made his decision.

As Truin closed on the lion, it released its grip on Hammer, and did the unthinkable. The lion, choosing between its two available targets of Truin and Christina, chose Christina.

"No!" Truin screamed as he realized the lion was accelerating away from him and directly toward his love.

"No! Run Christina, run!"

When Christina saw the lion bypass Truin and set its trajectory directly for her, a sudden rush of anxiety knocked on the door of her heart, but she refused to entertain it. Instead, she turned it over to the Lord.

"Father, help me, steady my hand, and make my aim true."

She reached over her shoulder to grasp another arrow and realized her quiver was empty. She had depleted her arsenal of arrows and was now without a human defense. The lion had already passed Truin and would soon be upon her. Again, anxiety knocked at the door.

What do I do now?

As the thought crossed her mind, she entertained her avenues of escape. As she did, her eyes discovered yet another lion emerging from behind her. She was now in the sights of two lions converging on her position from opposite directions.

Not good!

She ran as fast as she could across the clearing, the only hope she could see for escape. What she found at the other end of the clearing was instead a dead end, for the clearing ended in a steep cliff to jagged rocks far below.

She stopped herself just in time and teetered on the edge of the cliff. Christina knew she was in deep trouble. She was out of means to mount a defense against the beasts that approached; she was without an escape route, and Truin, as bravely as he was trying, would not reach her in time.

"No!" Truin screamed as he continued against all odds to get to his beloved.

"Please Lord, No!"

Tears filled Christina's eyes as she fought to hold on to hope in this most hopeless of situations. Confusion over what to do clouded Christina's mind, and the terror of the approaching lions fed her fears. Christina realized she was powerless to help herself; this was really nothing new.

Christina had learned long ago that she was helpless in the world to really alter her surroundings or better her situation in any significant way. Any misconceptions regarding her ability to change her fate drastically evaporated when the slave traders sold her into slavery so many years earlier. Since then, she had learned to rely on the Lord, the Creator of everything, for — everything. Though the Lord often gave her the tools to affect her surroundings, to praise her God, and to love those around her, she readily realized that he and he alone was the source of these gifts. In addition, many times in her life, as well as in the lives of Truin and their children, the Lord had directly intervened for their good. This was beyond any dispute!

Christina closed her eyes, fell to her knees, and bowed her head in prayer. This was not an act of weakness or despair. This was an act of humility and reverence, an appeal to a much higher power for intervention, and an acceptance of whatever the Lord willed the outcome to be.

Christina knew that this might be her last moment on the earth, and if it was to be, she wanted to give glory to her loving God one last time. She wanted to give witness to all that she was the Lord's, and that she knew everything, even her life — especially her life — was in his hands. Finally, she wanted Truin to know that she died in the faith, and would wait for him in their eternal home.

Truin could see now that he would never make it to Christina in time, and he instantly realized what a grave mistake it had been to leave her side. Truin could not live with the thought that the love of his life was about to be torn to pieces right in front of him by the lions.

What was I thinking? Father, forgive me. Please help her! You can help her! Please Lord, please! I'll do anything!

††††

The lions could almost taste the defenseless two-leg. A few more seconds and they would have.

From out of nowhere came a flash of light, a thunderous clap, and the time-space continuum unwrapping before them. Standing directly in front of the female two-leg was a glorious angel with six white, gold-tipped wings and a flaming red sword.

"No further!" The command blasted from the living being, uniting with the intense flash to overwhelm the lions' senses.

The lions, a moment before sprinting full speed toward Christina, experienced a violent force that threw them back, their momentum instantly halted by the angel's command. As the demons occupying and controlling their bodies writhed in torment, the lions screamed unnaturally.

"Release us! You cannot stop us! You cannot protect these. They are ours!"

"They do not belong to you, and you must not touch this one!" The angel responded in a voice so powerful that the sound sent shock waves rippling across invisible space. The angel outstretched his massive wings over Christina.

††††

From nowhere, the guardsman appeared, sword held high in hand. Christina jumped, startled when she saw him.

Where did he come from?

He looked familiar, but she couldn't place him. He didn't appear to be the guardsman that had accompanied them from the castle. Many years had passed since that day so long ago. Christina's memory, even her memory of that most important of events, had softened and faded over the years.

The guardsman turned his head to look at Christina. For a moment, their eyes met. His golden eyes pierced her soul as he spoke the words. "God is nigh. Trust him now."

Instantly her memory's cobwebs cleared, and Christina recognized the man with the blond hair, blonder at the tips.

"You, you're the, the —"

Christina's words tapered off as the man turned his watch toward the lions, which he had just tossed on their backs like rag-dolls.

Hope filled Christina's heart.

All will be well now. The Lord has sent us his protection.

Then, her protector spoke again and declared, "God is close. Trust him now. Be strong and courageous. We must endure this moment that God has ordained since long ago."

✝✝✝

Truin was in shock! He had asked the Lord to intervene and do the impossible, and it had happened. Something had knocked the lions backwards, and Christina was safe! There was no explaining such an event, other than the Lord had directly interceded.

But Christina was still in grave peril. Alone, she stood between the two lions. These monsters, though momentarily stunned, would soon recover and continue their attack.

Still at full sprint toward the two lions and almost certain death, no further thought was required about how his actions might affect his survival. This wasn't about thought. It was about love. Long ago, Truin had given his life to the service of God and family. If it was God's will that he give it all this day, then his life would be but a small sacrifice to pay.

As expected, the lions, having only been momentarily stunned, recovered and renewed their attack. Truin wasn't bitter that they had recovered so rapidly. Rather, he was thankful for God's intercession and the additional time he had to close on the beasts. Truin wished he was still as fast a runner as he had been when he was a young man. There was a time when he would have already closed the distance between him and Christina and been all over those lions, but the event in the forest so long ago had taken away much of his speed. With every step he took, Truin had to compensate for the effect his disability had on his running gait.

If I can just make it to Christina before they get there.

Though Truin was thinking about just getting to the fight in time, a small part of his mind started entertaining ideas about what he would do once he got there.

One man against two lions —

As soon as he realized the dilemma, he forced it from his conscious thought. There was really no viable solution.

The Lord is in control.

Truin's closing proximity to the first lion drew its attention. Without warning, it dug its claws into the dirt of the grassland, screeched to a halt, and spun around into a defensive crouch facing Truin.

Truin continued at full speed toward the beast. Even though every muscle in his body screamed in agony, Truin knew that this was most likely his last stand, and he did not want to be found lacking in courage or effort. He had to give it everything he had, everything that his body had left to give. He was aware of the pain, but the pain did not, would not, control him. Pain was fleeting, and he knew the pain would not last for long.

†††

Christina looked on in terror as the lion swung around to confront Truin.

"No, run Truin, run!" She screamed!

Can he not see my protector? Can he not see that I am safe? Why does he keep coming?

Christina, still on her knees, looked up to the guardsman that stood before her and begged him. "Help him! Please help my husband?"

The guardsman spoke. "Be strong. Have faith. Endure. It will be as it must be."

As he softly but firmly spoke the words, Christina saw tears fill the guardsman's eyes, as if he knew something she did not. She turned again to look upon her husband and what must be. Tears flowed freely from her eyes.

The guardsman, however, turned his attention to the forest.

✝✝✝

Daytona had never returned to the others after the slaughter of the bison. Instead, he had set out on his own. The others were no longer the same, no longer the lions he once knew.

As the big, gold and white cat moved stealthily through the forest, he caught wind of a familiar scent. Instantly, driven by instinct or some unseen force, he accelerated to a full charge through the trees. He exploded out of the foliage into the clearing and saw his target. He dashed at full speed to intercept it.

✝✝✝

This was it, the moment of truth. Truin stormed into the lion at full speed, with no strategy or plan of attack. He had directed all his efforts towards reaching Christina in time to make a difference. Now he had reached his objective, but he hadn't planned beyond this point.

Help me, Father, one last time?

Everything seemed to transpire in slow motion.

The lion had stopped about ten yards from Christina. Truin was close enough to Christina now to see her face, her beautiful face. He could hear her now, screaming for him to turn back, still caring more for his safety than her own.

Father, please protect her?

The lion was still in its low crouch as Truin flung himself into the air, directly at the beast. All Truin could think about was getting between the lion and Christina.

Truin's bold advance caught the lion off-guard, and the enormous cat crouched even lower to escape the two-leg's attack. As Truin flew over the top of the lion, he swung his sword, hoping to make contact as he passed. His hope was not in vain. As Truin passed over the lion, his sword found its mark slashing through the great cat's jaw and cutting it in half. Truin tumbled over the top of the lion and landed between it and Christina. Rolling as he hit, he came to rest on his feet, sword still in hand.

The injured beast went wild. The shock of Truin's sword taking off half its face sent the cat into a rage. It ran in circles, clawing at its face and rolling around in the dirt. Truin watched in amazement, trying to find the right time to land the final blow and put the wretched creature out of its misery.

Before long, the opportunity presented itself. The lion clawed at its own face, trying ignorantly to remove whatever was bringing it so much pain. As it did so, its face covered in dirt and blood, it surrendered many of its defenses. Truin pounced on the opportunity. Truin jumped onto the great cat's back. He lifted his sword and spiked the lion's neck to the ground, running his sword through the top of the cat's neck, down through its throat, and pinning it to the earth. Even then, the evil beast did not give up. Its jaw split open, its neck impaled and skewered to the earth; it still had the strength to catapult Truin off its back, while attempting to yank itself free. In vain, it struggled to do so, writhing in agony until the loss of blood and energy proved its time had ended.

Truin looked away from the beast just in time to see the unthinkable.

While Truin had been courageously battling the one lion, the other had recovered its footing and resumed its charge toward Christina. Christina, still on her knees and pinned against the side of the gorge, remained oblivious to the impending danger approaching her from the rear.

As the feline messenger of death reached terminal velocity, now but a moment away from hitting Christina, it launched itself into the air. It was at that instant that another miracle happened. From nowhere, another lion, gold and white, emerged from the forest, streaked across the clearing, and hit the airborne lion in mid-flight. Christina and Truin could readily hear the force of the impact as the golden lion caught the unsuspecting attacker completely unaware, fracturing half of its exposed ribcage on impact and redirecting its momentum away from Christina. The combined momentum of the lions sent them hurtling into the gorge. The golden lion continued its punishing attack on the second as entwined they ended their fatal dance in the rocky stream below.

Christina turned just in time to see the massive beasts catapult by her and out of view in an indiscernible blur of motion. A moment later, it was as if they had never existed.

✝✝✝

Smilodon leaped from the bushes at the edge of the clearing. The others had done their job of distracting the two-legs magnificently. Now it was his time, time to accomplish their true mission; time to end it.

He dashed across the clearing at full-speed. His prey, the one they had hunted for weeks, stood before him, exhausted, distracted, and completely unaware of his impending fate.

Smilodon could feel the piercing gaze of the mighty protector upon him as its blazing eyes tracked his movement toward the target. Why the protector did not intervene, Smilodon did not know, nor did he care.

Smilodon hit the two-leg from behind with enough force to crush its vertebrae. As he did, he sunk his long, sharp fangs into the two-leg's back, just below the neck. There was nothing the man-flesh could do but crash to the ground beneath the monstrous assault.

†††

Truin never thought he'd see one lion save Christina from another lion. He stood amazed, exhausted, and gasping for breath over the corpse of one dead lion as he watched two others disappear over the cliff behind Christina.

What manner of doing is this?

"Your will be done, Oh Lord."

Euphoria filled his heart as he realized both he and Christina had made it through the unimaginable ordeal.

Truin turned his focus to his beloved, and his eyes met hers.

I love you. Oh, how I love you. Thank God you are alright.

But something was wrong. As Truin looked to Christina across the clearing, he realized her face was not one of relief, but one of terror. She was screaming something at him.

Then the words reached his ears. "Truin, look out! Look out! No!" But her words arrived too late.

Before Truin could turn to see what Christina was so concerned about, he felt the impact. It was pain like he had not felt since his mishap as a young boy, the mishap that had maimed him for life. Intuitively, in that instant, Truin knew this would be worse, much worse.

Truin was well aware of the pain; intense pain shot through his body, overwhelming his nervous system as he hit face first in the dirt. An enormous weight then came crashing down upon him from behind. Truin was well aware of the pain, but somehow, he was separate from the pain. Though still in his body, he was also, somehow, not in it. The pain was fading.

†††

Everything was happening so fast.

Christina had just noticed the beasts hurl themselves over the ridge behind her. She turned back to Truin, and terror once again reached for her heart. By the time Christina saw the lion, it had closed to within lethal range. All she could do was scream.

Then the beast hit Truin, and he fell to the earth. His gaze remained locked on her, and she could see the love he had for her still blazing in his eyes. Truin hit the earth hard. The lion landed on his back, tearing ravenously into his flesh as if it was the culmination of its life's mission. At that moment, Jonn and three guardsmen, arriving in time to see the lion's attack but not in time to impede it, launched a melee of arrows into the lion, dropping it almost immediately. However, the damage had already been done.

Christina and Jonn rushed to Truin's side. Jonn and the guardsman pulled the lion off of Truin's broken and torn body. They carefully turned him over. Christina cradled him in her arms and rained tears of love down upon his face. "My love, my love, what have they done to you?"

Christina held Truin close to her and caressed his face. Truin's eyes opened. He saw his wife, the love of his life with him; holding him close, as she always had.

"Do not cry for me, honey."

Truin's voice was weak, and she could barely hear him. Her tears flowed all the more as she realized it was almost time for him to go.

"I will miss you and the boys. Tell them for me. Tell them their father loves them very much."

"I will, my love, I will," Christina tenderly whispered in his ear.

"Ka'el. You must tell Ka'el that I love him, and that I never held him responsible."

"I will," Christina repeated, barely able to speak through the tears.

"Tell him he must let go of the guilt. Tell him he now holds the light and must hold it high for all to see."

Jonn and Christina looked at each other, not sure what Truin meant by these words.

Jonn, realizing that the time must be very close, kneeled over Truin and softly touched Christina's shoulder, knowing the incredible grief that would soon descend upon her.

"I will."

"I must go now, honey. God is calling me."

Christina could barely hold back the flood of tears, but she did so, for Truin's sake.

"I love you, husband, and I always will."

"And I you."

Jonn quietly comforted Truin and Christina with the words of the twenty-third psalm. "The LORD is my shepherd, I shall not be in want. He makes me to lie down in green pastures, he leads me beside quiet waters, he restores my soul. He guides me in paths of righteousness for his name's sake. Even though I walk through the valley of the shadow of death, I will fear no evil, for you are with me; your rod and your staff, they comfort me. You prepare a table before me in the presence of my enemies. You anoint my head with oil; my cup overflows. Surely goodness and love will follow me all the days of my life, and I will dwell in the house of the LORD forever."

When he finished, a moment of silence passed as Christina held her love close for one last time, their hearts beating together in one last dance. As Truin's heart rate slowed, and the light faded from his eyes, he smiled and whispered. "Father, I'm home. Into your hands I commend my spirit."

Christina kissed Truin on his cheek as the life faded from his eyes, leaving only an empty shell where love had burned so brightly just a moment before.

Christina laid her cheek against Truin's; her long hair fell freely over his lifeless face. Unable to hold back the flood of tears any longer, she gave in to the unbearable realization that Truin had left the broken and battered body she held in her arms, and that he would never again return to her.

The dam broke, and an endless river of tears began their long journey from Christina's heart to that place where loving memories live on forever.

The guardsmen fell to their knees in disbelief that their leader had fallen. Jonn wrapped his arms around Christina and cried with her. Together they rocked back and forth with Truin in their arms, mourning the best friend either of them ever had.

†††

Time stopped for Truin. The temporal unraveled, faded, and something much bigger and much more beautiful appeared.

The last thing Truin saw was the face of his wife, his beautiful wife. Bright white light then washed over Truin's vision, drowning everything in unimaginable joy as Truin's understanding and concern for things taking place in the physical dimension faded, and the door to eternity opened.

Truin was aware of time. He was aware of Christina holding him and Jonn bending over him. His ears briefly heard Christina's cries, his skin the feel of her soft tears flowing over the cheeks he had left behind. But the sounds and the sensations grew fainter and fainter until they were gone.

Truin moved as if in a dream, in light and indescribable color, to a place of unseen and inconceivable beauty; the magnificence and splendor of what he saw, not with his physical eyes, but with his spiritual eyes, consumed his awareness.

He was moving to another place. His spirit was no longer troubled. The cares of the world dissolved until they dispersed like mountain fog before the morning sun. Any remaining sadness departed and gave way to feelings of overwhelming safety, warmth, peace, love, and joy.

A lifetime of faith gave way to the certain realization of hope — fulfilled.

It's all true. It is all true! The light! The beauty! My God!

Truin's new vision advanced to that of crystal clarity, and he entered the unimaginable light and fell into the arms of his first and truest love.

"Welcome home, Truin. Well done, my good and faithful servant!"

†††

The demons cheered in demented ecstasy as Truin drew his last breath. For so long, they had conspired and labored to this end. Now the day had finally come.

"We have nearly won the battle!" Lucifer proclaimed to his army.

"The defenses of Adonia are sure to collapse in the wake of Truin's demise. With no one left to lead them, their faith will shatter; their confidence and resolve will crumble before the overpowering forces we shall bring against them!"

The mighty throng of demons, assembled in the spiritual dungeon, roared in delight at his words; the sores and boils on their grisly and deformed bodies painted a clearly incongruent picture to the victorious finale their leader's words prophesied.

"Soon we will win the victory, and darkness will reign over all the kingdoms of man forevermore!"

CHAPTER 56

İΠCEΠSE

†††

The cool, soft breeze blew into the room through the open window where Evelin was peacefully dreaming. Abner lie next to her, also lost in the sweet rest of the night.

Evelin was dreaming of flying high through the cool night sky, looking down over the moon-shadowed forests and gently rolling hills below. It was hard to see anything clearly, for the hills, lakes, and trees were all sheltered by a low fog that was holding the terrain tightly in its grasp. Wispy clouds rushed by her as she soared through the darkness, urgently searching for someone in the soft light of the bright, full moon. She felt exhilarated by the flight but also anxious; she could not find the person she so eagerly sought.

Far in the distance, a fire was blazing on the ground below. Within no time she was there, hovering over the trees, watching.

Several shadows gathered around the fire. There was silent weeping as the powerful flames rose high into the sky, burning off the fog that had hung above moments before. The red and gold hues of the flames reflected off the trees that surrounded the gathering as the fire chaotically danced before them.

Suddenly, from the darkness of the night sky, seven golden stars fell from the heavens like meteors crashing to the earth. They approached the gathering at lightning speed, emanating a brilliant white light that would blind anyone beholding them — if it were not a dream.

Just before impacting the ground at the position of the gathering, they stopped abruptly, hovering over the flames. At that moment, they were no longer shapeless lights, but beautiful winged men of various colors and hue. Their brilliance combined to shower the entire area of the forest in intense light.

Evelin could now see the faces of those gathered around the fire; Jonn, Christina, and several of the castle guard. Christina was crying; Evelin could tell by the glint of the light reflecting off of the tears flowing down her face. Jonn's eyes, too, were sparkling in the firelight's radiance.

Evelin's heart sank. Grief and dread settled over her hovering spirit, like a thick blanket intent on suffocating her. Now aware of Christina's presence, Evelin searched for Truin, for they belonged together; they were one.

Where is Truin? What has happened to my Truin?

Her focus turned to the flames and to that which burned within. Her restless thoughts took flight within her mind, her eyes darting back and forth like specters in search of prey. Suddenly, a figure burst forth from the flames, exploding into the night sky as if abruptly unchained from prison and forever set free to soar unshackled through the heavens.

As the figure rose out of the flames, it hovered high above the gathering — high above Evelin. Evelin struggled to see the figure clearly, at first with little success. But as the figure hovered, it glowed — brighter and brighter. Soon its brilliance surpassed that of the seven winged men, and she could see him plainly. It was Truin. It was her son, Truin!

Her spirit leaped, instantly disintegrating the shell of dread and fear that had been crushing her from all sides, and immense love and joy surged through her being. She could see that Truin was once again whole, no longer restrained by the injuries he had sustained so long ago. He wasn't just whole; he had regained his strength and vitality, completely free from his injuries. Her son Truin, yes, but now so much more than the Truin she had known.

Then, as swiftly as he had emerged from the fire, he shot upward into the heavens, escorted by the winged men that had descended from there just moments before.

For an instant, Evelin thought she too would follow them, and though she tried soaring heavenward in pursuit, she soon realized she could not. It was not yet her time to go there.

As her son streaked across the sky, joining the millions of stars blinking in the heavens, she was aware of him speaking to her. "Where I go, you cannot follow, not tonight, Mother. But one day soon we will be together again — one day, soon."

Though she no longer saw him with her eyes, in her mind's eye, she watched him enter a city of perfect light and streets paved with gold. As he entered the city, he turned back to look at her, and he smiled. Then, continuing on, he faded into the intense light of perfection. Evelin heard a thunderous and yet still, quiet voice welcome Truin. "Well done, my good and faithful servant. Well done."

Evelin awoke. Her eyes opened to the twinkling of stars visible through the window in their castle room. They were so beautiful. It took a moment for Evelin to realize that she was no longer dreaming.

What a strange and beautiful dream. It felt so real.

Her dream faded, and physical reality again took control of Evelin's senses. She wondered what the dream could mean. Still focused on the millions of distant, blinking lights in the night sky, her mind gradually loosened its hold on her thoughts, and cuddling close to Abner, she drifted back to sleep.

†††

It was a bright day when Jonn slowly made his way up the path to Abner and Evelin's cottage. He dreaded having to be the messenger of such news. There was no worse news that any human being could bring to another than to inform them of the death of a son or daughter.

Evelin was working in her garden, tending to her vegetables and flowers, when she saw Jonn approach. Her first reaction was joy, but her spirit turned to sorrow and anguish as she read the deep sadness in his eyes.

As he spoke the words a mother should never have to hear, Evelin fell to her knees, feeling her heart being torn from her body. She instantly brought her hands to her face, trying in vain to hold back a flood of tears — a flood of tears that no mother could ever have held back. Jonn caught Evelin as she sank to her knees, holding her in his arms and wishing with all his heart that there was something he could do to ease her pain.

A few seconds later, Abner rushed out of the cottage and helped Evelin inside. The flowers would have to wait for another day to be tended.

Elin and Robinelle came to help comfort Evelin as soon as they heard what had happened, but Evelin was inconsolable for nearly two days.

Abner's heart was breaking as much as his wife's, but Evelin needed him to be strong, so he bottled up his grief, hiding it away in a room deep within his heart — a room whose door had been closed and locked for many years.

Once Evelin could sleep, Abner retreated to the small room of the cottage and the gloomy shadows cast by a solitary lantern to be alone with his thoughts. He sat in a cold, hard chair in the corner of the room and closed his eyes. That is when the weight of events hit him like a bolt of lightning.

My son is dead.

Grief that words simply cannot describe settled on Abner like a dense fog, suffocating him. He walked down that long hallway in his mind that led to the room — that room he had avoided for so long. Though he fought taking every step, the pull of the dark, cold room at the end of the hall drew him forward like the tow of a powerful river current, and moments later Abner opened the door and stepped inside. It slammed the door behind him, sealing him within.

Why God, why have you done this?

Abner felt lost in the pitch black room. It was a room void of all warmth, the scary room. But even without light, Abner knew he was not alone. He remembered the sinister shadow that made the room its home, and Abner searched frantically for it in the darkness. Cold currents of air circulated around Abner, sending chills through his bones.

"Why God, why have you done this?" Abner shouted into the darkness. "It is not right! It is not fair!" Abner's anger grew, competing with his grief and sorrow for the domination of his spirit.

Abner could feel the presence of the shadow growing closer. It now stood directly behind him. Its long, sharp fingers danced upon his shoulders, tightening their grip.

"He loved you, and you let him die!"

The fingers of the shadowy specter multiplied, becoming like the many tentacles of a giant sea squid. It strengthened its grasp around Abner's neck, torso, and legs.

"You abandoned him! You abandoned my son!"

The tentacles multiplied tenfold, slithering around Abner, covering his body, constricting. Their ugly black slime oozed over Abner, filling his pores and enslaving his essence. Only Abner's eyes and mouth remained unshackled.

The darkness grew thicker. Abner strained for any source of light within the pit of sorrow and death. The immense weight crushed his chest as he gasped for air, struggling for breath beneath the ever-increasing burden of his pain and grief.

Long, sharp needles emerged from the tentacles that bound him, piercing his flesh as they extended into his body.

With his last breath, Abner shouted into the void! "First you abandoned Ka'el and took him from us. Now you have taken Truin! Why Lord? Why do you abandon those who love you?"

The tentacles squeezed even tighter, seeking to crush the last remnant of lifeblood out of Abner. They covered his mouth, locking his words within so he could no longer speak. Caught within the cascade of rage and despair, Abner's hope dwindled like a tired flame in an icy winter wind. Nothing remained within Abner that could ever hope to free him. He was a prisoner of death.

Crushed, suffocating, dying, Abner searched the darkness for light, for hope, for the God he once knew and loved. At that moment, the smallest pinhole of light appeared in the top corner of the heavy door of the stronghold that held Abner captive, announcing a significant source of power just outside his prison cell. From the tiny source of light, a thin beam penetrated the darkness within and streamed across the room, hitting Abner squarely between the eyes.

Abner locked on to the light as his mind begged for deliverance from the menace that held him. His senses, now overwhelmed with pain and agony, thirsted desperately for help, for life.

From beyond the door, Abner heard the soft whisper that seemed to ride its way in upon the beam of light. "Abner."

Abner fought for breath. He pushed against his chains with all his remaining strength, but he could not answer the voice.

"Abner."

His mind reached for the door, reached for the heavy bolt that held the door shut, but he could do nothing. He could not move. The weight of the shadowy beast became too much for him. He had given it too much power, and now he was helpless to escape from it.

"Abner."

Abner could not speak, but his mind screamed out from within its prison.

I am here, Lord. Don't leave me! Help me, please, help me?

The whisper entered the dark cell and quietly filled the room, echoing softly through the darkness from all directions at once, like that of many voices. "My mind is not your mind, and my ways are not your ways."

Abner froze, giving up the struggle to reach the heavy bolt, to free himself. He realized he could do nothing. He let the words of the Lord's presence sink deep into his heart.

Then the reverberating voices united into one powerful voice emanating from the pinhole of light. "And I will never abandon those who love me!"

Like the sound of a thousand rushing rivers drawing closer and closer until finally they slammed against the walls of the room, the voice thundered in response to Abner.

Who is this that darkens my counsel with words without knowledge? Brace yourself like a man; I will question you and you will answer me. Where were you when I laid the earth's foundation? Tell me if you understand. Who marked off its dimensions? Surely you know! Who stretched a measuring line across it? On what were its footings set, or who laid its cornerstone — while the morning stars sang together and the angels shouted for joy?

Bound by dark despair, mired in sinful pride, and blinded to God's perfect purpose and justice, Abner's spirit shook.

The rivers pounded against the walls of the dungeon again as several beams of light penetrated the walls of the room.

Brace yourself like a man. I will question you and you shall answer me. Would you discredit my justice? Would you condemn me to justify yourself? Do you have an arm like God's, and can your voice thunder like his?

Still caught in the clutches of evil and nearly succumbing to death, Abner realized his sin. His life and the lives of his family were not their own, but existed to serve God and facilitate his plan. His life, Truin's life, and Ka'el's life; they all belonged to the Lord.

Abner had forgotten, but now he remembered. His life was not about his sinful desires. It was about serving the Holy Lord and about His-story. How arrogant he had been to think anything else. To question the justice of the almighty judge, to question the wisdom of the omniscient Creator of the universe, and to demand answers of God Almighty himself — how sinful his pride became. How foolish he had been! Surely he must die!

Abner's spirit trembled in awe and fear. "I know you can do all things; your plan is unstoppable. You asked, who is this that obscures your counsel without knowledge? Surely I spoke of things I did not understand, things too wonderful for me to know. Therefore, I despise myself and repent in dust and ashes."

Abner remembered the Lord, his first love, and the hope he had for his salvation. He replied, again, with the words of Job and the deepest longings of his heart. "Oh, that my words were recorded, that they were written on a scroll, that they were inscribed with an iron tool on lead, or engraved in rock forever! I know that my Redeemer lives, and that in the end he will stand upon the earth. And after my skin has been destroyed, yet in my flesh I will see God; I myself will see him with my own eyes — I, and not another. How my heart yearns within me!"

"Lord, forgive me? Save me? Have mercy on your servant, Abner? I am nothing without you!"

Instantly, thousands of slivers of light pierced through the walls of the cell and penetrated the darkness. The walls of the room melted away as the doors of the dungeon exploded outwards.

The tentacles that bound Abner recoiled immediately, withdrawing into the shadow that still stood behind Abner. Then, the ghoulish figure, like the dispelled darkness that had hastily retreated, had no choice but to flee from the presence of the light. It shrieked in terror as the light sent it away into oblivion, leaving Abner immersed in overwhelming light.

Abner opened his eyes. The room he had withdrawn to earlier was now filled with the light of a dozen lanterns, and several blankets covered him. Evelin kneeled beside him, caressing his temple with her hand.

His eyes met hers, and he could see the ready evidence on her face of the grief she had endured since learning of Truin's death, but instead of the sorrow that had so overwhelmingly become an unwanted tenant there, her face beamed with joy and comfort.

"Wake up, my husband. Let me tell you about a dream I had a few nights ago," she whispered to him. "In my grief, I had forgotten about it until now."

Evelin joined Abner in the large chair, held him close, and told him about her dream — the dream where the angels had taken Truin to be with God. Her face shone with a light of peace as her words soothed Abner's spirit.

"God is faithful. God has taken Truin home. There is no greater blessing than to be taken to be with God. There is no greater love that the Master can show."

Abner kissed Evelin on the forehead and wrapped his arms around her. "God is faithful indeed."

Abner's fever and chills soon subsided as they drifted off to sleep. They rested in the chair together through the rest of the night, basking in the warm glow of the lanterns and in the mutual love and companionship that God had given them to help soothe this life's many sorrows.

As the rising sun gave the dark blue sky the first sign of its imminent arrival, they awoke. Evelin looked directly into Abner's eyes and spoke with a sense of urgency. "We must pray for Ka'el."

Together they laid the blankets on the floor by the window that faced the western sunrise, and as the sun peaked over the horizon, Abner and Evelin humbled themselves before the Lord their God, the Creator and preserver of all things. Kneeling before The Almighty, they thanked God for calling Truin safely home to heaven, and asked for God's mercy on their son, Ka'el; they knew another storm was coming.

"Please almighty and merciful God, be with Ka'el. Show him the way, strengthen his faith, and help him be victorious in the battle that is coming. You, Oh Lord, are faithful."

CHAPTER 57

MERCY

✝✝✝

Tala sat alone in her cottage, contemplating the news she had heard earlier in the day at the market. Ka'el was conveniently out hunting again, and this meant there was no distraction from the feelings of guilt that had constantly bombarded her ever since Kala Azar's visit.

Tala felt overwhelmed with remorse. Until now, she had rationalized away her feelings of guilt over Truin's lost tunic; she had resolved that the tunic had not been important to Kala's plan. However, with the news of Truin's death and the lions hunting him down and assassinating him, that belief had shattered for Tala. Tala now recognized that she had played a key role in the chain of events that had brought about Truin's death and had brought unimaginable grief to her husband's family. Ka'el would never forgive her; none of them would.

At that moment, when Tala forever lost the love of Ka'el, she truly understood how much she loved him. Tala's eyes opened to all that they had shared over the years: falling in love, the birth of their sons, and their lives together.

Sure, there had been rough times, but those had been primarily the result of her pursuit of the dark arts and the trouble it had caused both their relationship and her relations with Ka'el's family. Ka'el had added to the chasm by being unable to forgive Tala for her earlier deceptions, and he still blamed her for his broken relationship with Truin.

Still, their lives hadn't been all bad. They had shared many happy memories together with their sons, Toro and Weiphal; before they had left home to make their own way; Tala had focused her memories on those happier times. But now, her involvement in Truin's death would forever shroud even those happy memories. Even her sons would not forgive her for her part in the death of their Uncle Truin.

Tala was confused. Tala's exposure and fascination to the dark arts and the power they held began when her brother, Pete, now the dark lord Karyan, discovered them. Short of any other instruction or influence, she hadn't known she was doing anything wrong. But over the years, Ka'el's witness to his beliefs in the one true God had been most influential on Tala. She had caught herself praying to Ka'el's God more and more often.

Tala found it difficult to stop using the dark words she had grown so accustomed to relying on all of her life. In addition, she feared doing so would forever separate her from her only surviving blood relative, her brother, Karyan. Yet, whenever she used the words, she felt like she was doing something wrong; she felt guilty.

And then there was the part she had played in Truin's death.

How could Karyan have known all those years ago that I would play such an important role in a future war — that my seduction of Ka'el would lead to the death of Truin?

Whether Karyan could have had the foreknowledge to know this would come to be or not, Tala knew she was responsible for the death of Truin. She had killed her brother-in-law, her children's uncle. The realization was unbearable!

Tala gathered up all her books of the secret arts, all the so-called knowledge of power she had collected over the years.

This cannot be the way. The ugliness that has come from all of this — the pain and the suffering — this cannot be the way!

Tala bundled it all up and hauled it out to the edge of the forest. There she built a fire.

What a waste — a waste of time — a waste of life!

As she tossed the books into the fire, Tala denounced the dark arts, the demons, and anyone having anything to do with their dark ways. She denounced Karyan.

He is not Pete. My Pete is gone. How could I have been so blind?

It was then that Tala remembered the words Ka'el had spoken of his God. So many times, Ka'el had tried to tell her of the God of love — the God of forgiveness. So many times she had let his words pass by her, through her, without latching on to them.

But unaware to Tala, some of Ka'el's words — some of his witness to the God he knew and loved — like seeds of love, had taken root. Without warning, these seeds sprouted and became fruit; they became faith.

As the smoke and flames of the bonfire rose tellingly into the clear, cool evening air, incinerating the wicked remnants of a past life and announcing the beginning of a new life, Tala proclaimed her freedom.

"I denounce my old ways, the evil ways, and turn to the new and only way! I throw myself at the mercy of the one, true God, the God of Abner, the God of Truin, and the God of Ka'el, my husband! Hear me, Oh true God, the great I Am, I believe in you and all Ka'el has taught me about you. Forgive me Almighty God, as only you can, for my many abhorrent sins against you and your servants? I throw myself at the foot of your throne. I ask for your forgiveness and trust in your mercy and promises. Use me as you wish. Direct my paths to serve only you. My life is yours."

Tears rolled down Tala's cheeks as she shed a lifetime of guilt and fear. No longer would she lie awake at night, tormented by her many demons. She was free of them, finally free!

The sun set and a new moon rose overhead. Tala sat in the empty field at peace and in awe of her merciful God, contemplating the amazing change that had just transpired.

What a tremendous feeling this is to be free of the guilt, free of the shame; I am free to serve God, not out of fear, but in thankfulness for who he is and what he has done.

For Tala, everything had changed. It was a new beginning. She was truly alive. She trusted in the promises of the ancient books that Ka'el had read to her over the years, and she knew she would live forever.

Joy filled Tala's heart. As the red-hot cinders had completely consumed the books of evil, so Almighty God had purged her of her sins and completely forgiven her. For the first time in her life, Tala felt clean.

The moon rose high in the sky, and a cool chill filled the air. Tala realized she had lost track of time. The fire had faded and the chilly night air reminded her she should not be alone in the fields after dark; there were too many wild animals about.

Tala stood and made her way back to the cottage. She couldn't wait for Ka'el to return home.

This will change everything!

But Tala was not alone. Several visitors had been watching her from the edge of the forest all evening long. Sent by Kala Azar — to tie up the loose ends — they had been waiting for darkness to fall before doing their evil deed, and Tala had made their job much easier by unknowingly coming out to meet them at the edge of the forest.

As Tala turned to walk back to her cottage, they made their move. She saw the trained assassins emerging from the forest trees, and she tried in vain to outrun them. She wasn't quite halfway back to the cottage before they caught her.

Tala did all she could to fight off her assailants. Had she used the dark words, she might have been successful, but she had rejected that life and all that went with it. No one would persuade her to return to the prison she had just escaped. They bound her and dragged her into the forest. She knew it would not end well.

Tala clung to her faith. She knew God had forgiven her for all she had done. But she also knew that her actions had consequences, and as much as God loved her, she now had to face the temporal consequences of her sins. Her conviction that God had a place waiting for her in the next life comforted her and gave her the ability to endure what was about to happen.

As her captives raised her above the fire in sacrifice to their god of hate and destruction, as the fire-beast had commanded them, Tala wished they had not gagged her. She so wanted to tell them about the true God and the freedom he had given her from the dark ways. She prayed for God to forgive them and show them the true way as he had shown her.

Tala thought not of the flames that burned her skin, but rather of the ones she so dearly loved. She prayed fervently to God that he bless Ka'el, Toro, and Weiphal. She prayed she'd see them again in their eternal home.

Tala considered it but a small sacrifice to give her life to the flame, if that was God's will. *This sacrifice is nothing compared to the joys that await me in heaven with you, Father.*

Her only regret was that she could not ask Ka'el for his forgiveness and to thank him for all he had done to show her the way to true life.

The smoke of the fire rose to the heavens like a sweet incense, along with the prayers of God's servant, Tala — a willing sacrifice from another whose name God wrote in the book of life.

†††

Ka'el returned home from the hunt the next day with enough food to last them through the winter, but he found Tala gone, along with all her books of the dark ways. It was unlike her to go without leaving a message saying where she was going and when she might return.

Though he searched for any sign of where she might have gone, all he would ever find was the smoking remnant of a bonfire by the edge of the forest. He would never hear from Tala again.

CHAPTER 58

Who Shall Stand?

†††

I t was the most stunning of mornings. As the sun carefully peaked over the trees to the west of Blue Lake, the morning fog noticed its approach, and not wanting to be caught, swiftly went into hiding. A gentle stream pleasantly flowed down one of the mountain valleys and emptied its life-giving waters into the lake, while a family of songbirds emerged from the trees nearby, sharing their morning lullaby with all who would listen.

Christina and Truin sat together on the shore of the lake, taking in all the surrounding beauty. They firmly believed that this place, at this time, was the most peaceful location on all God's earth. They had made a habit over the years to begin the day together, right here in this place. It was truly a window to heaven.

The couple watched the ducks fly in formation low over the water and the golden rays of sunshine slice through the retreating fog. Truin brushed back Christina's long, flowing hair and kissed her softly on the lips.

Time stood still and all life's fears and anxieties faded away. Peace, love, and joy — these were the rulers in this place.

I love you, honey, and I always will.

"I will always love you too," Christina replied, as she opened her eyes.

Something was wrong. Christina's heart sank as she realized she sat alone, alone in their special place on Blue Lake. She searched for Truin, but her husband was not there.

Those days had passed.

It had only been four days since they had taken Truin from her. The loneliness of an empty bed, the silence of a vacant cottage, and the pain of a broken heart had drawn Christina to the lake. There, in their special place, Christina had hoped to ease the pain; she hoped to connect just a little with her lost love.

Christina looked out over the lake and the mountains. It was so beautiful!

I know we will be together again, my love, in a place even more beautiful than this.

The moment was bittersweet. Christina thanked God for the time she had shared with Truin; the good times, the hard times, and the special memories they had shared here on Blue Lake would last forever. But, the memories, especially the special memories, hurt. Christina's heart hurt so much that she thought it could burst right out of her chest at any moment. The loneliness, the separation; it was nearly unbearable!

Christina knew that time would ease the pain and soften the sting of her separation from Truin. She had consoled many widows over the years — widows who had lost their husbands to combat or disease. She remembered the pain these women had endured, and she knew from their experiences that the pain was manageable — but also that it would be a long process of adaptation, a terribly slow process.

Christina would have given anything to share just one more hour with Truin, here on the lake. They had been so happy together; so very happy.

Christina closed her eyes again. Listening to the songs of the love-birds, the wind in the trees, and the crackle of the brook as it emptied into the peaceful lake, Christina could almost feel Truin by her side.

"I love you Truin."

"I love you too, Christina, and I always will."

†††

Deep within the pit of hell, the demons celebrated the death of Truin. The tremendous grief of the countless number of Adonians who mourned Truin's death was a bonus, feeding their perverted pleasure.

Putrid fluids and boiling flesh covered the floor and walls of the underground cavern. Noxious fumes and sulfuric gases bubbled out of pools of melting tissue that flowed sluggishly about the jagged rocks on which the winged demons rousted.

A demon known as Haught screamed in delight. "Master, the victory is ours! Without a leader, the Adonians will fall!"

At his words, the lesser demons around him nodded in agreement, doing all they could to win their master's favor. His favor translated to a better position in the feast of souls that followed every spiritual battle. The higher level demons decided who would dine first and those who would not dine at all.

"Indeed, it soon will be so," Satan hissed, arrogance oozing out of every word he spoke. "Abner is old, and Truin has fallen! There is no one left who can unite the Adonians and stand against the flood of darkness that will soon choke out the remaining light in the world of men."

Culpa forgot for just the briefest of moments that their master was not one to be questioned. "What about the brother, Ka'el?"

Satan's eyes flashed fire-red as his reptilian-like head snapped toward Culpa. The evil master's wings flared up and extended high above the other demons, spraying them with the rancid fluids and decaying flesh.

"He is totally ineffective! Distracted and confused by his lust for the sensuous beauty we arranged for him in his youth, he allowed himself to be misled and effectively neutered. He hasn't been a threat for quite some time."

The demons cowered low, covering their heads with their ragged wings and clinging tightly to the rocks on which they rested. The master was angry, and when the master was angry, demons got hurt.

"But are we sure?" the insubordinate minion thoughtlessly asked.

Satan cut short Culpa's foolish inquiry. Before the imprudent demon could utter another word, Satan had crossed the pit at lightning speed, knocking several demons in his path into the cesspools that surrounded them. Satan reached the rock where Culpa perched and violently seized him by the throat, yanking him up into the clammy air.

"He is lost!"

Culpa's wings and tail thrashed in panic as Satan's frothy, acidic spittle bombarded Culpa's face, instantly eating holes into its leathering skin.

"He is lost!" Satan wailed even louder as he flung the shell-shocked fiend across the pit into the far wall, shattering one of its wings on impact.

"Are there any more questions?" Satan screamed at his terrified host of warriors as he gyrated feverishly across the rocks, terrorizing his underlings and ensuring there were no others who wished to challenge his authority or wisdom.

Then he stopped.

Silence filled the dark dungeon. Only the sound of the condemned souls wailing in agony as they boiled in the hot trenches penetrated the musty and toxic air.

Satan scanned the depths of the pit with eyes that now burned like fire-red coals and darted about like lasers, focusing his glare on any discernible movement in his demented kingdom. His grotesque expression, now more contorted than usual, revealed his contempt for those around him.

"I didn't think so."

Flash!

"The pit is active. Darkness celebrates."

"Darkness by nature is blind. Its deceitful pride betrays itself."

"It is as it was meant to be."

"Indeed, as it was meant to be."

Flash!

†††

Ka'el sat alone in the dark. The sun had set an hour earlier, but he hadn't noticed. It had been two days since he returned home to find Tala gone. He felt lost.

Ka'el's emotions had always dominated his psyche, controlling his moods and determining his outlook on life. Now, Ka'el's feelings were driving him crazy.

In the last two days, Ka'el had run the full gamut of emotion. His first reaction to Tala's departure was apathy and relief. He momentarily convinced himself that life would be much easier with her gone. In all honesty, more than once, while away from home hunting, he had actually wished he would return to find Tala had left him. But he never really meant it. Rather, it was simply his bitterness over the past, over all the things that hadn't turned out the way he had planned — hadn't turned out the way he had foolishly idealized they should be — that plagued him. He had appeased this idealistic bitterness by wishing she was gone.

Now that Tala had left him, nagging questions continued to haunt Ka'el, depriving him of the peace he thought he would feel. First, there was confusion.

Why would she leave now, after all these years? Where did she go?
Then anger took the field.
How could she do this to me? I thought she loved me!
Finally, sadness and depression took over.
What was it all for? I lost my family for Tala, and then Tala left me. What do I have left to live for? I am alone.

Deep down inside, Ka'el knew it was as much his fault as Tala's that their relationship had been so rocky. Tala was wild — not like any woman his family would have wanted him to marry. She didn't share the upbringing, the values, and the beliefs that he did. The physical attraction they shared was tremendous, but the core differences between them ran much deeper than the passion. Those differences plagued their relationship from the start.

Ka'el had let passion and pride rule his life. Passion and pride had given birth to selfishness, envy, and anger. These flaws in his character had resulted in his alienation from the family and the failure of his marriage.

Ka'el now blamed himself for everything. His wish had come true, leaving him empty. He was nothing but an empty shell of a man; lost in gloom, despair, and self-pity. The grief was overwhelming and unrelenting.

The sun had set. Ka'el sat in the dark; the darkness made him feel better. The darkness brought him a strange comfort, like that of pulling the covers over one's head to shut out the world — if only for a little while.

In the dark, alone in the cottage, Ka'el drifted off to sleep. He didn't care if he ever woke up, and he figured it would probably be better if he didn't.

✝✝✝

The sun was just about to peek over the horizon when the knock came upon the door.

Ka'el still sat in a deep sleep on the same chair he had occupied for the last day and night. As his mind emerged from the dark place it had hidden, Ka'el became unsure of which world the knock belonged to.

Did it come from the real world or the dark, secluded world I have made my new home?

He ignored the intrusion, allowing his mind to drift back towards the black hole of his subconscious.

Again, the knock. This time, it arrived with much more urgency.

Ka'el's mind withdrew from the shadows and headed for the sliver of light making its way through the thick fog. Clumsily, resentfully, he moved towards the light as if treading through waist deep molasses, resolving to hastily turn away the intruder and blissfully return to the still and eternal slumber he so desired.

"Go away. No one lives here anymore."

A third time, the knock hammered authoritatively on the door and into the room in which he lay. His visitor refused to be deterred.

Ka'el fell out of his chair and stumbled to the door. His legs, long deprived of required circulation, protested in pain with every step.

"All right, I'm coming. I'm coming!"

Ka'el lifted the heavy latch and pulled open the heavy oak door. Before him stood a petite form wearing a dark, hooded, overgarment to protect its occupant from the icy rain. The hooded visitor stepped inside and pulled off the hood. It was Christina.

It shocked Ka'el to see Christina at the door for many reasons. Christina rarely visited him; never at night, and never alone.

He blurted his questions out blindly — awkwardly. "Christina, what are you doing here? You traveled in the rain, in the darkness, by yourself? Why isn't Truin with you?"

Ka'el couldn't see the tears that ran down Christina's face at the mention of Truin's name, tears forever lost in the rain. Perhaps it was better that way, for Christina had not journeyed perilously through the darkness in the middle of the storm for Ka'el's pity. She was on a mission.

Christina entered the dark cottage. The lantern she held flooded the enclosure with light, bringing life to the icy tomb that the enclosure became; causing the shadows within it to flee and offering new hope to all within who would embrace it.

Christina's heart was still breaking, trying to recover from the loss of her life-mate, but she would have to save those years of recovery for later. Many were the widows who would need to mend their lives after the war was over — but the war was not over, not even close. Adonia needed all of its inhabitants to stand and fight. That meant her and her sons. And that meant Ka'el.

Few in Adonia thought they could stay on the sidelines and pretend this war was unnecessary, but there were some. They foolishly pretended that Karyan would be merciful and that he would benevolently allow them to live as they wished under his rule. This was either insanity or a feeble attempt to cover their cowardice; sometimes, it was both. Karyan was anything but merciful, and his rule would mean nothing less than a heavy cloud of death and destruction that would suffocate everything that was virtuous and true in Adonia. To think otherwise was lunacy. Even now, the armies of Karyan continued to come ashore in the south, amassing for a final assault on the faithful.

The Adonian Guard, temporarily flattened by the death of Truin, was struggling to bounce back. The seven provinces were attempting to form a coalition to repel the overwhelming numbers of enemy troops preparing to advance against them, but this was proving to be very difficult. Though the sons of Truin loved each other dearly, their years apart had sharpened their individual wills and each of them believed he was more equipped to lead the coalition than the others. Each was a leader in his own right and had loyal followers within their respective provincial guard, as well as throughout their respective populations. Thus, the success and popularity of each of the sons of Truin now presented a problem, an impediment to the formation of a coalition.

They formed the 777 by combining seven individual Provincial Guards to create the Adonian Guard. However, everyone understood that one son of Truin would command each of these Provincial Guards, and Truin himself would command the all the Provincial Guards together.

None of the provinces wanted to transfer their provincial flag of command to the commander of another province. The thought of surrendering their provincial sovereignty to a commander that might prioritize another province's interests above their own was unacceptable to a majority of the Provincial Guards, even at a critical time like this. Adonians, a freedom-loving people, had to ensure that they protected the continued sovereignty of their individual provinces at all costs.

However, as anyone in a military organization knows, there must be a chain of command, and there can be only one commander. Invariably, there will be disagreements on strategy, tactics, and the next move. Someone must make the final decision, and everyone must respect and implement the commander's call, right or wrong. That is why he wears the hat of the commander. If the military organization cannot make a decision, it will become paralyzed. When the survival of an entire people is on the line, paralysis is not a great option.

And so, there was an impasse. The provincial commanders were aligning their defenses as best possible to repel Karyan's forces, but there remained serious concerns. How might the nonexistent Unity of Command jeopardize the efficiency, effectiveness, and ability of Adonia's Guard to repel the invasion — to ensure victory against Karyan's next assault?

Adonia needed a leader. Truin was gone, and someone else had to be trusted with the life and death decisions; the survival decisions.

Christina held the lantern up to Ka'el's face. He looked terrible, like death itself. Ka'el squinted as the light poured over him, still unsure of what was going on. Ka'el looked down into Christina's big, wide eyes. "How can you be here?"

Tears poured from Christina's eyes; continuing the struggle without Truin was difficult. It would have been much easier for Christina to just give up. It took every ounce of her will to not give up and to do what was necessary to stand and fight.

Christina knew penetrating through the years of anger, guilt, and pride that had entombed Ka'el spirit would not be a simple task. Humanly speaking, most would say it was impossible. But Christina also knew that she was not alone.

Truin's death had not shattered her hope. She had fearlessly made the journey through the darkness to Ka'el's cottage, and she now found herself in front of Ka'el with the will and determination to awaken him from his long spiritual coma; these were all the signs she needed. She was not alone. By herself, Christina knew she would not have had the strength to do any of these things. But in her weakness, God's strength was even more visible.

Indeed, Ka'el too, though he did not yet realize it, must have also sensed the reality that something greater than that which meets the eye was at work here. This was obvious to Christina by the way Ka'el had asked, "How can you be here?"

Christina turned away. She quietly crossed the room and placed the lantern on the table by the chair Ka'el had been sitting in a moment earlier. As she moved across the room with the lantern, the light forced the darkness to flee its gloomy hiding places and seek new ones.

Christina wiped away her tears, turned, and faced Ka'el. Strengthening her resolve, she looked him directly in the eyes.

Ka'el, still only semiconscious, continued to stand in front of the open cottage door. The wind and rain still penetrated the dark and chilly cottage at will.

Christina steeled herself and spoke the words. "Truin is dead."

The words rolled off her lips and landed in the center of the cottage like a meteor crashing to the earth. The meaning inherent in these three words sent a shockwave out in all directions, crashing against the walls of the cottage and hitting Ka'el like a ton of bricks.

Ka'el had, over the years, become totally consumed with self. His world had shrunk down to include, little, outside those things that directly affected his immediate circumstances. For too long, Ka'el had not been concerned about the troubles of the world. His preoccupation with his own life and his own unhappiness had dominated his time and his thinking, leaving little room for anything else.

Christina's words unleashed a landslide of thoughts from a long-neglected corner of Ka'el's mind — a region he had sealed off forever. An army of thoughts invaded his understanding, assaulting it from all directions, overwhelming his mental defenses, and instantly snapping him out of his stupor. Then the thoughts catapulted him into an even deeper valley of shock and confusion.

Truin, dead?

461

This wasn't a concept that Ka'el's mind could wrap itself around. Truin was the successful son, the one who had done everything right, the hero and leader of Adonia.

He cannot be gone. This simply cannot be.

Ka'el almost could not get the word out of his mouth. "What?" He stared at Christina as if she had spoken in some unintelligible language.

"Truin is dead," Christina repeated. The words were just as hard to mouth the second time as they had been the first.

The shockwave hit him again. Ka'el fell to his knees, then to his hands and knees. Gusts of wind continued to blow the sheets of rain through the open door behind him. The relentless onslaught of raindrops pelted Ka'el's body mercilessly, then pooled on the wooden floor where Ka'el now kneeled.

This cannot be. It just — can't be.

"How?" Ka'el's question resulted in nothing more than a whisper.

"Assassins. Lions. He died protecting me." Christina responded slowly, the words continuing to cling to her throat as she forced them out of her mouth. "He died protecting Adonia."

The words swept over Ka'el like a heavy cloud of poisonous gas, covering him, pushing him down, and suffocating him. Shadows in the room danced about like ghoulish bullies as chaotic drafts invaded the small cottage and ruthlessly assaulted the flame in Christina's lantern, trying ever so hard to extinguish the light.

All the guilt that had ravaged Ka'el for years battered him again.

If Truin had been whole, he could have fought off the attack. I should have been there. I should have protected him. This is my fault. My fault!

Ka'el held his face in his hands. "No. No. This cannot be. It is my fault. It is all my fault!"

Sinister winds blew in through the open door, striving again to reach and extinguish the flame that burned brightly within the cabin. They carried with them a torrent of heavy rain that hammered Ka'el. He fell over on his side, still sobbing and screaming into the darkness. "This is my fault!"

Christina ran to Ka'el, throwing her arms around him and consoling him. "No, no Ka'el, this is not your fault. Truin did what he had to do. He did what God created him to do."

She threw her cloak over Ka'el, struggling in vain to lift him off the floor. Kneeling beside a broken Ka'el, Christina gently cradled his face in her soft hands. "He told me to tell you he forgives you. He told me to tell you he loves you."

Ka'el felt as if someone had thrust a sword through his heart. Christina's words, intended to impart forgiveness and peace to Ka'el, instead brought a deeper heartache. Ka'el's spirit plummeted to a much deeper valley of sadness and grief.

My little brother; my only brother is gone. I wasted all that time! What have I done? I am sorry. I am so sorry!

The darkness threw everything it had at the small cottage as Ka'el wept uncontrollably in Christina's arms. Years of pain and guilt hemorrhaged out of Ka'el as the wind and rain assaulted the small cottage.

When Ka'el could cry no more, he looked up at Christina, for the first time showing signs he was once again in control, freed from much of what had haunted him.

"I am so sorry, Christina."

"I know Ka'el. I too have regrets, but this is not about us." Christina pulled on a still lethargic and defeated Ka'el. "Get up."

Ka'el did not respond. He didn't want to get up. He did not want to STAND.

"Get up, Ka'el!" Christina said sternly, surprising Ka'el with the firmness in her voice and the strength with which she now lifted him to his feet.

"Truin told me to tell you one last thing."

Ka'el raised his head, hanging on her every word as he thirsted for one last connection with his brother, Truin.

"Truin said, 'Tell Ka'el he must let go of the guilt. He now holds the light and must hold it high for all to see.'"

As she spoke the words, the sun rose. With the arrival of dawn, the storm abruptly ceased and the fierce wind and rain that had battered the small country cottage retreated. The powerful rays of the sun raced across forest and plain, effortlessly piercing through the windows and open door of the cottage, illuminating it in vibrant shades of orange and gold. The brilliance of the light from Christina's lantern swelled a thousandfold with the flood of sunshine. Christina and Ka'el both covered their eyes, attempting to shield them from the sudden and intense power of the sun.

At that moment, the Spirit stirred within Ka'el, and he recalled the Word of the Lord that he had learned in his childhood.

You, Oh Lord, keep my lamp burning; my God turns my darkness into light — for who is God besides the Lord? And who is the Rock except our God? It is God who arms me with strength and makes my way perfect.

Ka'el stood. "This is not about us, it is his-story."

Christina smiled. "That is right. His-story, not ours."

Christina gazed at Ka'el, and she could see everything had changed. His face glowed in the morning sun. His stance was strong and secure, like that of the Ka'el she once knew. Most strikingly, Ka'el's eyes now burned with an intensity she had never seen in them before.

Ka'el remembered Psalm 69.

Let those who trust in you not be put to shame because of me.

A flood of lessons from his childhood engulfed him. He remembered what his father, Abner, had taught them.

The past is gone; our future is secure in the Father's hands; now — the present — is life. Life is to be lived. We must do — now — what needs to be done! We can only accomplish the doing in the present.

Christina stoked the fire that grew in Ka'el's eyes. "Wake up, Ka'el. For too long, your spirit has slept. For too long, you have slumbered as the battle has been raging!"

Ka'el remembered his father's instruction.

There are three types of folk; sheep, wolves, and sheepdogs. For the sake of the sheep, the sheepdogs must STAND!

Ka'el thought.

Twice, my brother has saved my life: in my place — he stood where it was not safe to stand; and he stood when I was not prepared to stand. Now he needs me to do what he cannot. He asks me to fulfill my calling. It is time for me to STAND.

Christina could see Ka'el transforming from a broken, empty shell to the warrior that Truin had so often told her still existed. It was as if the breath of God had filled his body and ignited a raging furnace within him. "Ka'el must awaken!"

Ka'el looked down into Christina's eyes. He now stood immoveable before her, a mountain with eyes ablaze. Christina then recognized the fire that burned in Ka'el's eyes. It was the same fire that had burned so brightly in Truin's eyes.

"Ka'el is awake. The sleeper has awakened."

CHAPTER 59

SHOWDOWN

†††

The fighting raged. Omentian invaders, augmented by thousands of conscripted Heathian and Parlantian foot soldiers, drove south and west into Adonia, destroying everything in their path.

These massive armies of men, deceived by the delusions of demons, put their trust and allegiance in the hand of sorcerers and mad men. The dark magic at their disposal was indeed convincing. With it, the disciples of Karyan wielded the power to move inanimate objects, alter the physical environment, cast spells on the feebleminded, and free the consciences of their followers of any remorse they might have had for the senseless destruction and plunder of countless villages — the merciless slaughter of innocents.

The dark army of Karyan became more and more sinister with each passing moon, until it no longer bore any resemblance to an army of men, but a massive throng of mindless brutes, capable of unimaginable savagery.

Also, adding to the ranks of an already formidable foe were the monsters of the land now under Bestia's control; the dragons, the lions, and the giant flesh eating worms. Together these dark forces assaulted and defiled the countryside of Adonia, and though the remaining elements of the Adonian Guard, led by the courageous sons of Truin, fought fearlessly for every foot of their homeland, evil established a firm foothold and sank its determined talons into the heart of Adonia.

The sons of Truin had individually gathered and maneuvered their defensive forces to the south of the main Omentian horde, each hoping divisions from the other provinces would assist them. Hundreds of faithful guardsmen had answered their prayers responding to the call, refilling the ranks of the 777 and rekindling the hope that they were not fighting a losing battle.

The 777 converged in southern Adonia, between the western foothills of Kandish and the forests of Tobar, well prepared to make their last stand. The Adonians knew that this would be their last chance to thwart the Omentian offensive and save their homeland. They knew that failure in their task would mean the unspeakable for their wives and children. What they did not know was the current strength of the enemy forces that would soon confront them.

The Great Struggle had raged for months across Adonia. Due only to the Lord's direct intervention, the Adonian Guard's casualty count had been much lower than that of the Omentian horde. But the Omentians' numbers, supported by Parlantian and Heathian conscripts, were vastly superior to that of the Adonian Guard, and in a war of attrition, Adonia could ill-afford many more losses. The ranks of the 777 were full once again, but there would be no more replacements in the future. Adonia was "all in."

The 777, now defensively positioned in the relatively narrow gateway to southern Adonia, held back a vastly superior force, roughly estimated at well over ten thousand troops. How the enemy had landed such a large force on Adonia's shores without the Adonian Guard's knowledge was puzzling, to say the least. However, the Adonian Guard had been persistently engaged in battle for months throughout Adonia, stretching its intelligence, surveillance, and reconnaissance resources to the bare minimum. So, meeting further requirements was sketchy at best. No doubt Karyan had planned it this way, and his plan had worked well. The 777, though exhausted from battle, fought on, but the outlook was less than enthusiastic considering the overwhelming disadvantage they faced in the upcoming battle.

The enemy gave the Adonian defenders little time to consider their predicament. While Karyan continually marshaled more and more troops for the final assault and destruction of what he considered being nothing more than the final pocket of Adonian resistance, he also sent wave after wave of infantry attacks against the Adonian line to soften its defenses, destroy its morale, and deplete the strength of its defenders.

The most effective attacks came from the possessed beasts that now accompanied the forces of darkness on their endless endeavor to subjugate all of mankind. Karyan's ambassadors mindlessly carried out Bestia's commands; directing the dragons, lions, and worms to besiege the 777 constantly, leaving only a few precious moments for the Adonian Guard to rest and pray. By day and by night, the attacks came, never in the same way and never at the same time.

The attacks always began with the worms. They appeared out of nowhere. Perhaps they were called up from the depths of hell itself to serve just this purpose, at just this time. No one knew. No one in Adonia had ever seen them before the Omentians arrived.

The worms attacked by day. As the Adonians were setting up barrier defenses across the flat prairie that runs between the foothills of Kandish and the lush forests of Tobar, the dreadful creatures struck. There was little to no warning. Capable of burrowing through the earth at high speed, the worms emerged from the ground beneath them, latching onto the feet and legs of the working soldiers, tearing through their flesh and bone with razor-sharp teeth, and dragging them down into the worms' deep, dark dens below.

This menacing threat struck their defensive lines, causing the men to scream in surprise and terror and prompting the engineers to scramble for higher ground.

Skottie was supervising the lines when the worms first struck. While dozens of men ran toward him and up the foothills to find safety, he charged the opposite direction, long spear in hand, to save a soldier caught in the jaws of one of the hellish creatures. By the time Skottie made it to the unfortunate man, only his upper torso remained visible above the ground. The man groped frantically for anything to hang on to, screaming in agony from the fatal wounds being inflicted on him below the surface. As Skottie approached him, the man reached out, pleading to Skottie for help.

Skottie's first instinct was to grab hold of the man and pull him from the jaws of death, but Skottie could see the force at which the other men in the same predicament were being pulled under. Even now, this man was being tugged mercilessly further and further into the depths, the earth engulfing more of his torso with each yank of the beast. Skottie knew that trying to play tug-of-war with the worm, while using this poor man as the rope, would not end well for the man. He also doubted he could match the strength of this dark monstrosity.

Skottie ignored the man's heartbreaking cries for help as best he could and resorted to a backup plan. He fearlessly stood over the man, grasped his spear firmly in both hands, pointed the tip toward the ground at his feet, and making his best estimate of where the wretched worm's head might be below the surface, speared the ground between his feet with as much force as he could muster. As Skottie raised his spear and plunged it into the ground, he could tell by the terrified look on the man's face that he did not like the idea. Skottie shared the man's reservations, but he had little choice or time to contemplate the gamut of alternatives. He had to act immediately if there was any hope of saving this man. Though the man might have been hoping the spear would put him out of his misery, Skottie hoped and prayed that the Lord would guide his aim and deal a big enough blow to the worm to make a difference, forcing it to release the pitiful man at his feet.

First indications were not great. As Skottie thrust the spear into the soft ground below him, the tip penetrated one to two feet into the earth and stopped. Instantly, the man's screams intensified as he writhed in pain. Thinking he had missed the worm and struck the man instead, Skottie's heart broke.

An instant later, everything changed. The ground below Skottie's feet exploded upward, sending Skottie, the man he was trying to save, and five-hundred pounds of earth bursting skyward. Everything was a blur. Skottie landed flat on his back, the air knocked out of him. While struggling to breathe, Skottie caught sight of the besieged man as he landed beside him, blood spraying from one of his thighs where the worm had inflicted a terrible wound. An instant later, Skottie saw the most horrific creature he had ever seen. It thrashed about in the crater of dirt from which it had just emerged; a spear embedded in its head.

The worm was eight to ten feet. Its clammy, gray body was like that of an enormous eel with an enormous head and a long, slimy tail. It didn't appear to have any eyes; no distinguishing features were visible apart from its massive jaws and multiple rows of small, jagged teeth.

Skottie, still unable to breathe, leaped to his feet and, grabbing the man beside him, dragged him away from the colossal worm that continued to toss about in its final death-throes.

Jacobin and two other guardsmen were rapidly on the scene, helping Skottie and the injured man to safety on the higher grounds of the rocky foothills. The man would live, but the horrific beasts in darkness' employ would claim the lives of many others through countless attacks.

Still, the 777 held the line.

†††

Day and night, death rained down on the defenders of Adonia. Change had come, and the change was terrifying. The day, and especially the night, held a dread that few of Adonia's inhabitants had ever known before. The changing circumstances constantly forced the Adonian Guard to adapt since the constant skirmishes with the invaders left them little time to regroup.

Karyan's tactics were wearing down the Adonians; but the Adonian Guard continued to stand. Though their numbers were few in relation to the enemy, they did not stand alone. The prayers of another army, a throng of many thousands of Adonia's citizens, were being offered continuously to the God of the heavens. Their prayers, filling the heavens like a sweet aroma, reached the throne of the King, and he heard their cries for help. The far ends of Adonia sent a mighty army of orn and wolf to combat the dragon and the lion.

Light and darkness battled, and the creatures of the earth were their pawns. The magicians of Karyan attempted to use the light of the sun to deceive the eyes of the Adonians with the illusions that had worked so well on the Parlantians and Heathians. But the orn, commanded by the Creator, arrived in such large numbers that they eclipsed the sun and denied darkness its deception. As more of the tannin crept out from their underground dens, more of the gorn stood against them. As the number of lions infiltrating the lines of the Adonian Guard increased, so did the wolf-pack patrols, intent on seeking and destroying the lions. And as the dark ravens attempted to intercept the songbird messengers that so faithfully served the Adonian Guard, the mighty eagles flew combat air patrol high overhead, ensuring the peaceful "bird-speak" messengers reached their destinations. The 777 continued to dominate the observe, orient, decision, and action (OODA) loop.

After weeks of fighting, neither side gaining much ground, the army of Karyan finally surrounded the Adonian Guard, cutting off its supply lines.

The Adonain Guard stood its ground, singing praises to God, day and night. The men of the 777 built each other up with the psalms, hymns, and spiritual songs that they had learned from their mothers as children. Exhausted and injured, they sang and made music in their hearts to the Lord, understanding — perhaps more clearly than ever — that every moment of their lives was a gift from the God of Creation. They gave thanks to him with every single breath they took, knowing each breath might be their last.

The demons shrieked in agony as they heard the songs of the Adonian Guard rise into the heavens. The sound burned through them like acid, torturing their lost souls and reminding them of their ancient fall. Unwilling to suffer alone, they tormented their Omentian hosts mercilessly, driving them into a frenzy of self-mutilation and bloodletting.

In sharp contrast to the praise of the saints, the Omentian wails of anguish and misery tainted the skies over the battlefield, forming an unseen but distinctive spiritual and metaphysical barrier between the opposing forces.

The heavens further accented the wall of separation that existed between the two opposing forces. Dense, dark clouds formed over the forces of Karyan by day and by night, immersing the evil horde in a blanket of gloomy shadow and battering the dark army pitilessly with heavy wind and freezing rain. In sharp contrast, the sun and moon continuously shined their light on the Adonian Guard, warming their bodies and their spirits. In addition, manna and quail appeared daily for the nourishment of the faithful. Though the most learned men of Karyan could not see how these events could take place, the soldiers of the Adonian Guard — to the very last man — could clearly see.

Donstup and other shepherds of God moved tirelessly amongst the injured soldiers of the light, ministering to them and strengthening their resolve with words of truth.

"Adonians, today you are going into battle against the enemies of the light. Do not be fainthearted or afraid; do not be terrified or give way to panic before them. For the Lord, your God is the one who goes with you to fight for you against your enemies to give you victory."

Donstup continued, pointing up into the ring of clouds in the sky and the clear view of the heavens above the Guard. "To whom will you compare me? Who is my equal says the Holy One. Lift your eyes and look to the heavens: Who created all these? He who brings out the starry host one by one, and calls them each by name. Because of his great power and mighty strength, not one of them is missing."

"Do not fear the enemy or those that fight with him, be it in the spirit world or the physical! There is no room for demons or their deception in your hearts or in your minds! They have no power over you!"

Donstup had learned long ago that the Lord showers blessings on his faithful — many more blessings than they could ever even know to ask for. He often said that the Lord's hand to give is much larger than his people's hands to receive. Losing his one eye early in life had blessed his many years with the constant reminder not to trust in physical sight, which is all so often deceptive. Rather, he urged the faithful to place their trust in the God of Creation, the God who created everything and can operate beyond what they can see or understand. The insight of this Nomen was a great blessing to all the faithful gathered for the ultimate defense of Adonia.

Donstup raised his hands to the heavens below a noonday sun that shared its light with only the faithful. "The Lord speaks plainly to you, defenders of the faithful, not with trickery or illusion. See his majesty. Listen to his words. The Lord will be victorious! The will of the Creator will be — here in this place and everywhere! Put your trust in him! Your faith is from the Lord! You have not received a spirit of fear; you have received a spirit of power! No one can mock God! God is and will always be faithful to those who love him, and his will — will be done!"

Thanks to the mercy of the almighty and the efforts of men like Donstup, the 777 fought on, holding back the constant onslaught of the darkness that surrounded them.

But evil was not idle; knowing that much of the Adonian Guard's strength lie in the leadership of the seven sons of Truin, Karyan dispatched his sorcerers to focus their attacks directly on them. The next morning, darkness put the plan into play. Geoff, Skottie, Daniel, Bigaulf, Gareth, Cusintomas, and Moesheh all met at sunrise around the command fire at the center of the encircled and besieged divisions of the Adonian Guard. Truin's sons had met to discuss the current situation and revised their defensive strategy to offset the enemy's ever-changing tactics. Without warning, a visual illusion of countless enemy campfires, soldiers, and beasts simultaneously bombarded them. Momentarily blinded and off balance, the seven joined hands and prayed to God to repel the attack and give them back clear vision of the battlefield. They received in return much more. As the dark illusion fled before their eyes, the seven sons of Truin miraculously gained the ability to see the invisible army of angels surrounding their positions and protecting them from the Omentians. They saw the hills full of horses and chariots of fire, the flames of which burned of jasper, sapphire, chalcedony, emerald, sardonyx, carnelian, chrysolite, beryl, topaz, chrysoprase, jacinth, and amethyst. Departing the campfire and returning to their respective divisions, the faces of the seven sons glowed with a light that awed and inspired their troops. The all-knowing and all-powerful hand of the Creator again thwarted the evil intentions of darkness in answer to the prayers of his faithful servants.

Thus, it was at every turn. As evil implemented its dark plans, the Creator used his power to turn evil's actions into blessing for the faithful.

Though the invaders encircled and outnumbered the Adonian Guard, it was the Omentians, the Parlantians, and the Heathians that feared battle. Crazed monsters on the outside, their wretched spirits within them cried out in terror for their immortal souls as their enslaved bodies followed the commands of their dark master; they were nothing more than possessed and pathetic puppets dancing to a merciless puppeteer.

In stark contrast, the Adonians had already given their lives over to the service of their master, protecting their families, and the cause of freedom. They had considered the likely outcome of their service on the battlefield, and they had determined, to the last man, that their sacrifice, whatever it might be, would be insignificant relative to the rewards of serving the Master of the Universe. The Master was worthy of whatever they offered, even their lives! Though they wanted to live, they did not fear the battle or death itself. They already knew their victory was sure and their inheritance secure in the hands of their God.

Still, to the human eye, the Omentian held the upper hand in this battle, and it was this battle that would decide the fate of Adonia.

††††

Ka'el moved swiftly through the steep mountain pass. Urgently departing after Christina's visit, he hadn't packed for the journey; he didn't bring weapons, special clothes, or food. Though his many years of hunting had well prepared him for the trek, both physically and mentally, something else — something bigger than the physical or mental — now drove Ka'el.

The events of the last two days had drastically changed Ka'el's life, and they had drastically changed Ka'el. For many years, Ka'el had searched for a purpose, a reason for his continued existence. For a period, he had supposed that enjoyment, happiness, and pleasure were suitable reasons to go on; but he soon discovered these to be empty. He tried over and over to make his relationship with Kala the centerpiece of his existence, only to find repeatedly that this, too, was an elusive dream. The seasons of Ka'el's life had come and gone, passing by in a forgettable succession of insignificant days, months, and years that Ka'el could no longer remember. Still, he had found no answers.

But that had all changed overnight. Tala's unexplained departure had been the silent earthquake, the unannounced tsunami, which had finally knocked Ka'el off of his fragile foundation and swept him away. Instantly peeling away the many layers of superficial strength and boastful bravado that he had clothed himself with over the years, the event had exposed the raw weakness, insecurity, guilt, and regret that truly defined the man known as Ka'el. The event forced him to see himself as he truly was, and the ugly self-portrait was too much for Ka'el to bear. He had given up. Empty, exposed, and too weak to replace the all too familiar facades, he had surrendered his fate to whichever invisible force would have him. Then, sinking to the depths of despair, he had been powerless to save himself.

But then love had knocked on the door. Christina had brought a message of forgiveness from beyond the darkness and from beyond the curtain of death. Out of nowhere the sun had suddenly risen, dispelling the gloom and thawing Ka'el's ice-covered heart. Like a defenseless child, plucked from the jaws of certain death by a loving father, everything had changed. Clarity replaced obscurity, wisdom replaced folly, and purpose swept away the emptiness, instantly transforming Ka'el from an insignificant observer of the life and death conflict that surrounded him to an active participant.

Ka'el was not sure what role he played or if it was even possible to alter the course of events and contribute substantially to the defense of Adonia, but he knew he had to try. Reason would tell him that there was nothing one man could do to change the outcome of this war. It, reason, was master of all that men could see and measure. The reality of the situation — what men could see — was that a vastly superior force had invaded Adonia. This dark scourge had encircled the Adonian Guard, the last remaining hope of the Adonian resistance, and at any moment the end would surely come. This was reason's sure verdict.

But Ka'el was no longer listening to the voice of reason. Reason, despite being wonderfully unique to mankind, had limited abilities and usefulness as a tool. In situations such as this, where much more was involved than what men could see or measure, relying solely on reason was a liability and a mistake. Events like this required gifts beyond the limited abilities and reach of reason. Happenings like this required a sight beyond that which men could see with human eyes and witnessed with human senses. These situations required a deep understanding of what was beyond physical sight; they required faith.

For many years, Ka'el had not understood the puzzling course of his life, the seemingly unrelated events that had altered his path, and the true purpose of his existence. Suddenly, like a puzzle, some omniscient, all-knowing architect had methodically assembled before his eyes; it all made sense. Each piece of the puzzle had a different shape, a different color, and a different location in the overall picture, but each depended on the others for purpose, and they all depended on the puzzle maker for order and design. It had taken many years for all the pieces of the puzzle to fall into place, but now, enough pieces had done so for Ka'el to see his part in the overall picture — his part in the plan.

Ka'el realized that for too long he had sat idly on the sidelines, observing the construction of the puzzle, thinking himself not part of the picture. For too long, he had thought his brother Truin's pieces would complete the portrait. But no one man dominated all the pieces of the puzzle — not his brother Truin, not his father Abner. They were all important, each for their own purpose, each for their own time. And now it was his time. Ka'el knew that the time had come for him to fulfill his purpose and embrace the man he was created to be. Armed with absolute assurance and despite all the judgements of reason, Ka'el blindly followed faith's direction. He entered the fight.

Ka'el had expected to meet resistance as he penetrated the enemy perimeter, the enemy shell that had circumvented the 777. He had wondered how he would fight his way through them without a sword or armor. The answers to his questions came quickly.

As Ka'el entered enemy territory, he encountered the dismembered bodies of dozens of Parlantian guardsmen. Ka'el only supposed that a great number of wolves were responsible for savagely tearing apart the men limb by limb. The bloodied and mutilated torsos of the unsuspecting Parlantians littered the hills, marking an obvious path of carnage through the trees. Ka'el, suspecting that the path was for him, followed the corridor that was clear of all armed resistance.

The sun rose over the distant forests of Tobar, and Ka'el soon approached the embattled Adonian front lines in the Valley of Brann. The Omentians had disengaged from the fight some two hours earlier, and the Adonians were busy withdrawing the wounded to the rear, where medics could treat their bodies and Nomen could comfort their souls. Still, Ka'el's arrival instantly caught the attention of the Adonian sentries.

"Halt!" ordered Joust, commander of the watch.

Ka'el lifted his hands high in the air to show he was no threat. Mattus, Grahmulan, and Thomar surrounded him; the three battle-weary yet formidable guardsmen with their shields held high and their swords ready to strike at any sign that Ka'el was part of an enemy attack.

"Identify yourself!" Joust commanded.

Ka'el understood and approved of the guardsmen's diligent precautions. He knew that although he held no weapons, his size alone demanded the soldiers be ready to engage him. Hands still held high over his head, Ka'el was careful not to make any movement that these combat veterans might misinterpret as an aggressive act. He answered them. "I am Ka'el, son of Abner, brother of Truin."

The men froze in their tracks and then looked at each other in disbelief. True, they had heard of Ka'el, the brother of Truin, but it had been many years since anyone had seen him in public, let alone on the battlefield. Some had postulated that he was dead; others that he was never anything more than a legend.

Thomar, doubting Ka'el had spoken the truth, extended his sword and challenged Ka'el. "Prove it!"

Ka'el thought for a moment and then lowered his arms. "I cannot. Do what you must do."

Mattus and Grahmulan converged on Ka'el, deciding that they had no choice but to subdue him. They could not let this giant walk freely among them without knowing if he was friend or foe.

Ka'el did not resist. It was not a simple thing for him to do. Though he had undergone a profound change in the last two days, part of the old Ka'el remained within him and allowing these men, or any men, to subdue and bind him without a fight was something he had never allowed before. Ka'el could feel his blood boil, and for a moment he thought he would explode. But then he remembered the puzzle.

Surely, I am not here to fight my own countrymen. My part in the story cannot be this.

A peace blanketed Ka'el's spirit as the men bound him.

Joust ordered the men. "Take him to be interrogated. We will find out who this spy is."

As they led Ka'el off in chains, Ka'el knew the Lord was with him and that somehow this was part of the plan.

Far away and across the land of Adonia, the faithful raised their prayers of intercession to the Lord of the heavens. Abner and Evelin prayed. Christina and Elin prayed. Salli, Kaye, Marilu, Susanni, Ahnettia, Kharin, Lorih, Robinella, Gina, Margerie, and Sandrah prayed. All the faithful women and children of Adonia prayed the Lord would protect their land and safely bring the men of Adonia back home to them.

✝✝✝

"Release him!" the command thundered from the Captain of the Guard. "Release him now!"

A powerfully built soldier with an enormous golden shield had suddenly appeared before the detachment of soldiers escorting Ka'el to interrogation. The soldiers looked at him in shock.

"But sir," Joust retorted, confrontationally, "we don't know who this man is! We captured him as he tried to infiltrate the line, and —"

"Release him now!" the Captain of the Guard ordered again before the guardsman had finished his unrequested explanation. "This man is Ka'el, son of Abner, brother of Truin!"

The three guardsmen, overwhelmed not only by the officer's rank but by the authority with which he spoke to them, anxiously loosened Ka'el's chains and freed him. They stepped back sheepishly, unsure of what punishment might await them for their grave mistake.

"No harm done, men," Ka'el offered, extending his arm to each of the men, in-turn. "You were only doing your duty in holding the line, and I salute you for it."

"Resume your duties. Return to the line!" their commander ordered them as he approached Ka'el.

Joust and the others immediately responded and hurried off toward the perimeter. Ka'el turned to the officer, eager to see who it was that had recognized him, and curious how.

The officer approached. Ka'el had never met this man before. Yet, as the strong, blonde man with the golden shield stopped and stood before him, Ka'el realized he knew him.

A week earlier, Ka'el would not have accepted what was happening. A week earlier, Ka'el could not have seen beyond the ordinary, physical world around him. In fact, he had been blind for most of his life. He had looked upon the world around him, the people in his life, and the events of his life with the eyes of a child; seeing without depth and observing without true discernment.

But this had all changed unexpectedly. After a lifetime of blindness and ignorance, Ka'el suddenly had vision. In an instant, the blind man had understanding, and the simpleton became a sage.

That he recognized this man, a man whom he had never met before, did not surprise Ka'el. Unexplainably, he expected it.

"Have faith, Ka'el, in the Lord your God. Do not trust your sight, your emotions, or your reason. Trust only in God to deliver you!"

A deep peace came over Ka'el as he walked with the warrior into the midst of the Adonian camp.

"Will you be accompanying me?" Ka'el looked at his golden companion?

The Captain of the Guard stopped and turned to Ka'el. His eyes burned a brilliant reddish gold, and he spoke with authority. "Before your very conception, God designed you to do what you go to do now. You have never been alone, and you are not alone now. He is with you, and we are all around you."

They continued on deliberately, with quiet resolve, through the Adonian ranks, toward the field of blood that lay before them. Though eager to do the Lord's bidding, part of Ka'el was still reluctant to answer the morbid call that had beckoned so many before him to their grisly deaths. The battlefield ahead displayed the lifeless bodies of Omentian, Heathian, and Parlantian, scattered before them — the scavengers of the air ravaging their fallen bodies.

More and more of the Adonian Guard recognized Ka'el as he walked through the camp. Word rapidly spread that Ka'el, the son of Abner and brother of Truin, had returned to join the fight.

As Ka'el reached the front lines, the eyes of the guardsman watching the perimeter turned to him. The warrior, the Captain of the Guard, had vanished into the fog. Ka'el stood before them and at that moment couldn't help but feel alone.

But I am not alone. This is my purpose. It is my time, and they are all around me. I am not alone.

†††

The living beings invisibly gathered in the skies overhead. Though time had no meaning for them and did not affect the dimensions in which they moved, time for those upon the earth all but stopped as Ka'el surrendered his will to the purpose for which his maker had called him. He entered the conflict armed solely with the faith given to him by the Master.

They kept vigilant eyes on Ka'el and the faithful in their charge. Ever ready to respond, the living beings watched in awe as the Master's plan unfolded before them.

†††

There was no wind, no breeze at all as Ka'el stood side by side with the Adonian watchman on the front line of the Adonian defensive perimeter. Ten feet in front of them was a wall of fog. Beyond the fog was death.

A young warrior named Darshe had been the last one to venture through the wall before them. Bravely announcing his intent to thrash the Omentian fiends that had killed many of his brothers, Darshe impulsively dashed out into the murky void, only to be mercilessly cut down somewhere beyond the dark shroud. The shrieks and wails of the suffering, those still left unattended within, poignantly accented the morbidity of the battlefield that waited.

"You cannot defeat me!" The voice screeched from beyond the dark veil of fog. "No one can defeat me!" The voice sounded eerily strange, like it might not even be a human voice.

As Ka'el gathered his resolve and stepped out onto the field, his movement disrupted the stale air over the plain of death, assaulting the wall of fog before him and sending several small vortices of vapor slowly spiraling off in several divergent directions.

"Who is next? Who is the next little sheep being sent to the slaughter?"

Ka'el took another step, again disrupting the sea of stagnant air and shadow in front of him that seemed to suck in and destroy all the light.

"I see you," the voice snarled, now in a low rumble. "I see you, little lamb."

Most of the 777 had quietly gathered on the front lines behind Ka'el. The news of Ka'el's arrival spread through the camp, igniting renewed hope in everyone that the battle might soon conclude, that the seemingly endless siege might soon end.

"I know you!" the voice suddenly thundered!

Ka'el's resolve was unshaken. He took another step.

I am not alone.

His step took him into the darkness, into the wall of thick fog. He could now see nothing in front of him. It was as if he had fallen into a great abyss. He was blind.

Help me Lord. Be with me, my God?

The voice cried out again. "I see you and I know you! You are Ka'el, and you are nothing!" Freakish laughter erupted after the pronouncement, followed by a cascade of spine-tingling voices as the many fiends from within joined in ridiculing Ka'el, echoing their master's sentiment.

Ka'el looked with spiritual eyes. "And I see you!"

Laugher erupted from the fog. "You can see nothing!"

"I see your defiance of Adonia; I see your disdain for all that is noble and right; and I see your rebelliousness against the one true God! I see you, and I know you!"

Thunder rumbled in the distance as Ka'el spoke the words. At first, no one paid any attention to it, as the events before them dwarfed the sounds of the approaching storm, but as the thunder grew louder and louder with each of Ka'el's words, it soon captured everyone's attention.

"I see you." Ka'el repeated.

As he spoke the words, the thunder cracked above them and a massive burst of air crashed down from the hills onto the plain, sweeping the fog away from east to west. Both armies watched in amazement as an invisible river of air swept the plain clear in a matter of seconds, transforming it from total darkness and fog to clarity.

Then, a deafening silence. The thunder had ceased, the torrent of wind had dissipated, and the two armies stared each other down under a cloudless, blue sky; the leaders of each standing alone, well ahead of both of their battle lines.

"And I know you," Ka'el whispered. The whisper echoed through the silence to the ears of every man on the battlefield.

"You know nothing!" Karyan retorted! "You are a fool! Look at the army that stands amassed against you, a multitude one-hundred times that of your ragtag bunch of misfits. My army is unstoppable! It swept across Omentia, Parlantis, Heath, and now Adonia with ease. My army crushes all who stand in its way!"

Ka'el stood silently.

Karyan continued. "I know you, Ka'el. I know what you like, and I know what you want. Did you not enjoy the wife I gave you? Did she not bring you pleasure? I have many more like her that will serve you, Ka'el. All you have to do is ask. Join me, and I will show you pleasures you have never dreamed of."

Still, Ka'el did not reply.

"You have nothing to say? Karyan continued, agitated at Ka'el's silence. I offer you the world, and you have nothing to say? Join me, Ka'el. Join me or die like the rest of these mindless peasants that helplessly cling to the ancient words of their God — a God that is surely dead."

Ka'el remained silent no longer. "I know you."

"Yes, you know me! I am Karyan, master of the world, and you are a fool! We are many, we have many powers, and we will destroy you!"

As Karyan spoke, the dirt and debris around him rose off the ground and swirled in an ever-expanding circle around him.

"You are no doubt shaking in your skin, you and your pathetic army. You are weak and you serve a weak God!"

Branches and dirt, the swords and armor of the fallen, and even the dead bodies littering the field circled through the air around Karyan. The grass of the field and the branches of the trees all bent toward the swirling vortex. Even the sand beneath the feet of the Adonian soldiers gave into the vortex's tow and slid across the fields towards it.

Karyan rose off the ground, levitating in the deadly maelstrom of solid matter whirling about him. His voice changed from human to something other than human. "Join me Ka'el! Worship me!"

"I know you!" Ka'el said, his voice echoing like an explosion across the plain at Karyan and his army. "You are Potentus, Bestia, Metus, Lucious, Arrogante, Scire, Glutonus, Pecunius, Doldrus, Viscere, Fractos, Terrus, Soluson, Dubitare, Colera, Disperato, Obaminus, and Scum! You are Legion!"

"Yes!" cried Karyan, his face distorting in unimaginable ways as his arms outstretched and his head lurched back. "Yes, we are Legion and we want you to join us! We demand it!"

In that moment, Ka'el recalled the lessons that Truin, Elin, and he had learned so long ago in the small cottage in Omentia where they had grown up.

Whether we live or die, we are the Lord's. We have nothing to fear, for the Lord is with us. Trust and obey.

Without warning, dark, heavy clouds once again replaced the blue skies overhead, rolling low across the sky. They covered the sun, swallowing its light, and dropped a blanket of darkness over the battlefield.

Ka'el walked across the battlefield, directly towards Karyan and the swirling torrent. The Omentian army, now assured of their master's power, observed with elation as the champion of the Adonians gave in to their master's demand. The Adonians stood like dead men; mortified by what they observed to be Ka'el's surrender.

"Come, my son, come to us. We have much to give you. Reign with us. You will be a king!"

The lightning flashed and thunder cracked overhead as Ka'el drew within one hundred feet of the dark lord. Ka'el's body swayed as the winds of the irregularity hammered against him.

Ka'el stopped.

Twisted voices cried out from Karyan's mouth. "This one is strong! We will enjoy him!"

"He is mine!"

"No, he is mine!"

One by one, the Adonians fell to their knees. Within moments, the entire line of the Adonian Guard kneeled before the Omentians.

The demons of the legion took turns speaking from Karyan's mouth.

"You see, no one can stand before us! Bow now, Ka'el. Yes, bow before us!"

"There is no shame in it. We will make you ruler over this land and its people; though why anyone would want to rule them, we do not know."

"They are pathetic! They surrender without a fight. Behold even now, they bow before us!"

Ka'el lifted his head and looked directly into the eyes of Karyan. "They are not weak, and they do not bow to you."

The Legion spoke. "You are wrong, Ka'el! Turn around, look, and see! They are weak!"

Ka'el turned and looked upon the Adonian line, on the 777, and tears ran from his eyes. To the last man, the entire 777 had fallen to their knees. They bowed their heads. Their eyes were closed.

The lightning flashed across the sky, drawing Ka'el's attention to it. He raised his head and looked straight up into the clouds that rolled by overhead at a speed he had never witnessed before. As Ka'el watched the continuous flashes, he realized that this was no ordinary lightning. The flashes continually changed color. First there was jasper, then sapphire, then chalcedony.

The voices cried out to Ka'el. "Turn, Ka'el. Turn and bow to us!"

Ka'el continued to stare up into the skies. Emerald, sardonyx, and carnelian flashed above him as the skies continuously rumbled.

Ka'el dropped his gaze to the Adonian line. As he did, he saw the flashes of lightning reflecting off the 777: chrysolite, beryl, topaz, chrysoprase, jacinth, and amethyst. Then he noticed something else, something he had missed the first time he had looked upon the Adonian line. Yes, they were kneeling. Yes, they bowed their heads. What Ka'el had missed the first time was that they had folded their hands. All of them had dropped their weapons, shields, and armor and folded their hands.

Ka'el turned to Legion and spoke. "You have failed."

Legion responded with laughter and scorn. "You have gone mad, Ka'el!"

"I will not bow to you; not now, not ever."

"Then you shall die! You shall die alone! The rest of your comrades have already given themselves over to us! They have already chosen the better way!"

"Indeed, they have chosen the better way, but they do not bow to you. They are stronger than they have ever been."

Ka'el looked to the skies overhead. "Even now they pray to the one, true God." Ka'el raised his arms until they pointed up into the heavens.

The voices cried out, "No, we are god! Bow to us, Ka'el! You are nothing! You cannot resist us!"

"Alone I am nothing, but I am not alone. He who is with me is greater than those who are with you!"

"Bow to us!" Legion cried out in rage as the body of Karyan contorted and writhed in agony.

"Today, the carcasses of the Omentian army will be given to the birds of the air and the beasts of the earth, and the entire world will know that there is a God in Adonia. All those gathered here will know that it is not by sword or spear that the Lord saves; for the battle is the Lord's, and he will give all of you into our hands."

The lightning flashed! The thunder cracked!

Karyan was furious. "Destroy them!"

The Omentian army advanced as one on the Adonian line. Their advance shook the ground as they marched in step closer and closer to the Adonians. The Adonians did not respond, but remained kneeling with their heads bowed.

Ka'el, keeping his eyes to the skies, called to the Lord of creation. "Oh Lord, God of our fathers, show the world today that you are the God of Adonia. Hear your servant's cry, Oh Lord. Save your people?"

As Ka'el spoke, the skies erupted again in thunder and brilliant flashes of light. The clouds churned and boiled above.

Suddenly, Karyan screamed with the sound of a thousand voices. His body writhed and contorted in indescribable ways. Then, as if some invisible force had suddenly weighted him down, Karyan and his swirling whirlwind crashed to the ground. The lord of darkness was on his hands and knees.

The Omentian army's advance came to an abrupt halt as they saw their master's power stripped from him.

Shocked at what had just happened, Karyan raised himself up off the ground and stood. He faced Ka'el with a bewildered and terrified look on his face.

Karyan begged some invisible entity that only he could see. "You promised! Where are you? You cannot leave me! You promised!" Karyan's voice had lost all of its powerful tone, now resembling more that of a teenage boy than that of a powerful commander.

In another dimension, laughter echoed through the fiery chambers of hell.

Ka'el lifted his arm and in the name of the Lord, pointed to Karyan. "You have made your choice! Go to your master!"

The ground around Karyan began to shake and vibrate intensely as Karyan's armor crumbled, and he again fell to the ground. Karyan's eyes widened as he pleaded to the God he never knew. "No! Please, no! I didn't know what I was doing! I didn't know!"

Smoke oozed from the cracks now forming on the ground around Karyan's hands and feet as the hidden dimensions merged. Rising with the smoke were a great multitude of cries from those suffering in an eternal agony beyond; those who had made the same choice. The cries grew louder and louder.

Karyan looked up at Ka'el, and it appeared as if his face had transformed back to that of the young boy who had blindly stumbled into the jaws of Hades so many years ago. With terror in his eyes, Pete pleaded with Ka'el for mercy. Ka'el looked at the boy in pity, but he could do nothing. It was not Ka'el that Pete had despised and rejected.

Thousands watched as the fearless dark lord, now a helpless fool, begged for mercy. But the time for mercy had passed; Pete's time of grace had ended. Without warning, innumerable arms and hands, burned and bloodied from eons in hell, emerged from the pit below Pete, like the tentacles of a giant squid. They wrapped themselves around Pete's arms, hands, legs, and feet, anchoring him in place. He screamed in terror!

The Adonians raised their heads as one, watching. They would remember this day and how the Lord had defended his faithful. They would surely pass the lesson down to their children and their children's children. Adonia must never forget.

Pete sank into the moist, blood saturated mud as the bloody hands dragged him down into the earth, into the fiery flames now erupting from the chasm that had formed around him. His screams of sheer terror pierced the souls of everyone on the plain. As the earth swallowed him, Pete's fingers clawed and tore at the surface for one last hold, one last second of hope before an eternity of suffering.

"I didn't know!"

His efforts were in vain as he gave in to the inevitable, and sinking below the earth, he succumbed to an eternal separation from the love of God and everything that is good. Then the earth closed over Pete, and his screams were silenced. His time upon the earth was no more.

Thunderless lightning flashed across the sky.

Ka'el turned to the Adonian line. "Remember well what you have witnessed and what you have yet to witness here today. Remember and tell your families how the Lord has delivered his people and saved our land."

Ka'el returned to the Adonian line. The 777, replacing their armor and taking up their weapons in hand, stood at the ready. All eyes turned back toward the Omentian trespassers.

CHAPTER 60

HOLY FIRE

†††

The two battle-hardened armies silently stood facing each other beneath the angry skies. By human standards, the Omentians held the distinct advantage, because of their overwhelming numbers, but they had just witnessed the unbelievable ousting of their commander, Lord Karyan, by some unseen power and did not know what to make of it.

Karyan's many apprentices, long awaiting any opportunity to move up in the ranks of the arts, realized that this was their opportunity. Craving the power that Karyan had held over them for so long, blinded and indifferent to the fate it had ultimately bought him, Karyan's former minions worked themselves into a frenzy chanting and pleading to the demons to intercede for them and make them Karyan's successor. They convinced themselves that it was so, and each one of them approached the Adonian lines, in-turn, mumbling their dark words and displaying their tricks of magic.

Sebil was the first. From a young age, Sebil worshipped snakes, burning their image onto her body, and sleeping with them in the dark, cool nests where they made their home. Those who embraced evil and stole young babies from their mothers in the night and fed them to her brood followed her. Her skin was almost transparent from the years of being hidden from the sun.

Hundreds of Omentian snake worshippers accompanied Sebil as she approached the Adonian line. Snakes slithered around her body, beneath her cloak, and through her hair as she uttered the demonic words. As she spoke, her minions dropped their staffs upon the ground and they became ravenous vipers, many times larger than those the Adonians had ever seen. The crimson serpents glided at high speed across the plain towards the Adonian line, their deadly jaws snapping at the air as they closed in on their targets.

But the 777 did not retreat. They did not even budge. Skottie and his six brothers joined Ka'el at the front of the Adonian line. "Throw down your spears."

Instantly, the spears of the Adonian Sixth Division became white snakes and rushed forward as one to intercept the crimson onslaught. As the two great masses of serpents collided, the horrific sound of high-pitched squealing and gnashing of teeth ripped through the hot, dry air as the outnumbered Adonian snakes devoured the crimson tide. Not one Omentian serpent remained. When they had finished, the white snakes returned to their masters and then to the shape of Adonian spears, lying motionless upon the blood red prairie where their warriors retrieved them once again.

Sebil screamed in terror at the sight of her serpents being consumed. She crumbled to the ground in misery. The serpents that covered her body then turned on their master and tore her to pieces. Sebil's followers turned and fled to the rear of the Omentian formation.

Next came the creature wizards, Mansen and Sanger, calling on the lion and the tannin to join the fight. In response, Toro and Weiphal stood ready to call out the graptor and the wolf in the name of the Lord. But the lion and the tannin no longer responded to their dark masters' calls.

Mansen and Sanger tried to return to the Omentian ranks, pleading with their comrades for mercy, but the Omentians were not a merciful bunch. When the Omentians saw that Mansen and Sanger had lost their powers to control the magnificent creatures, they decided the two had outlived their usefulness and unleashed the Heathian archers on them, cutting them down where they stood.

Next was Mirare. After many years of having her way with men, Mirare thought she could cast her spell over the Adonians. She strutted alluringly out onto the field. "Brave men of Adonia, lay down your weapons. There is no need to fight. I have just what you need. Lay down your weapons and come to me. I and others like me will satisfy you."

The Omentians, Heathians, and Parlantians watched in amazement as the 777 resisted her advances and invitations to lay down their arms and join her. Every man in the Omentian line would have given their life at her request.

But her advances did not deceive the Adonians. Her deceptions would not work on those who saw through the eyes of the Spirit. They saw her as she truly was, and they cringed at the thought of being with someone so ugly and vile.

"Return to the pit, harlot!" Daniel cried out. "How could we ever even consider such wickedness and sin against our God?"

Mirare covered herself and, sinking deep within her hooded cloak, returned rejected to the Omentian lines, where the men there gladly received her back, their eyes remaining covered with the scales of her deception.

And so it continued, with each of the Omentian wizards and witches taking a shot at the 777.

Finally, one last evil wizard stepped out from the Omentian horde. He approached the Adonian line with his arms stretched out to his sides, his hands palms up toward the blazing sun.

He announced to the 777. "One last chance. Surrender or die!"

As he walked toward the 777, burning flames appeared in the palms of his hands. He stopped halfway across the field of death, his arms outstretched, and his hands on fire.

At the sight of it, the sons of Truin remembered the Word taught to them as children.

For the Word is living and active.

They spoke the verses quietly and with reverence. Moesheh spoke first. "Love the LORD, all his saints! The LORD preserves the faithful, but the proud he pays back in full." Geoff said, "The LORD is my strength and my shield; my heart trusts in him, and I am helped. My heart leaps for joy and I will give thanks to him in song." Skottie added. "Because he loves me, says the LORD, I will rescue him; I will protect him, for he acknowledges my name. He will call upon me, and I will answer him; I will be with him in trouble, I will deliver him and honor him."

The wizard offered his final ultimatum. "Serve our master or burn!" The flames in his hands grew larger, now rising two feet above his palms.

The 777 stood firm, each of the men meditating on passages from the Word.

"Very well then, you have made your choice!" As he spoke the words, he brought his hands together in front of his face with a large "clap!" and the fields around the 777 burst into flame!

The Omentian line erupted. "Death to Adonia and death to Adonia's God!"

"What manner of illusion is this?" Gareth cried out as he saw the Adonian Guard's perimeter surrounded by flames.

The Adonians, understandably agitated and confused by the display, broke formation.

"Men of Adonia, hold the line!" Bigaulf commanded!

"Is this illusion or is the fire real?" Gareth knew full well the answer by the rapid rise in temperature.

The 777 watched the flames consume all the grass and bushes surrounding them. Ka'el and the sons of Truin searched for an exit strategy, but there was none.

"I have been here before," Bigaulf announced. "Do not be afraid of the flames! That which burns in your hearts is hotter! Trust in the Lord, and he will carry you through the flames!"

"It is true!" Ka'el said, "Remember, well, Adonians, what you have seen this day and what you are about to see! Tell it to your children and to your children's children. There is but one God!"

At that, Ka'el commanded the advance. "Your will be done, Oh Lord! Forward, march!"

The Adonian formation advanced as one toward the flames and toward the Omentian horde; not a man even hesitated.

The Omentians' mocking and ridicule grew silent. They did not know what to think of what they were seeing.

What army would be so foolish as to march toward the flame?

The Adonians marches while proclaiming the twenty-third psalm. "Though I walk through the valley of the shadow of death, I will fear no evil, for thou art with me!"

Then came the moment of truth; as the front echelon of the Adonian Guard's formation hit the wall of flames, the unthinkable happened — nothing.

The Omentians were stunned. "This is not possible! Why are they not consumed? How can it be that the vegetation is ablaze, but the men are not affected?" In mass, the entire Omentian army withdrew, away from the approaching Adonian Guard. Confusion and fear settled over the Omentian ranks as the Adonian Guard continued their advance through the flames. The sound of the marching formation, the beating of their drums, and the anthems they were singing to God were deafening!

The 777 emerged through the wall of flames, and everyone could clearly see that the fire had not harmed their bodies, the hair on their heads, their armor, or even their tunics.

The invaders had seen enough. They had seen their leader pulled to the depths of hell before their eyes, the best magic of their wizards vanquished by the Adonians, and now the 777 emerge from raging fires unburned. They prayed for the darkness to cover them, to conceal them from the army of Adonia. Instead, they could no longer summon the shadow that had hidden them for weeks whenever they had requested it; and a mighty sun, a sun that seemed to burn hotter than ever before, scorched their skin. The sun froze in its position directly overhead, baking the army of Omentia below it.

Panic spread through the Omentian ranks. "How can we fight an army that does not burn?"

"Adonians, halt!"

The 777, having fully emerged from the fire, now stood within archer range of the Omentian line. Only Donstup, flanked by his protectors, Jhim the Sword and his brother, Wristo, continued forward into the no-man's-land between the two armies. There Donstup, the Nomen, addressed the Omentian, Heathian, and Parlantian invaders.

"Choose this day who you will serve! Reject the dark ways, repent, and serve the Lord of the heaven and the earth."

At his pronouncement, the Omentian lines collapsed. Despite the Omentian elite's attempts to stop the massive flight of Parlantian and Heathian infantry by striking down any man that turned to run, the soldiers fleeing overwhelmed them as they dropped their weapons and headed east for the shore, choosing to live in exile rather than endure the wrath of Adonia's God.

"Serve the true God or go to be with your masters in hell!"

Approximately one-third of the horde deserted; two-thirds of the invading host remained. Led by Gorus and Kala Azar, the remaining forces were overwhelmingly Omentians that demons had completely overcome and blinded to the truth. Still, liking their chances against the smaller army of the Adonians, they stood their ground, determined to fight the 777 to the end.

Not wanting any man to perish, Donstup looked upon the Omentian army and again called for them to reject the demonic dark arts, to repent of their evil ways, and to live! But the Omentians cursed Donstup, hurling a barrage of insults at him and speaking blasphemy against the God of the Adonians.

"So be it. You have made your choice."

At Donstup's direction, they brought lamb's blood to the front line of the formation and poured it out upon the ground, dividing the field in half. The Lord's faithful on one side, those who rejected the true God on the other.

The enemy continued to jeer and ridicule the men as they carried out Donstup's instructions, attempting to cut them down with their bows, but the arrows could never find their mark.

Donstup raised his hands to the heavens and cried out to the one true God. "Oh Lord, let it be known today that you are the Lord, the only true God." Burning high over the battlefield, the sun released its fire down upon the invaders. The flesh of the blasphemers melted from their limbs as the fires of heaven completely incinerated their bodies, sending them prematurely to meet their demonic masters. The fires of heaven entirely consumed the ground on which they stood, the trees, the bushes, the sand, and all the rocks. As God removed them from the earth — forever — their screams echoed across the plain.

In that place, the fires of heaven set ablaze a great cauldron of molten fire and burning rock. It would burn perpetually, without quenching, for as long as the earth remained — a warning to all future generations that might choose to stand against the one true God.

†††

Engel and the living beings descended en masse upon Potentus and the demonic horde, striking them down and sending them back into the pit with their master.

CHAPTER 61

Puпishmeпt

†††

The charred remains of those who had refused to turn from the rebellion against the Lord covered the entire area before them. Their smoldering corpses floated on the red and orange lake of molten lava that was a moment before a battlefield. The flames still burned on many of the Omentian corpses as their flesh and bone dissolved and sank into the sea of fire. Their spirits had already departed for their eternal destination.

To the 777, the apocalyptic sight was as dreadful as it was miraculous. The dichotomy between the horrible fates these poor, lost souls had just begun and the marvelous deliverance the faithful had just received was clear to all. They realized that, but for the grace of God, they too might lie in that burning sea of death. This made them stand in awe, speechless before the awesome power, justice, and mercy of their God. They swore to tell everyone what they had seen and to never forget.

But not all the invaders died there that day. Many of those who fled God's judgment reached the eastern shore and, through various means, returned to Omentia. That land then became known to the Adonians as Dexilia, the devil's exile.

Though the many who fled gained for themselves a temporary reprieve from the fires of hell, they lived out their lives amidst famine and pestilence, never able to regain that which they had lost. They were a poor and bitter people, swearing their vengeance on the children of

Adonia. Their bitterness carried over like venom to every aspect of their lives, and it poisoned generation after generation of their offspring. In this way, their children and their children's children paid dearly for the rebellion, cowardice, and unrepentant sins of their fathers. Each generation learned and turned to the same evils that their fathers had before them.

The dragon and the lion rarely made another appearance. As rapidly as they had made their presence known in the land, they had departed, dissolving again into the shadows whence they came. Many held that they became extinct as a punishment for their part in the Great Struggle, but no one knew for sure.

The boiling cauldron continued to rage, perpetually lighting up the night sky of southern Adonia as a testament to God's power and his deliverance of the faithful. Extending its fiery reach to the nearby Kandish Mountains, the molten fire from the cauldron bled underground through great fissures below the plain. The tremendous heat of the magma separated out a strange, bluish liquid from the heavy rock in the mountains. This liquid then filled pockets of porous rock, illuminating the walls of countless subterranean caves and forming beautiful crystals. Infused with the power of the heavens, this glowing ore would someday offer more than simply beauty to the inhabitants of Adonia.

†††

In the shadows of many dimensions, a solitary figure moved clandestinely, hoping to remain unseen by the protectors that now dominated the skies overhead. His heart was as dark as the blackest of coal, and his intentions were that of the purest evil. Lucious would accompany the exiles to Dexilia, and one day he would lead them back and to the victory they so rightly deserved.

That day, he thought, the sons of Truin will join their Omentian, Heathian, and Parlantian brothers that even now are being given their reward below. The Adonians also deserve a home with my master in the pit.

Lucious faded into the darkness. As he disappeared, his whisper lingered, echoing through time. "My master will be so pleased!"

†††

The living beings filled the skies, proclaiming the glorious victory over the demons of darkness. As they did, unimaginable colors of light streaked, ballooned, and exploded across all the dimensions of the universe. Their announcement penetrated the farthest corners of the limitless expanse, echoing through space into the deepest and darkest pits of hell and leaving no doubt who it was that still sat upon the throne.

"The earth is the Lord's, and everything in it, the world and all who live in it; for he founded it upon the seas and established it upon the waters… Lift up your heads, O you gates; be lifted up, you ancient doors that the king of glory may come in. Who is this King of glory? The Lord strong and mighty, the Lord mighty in battle. Lift up your heads, O you gates; lift them up, you ancient doors that the King of glory may come in. Who is he, this king of glory? The Lord almighty — he is the King of glory."

The demons shrieked in agony as the awesome words thundered over and through them, shaking and crumbling the rock walls of the pit. The voices of the mighty ones in heaven pierced through their broken and wretched bodies, tunneling through their dark understandings, and reconvicting them of their futile struggle against those who would ultimately be victorious in the war; those who fought for the Lamb and whose victory was sure, though it had not yet happened in time.

The living beings with their many eyes scoured the skies, ensuring that all was as it was meant to be. A subtle incongruity caused a ripple in the continuum and caught their immediate attention.

"I see him."

"Should we —?"

"No, that one will serve his purpose and be dealt with at the appointed time."

CHAPTER 62

JUBILEE

✝✝✝

J oy overwhelmed Adonia!
The news spread across the land; the Lord had miraculously delivered his people from their enemies! Not only did the news answer the
thousands of prayers that the people had raised to the throne of heaven,
but it also marked the safe return of Adonia's courageous guardsmen to
their loved ones. All across the land of Adonia, the people sang praises
to God in celebration.

"Sing to the LORD a new song; sing to the LORD, all the earth.
Sing to the LORD, praise his name; proclaim his salvation day after
day. Declare his glory among the nations, his marvelous deeds among
all peoples. For great is the LORD and most worthy of praise; he is to
be feared above all gods. For all the gods of the nations are idols, but
the LORD made the heavens. Splendor and majesty are before him;
strength and glory are in his sanctuary. Ascribe to the LORD, O families of nations, ascribe to the LORD glory and strength. Ascribe to
the LORD the glory due his name; bring an offering and come into
his courts. Worship the LORD in the splendor of his holiness; tremble
before him, all the earth. Say among the nations, 'The LORD reigns.'
The world is firmly established, it cannot be moved; he will judge the
peoples with equity. Let the heavens rejoice, let the earth be glad; let the
sea resound, and all that is in it; let the fields be jubilant, and everything
in them. Then all the trees of the forest will sing for joy; they will sing

before the LORD, for he comes, he comes to judge the earth. He will judge the world in righteousness and the peoples in his truth."

†††

As the clouds of gloom and death lifted from the lands of Heath and Parlantis, so also the sadness over the loss of his brother lifted from Ka'el's heart. Early one morning, kneeling over Truin's grave beneath the great oak tree on Blue Lake, Ka'el spoke aloud to his brother. "Thank you, Truin, for never giving up on me. Thank you for continually taking your prayers of intercession to our Lord in heaven. I always thought it was I who watched over you. In the end, it was you little brother who was watching over me. Thank you for your faithfulness. I know I will see you again soon. Until that day, I will faithfully run the race that our God has set before me, eager to make up for the time that I have lost."

The sun rose over the land of Adonia, the flowers bloomed, and the birds sang their songs of joy.

And Ka'el was reborn. Somehow, over the years, he had stopped hearing the joyful songs of the birds waking him at sunrise. He had stopped feeling the warmth of the sun's rays as they caressed the golden grains of wheat, gently waving in the cool evening breeze. He had stopped appreciating the glorious beauty that surrounded him in this wonderful land, and he had stopped thanking God for his mercy and all of his blessings.

In a heartbeat, that all changed. Ka'el now lived every moment of his life in awe of God! Psalm 118 became his anthem, his message to everyone he met. He proclaimed it, and he lived it for the rest of his days.

"Give thanks to the Lord, for he is good; his love endures forever... In my anguish I cried to the Lord, and he answered by setting me free. The Lord is with me; I will not be afraid. What can man do to me? The Lord is with me; he is my helper. I will look in triumph on my enemies. It is better to take refuge in the Lord than to trust in man. It is better to take refuge in the Lord than to trust in princes. All the nations surrounded me,

501

2

but in the name of the Lord, I cut them off. They surrounded me on every side, but in the name of the Lord I cut them off. They swarmed about me like bees, but they died out as quickly as burning thorns; in the name of the Lord I cut them off. I was pushed back and about to fall, but the Lord helped me. The Lord is my strength and my song; he has become my salvation. Shouts of joy and victory resound in the tents of the righteous; The Lord's right hand has done mighty things! I will not die, but live, and will proclaim what the Lord has done... The stone the builders rejected has become the capstone; the Lord has done this, and it is marvelous in our eyes. This is the day the Lord has made; let us rejoice and be glad in it. The Lord is God, and he has made his light shine upon us. With boughs in hand, join in the festal procession up to the horns of the altar. You are my God, and I will give you thanks; you are my God, and I will exalt you. Give thanks to the Lord, for he is good; his love endures forever."

CHAPTER 63

BIRTH OF THE REPUBLIC

†††

I n a quick response to the need for common defense, the people of the new republic, formed during war, hastily drafted an agreement to unite the provinces under one flag. The first major event of the new republic was a state funeral for Truin, a genuine hero of Adonia. The people of Adonia traveled to Aanot in massive numbers from across the land to pay tribute to Truin, son of Abner.

All the Adonian Guard, ten divisions, otherwise known as the 777, assembled in military formation to give honor to Truin. The First, Second, and Third Divisions of Aanot; Fourth Division of Delvia; Fifth Division of Chastain; Sixth Division of Kandish; Seventh Division of Plattos; Mighty Eighth Division of Tanshire; Ninth Division of Tobar; and the Tenth Division of Rothing, all dressed out in their newly established Adonian uniforms. They flew their newly established colors of jasper, sapphire, chalcedony, emerald, sardonyx, carnelian, beryl, topaz, jacinth, and amethyst, rendering full military honors to the one who became known as the "Father of the Provinces," and the "Father of Adonia."

The throng of thousands stood as Christina read a message of hope and promise from the book of Isaiah, chapter 25.

"On this mountain, the LORD Almighty will prepare a feast of rich food for all peoples, a banquet of aged wine — the best of meats and the finest of wines. On this mountain he will destroy the shroud that

503

enfolds all peoples, the sheet that covers all nations; he will swallow up death forever.

"The Sovereign LORD will wipe away the tears from all faces; he will remove the disgrace of his people from all the earth. The LORD has spoken.

"In that day they will say, 'Surely this is our God; we trusted in him, and he saved us. This is the LORD, we trusted in him; let us rejoice and be glad in his salvation.'"

At Jonn's command, the Adonian Guard presented arms, offering their final salute to their fallen commander, and Kory read the words Toro had written for Truin's funeral. They spoke tenderly of the love Truin and Christina had shared.

"This day in battle a warrior falls and to the sky his Maker calls. As from his body his spirit flows, he leaves behind here all he knows. His thoughts then turned to his one true love as he looks down now from high above, upon the corpse lying in the sand and the wedding band upon its hand. As to Heaven his soul soared, this fallen warrior to his Lord, one last wish this man was given to touch once more his wife yet living. A soft breeze blew in from the plains and to the home came peaceful rains. A gentle mist caressed her face and on her lips left but a trace. As she gazed on the setting sun, at that moment knowing what was done, quietly to her knees she fell for she had felt his last farewell."

Khory read the lines of the salute, and a breeze blew in from the southern plains, gently flowing over the solemn assembly in the twilight of a setting sun and softly caressing Christina's dark veil, causing it to lightly flutter. Lost on no one in attendance and nothing short of a gift from heaven, Truin's last goodbye was witnessed by all in attendance that day. Behind the veil, Christina's tears flowed freely.

As they moved Truin's coffin to his favorite place, below the great oak overlooking Blue Lake, Melkione led the gathering in a song of prayer for their new home.

"God bless our native land; firm may she ever stand, through storm and night: when the wild tempests rave, ruler of wind and wave, do

THE FAITHFUL

thou our country save by thy great might. For her, our prayers shall rise to God above the skies; on him we wait; thou who art ever nigh, guarding with watchful eye, to thee aloud we cry, God save the state!"

As they sang the hymn, archers from all the Adonian Guard divisions simultaneously launched seven volleys of flaming arrows into the air over Blue Lake. Not an eye was dry. They would all feel the absence of Truin.

††††

Ka'el stood alone in the backyard of Truin and Christina's home — now only Christina's home. It had been a month since the funeral, and he visited Christina to see how she was doing.

While Ka'el waited for Christina to return, he sat on the large oak bench that overlooked the apple orchard and Blue Lake. He relaxed and took in the beauty all around him. After gazing on the lake, the rolling hills, the abundant wild flowers, and the mountains of Chastain in the distance, his eyes turned to his immediate surroundings, and he noticed the etching on the top of the bench on which he sat. He looked closer and read the words carved there. He realized it was a poem. It read:

Constantly under attack, the world you choose to live, your surroundings —

So hard to stay on track, returning what they give, so confounding —
It should be easier than this. I struggle with control —
I fall short so many times each day —
It weighs heavily on my soul.

Relying on my strengths, and on my own authority, I fail —
Alone, I try strenuously to remain free, to no avail —
My effort is in vain, I do not possess the skill —
Whereby with simple flesh and blood, to defend against their will.

505

One critical oversight, one fatal flaw to my endeavor —
They more than match my might, their strength beyond my measure —
Alone, I'll defeat them never; they are not as they appear, in this
world of illusion —
But rather, they are a united host, intent on my destruction.

They are the servants of the enemy, defenders of his lies, of all
depraved —
Look closely and you'll see, their devious methods try to attack
the saved —
They do all that they can, in allegiance to their condemned king —
To deny the heavenly plan, and to the Saints distraction, bring.

There is a way that's sure to be victorious in this fight,
walking tall —
A way we can endure, remaining in the light, and answering
the call —
Equipped with the armor of God, led by the sword of the Spirit —
On the demons, the Saints will tread, their numbers we
will attrite.

So do not be deceived into thinking there is no battle, that
all is well —
While those who believe the lies are gathered like cattle, to the
eternal slaughter of hell —
It is our call to arms, in prayer and supplication —
To lead them from all harm, to tell them of salvation.
A host of heavenly warriors, in service to their Lord, will aid in
this endeavor —
He promises a heavenly place that is yours, and we are
His forever —
There all the Saints will be blessed, salvation through the blood of
the lamb —

Singing praises to God in the highest — Victory eternal to the
great "I Am"

Tears filled Ka'el's eyes as he read the words of the poem and realized the tremendously challenging road his brother had walked in his
life. For so long, Ka'el could only see his own life and his own troubles;
he didn't truly see what his brother was going through.

Truin had always seemed to be so together and so in command.
Truin made it look like his walk in the light had always been easy. But
the words of this poem told a fuller story. They told of the tremendous
conflict and spiritual attack Truin had to overcome daily. Truin's physical challenges had been quite formidable, but his spiritual struggle to
stay on the narrow path had also been quite challenging. He had just
kept it well hidden.

Aware of his own weaknesses, he had never allowed pride to take
hold or arrogance to gain a grip. Truin had always trusted in God to
provide him with the physical and spiritual strength he needed for his
daily journey through life. The deceitfulness of worldly things had
never clouded over his clarity of spiritual vision. His focus in life had
remained fixed on serving his God and his fellow man; this drove his
action in every aspect of his life. His peace and hope had rested solely
on the promises of God, and because of his unwavering faith, he had
left behind a beautiful legacy.

Ka'el could not take his eyes off of the bench. His brother's hand
had eternally changed the bench, like so many of the lives Truin had
touched. The bench and the poem upon it now truly served as a timeless tribute to Truin's purpose, his struggle, his faith, and his victory.

A smiled crossed Ka'el's face as he slowly ran his fingers over the
precious words his brother had left behind; words of instruction, faith,
and truth. In life and in the face of death, Truin had held nothing of
himself back. Selfless love had directed his daily path and selfless love
had guided his last act. He had lived his life as a servant to others, and

there was no doubt in Ka'el's mind that Truin was now resting in the hands of God.

"Well done, little brother, well done."

†††

Within a month, Adonia's elected representatives, or "Council of the Ten Provinces" met together at Castle Armon to establish more formal covenants between the provinces regarding trade, diplomatic dealings with foreign dignitaries, and provisions for the common defense.

The council chose Gladsel to be their leader or their "First." Guided by an earnest love for God and a strong faith, Gladsel opened the first council of the new republic with prayer.

"Almighty God of all that has been, all that is, and all that will ever be, we, the chosen members of this council, citizens of this new republic, humbly bow before your throne on this truly historic day.

"Today, a new republic is born in the land. It is a republic born out of trial and testing; a republic birthed in freedom and equality for all its inhabitants; but most of all, a republic of your children, dedicated to the preservation of the truth, the safeguarding of your Word, and the cultivation of the faith that you have in your infinite mercy so graciously given to us.

"We praise you for all that you are; your infinite wisdom and power; saving us from our enemy; delivering our land from the evil ones that sought to devour it; and preserving the truth for the generations of faithful believers to come.

"We reverently bow before you this day as your humble servants. Please give us the strength to always follow your precepts; choosing the path of righteousness over the paths of pleasure, riches, or fame. Grant us the wisdom to serve the Republic and its citizens well. Bless us with a selfless love for you, for each other, and for that which you have called us. Help us gladly give our lives to doing what we know to be right and true.

"Dispel any arrogance or pride from our being before it can ever wrap its destructive tentacles around our minds and use us for its bidding. Guide our minds day and night that we stay close to you in everything we do; close in thought, word, and deed. Deliver us from the evil that lurks behind every door and within every shadow, stalking those who love you and waiting to take advantage of any complacency. Help us always to stay vigilant; the evil one and his followers never sleep. We are nothing without you, Oh God. We cannot be happy, cannot be prosperous, and cannot remain free without you. Without you, we will surely fall.

"Almighty and loving Father, please keep us always in your care. Never let us wander from you. Never let us put our trust in anything or anyone other than you and you alone. And if we ever wander from you, foolishly trusting in any of the created things instead of you, the Creator; strip us of your blessings and all the false idols of our fancy; in so doing, bring us back to you.

"You are our God; we are yours and yours alone. Please equip us to do the work you have prepared for us to do. Keep us faithful. Amen."

And all the men of the council echoed the word together. "Amen."

As Gladsel's first official act, he recommended they name the newly formed republic, the Republic of Truinean — in honor of Truin, the father of the republic. All the provinces unanimously supported the suggestion, and from that day forward, Adonia became known as Truinean.

The Council of Truinean vowed to the last man to never forget the one, true God; to never forget who had delivered them from their enemies and established their new home in this beautiful land. Gladsel, an honest and principled man, led the council with honor and wisdom for many years, and under his watchful eye, the council held true to their vow.

Over time, the exact when or why is unknown, the people changed the name of their land to Trinian. Anchored in God's commands; protected and blessed by their Creator, Preserver, and Keeper; the Republic of Trinian prospered. It became a great beacon in the world for all who loved freedom, truth, and justice. Known throughout the world for its love and charity, the Trinians lived lives of faith and community, gladly sharing all that they had with one another.

Christina lived out the rest of her days without taking another for a husband. Death could not break the bond that she and Truin had shared. Though her heart often yearned for the warmth of her husband's touch, her sons and their families did much to fill the void that Truin's absence had created in her life; they took good care of her. There was never a day when Christina laid her head down to sleep where she did not consider herself blessed and loved.

Toro and Weiphal became famous for their legendary adventures, settling the uncharted lands of southern Trinian. Their travels could fill many books.

The Valley of Fire, where God had poured out his wrath from the heavens on the evil ones, continued to burn incessantly, illuminating the night sky for over fifty miles in all directions. It became known throughout the land as the Great Cauldron.

The Dragon-kind disappeared from the land. Many people widely believed that extinction was their punishment for having served the evil ones. It didn't take long before the inhabitants of Adonia forgot about the dragons, even claiming they had never existed. It was usually about that time that some unsuspecting farmer or miner would dig up a fossil or skeleton of one of the beasts, and the brightest of Adonia would insist the skeletons were proof of beasts that lived many millennia earlier. The faithful, however, knew better than to follow the fallible folly of their fellows and continued to trust in God's Word for truth.

The wolves moved freely throughout the land. Never forgetting the part the wolves had played in the Great Struggle, men welcomed the wolves onto their lands and even into their homes. Domesticated over time, they became pets, playing a permanent role as guardian and earning the title of man's best friend.

In contrast, much smaller remnants of the lion eventually appeared in the land; they were nothing like their former cousins. People did not revere these cats, as they became commonly known, the way they revered wolves, since there was not even one claim they had ever saved a human or even attempted to help one. In addition, no one ever claimed that they were man's best friend. Seldom trusted, they cohabitated with human families as a curiosity only.

✝✝✝

Abner and Eve sat together on a bench under the giant oak tree on the knoll overlooking Blue Lake. They had come to see their son. They sat on the love seat Truin had made for them years earlier. At Abner's request, Ka'el had placed it next to Truin's grave; so Abner and Eve could feel close to Truin on sunny, summer days; days when they could sit and visit — dream and reminisce of days gone by.

After being lost for so long, Ka'el was finally home. Their son, Truin, faithful in his walk all the days of his life, had been called to his eternal home.

They sat and spoke of their son, reminding each other of the many happy memories of him they shared. Eve pulled an old piece of parchment from her pocket. It contained a poem that Truin had given to Abner on Truin's tenth birthday. Abner had cherished the poem ever since. Tears formed in their eyes as she read the poem aloud.

To a stranger, it would look like they were mourning their son's death. Perhaps they were a little. It was so hard to let Truin go; they missed him so much!

But most of all, they were remembering; remembering all the love Truin had given to his family, friends, and even strangers he had encountered along his walk. Truin had lived his life well. He had lived his life fully. He had lived his life faithfully. And though his time had ended before Evelin was ready to say goodbye, as certainly any mother would say of a lost son, she was sure through the eyes of faith that her baby boy was now resting in the Lord's hands and that she would soon see him again in their eternal home; a place that knew no goodbyes.

Peace settled over her heart, mind, and spirit as the Father's heavenly host ministered to her.

They sat together in the shade and listened to the sounds of the birds singing their sweet melodies high above them in the branches of the giant oak. Basking in the day's warmth and the memories of their son, they knew no worries, only peace.

CHAPTER 64

✝wiLiGH✝

✝✝✝

A bner sat alone beneath the multicolored trees that grew straight and tall behind the cottage where he and Evelin had spent the fall of their lives. The sun was setting, and it mirrored the reds and oranges of the leaves falling from the surrounding trees.

Abner reached into his coat pocket. His old and tired hand removed a small object wrapped carefully in a soft cloth. He cupped it in his hands before unwrapping it. The setting sun's rays glinted off the smooth, glass face of the timepiece as the beauty of it, once again, captured Abner's full attention.

The timepiece was circular and primarily consisted of polished gold. The finest clockmakers in the land had meticulously crafted the internal mechanisms of the timepiece, and it was truly a marvel in its time. Beneath the glass face of the timepiece were eight stones — seven brilliant stones representing the seven sons of Truin and a diamond at the twelve o'clock position representing Truin, himself. Each of the stones represented the richness of a different province of Truinean. On the back of the timepiece, the watchmaker etched the name of each of Truin's sons opposite the stone from his respective province.

Truin had treasured the timepiece. His sons had given it to him many years earlier, before the Great Struggle. He had carried it with him everywhere. It was a symbol of their unity, a symbol of their family, and a symbol of their love.

Abner remembered the day Christina showed up at the cottage with the news of Truin's death; he remembered it like it was yesterday. He could still see the tears rolling down her cheeks as she lowered her gaze to her fragile and shaking hand, slowly opening a cloth to reveal the orphaned timepiece. She didn't need to say the words. Abner knew Truin would never have parted with the keepsake, not while he was still breathing.

The timepiece had stayed with Abner ever since that day. He had carried it with him everywhere. It was a way of being close to Truin and close to his grandsons. It was a symbol of their unity, a symbol of their family, and a symbol of their love.

Abner ran his fingers over the smooth face of the timepiece, and his eyes began to tear up.

So many happy memories.

Evelin joined him in the twilight and wrapped her arms around him, consoling him with her presence. Together, they dreamed of days past and days to come when they would all be together again.

"I can't wait till we see him again. I can't wait until we are home."

"Soon, soon enough, it will be so, my love, but not yet. Come in now, I have a warm fire going, and your favorite pork-pot stew should be about ready. Come."

Together, they hobbled up the stone path to the open door of their small cottage. The warm rays of golden candlelight shone warmly from the entrance, welcoming them and guiding them through the darkness to the safety of their home.

As they snuggled in their big, cozy chair in front of the fire, Abner thanked God for his wife. Where would he have been without her love? They had been through so much together, and she had always been faithful. Through her love, Abner saw a glimpse of God, their Father in heaven. She exemplified his caring, his love, and his faithfulness.

Thank you, Lord.

†††

The days passed, and Evelin was called home first.

Three days after burying his wife on the small hill with the large, oak tree that overlooked Blue Lake, Abner, now an old man, kneeled in the tall grass of the mountainside hill that overlooked his modest countryside home. It was a moonless night, and he was alone beneath the stars.

As he did most nights, he dreamed of his wife, his children, and the countless happy memories God had blessed him with over the many years of his life.

Despite the temptation to go down the hallway of his mind and open the door to the dark room of fear, sadness, and despair that had plagued him so often in his early life; he closed and locked the door to that dark room forever.

Abner thanked God for his faithfulness. God had been faithful to him all the days of his life. As he rested peacefully on the soft grass below the stars, gazing into the night sky in awe and wonder, Abner marveled at how the Lord had kept his promises and worked his omniscient purpose throughout his life. *"You, Oh Lord, are faithful."*

Abner thought of his life:
The journey begins — in tears,
Cold and naked — fear,
Then warmth and love rescue me and keep me safe.

On my own — alone again,
Must make my own way — fear,
I find her — warmth and love.

Their journey begins — in tears,
Cold and naked,
They are given to us — our greatest blessings.
We give them warmth and love,
Protect them.

A lifetime past — memories,
She is now gone — alone,
Yet not alone.

It is my time now,
Warmth and love,
Home.

Abner pondered the words of the 73rd psalm, as he had so many times before in his life. "Yet I am always with you; you hold me by my right hand. You guide me with your counsel, and afterward you will take me into glory. Whom have I in heaven but you? And earth has nothing I desire besides you. My flesh and my heart may fail, but God is the strength of my heart and my portion forever."

A little bird with a yellow belly landed above Abner on a branch of the old oak tree. It sang a soft, gentle song as Abner closed his eyes. Below the night sky, the boy of one hundred and ten years smiled. Heaven smiled with him and welcomed him — home.

CHAPTER 65

THE TRUTH KEEPERS

†††

As Trinian developed, it became clear that the preservation of its history was necessary. So they formed a Scribe Clan to protect the truth and pass it from generation to generation.

The scribes were especially meticulous, excessively careful to preserve the truth of Trinian history in the face of each generation's foolish and sometimes malicious attempts to rewrite it. God, through the truth keepers, simply did not allow the truth to be lost.

Thus is the lineage of one such scribe named Norman, the son of Geoff. Geoff and Annette had a son and named him Norman. Norman and Rosemary had a son and named him Gaylord. Gaylord and Soccorro had a son and named him Melhvin. Melhvin and Margie had a son and named him Eughene. Eughene and Laurah had a son and named him Herman. Herman and Mildred had a son and named him Pahl. Pahl and Shirley had a son and named him Wilhelm. Wilhelm and Alice had a son and named him Roy. Roy and Judith had a son and named him Veteris.

CHAPTER 66

ALL ABOARD

†††

"Thus is the history of our land; the time of Abner, Truin, and the sons of Truin; or sons of Trinian, as they are now known. It did not unfold the way any would have expected it to unfold; but then the thoughts of God are not the thoughts of men.

"There is so much more to God than what He has told us in his Word, so much more than we can ever fathom. Still, too often we try to put God in a box; in a box that our puny minds can imagine.

"Do not make this mistake, my children. Never doubt what the Lord can do. Never shackle your God with the limitations of your human thoughts, dreams, or imaginations. Our God is an awesome God!"

They all shook their heads in acknowledgement.

"We have quite the advantage, don't we? We have the history of God's incredible plan of salvation recorded for us, whereas our ancestors did not. They faithfully looked forward to the coming of the promised Savior, but we can look back on history and take comfort in the fulfillment of God's promise.

"Of course, as you all know, our Savior has come, our deliverer has saved us from the curse of sin, and we can rest in the sureness of God's forgiveness."

They nodded in agreement and smiled.

"Much more than a promise, we now know our Savior's name; Jesus, God's only Son."

One of the tiniest toddlers spoke. "Jesus loves me."

"That is right. He loves all of us very much, and he has prepared a place for us in his heavenly home. We know this by faith, and what is faith?"

"Now faith is being sure of what we hope for and certain of what we do not see. This is what the ancients were commended for," they all replied together.

"That is right, children," Veteris said, smiling lovingly as he looked into each of their childish faces. Seeing the seeds of faith budding right before his eyes, he continued. "The Apostle Paul told us that in his letter to the Hebrews."

"It certainly will be wonderful at the end of our journey, when we can at last have rest and peace in our eternal home. How wonderful that will be."

Veteris gazed into the distance as he spoke the words and, through the eyes of faith, saw his eternal home in the distance. His voice had a certain peace about it as his eyes slowly closed. A soft smile formed on his face, and his head slowly sank to his chest.

Most of the children thought he had nodded off again, as it was customary for him to do about this time of the day. The youngest of the children scrambled off to play games, and most of the older children began a walk along the lake, talking quietly with each other.

It wasn't until hours later, as the sun set in a portrait of glorious colors far off on the horizon, that they discovered the old man had left this world behind for one much better. After he had passed Trinian history on to the children of the future, Veteris had drifted off, still leaning against his time-tested friend, the old oak tree which overlooked Blue Lake and the ancient cemetery of his ancestors.

So began Veteris' long voyage to another time and another place, a place where he would once again join the friends and loved ones that had left him behind so many years earlier.

The young men ran back to the hill where Veteris peacefully rested. They carefully approached and reverently bowed their heads. They realized they would never again see the old man's eyes burn intensely as he told them the history of their land. The young woman with them cried.

One young man, named Jonnas, put his arm around the young woman, Tessia, and consoled her. "Do not cry for him, Tessia. He is walking with the Master now, and he is very happy. He is home."

"I know, but I will miss him so much."

Jonnas' voice cracked. "We all will. But we will see him again someday, someday when we are there."

"Yes, someday, when we are there."

At that, they all realized that the old man whom they had taken for granted for so many years was now gone, and with him, a great treasure of wisdom. They would all miss him very much.

"I guess you never really realize how special people are until they are gone," Tessia offered as she turned and began down Outlook Hill, still trying to stem the flow of tears. "Even in his passing, he shared with us this one, last, pearl of wisdom."

"We will never forget Veteris or his words. They will burn in our hearts forever." He turned and somberly followed Tessia down the hill.

The sun sank in a rainbow of colors on the horizon as a sweet little girl with freckles and a turned-up nose drew close to the old man to say her last goodbyes. The little girl was Jonas' little sister. Her name was Ka'elee, named after her great ancestor, Ka'el.

As she gave Veteris the soft hug she always gave him at the end of the day, she noticed he was cradling something in his hands. She looked closer. His rough, chilly hands still held a golden timepiece on a long, golden chain. It had a brilliant diamond at the top of its face and seven other beautiful stones of various colors, arranged in a circular pattern around the outside of the face. Engraved on the back of the timepiece opposite each of the stones was the name of one of the seven sons of Truin. She smiled widely when she saw it.

She softly tugged the old man's beard one last time, and whispered in his ear, "Foggy, winter nights and early morning dreams."

Then she lovingly kissed his cheek, and with the gold chain of the timepiece swinging from her pocket, she ran to catch up with Jonnas, who was waiting for her at the bottom of the hill.

As the sun set over the clear, still waters of Blue Lake, the ancient and majestic oak tree sat alone at the top of Outlook Hill, guarding the ancient stones which still marked the resting place of Trinian ancestors and welcoming home a dear, old friend that now slept peacefully below its strong, protective branches. They faded together into the night.

Veteris' time on earth passed, and he was no more.

But he was not gone.

CHAPTER 67

The Line of Moesheh of Rothing

†††

T hus is the lineage of Moesheh, the first Governor of Rothing. Moesheh and Sandrah had a son and named him Gabe. Gabe and Laura had a son and named him Morris. Morris and Rose had a son and named him Charles. Charles and Dorthy had a son and named him Arnold. Arnold and Helen had a son and named him Vernon. Vernon and Dorissa had a son and named him Earl. Earl and Pearl had a son and named him Russell. Russel and Ruthie had a son and named Adrian. Adrian and Alicea had a son and named him Johon. Johon and Mary had a son and named him Gordohn. Gordohn and Juneth had a son and named him Rhobert. Rhobert and Joanneh had a son and named him Clayton. Clayton and Mabella had a son and named him William. William and Helda had a son and named him Henry. Henry and Lene had a son and named him Henry II. Henry II and Arlene had a son and named him Teroth. Teroth married Therisa, and they had two sons, Tanner and Thomas.

CHAPTER 68

PROTECTED

†††

A millennium had passed since the Lord had freed Adonia from the powers of darkness. In that millennium, the Republic of Trinian had grown and prospered. But the Republic lost its way, and Dexilia planned its vengeance.

Still, the new Republic of Trinian continued to thrive, for the Lord was slow to anger. Young men and women entered marriage and embarked on starting their own families. One such couple, Jonnas, from the line of Ka'el, and his wife, Tessia, from the line Elin, were married and moved to Delvia. They settled down, built a homestead, and had a son. They named their son, Louis.

One day, while Louis was out playing in the fields, a scouting party of Dexilians, under the command of a youthful scoundrel named Scimitar, came ashore near his family's farm. Jonnas and Tessia accidentally stumbled upon the intruders, and though Jonnas put up a fierce fight, the evil band of Dexilians took both him and Tessia captive to preserve the secrecy of their reconnaissance mission. Jonnas and Tess never told their captors that they had a son.

Though they had saved their son's life that day, Louis would never know it. There had been no chance for his parents to say goodbye, and he would never see them again. Their sudden disappearance would haunt Louis all the days of his life.

Louis being spared that day was not an accident. God had a plan for Louis, and God was faithful.

To be continued…

Note: Watch for *Forever* and the second edition of *Stand (2005)* to be released 2024.

The Faithful Stand Forever

İNDEX OF NAMES
(THE FAİTHFUL)

Achilles (pain): Fighting man.

Adonia (the Lord is my God); The land the Lord gave to Abner.

Abner (believer in truth, father of light): Farmer in Omentia, who brings his family across the Sea to Adonia; Father of Truin, Ka'el, and Elin; Husband of Evelin.

Aanot (light): Capital of Adonia.

Abrahm (illustrious father): Youngest son of Bigaulf.

Adonia (God is my Lord): Land to the West that remains faithful to the true God. It becomes the Republic of Trinian.

Ahnettia (grace): Wife of Geoff and Mother of Samuell.

Anak (necklace): Hanjian's second in command; leader of the Anakim; best of the Dark Knights.

Andru (man): Oldest son of Bigaulf.

Anders (man): Abner's father.

Armon (castle): Fortress in Aanot, Chastain.

Arrogante (arrogance): The demon of pride.

Ashwin (star, spear): Stallion.

Atlantia (mighty opponent): Seaport on the west coast of Omentia.

Austinian (great): One of Weiphal's exploring party.

Baldrus (prince): Heathian Commander.

Balok: (owner of the field): Murderer.

Barbille (mysterious): Missionary to Christina's village as a child; wife of Juddin.

Benhjami (son of the right hand): Advisor to Daniel.

Bestia (beast): A demon of the beasts.

Bigaulf (counsel): Son of Truin.

Black Bart: (from the farm): One of The Brothers of a Lion.

Buke: (wise, old person): Faithful friend of Toro; one searcher who rescued Toro in the Strange Lands.

Chase: (hunt): One of Weiphal's exploring party.

Chastain: (pure): The mountainous land in northern Adonia.

Christina: (anointed): Wife of Truin; mother of Truin's seven sons.

Colin: (young creature): Parlantian foot-soldier.

Colera: (anger): The demon of anger.

Crastis the Cruel: (cruel): Ometian Fleet Commander.

Culpa: (guilt): The demon of guilt.

Cusintomas: (twin): Son of Truin. Nickname: Surge.

Daniel: (God is my judge): Son of Truin.

Dark Sea: Sea between Adonia and Omentia.

Daev: (beloved): Brother of Khory (both "smiths.").

Daytona: (speedy): An independently minded lion.

Delvia: (dig): Peninsula on the northeastern corner of Adonia where Abner and family came ashore; known for its fertile lands.

Devon: (poet): Lifelong friend of Samuell.

Dexilia: The devil's exile.

Disperato: (hopelessness): The demon of hopelessness.

Doldrus: (sadness): The demon of sadness and depression.

Donstup: (Respect) Man of God; one of the Nomen.

Drakon: (serpent): The leader of the dragon.

Dr. Phil: (brotherly Love): Abner's family doctor.

Dubitare: (doubt): The demon of doubt.

Elin: (light): Daughter of Abner and Evelin; sister of Truin and Ka'el; wife of Khory.

Engel: (messenger): Angel of the Light.

Evelin: (life-giving): Wife of Abner; mother of Truin, Ka'el, and Elin.

Farkus: (wolf): Commander of the Wolves.

Fractos (division): The demon of division.

Gareth: (spear): Son of Truin.

Geoff: (peace of God): Son of Truin.

Ghurgania: (strange chief): Part of the Strange Lands explored by Weiphal; where K-7 was mined.

Gina: (queen): Wife of Captain PJ.

Gladsel: (glad soul): Brother of Jonn; Ambassador of Adonia; first leader of the Republic of Trinian.

Glutonus: (hunger): Demon of the stomach, hunger, and gluttony.

Gorus: Heathian Commander in charge of Tanshire Campaign.

Grahmulan: (home): Adonian sentry.

Granus: The Heathian god of the harvest.

Graptor: (giant raptor): The Giant Raptor, ancient relative of the orn; also known as gorn or great orn.

Gwair: (grass): Capital of Heath.

Hanjian: (traitor): Commander of the Dark Knights.

Haught: (pride): Demon of pride.

Heath: (wasteland): Land far north of Adonia where Christina was born.

Hussein: (good-looking): Omentian; disciple of Karyan; agent of deception, magic, and evil.

Isaak: (laughing one): Son of Jonn.

Jacobin: (held by the heel): Lieutenant of the Sixth Division.

Jhim the Sword: (substitute): Man of God.

Jonn: (God is merciful): Friend and advisor to Truin; expert in trade.

Jonnas: (dove): Husband of Tessia and father of Louis.

Joust: (to engage): Commander of the Adonian Watch.

Juddin: (praised): Missionary to Christina's village as a child; husband of Barbille.

Kandish: (kan-like): Land of rolling hills, valleys, and caves to the east and southeast of Adonia; known for the kan found there.

Ka'el: (mighty warrior): Firstborn son of Abner; older brother of Truin.

Ka'elee: (pure): Descendent of Ka'el; cute little girl with freckles and a turned-up nose.

Kala Azar: (black fever): Lieutenant of Karyan.

Karyan: (the dark one): Leader of the fallen Omentians; previously Pete.

Kaye: (pure): Oldest daughter of Elin.

Kharin: (pure): Wife of Daniel.

Kieron: (dark): Heathian farmer and citizen.

Koldas Ice: (island): Another name for Gareth.

Khory: (spiritual): Truin's most trusted and faithful friend; husband of Elin.

Khorygen: (K-7): Flammable, tar-like mixture of organic chemical compounds found in the Strange Lands.

Krieg: (war): Karyan's Lair.

Kristof: (Christ bearer): Friend and advisor of Truin.

La Gina: (the queen): Captain PJ's ship.

Land's End: (end of land): Part of the Strange Lands in the south of Adonia.

Lorih: (crowned with laurel): wife of Skottie.

Louis: (famous warrior): Son of Jonnas and Tessia.

Lucious: (light): Demon, whose story is another day.

Mansen: Omentian; disciple of Karyan; agent of deception, magic, and evil.

Margerie: (pearl): Wife of Melkione.

Marilu: (star of the sea): Faithful prayer warrior.

Mathias: Chastainian Signal Corps soldier. Call sign: Caveman.

Mattus: (gift of God): Adonian Sentry.

McBob: (God is my judge): One of "The Brothers of a Lion."

Mellon: (small pleasant one): Deputy Commander of the Adonian Fleet.

Metus: (fear): The demon of fear.

Melkione: Assistant to Noa; trainer of Adonian Army.

Mikole: (one who resembles God): Captain of the Sirenian and Captain PJ's partner.

Mirare: (to appear, to seem): Omentian witch of deception.

Mitch: (who is like God): One of Weiphal's exploring party.

Moesheh: (drawn out): Son of Truin.

Mobjack Mound: (desolate wasteland): Center of the Great Desert of Tanshire.

Molech (king): The demon that demanded human sacrifice.

Noa (Noah): A wise and talented mentor to Truin's sons.

Nomen: Man (men) of God.

Obaminus: (hate): The demon of hate.

Omentia: (prophesy): Land of the East that falls to darkness and unbelief.

Ormand: (serpent): Commander of Parlantian invading force.

Orn: (Eagle): Large eagle.

Parlantis: (son of the plow): Land south of Omentia.

Pamela: (all honey): Mikole's wife.

Pax: (peace): Capital of Plattos.

PJ: (Peter Joseph): Short for Papa John; Captain of the La Gina.

Pecunius: (wealth): The demon of materialism.

Pferd: (horse): Capital of Parlantis.

Phillip: (lover of horses): Parlantian doctor who brings word of Parlantis' fate.

Plattos: (flat): The flatland region of Adonia.

Potentus: (powerful): Demon of power.

Republic of Trinian: Land of Adonia following the Great Struggle; federation of the provincial states of Adonia.

Reynold: (ruler with counsel): Faithful man in Omentia.

Robinelle: (bright fame): Jonn's wife.

Rothing: (red pasture): The southwestern region of Adonia known for its red pastures.

Sandrah: (defending men): Wife of Moesheh.

Salli: (princess): Youngest daughter of Elin; wife to Willieim.

Samuell: (his name is God): Son of Geoff.

Sanger: Omentian; disciple of Karyan; agent of deception, magic, and evil.

Satan: (adversary or enemy): The archangel cast from heaven for leading the revolt of the angels. He disguises himself as an angel of light. Also known as the Devil (liar or slanderer); the father of lies; Abaddon or Apollyon (the destroyer): Beelzebub (lord of the flies); Belial (worthlessness); murderer; red dragon; ancient serpent; prince of this world; ruler of the kingdom of the air; evil one; tempter; roaring lion; and god of this age.

Scum: (worthless): The demon of uselessness.

Scire (knowledge): The demon of human knowledge and logical deception.

Sebil: (female prophet): Serpent queen; killer of babies.

Serendopolus: (king of titans): Part of the Strange Lands explored by Toro.

Sifu Rodriguez: (Edible): Master of martial arts in Glen of Braden.

Sir Adrian the Bold: (rich): One of Castle Armon's heavy infantry commanders.

Sir Briean the Brave: (noble): Commander of the Parlantian Guard.

Sirenian: (fair charmer): Captain Mikole's ship.

Skottie: (tattoo): Son of Truin.

Smilodon: (knife-tooth): Alpha Commander of the lions.

Soluson: (alone): The demon of loneliness.

Spencer: (steward): Faithful sailor aboard the La Gina.

Susanni: (lily): Faithful prayer warrior.

Tala: (the goddess of stars): Wife of Ka'el.

Talon: (claw): Leader of the orn.

Tannin: (dragon): The ancient dragons of the Strange Lands.

Tanshire (tan horse): The northwestern region of Adonia known for its wild, tan horses.

Tessia (loved by God): Wife of Jonnas; Mother of Louis.

Terrus (anxiety): The demon of anxiety.

The Susanna (Lily): Captain Mellon's ship.

Thomar (twin): Adonian Sentry.

Thor (thunder): Abner and Evelin's sheepdog.

Toro (bull): First son of Ka'el.

Travish (to cross over): Cusintomas' second in command.

Truin (truth): Trin; Second born of Abner; faithful to God.

Trinian/Truinean: The land of the descendants of Truin; Adonia's new name.

Valley of Brann: The Valley of Fire.

Veteris (truth): Truth speaker; carrier of the light.

Viscere (visual): The demon of lust and visual illusion.

Weiphal (mighty brother): Second son of Ka'el.

Wendal (wanderer): Heathian force commander.

Wezen (creature): Giant, multi-legged sea creature.

Willieim (protection): Apprentice of the Brothers of a Lion; husband of Salli.

Wristo: (Christ bearer): Man of God.

Xenon: (Stranger): Fighting man.

POEMS OF ADONİA

Beauty (Abner's Song for Evelin)

I watch her from the window; she's working in the yard,
I love her so very much it hurts, but telling her can be so hard.
We rarely seem to really touch; so many things get in the way,
With all these things we *have* to do, and so little time day-to-day.

She's working in her garden; her face is all-aglow,
She's planting new spring flowers. I wonder if they know that,
No matter the hues or colors, their brilliance we behold,
Not one or all together. Her beauty will they know.

So gentle and so fragile, yet supple and so fair,
Nature and all its grandeur, to her, never will compare.
Her beauty is eternal; it flows from deep inside,
Our maker placed there it, and there forever will abide.

From her beauty, has flowed life; it's all around to see,
She's given life to two strong sons, and she's given life to me.
So, I wonder if those flowers know who cares for them above,
And if they too feel in her touch, the wonder of her love.

For God gives soil and light and rain, in His hands their life is kept,
But she gives to them purpose, her beauty to reflect.
So, though I cannot hold her, and her touch, I seldom see,
Her beauty and her warmth continually encompass me.

She (Truin for Christina)

I've known of her — forever, yet her name, only twenty-seven years,
This name, with mine, since the beginning of time,
Hidden for a while, but now so clear.

To speak of her is so easy, yet to describe her — very difficult, I must say,
I'm not readily able to outline the inexpressible,
For she changes every day.

She's the pitch black darkness of midnight, keeping a tight grip on
whatever she hides.
She may surrender just a little, never a complete piece, but perhaps a nibble,
Slivers of moonlight, your only guides.

She's the seasons, but not in set order. Springtime may not always
bear summer,
No one can for sure say what she will be like today,
It will be what you expect — or some other.

She's the fog in mountain valleys, the flowers' morning dew,
Sheltering her beloved with the umbrella of her love,
And bringing needed nourishment too.

She's the cool shadow in the heat of day, the gentle breeze under the
setting sun.
Encouraging a stand while the task is at hand,
And carrying peace when the day is done.

She's the wind that stirs up oceans' waves, breakers crashing against
the shore,
The ability to see everything you should be,

And the wisdom to help you be more.

She's all the colors of the rainbow, ah, but perhaps most of all the gold,
That follows springtime showers, revealing its powers,
And illuminating the world that it holds.

A complete portrait of my love I'm not able, but a few strokes of the
brush can I portray,
Like a fleeting glance, I attempt to enhance,
There is just so much more left to say.

God placed her on earth as a helper, and without her "we" wouldn't be,
God gave meaning to "she," and I hope my she sees,
She means everything in this world to me.

TERRENCE L. ROTERING

The Spell (Ka'el's Warning)

Words cannot say, only time will tell,
The full effects of current spells.
What once was real, now is the past,
Yet in memory's web, forever lasts.

As life treads on, much goes unseen,
With distant song and hidden dreams.
When once we've felt never again the same,
For deep inside, we cannot tame —
The passion known, the contact made,
The seed we sowed, and the card we played.

So beware, my friend, and guard the heart,
Once affection we send, we become a part —
Of another's world, and another's life,
Our thoughts we hurl into secret strife.

Like the hidden virus infects the machine,
What attacks the heart will go unseen,
Forever secret and forever hidden —
Hearts away — Hearts away.

Time (Mikole's Lament)

Youth.
Filled with fancy and senseless notions.
When it seems that all we do and say,
Is driven by emotions.

At this time, I could not see,
What time would have in store for me,
And that with all its subtlety,
Time would someday flee.

A busy life, so much to do,
Always on the move, or lest I stall.
I will not slow or fall off the pace,
Oh, I can do it all.

Blind this time, I didn't see,
That time was then besieging me.
And that in assured subtlety —
I stood convinced; it had no hold on me.

Then one day I awoke to find,
That, in reflection, I spotted time.
And though the distraction quickly changed the song,
Ignorance was forever gone.

Though for a moment, I could see,
I chose to think it could not be.
Ignore it, and it will go away,
I'll worry about time another day.

Now I stand in the twilight years,
Though many are gone, time brings new fears.
And failing, I plead through heavy tears,
"Time — I need more time!"

All this time, it took to see,
That time was only teasing me.
And that with no more subtlety,
Time — is — gone.

Freedom (Parlantis' Cry)

Entering the skirmish, I hear the battle cry.
And know it is for certain that many men today will die.

But not for want of glory, as it is sure for some.
That I today will fight; it is alone for our freedom.

So tell not of this day with pride, for what this hand has done.
But rather of my dream for peace, this song my heart has sung.

Goodbye (Heathian Lament)

The sun in rainbow slowly sets and softly caresses the clouds —
That twist and turn beneath its gaze in endless colors found.

I, like the sun, have had my time; I've shared my reds and blues.
But now they fade, darkness comes and steals the life they knew.

Who will remember the unique shades or the portrait that they made?
What is the gain to those I love for the life that I now trade?

Goodbye my love, goodbye, — and please try not to cry,
Remind my sons I love them so,
I go away to die.

This World (Adonian divisions depart Castle Armon)

I leave the world, my world; the world as I know it.
Though I feel the pain, convention dictates that I do not show it.

To require a man to leave his home,
To leave behind his family and all he's ever known,
Though I've done this before, sure to do this again,
Each time leaving gets harder, truly harder than ever been.

Saying goodbye to their little faces — faces that echo those little hearts.
Wondering if inside they're breaking — knowing yours is — this is the
hardest part.
I leave now the world, my world; the world as I know it.
Though I feel the pain intensely, convention dictates I do not show it.

Wishing It Away (Truin's Lament)

The Lord says every day is grace,
A chance to serve Him in this place,
Though I know that this is true,
I see a different aspect too.

I find that when I go away,
To some far distant land, to stay.
It doesn't take long until I'm blue,
Realizing how far I am away from you.

Then I find you're on my mind,
So hard to leave those thoughts behind.
Of wife and kids and our warm home,
So far away, so all alone.

But know it's true, alone I'm not..
Nowhere on earth by God forgot.
He guards my thoughts; he guides my way,
He promised by my side he'll stay.

Now, to do what He has planned,
Directed by his almighty hand.
And though his guidance I obey,
I find the time I wish away —
So I can be home with you.

A Man (Who shall stand?)

What is it that makes a man?
Is it the muscle and tendons that guide his movement?
Is it the flesh and bone that help him stand?
Is it the heart that drives his emotion?
Is it the mind that gives the command?

Is it the will that pushes him on?
Is it the conscience which holds him back?
Is it the drive that moves him forward?
Is it a voice that's never heard?

Is it his accomplishments now written?
Is it the pride that shows on his face?
Is it the memories of today and tomorrow?
Is it the glory of days long past?

Is it the ability to handle the pressure?
Is it the strength he has in his hand?
Is it the power he yields before him?
Is it the treasure he has on his land?

Is it the children that play before him?
Is it the one that bore them in pain?
Is it the family that surrounds him?
Is it the sunshine before the rain?

Is it the fear of what could happen?
Is it the hope of what might be?
Is it the faith of a bright tomorrow?
Is it the desire to be happy?

Is it his spirit, his love, his faith?
Is it his mind, his soul, his heart?
Is it the future, now, or is it the past?
Is it the things which never last?

One thing it is for certain, all these things make up a man.
But it depends which parts are strongest, that decide just where he stands.

For some things, yes, are fleeting; they last for but a day.
Then surely crack and crumble, and they quickly blow away.
Others will last awhile, no one knows just how long,
Then they too leave the picture, just like one's favorite song.

But some things are eternal; yes these they are the kind,
That man should give the very best of his long life to find.
God gave him all to ponder; it's up to him to decide,
Woe on the man who wastes his life, there'll be nowhere he can hide.

So take this simple message and decide whom you will be,
Don't let the parts decide the whole, don't gamble on what might be.
Let the good things make you happy, deny the bad, which makes you sad.
Take the best of what you offer and throw away all that is bad.

For a man takes charge of his life, he knows the battle is won,
If he indeed denies other men from deciding his direction.
Some say there's strength in numbers, but others make it known,
That sparrows fly in numbers, and eagles fly alone.

If standalone, it must be it's not the worst of times,
As long as angels guide my way, when death's bell softly chimes.
So think of me not with riches, no treasures in my hand,
Think of me only as a message to spread across this land.

Take charge of what's around you; fear not to take a STAND,
Decide what you believe in, step forward and be a MAN.

The Warrior's Farewell (Toro's ballad for Christina and Truin)

This day in battle a warrior falls,
And to the sky his Maker calls,
As from his body, his spirit flows,
He leaves behind here all he knows.

His thoughts then turn to his one true love,
As he looks down from high above,
Upon the corpse lying in the sand,
And the wedding band upon its hand.

As for heaven, his soul soared,
This fallen warrior to his Lord,
One last wish this man was given,
To touch once more his wife yet living.

A soft breeze blew in from the plains,
And to the home came peaceful rains,
A gentle mist caressed her face,
And on her lips left but a trace.

As she gazed on setting sun,
At that moment, knowing what was done,
Quietly to her knees, she fell.
For she had felt his last farewell.

Truin's Struggle (Poem of Victory)

Constantly under attack, the world you choose to live, your surroundings.
So hard to stay on track, returning what they give, so confounding.
It should be easier than this. I struggle with control,
I fall short so many times each day,
It weighs heavily on my soul.

Relying on my strengths, and on my own authority, I fail.
Alone, I try strenuously to remain free, to no avail.
My effort is in vain, I do not possess the skill,
Whereby with simple flesh and blood, to defend against their will.

One critical oversight, one fatal flaw to my endeavor.
They more than match my might, on my endangered soul they gnaw.
Alone, I'll defeat them never, for they are not as they appear, in this world of illusion,
But rather, they are a united host, intent on my destruction.

They are the servants of the enemy, defenders of his lies, of all depraved.
Look closely and you'll see, their devious methods try to attack the saved.
They do all they can in allegiance to their condemned king,
To deny the heavenly plan, and to the Saints distraction bring.

There is a way that's sure to be victorious in this fight, walking tall.
A way we can endure, remaining in the light, and answering the call.
Equipped with the armor of God, led by the sword of the Spirit
On the demons the Saints will tread, their numbers we'll attrite.

So do not be deceived into thinking there is no battle, that all is well.
While those who believe the lies gather like cattle to the eternal slaughter of hell.
It is our call to arms, in prayer and supplication,

To lead them from all harm and teach them of salvation.

A host of heavenly warriors in service to their Lord will aid in this endeavor.
He has promised there is a place that is yours; evil cannot sever the cord, for we are His forever.
There all the Saints will be blessed, salvation through the blood of the Lamb,
Singing praises to God in the highest —
Victory eternal to the great "I Am."

The River of Time (Veritas' Instruction)

As a child, I knew her not; not yet a keeper of truth. Life had no plot.
Now a man of many, many years, through the haze she sometimes appears,
Softly, slowly her pages turn, and yet little of her, still, we learn.
Reflecting all she passes through, her image changes from every view.

She takes her color from the sky; it gives nothing of her away; it is all a lie.
Though she feeds all the surrounding life, her current causes all our strife.
Though some above, and some below, and some all around her grow —
We pass through cloud and then through sun, memories of pain and
memories of fun.

How much evil lies within? The ripples hide from us her sin.
How much good lies within her, will good follow when she turns?
You can try to plan for where she'll flow, but none can tell where next
she'll go.
I cannot hold her, she is not mine, but only a few drops at a time.

She touches all with each new mile and takes us with her for but a while.
Some with her move all around, some will fail and quickly drown.
Settling in the murk below —
Light again to never know.

Sometimes peaceful, sometimes still, all she passes over she fills.
Whether over, under, or around we tread, she provides us with the
common thread.
She maintains the plane we live upon, and she'll be there when we are
long gone.
Do not be bitter and angry about this, though time before or
after you miss.
She holds no malice; there is no crime —
Justice to all — the river of time.

SONGS OF ADONIA

Lead You Home
When I was just a little boy,
Playing with my little-boy toys,
My Father took me on a walk,
He said it was time to have a talk.
Walking slowly with my dad,
He bent down close and took my hand.
And looking just a little sad,
He spoke these words to me:

He said —
Son, you got to know,
I will always love you so,
Don't you put your trust in me,
I won't always be here with you.
Put your trust in the Lord,
Walk, my son, by His word,
And He will lead, He will lead you home.

I always doubted what I'd heard,
When I remember my daddy's words,
'Cause he had always been there for me,
So, I refused to see.
Then suddenly that day was here,
That day that all sons have to fear,
As I kneeled down by his side,
I held his hand and cried

He said —
Son, you know, I have to go,

Son, you know, I love you so,
And you know I can't always be,
I can't always be here with you.
Put your trust, Son, in the Lord,
Walk now son, by His word,
And He will lead, He will lead you home.

Mom and Dad have now gone home,
And on this land below, I still roam,
Blessed with sons now, I can see,
Clearly, what will be.
So, feeling just a little sad,
I found those words I've always had,
I sat my sons down on my knee,
And told them, like my dad told me.
I said —
Sons, you've got to know,
I will always love you so,
Don't you put your trust in me,
I won't always be here with you.
Put your trust in the Lord,
Walk, my son, by His word,
And He will lead —
He will lead you home.

Remember the Trees

In the cool of the trees, in amongst all the leaves,
There's a buzzing of the bees, and the laughter of monkeys,
In the calm of the day, as they all swing and sway,
There are no worries today, only peace.

As the sun starts to set, and the sky turns to red,
No fears in their heads, as they snuggle into bed,
In the shadows of the night, they know that all is right,
There are no worries tonight, only peace.

They don't worry; they don't stress,
They aren't anxious; they aren't depressed,
They know who's up there, high above the nest,
They do their part; He does the rest.

As we go through our lives, many trials will arise,
Our Lord reigns high above, and our God, He is love,
Let us always remember that He loves us more than ever,
There are no worries then, only peace.

We don't worry; we don't stress,
We aren't anxious; we aren't depressed,
We know who's up there, high above the nest,
We do our part; he does the rest.

Out of the Depths

Out of the depths, out of the depths I cry to you, Oh Lord. Oh Lord, hear my voice.
Let your ears, let your ears, Oh Lord, be attentive to my cry.
I wait, I wait for the Lord, my soul waits. In his word, I put my hope.
I do not concern myself with this world; you have stilled and quieted my soul.

Keep falsehood and lies far from me. Give me neither riches nor poverty. But give me only my daily bread. So I may not disown you, or dishonor thy name.
The name of my God.

Praise the Lord, praise the name of the Lord our God. Praise him, you who serve the Lord.
Praise the Lord, praise the Lord for he is good, his name will last always.

Keep falsehood and lies far from me. Give me neither riches nor poverty. But give me only my daily bread. So I may not disown you, or dishonor thy name.
The name of my God.

Light (Prophecy)

Oh, what a quiet night; Oh, what a peaceful night; One like all others, yet none ever before.
For in the heavens doth burn a new light; high above us, it's burning bright.
With love, its radiant beams to earth soar.

Thousands of years for this night, men waited; they sleep while the moments quietly pass.
Angels now bring to earth their heavenly King; as all creation so quietly sings,
In a lonely manger, His glory is masked.

Oh, so serene yet miraculous night; the most spectacular, yet hidden from sight,
This night the Savior comes, and night will soon — succumb.
For so long darkness, now "Let there be Light!"

Though man has been blind through the ages and more ages of blindness, he'll see,
The remnant of God's glorious creation — pausing in bridled anticipation,
This night in silence bows down — bended knee.

His Word had given life to creation, but man's rebellion then gave birth to death,
Atonement demanded the sacrifice; only the Son of God could pay the price,
Be still, the infant now takes His first breath.

Oh, so serene yet miraculous night; the most spectacular, yet hidden from sight,
This night the Savior comes, and night will soon — succumb,
For so long darkness, now "Let there be Light!"

Be still, the infant now takes His first breath.